THE HOLY CONTINENT
LIGHTHAVEN
PORT BELFAIR
N
W
E
S

ALSO BY TESSONJA ODETTE

ENTANGLED WITH FAE SERIES

Curse of the Wolf King

Heart of the Raven Prince

Kiss of the Selkie

A Taste of Poison

A Dream So Wicked

THE FAIR ISLE TRILOGY

To Carve a Fae Heart

To Wear a Fae Crown

To Spark a Fae War

FAE FLINGS AND CORSET STRINGS SERIES

A Rivalry of Hearts

My Feral Romance

The Lies That Summon the Night

A Songs for the Sinless Novel

Tessonja Odette

DELACORTE PRESS
NEW YORK

Delacorte Press
An imprint of Random House
A division of Penguin Random House LLC
1745 Broadway, New York, NY 10019
randomhousebooks.com
penguinrandomhouse.com

Hardcover ISBN 979-8-217-09490-5
International ISBN 979-8-217-30099-0
Ebook ISBN 979-8-217-09491-2

Printed in the United States of America

1st Printing

First Edition

Book Team: Production editor: Kelly Chian • Managing editor: Saige Francis • Production manager: Nathalie Mairena • Proofreaders: Lara Kennedy, Cyrus Chin, Tess Rossi

Book design by Caroline Cunningham

Title page background art: Salomi art/Adobe Stock; chapter opener art: needle & thread: HaqueMukul/Adobe Stock; potion bottle: kssss/Adobe Stock

Endpaper map: Charlie Arpie

The authorized representative in the EU for product safety and compliance is Penguin Random House Ireland, Morrison Chambers, 32 Nassau Street, Dublin D02 YH68, Ireland. https://eu-contact.penguin.ie

AUTHOR'S NOTE

The Lies that Summon the Night is an adult romantasy intended for mature readers. The romance between the main couple is *not* dark, but the fantasy world it takes place in *is.* This book features monsters, gore, and dark themes. Please take care when reading.

Below is not an exhaustive list, but this book contains the following content:

- Adult situations.
- Explicit language.
- Open-door descriptive sex scenes featuring coarse language, shadow play, and blindfolding.
- Religious and political corruption.
- Violence, blood, and gore, including blood drinking by a vampire-like species.
- Drug-like blood addiction and withdrawal.
- Body horror and frightening scenes.
- Mentions of parental neglect in the past.
- Mentions of sexual assault in the past.
- Mentions of murder, physical abuse, and mutilation in the past.
- Grief and the loss of loved ones.

GLOSSARY

PLACES:

THE HOLY CONTINENT—the only continent in the world inhabited and ruled by the Sinless.

SACRED CITY—a city ruled by a Sinless royal, protected beneath a Holy Brazier's dome of light, and surrounded by silver walls. This is the safest location for humans to live, since Shades cannot enter the walls. There are currently eight sacred cities, including the royal capital, Lighthaven.

PROTECTED VILLAGE—a village ruled by a Sinless duke, protected beneath a Holy Brazier's dome of light. Unlike the Sacred Cities, protected villages are not surrounded by silver walls. Nevertheless, they are the second-safest locations for humans to live.

MAGIC:

ASTROTHEURGY—magic that utilizes the energies of the gods and cosmos to draw down blessings onto mortal earth and effect a desired outcome.

ASTROTHEURGICAL DIAGRAM—a ritual circle featuring angles,

geometric patterns, and glyphs that harnesses the energies of the gods and cosmos in specific ways to work astrotheurgy.

SOLAR ASTROTHEURGY—a type of powerful astrotheurgy that only Sinless and Shadowbanes can perform, which harnesses the energy of the god Bastien and the properties of the sun. It requires a blood sacrifice, and the more demanding the feat, the more the blood or death that is required to fuel it.

COMMON ASTROTHEURGY—a type of astrotheurgy that was widespread before One Hundred Days of Darkness, utilized for everyday feats such as infusing potions and tonics or instantaneously delivering communications across great distances. In the modern day, all forms of astrotheurgy are forbidden to the common folk and are closely guarded by the church.

HOLY BRAZIER—a wide, shallow bowl with an astrotheurgical diagram etched inside. When lit, it creates a massive dome of light over a designated area, through which Shades cannot pass. Lighting a Holy Brazier is one of the most powerful feats of solar astrotheurgy, and it requires a heart sacrifice at regular intervals to maintain the light.

ABSOLUTION—the astrotheurgical ritual that turns a human into a Sinless by stripping their soul of sin.

PARTIAL ABSOLUTION—an astrotheurgical ritual reserved for Shadowbanes that strips a human's soul of only half its sins.

PEOPLE:

SINLESS—a former human who has undergone the Absolution ritual and now consumes blood regularly. They are considered immortal and incapable of attracting Shades.

SHADOWBANE—considered to be half Sinless, Shadowbanes undergo a partial Absolution, which strips their soul of half its sins. They consume blood, though less regularly than pure Sinless. They experience a lesser range of emotion than humans do.

HALFSOUL—another term for a Shadowbane.

SINLESS HIERARCHY—King Kaelum rules the Holy Continent as its sovereign. The church, royals, and dukes serve directly beneath him.

The Sinless Princes are the second-most-powerful Sinless beneath the king. They were made royal by sacred appointment after their Absolutions. There are currently seven Sinless princes, each of whom rules over their own Sacred City. The Sinless dukes are the third-most-powerful Sinless, beneath the royals. They are appointed to the position as reward for merit and piety and given a territory to rule over as its duke. The king, princes, and dukes can all perform solar astrotheurgy to light their Holy Braziers, but are not permitted to perform any other kind of astrotheurgy or for any other purpose. The next-most-powerful Sinless are the Shadowbanes. Even though they are only half Sinless, their position as protectors of the continent, bounty hunters, and Shade slayers, as well as their permitted use of astrotheurgy, makes them highly respected and feared by the common folk. At the bottom of the Sinless hierarchy are the Sinless lords and ladies. They are given their titles as rewards for merit and piety and often take on positions of leadership and honor above the common folk. They are not privy to any knowledge of astrotheurgy. All ranks of Sinless consume blood and are above the law when it comes to their actions and behavior, including in choosing their blood sources.

THE CHURCH—in direct service to King Kaelum, the priests are the most powerful humans on the Holy Continent. They are keepers of all knowledge of astrotheurgy and oversee judicial and military functions of the government. They are the only ones permitted to perform the Absolution ritual, as well as some forms of common astrotheurgy under strict regulations.

MONSTERS:

SHADE—a semi-sentient shadow born from human sin. Often humanoid in appearance, though sometimes seen in animallike forms, they stalk humankind and are drawn to sin. When provoked, they turn violent. During the day, they are relegated to dark places and cannot stand direct sunlight. They are sensitive to silver and cannot walk past walls or barriers composed of the metal. They can be banished beneath daylight or cut down by a flaming sword, but they will re-form—quickly if it is past nightfall. The only way a Shade can be permanently killed is if it becomes Incarnate and is dispatched by a Shadowbane.

INCARNATE—a Shade that has taken a keen interest in a specific human, subsequently copied their likeness, and then consumed them. Afterward, the Shade becomes corporeal, with their victim's copied likeness and memories. They have convinced themselves they are human, and anything that reminds them they aren't will provoke them to violence.

HISTORY/LORE:

ONE HUNDRED DAYS OF DARKNESS—legend states that five hundred years ago, humankind grew so wicked that the nine gods sought to punish them by plunging the world into darkness for one hundred days.

THE YEAR OF BASTIEN—the eighth year of every decade, during which Bastien is considered the patron god of the year. He is honored at the capital on the summer solstice with an atonement ritual, meant to beg the god's forgiveness and end the threat of Shades.

SEVEN HUMAN SINS—considered the seven darkest aspects of humanity: pride, lust, sloth, gluttony, greed, envy, and wrath.

SEVEN HOLY VIRTUES—considered the seven highest virtues humanity must embody to earn the gods' forgiveness: humility, compassion, diligence, temperance, generosity, awe, and patience.

LUNAR ENERGY—also known as *sin,* lunar energy is the aspect of the gods, cosmos, and humanity that was born from Vanna, Goddess of the Moon, representing the shadow side of all things, the natural end of all cycles, and the necessary opposite and counterpart to solar energy. In the modern day, lunar energy and all things related to the moon are considered sinful and evil.

THE NINE GODS

Parent gods:

- Bastien, God of the Sun, representing life, light, and creation.
- Vanna, Goddess of the Moon, representing death, darkness, and destruction.

Their children, the seven minor gods:

- Herald, God of Prosperity, representing energies from greed to generosity.
- Serafina, Goddess of Love, representing energies from lust to compassion.
- Malen, God of Wisdom, representing energies from pride to humility.
- Lilith, Goddess of Justice, representing energies from wrath to patience.
- Sylas, God of Harvest, representing energies from gluttony to temperance.
- Dian, Goddess of Beauty, representing energies from envy to awe.
- Kole, God of Purpose, representing energies from sloth to diligence.

For anyone who has ever mended a broken heart

and come out stronger for it.

The Lies That Summon the Night

CHAPTER ONE

Inana

The first time I whispered a story to the wind, it was with the certainty that it would end in my death. I may have been a child then, but I understood the implications of the crime I was committing. To perform art is to lie, to lie is to sin, and to sin is to attract the shadows that haunt the dark. Still, instead of running from what I'd done, I waited with bated breath, safe in the sunlight, while my eyes were locked on the woods at the edge of my village. I hardly dared blink for fear I'd miss the telltale sign of movement darkening between the trees. Some indication that I'd stirred a shadow monster's hunger.

When an hour passed and no such danger presented itself, I wasn't relieved.

I was disappointed.

Not because I wanted to die; I wanted to feel alive. To quell the longing inside me, instilled not by sin but by holy scripture.

There is no lie greater than fiction,
No sin more beautiful than art.
Stray not unto these pleasures,
For the devil is their muse.

Gods, the way those lines moved me back then. Though they were meant to serve as a warning not to partake in the forbidden arts, they never sounded like one to me. They sounded like a calling. A challenge. Could I weave a tale so fascinating the devil would take notice? One so beautiful the Shades that plague humanity would seek my death?

That wasn't the last time I breathed fiction into the world. It was only the beginning, and eventually storytelling spelled my doom. Twice I was caught for my crimes.

The first time, it cost me the man I loved.

The second time, my freedom.

Yet it's funny how captivity is the place I've felt most free. On nights like tonight, at least.

A windowless room beckons me from up ahead. I keep my breathing steady as my companions and I proceed down the dim corridor toward it. We're silent save for the soft padding of our slippered feet, the air between us buzzing with a palpable blend of terror and anticipation. We know what awaits us, for none of us are new to performing at the Wretched Lair.

There are more than a dozen of us tonight, all of us artists and outlaws. At age twenty-six, I am neither the youngest nor the oldest. My colleagues range from a girl in her teens to a man twice my years. Most, like me, are indentured to Mr. Rockefeller, the well-dressed gentleman who leads our entourage. The rest have already earned out their contracts and are here by choice to make a living. In two years I'll be among them. Another year after that and I'll have earned enough to buy safe passage off this fucking continent.

I just have to survive until then.

A shiver crawls up my spine as the first strain of music reaches my ears, a lilting melody plucked on some stringed instrument. Such a chilling sound when all forms of imaginative art are forbidden. I should be used to it by now. After one year in Mr. Rockefeller's custody, one year of performances at the Wretched Lair, I've heard my share of music. Yet I don't think it will ever sound less haunting. Less enchanting.

The closer we draw to the doorway, the louder the melody grows, as do bursts of laughter and chatter. I brace myself for the sharp scent of liquor that floods my nostrils, hoping I don't smell the iron tang of blood along with it. If there are any Sinless in attendance tonight . . .

I swallow the ball of fear that rises in my throat. Mr. Rockefeller may hold enough sway over his fellow aristocrats to keep us safe from them, but he cannot promise the same with the Sinless.

At least all of us are masked, our identities further obscured by identical garb: silk robes in deep scarlet with ribbon closures from waist to neck and matching veils over the backs of our heads. No one will see my red-blond hair or freckled cheeks. They'll hardly notice my gray irises through the eye slits. All they'll see are the different designs on our masks—the only things that set us apart, save for our varying heights and builds. My mask is embellished with an elegant floral filigree and a halo of narrow spikes that resemble sunbeams, all of which trail bronze beads that rustle and sway with my movements.

We cross the threshold at last, the transition from the dark corridor to the brightly lit room temporarily blinding me. I blink to adjust to the glow of the glittering crystal chandeliers suspended overhead, their golden light made even more brilliant by the gleam reflected off the silver walls, floor, and ceiling. It's bright enough to send a throbbing ache to my temples, though I should be grateful. Silver and light are the two things that ward off Shades—shadow monsters that manifest from human sin.

That was the original purpose of this room, to serve as an underground emergency bunker. Sacred Cities like Nalheim are surrounded by towering silver walls as well as a dome of light cast by a Holy Brazier at the city's center. Bunkers like this one provide a haven for the aristocracy to flee to should Nalheim's primary protections be compromised. Yet instead of reserving his sanctuary for such a cataclysmic event, Mr. Rockefeller turned it into a social club for the upstanding city elite. A place to safely give his peers a taste of sin.

Rockefeller leads us to the center of the party, where we fan out to allow our audience a full view of tonight's entertainment. Despite the lack of windows, the room is what I imagine a parlor in a palace would look like, with velvet-upholstered wingback chairs and tables laden with decadent food. The silver walls are etched in a damask pattern, the silver ceiling is coffered, and the silver floors are polished to a shine. Such an extravagant display of the continent's most coveted metal.

A few sets of eyes dart our way, but most of our patrons are still engaged in conversation or deep in their drinks as they sprawl about on the furniture. They're dressed in their finest frock coats, top hats, and ball gowns in bright silks, laces, and brocades. Like ours, their faces are hidden behind masks, but theirs are featureless porcelain where ours are works of art, proof that they are not sinners like we are. They don't participate in the unlawful arts. They only watch. Judge. Bask in the splendor of the very thing they publicly condemn.

The melody shifts to a new tune, and I catch sight of the musician, seated in the lap of a slender male. She wears no mask, her eyelids heavy, pupils blown wide. Her fingers remain lithe and active on her harp despite her slumped posture, the bleeding punctures on her neck, and the roving pair of hands that climb up her petticoats and over her stockinged thighs.

My blood goes cold.

I recognize her. She only worked at the Wretched Lair on occasion, having earned out her contract with Mr. Rockefeller years ago. I haven't seen her in months. Now I know why, just like I know what kind of man sits behind her, even without looking at his face. It's written in the effortless grace that lines his posture, in how brightly he seems to shine, as radiant as the chandeliers and silver walls around him. But that's merely because he's the only person in the room who doesn't cast a shadow.

For the Sinless have no shadows.

Absolved of sin, freed from aging and death, the Sinless reign over humanity as the purest of us all. Since they are the only beings who don't attract Shades, they are above reproach.

My jaw tightens. I lift my gaze from the puncture wounds on the woman's neck to the bloodstained lips of the Sinless male. Like the musician, he wears no mask, revealing his sharp cheekbones and empty blue eyes, his golden hair that falls over his forehead. He has no reason to hide who he is or what he does. No reason to feed from his sacrifice in private. He can claim who he wants as his blood source and force them to consume his blood in turn, making them his obedient thralls.

Mr. Rockefeller welcomes his guests and announces the start of tonight's entertainment. Forcing my attention away from the Sinless and his thrall, I stride to an empty marble box, lifting the hem of my robe as I step up on it. Throughout the room, my companions do the same, some with musical instruments, others holding paintbrushes, sketchbooks, or other artistic tools. A few are empty-handed like me, though I won't remain so for long.

Clasping my fingers at my waist, I stand tall. Pretend to be fearless as I make myself a target of interest. Despite the anonymity my mask provides, I always feel naked during this part. Too seen. Too vulnerable. But I refuse to let it show.

Mr. Rockefeller weaves through the crowd, whispering temptations to our patrons.

The Blade juggles knives without drawing a single bead of blood.

The Bard has the scarred hands of a killer yet the voice of an angel.

The Lover waltzes like a prince from the forgotten faerytales of old.

The Harlot has thighs as smooth as silk and a pen that will draw you between them.

The Seamstress stitches a tale of horror and hope that will tug on your heartstrings.

None of us go by our true names, not even with one another. Long gone is Inana Westwood, replaced by the Seamstress. Thanks to the gossip my master spreads, a small audience soon grows around me, hungry for the Seamstress's fare.

My patrons maintain a modest distance, bodies angled slightly away as if they fear they'll catch my vileness by proximity alone. If they were truly worried, they wouldn't have come to the Wretched Lair. In truth, their disgust is feigned. I can see the excitement that flashes behind their masks, the anticipation that dances in the shivers that roll through their beautifully clad bodies. They're as thirsty as the Sinless, though not for blood. As hungry as the Shades, though not for flesh.

The harpist's tune slows, and our patrons make their final selections. Some attendees keep to the walls to more convincingly maintain an air of indifference, like the Sinless male, who hasn't left his chair—thank the gods. I hazard a glance his way, a ball of tension easing from my shoulders. So long as he keeps to himself, I can give my performance my all. Otherwise, I would have to walk a fine line between entertaining my audience and remaining unmemorable. It's the most talented ones the Sinless seem to favor on their rare visits to the Wretched Lair.

My heart falls as I lower my eyes to the harpist once more. Her smile is so peaceful, her gaze so empty. What does it feel like to be drunk on a Sinless's blood? Is there a part of her that remains lucid, slamming helplessly against the cage of her mind? Is that the part of her that continues to play so well, her only act of rebellion while the rest of her body obeys?

I don't want to know. Only someone in her position could answer that question, and I would never wish her fate upon myself. Perhaps it's selfish to be grateful that I'm not her, but outlaws don't survive this long by being selfless.

As the Sinless lowers his lips, pressing sharp canines to the gaping bite marks on his thrall's neck, his eyes lift and lock on mine. Or perhaps I only imagine they do. Surely he can't see my eyes from where he sits. I tear my gaze away. Just as quickly, the harpist's song cuts short. My pulse hammers in the wake of her silenced tune.

She might not be dead, I tell myself. She could have temporarily lost consciousness from blood loss. Not all Sinless drain their sacrifices to death. Some keep pets.

Not all Sinless stop at drinking blood, my darkest side whispers back.

I resist the urge to rub the scar on my chest, hidden beneath my robe, and remind myself why this is all worth the risk. Why I will choose to return here, even after I've bought out my contract.

Because this is my best chance at funding my escape from the continent.

And the one way I can satisfy my darkest longing.

Gathering a bracing breath, I lower my eyes to the audience that surrounds my tiny marble stage.

"Mine is a story of a woman who lost her heart," I say, my wistful tone barely carrying over the din that has risen as each performer starts to spin their craft. Unimpressed eyes droop behind their masks, my patrons second-guessing whether they chose the right performer. An intentional diversion on my part, as I loosen the top closures of my robe. Then I claw my fingers beneath the garment, letting the front sag open enough to reveal the puckered line of flesh that runs from my sternum to the upper curve of my breast.

My audience's eyes widen on seeing my jagged scar. Their interest is piqued.

I lower my voice to a harsh rasp.

"Mine is a story of a woman who lost her heart," I repeat, more sinister this time.

From beneath my robe I extract the still-beating organ in question.

"Mine is a tale of the treachery of love."

CHAPTER TWO

Inana

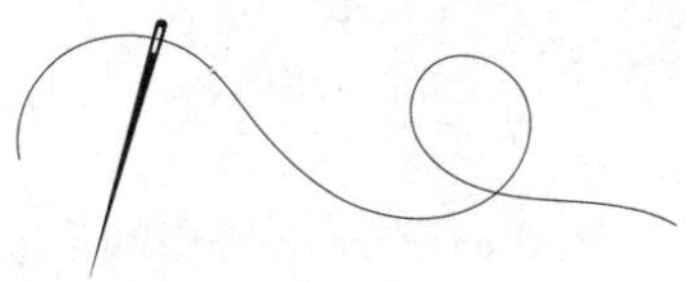

My crowd huddles closer as I flourish the beating heart in my palm. It's constructed of red silk stitched with sparkling faux rubies that give the impression of blood. The threads looped around my fingers trigger the miniature bellows that fills the heart with air. With every tug of my pinkie, the heart pulses. Pulses. Pulses.

It took me two months to create this. Several iterations and much trial and error before I finally got it right. I could tell my story without it, but if I'm going to risk my life for art, I might as well do it in style.

"The first time I lost my heart," I say as I lift my silk organ with great reverence, inflating it with a calm and rhythmic thud, "it was taken gently. A theft so soft and sweet. One of breathless whispers and chaste kisses. I relinquished my heart with a smile. But the second time . . ."

I tug the threads, harder this time, working the bellows in uneven lurches. My voice dips low again.

"The second time it was stolen by force." I crush the heart in my palm and press it against my scar. My audience lifts their eyes to mine, pupils widening behind the slits in their masks. "The thief's identity was one and the same, yet he'd changed in every way. Once beautiful, he was now grotesque, a beast of fang and claw. Four years we'd been apart, and in that time he gave his heart to another, the dark and wicked moon."

Resentment burns my blood as the last words leave my lips in a lie that tastes like acid. It would be more accurate to say my love gave his heart to the sun, but it's the moon the people are taught to despise. And not without reason. We all grow up reading the same holy texts that describe the moon goddess's villainy. We all know what happened five centuries ago, when all nine gods turned their backs on mankind when we grew too wicked. They withheld their ruling planets' light, plunging us into a time known as One Hundred Days of Darkness. But it was Vanna, Goddess of the Moon, who gave solid form to humanity's sins, allowing them to materialize as Shades. It is under her night sky that the Shades continue to flourish, safe from the sunlight that forces them to hide during the day.

The only deity who showed mercy was the sun god, Bastien. After One Hundred Days of Darkness ended, he created the first Sinless, King Kaelum. He stripped the king's soul of sin, gave him immortality, and taught him the Absolution ritual that could turn other humans Sinless thereafter. Then he gave the king a special kind of astrotheurgy—divine celestial magic—that allowed him to harness the power of the sun as protection from the Shades. Bastien's only lasting punishment was that all Sinless would feast on sinners' blood.

The holy texts claim that when the Sinless lose their thirst, the Shades will disappear. It will mean we've atoned and are blessed by the gods once more. But first, humanity must put an end to sin.

Tonight is evidence as to how well that's going.

My patrons curse Vanna's name under their breath at my mention of the moon.

"I never knew love could change a man into a beast," I say, "but his dedication to the queen of the night was steadfast. All-consuming. Only one thing kept him from merging fully with his beloved, and that was the heart I'd given him."

With my hand still pressed to my chest, I tuck the silk heart into the top of my chemise and exchange it for a different creation.

My voice takes on a darker edge. "Now love came to me as a devil. Gone were his gentle hands and sweet promises. When he reached deep inside my chest, he did so with razor-sharp talons. He clawed open my flesh, broke through the cage of my ribs, and split my heart in two."

I heave forward, my palm splaying open to reveal the shriveled clump of red silk within. Crimson ribbons spill over the sides of my hand, strung with more sparkling red stones.

"But cleaving it in two wasn't enough," I say, "for a heart severed in half can easily be stitched back together. My love was a thorough beast indeed, piercing that which he'd once claimed so sweetly only to tear it to shreds, piece by piece by piece."

I turn my palm to the ground, and the heart flutters to my feet in minuscule shards while red threads dangle from between my fingers like delicate tendrils of blood.

As I press my free hand to my scar once more, my viewers discover more scarlet ribbons streaming from where my robe gapes open.

"Love was thorough," I say, my voice so quiet my audience leans closer. "Love was deadly. And in the wake of his violence, my life was bled dry. It was the end for me. Or it should have been. For what is life without a heart? How does one breathe when there is nothing left to inflate your lungs? No one was going to save me. No one could piece me back together. No one could possibly make whole the heart that had been so terribly rent.

"At least, that's what love thought. He'd made a mistake in leaving even a shard of my heart intact, when he should have devoured me blood, bones, tissue, and all. For who better to repair that which is broken than a seamstress?"

I shift my focus to my hand and the threads looped over my fingers. This next part takes precision, order.

"There may not have been a heart in my body, but there were threads of life, a needle of hope." I lift one string, then another, looping them around my fingers, then together, until the pieces of fabric at my feet stir to life. "That was all I needed to stitch and stitch and stitch. Even though pieces of my heart had been irretrievably lost, I made do with what I could forage. A dried flower I'd kept from one lovely spring past. A lace ribbon I'd treasured as a girl. A worn letter I'd read a thousand times over. A blanket that had always kept me warm."

Sweat beads behind my mask as I continue to carefully weave the threads, praying to gods who don't listen that my creation won't get tangled. To my great satisfaction, the pieces come together, and as I loop the final thread, tugging the mass of cloth toward my hand, the heart is whole once more, though it is no longer red silk, but a collage of mismatched prints that had been hidden on the reverse side. My grin grows wide as I flourish the heart upon my palm, pride igniting in my chest. This took even longer to construct than my beating heart. I'm not sure how I managed enough patience to see it through.

I glance away from my craft to take in the impressed eyes of my audience. My pride swells tenfold.

Gods, this feels good. To know I've entranced them. This is what I've craved, ever since I told that first tale when I was young. To balance on the knife's edge between beauty and danger is the best feeling in the world. Better than any other accomplishment. Better than verbal praise. Better than sex.

Maybe the priests are right about artists.

They say our greatest sin lies not in our temptation to create but in our inability to resist the devil's call. Our slothful disregard for the dangers, laws, and consequences. Our lust for that which is forbidden. Our pride in our illicit craft. According to the holy texts, all seven sins are present in art: greed, envy, gluttony, wrath, sloth, lust, and pride. Every brushstroke is a lie. Every line of poetry a fabrication. Every act of creation a mockery of the gods who had forsaken us. And we keep doing it again and again.

For that I am guilty.

I could have learned my lesson the first time I was caught for my forbidden art and consequently sentenced to death. After I escaped imprisonment, I *should* have turned my back on storytelling for good, but I didn't. Not even after I took a new name and started my life over at a textile mill. I shouldn't have stolen scraps of silk, nor should I have sewn daisies on them when my fellow workers were sleeping in their bunks. I most certainly should not have muttered stories while I stitched, for that was what got me caught for my wickedness the second time. After that, I was sold off to Rockefeller—a mercy compared to what normally happens to criminals. An even greater mercy compared to what would have happened if anyone knew of my previous crime.

"Mine is a story of a woman who lost her heart." I speak slowly this time, serenading my audience with the sway of my spoken tempo. "Mine is a tale of the treachery of love. But when love left me bleeding, I stitched myself back together, turned wounds into seams and sinew into threads."

I let hope infuse my tone, which is perhaps my greatest lie of all. The truest version of my story isn't one of hope. It's one of hatred and pain and a heart that never healed. Of blood pooling on the floor of a dusty jail cell, a needle in my hand. Of the urge not to repair but to break. To wound. And, if I could, to kill.

But that isn't the story I've promised my audience. My patrons may be a privileged lot, but they still value hope and happy endings.

I blink away broken memories and melt into the comfort of my fiction. "A monster cleaved open my chest, tore out my heart, and ended my life. But I clawed my way back from death and stand before you now. A patchwork heart may not be what I was born with, nor is it what I wanted . . ."

I force a liar's smile to my lips, one my audience can't see through my bronze mask but can hear in my gentle tone. In the fallacy of hope I leave them with.

"But a patchwork heart is like any broken thing that's been mended. Beautiful. Stronger. New."

I lower my head and dip into a curtsy while a few of my patrons offer a smattering of applause. No matter how much I may have entertained them, they aren't known for their acclaim. To praise any artist too effusively would be akin to suggesting maybe art is enjoyable after all. Maybe it shouldn't be considered a sin.

Yet even if anyone were rash enough to argue such a thing, it would matter not. The fact that Shades are drawn to artists more than anyone else—more than murderers, adulterers, and thieves—is proof of its wickedness. For the Shades were born from humanity's sins, and to our sins they are drawn.

By the time I rise from my curtsy, most of my audience has dispersed, though one couple remains. Most likely they stayed not for an encore but because they're so engaged in conversation they haven't noticed my performance has ended. Turning away, I prepare to repeat my story for the next crowd. I gingerly smooth out both silk hearts, tucking threads and ribbons in all the right places, especially my second heart. There's a precise order for each thread so that the piece unravels and merges back together with relative ease. I tuck them back beneath my chemise, along with my bloody ribbons, and seal the front of my scarlet robe.

When I face forward, I find my new audience has already gathered. Not only that, but newcomers have entered the party, making the room even more crowded than before. I open my mouth, ready to speak my starting line—

My jaw snaps shut.

A pair of dark eyes snag mine, rendering me mute. My pulse quickens, though it takes several rapid beats of my heart before I understand why. It isn't because the man is new to the party, or that he towers over the figures around him.

No, it's his lack of a mask.

The hilt of a silver sword at his back.

The black linen shirt and dark leather jerkin he wears when everyone else is dressed in bright finery.

Of all the different ranks of Sinless, he's the last I'd want to meet.

A fucking Shadowbane.

CHAPTER THREE

INANA

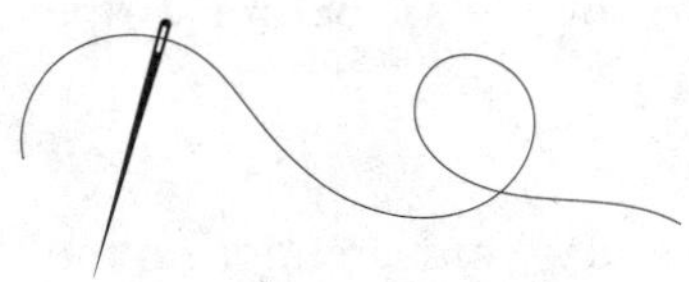

There's a hierarchy among the Sinless.

The original Sinless, King Kaelum, rules from the capital Sacred City at the heart of the Holy Continent. Beneath him are seven Sinless princes, made royalty not by birth or bloodline but by sacred appointment following their Absolution. Each prince rules over a walled Sacred City of their own, like Nalheim, where I reside now. Below the princes are the Sinless dukes. All three ranks are bestowed with solar astrotheurgy, the divine magic that allows them to ignite the Holy Braziers that dome their cities in light. The dukes' lands, however, are not protected by silver walls, making them more susceptible to the threat of Shades. Still, they're safer than unprotected villages.

At the bottom of the hierarchy are the Sinless lords and ladies. Neither are they royalty, nor can they perform astrotheurgy. Instead of ruling over land, they head the aristocracy. All good citizens aim to be turned Sinless, regardless of rank. They seek to be rewarded for their devoutness with the Absolution ritual that rids their souls of sin. Since royal positions are hard to come by, most aspire to simply reach the bottom rung of Sinless gentry.

The Sinless male with his harpist thrall is one of these lords. While he may rank low among the Sinless, he's the highest among the gentry and common folk, and the last person I'd want to attract attention from. At least, that was before the Shadowbane entered the soirée.

The Shadowbane stands at the back of my crowd, his dark gaze too keen, too penetrating, and locked straight on me. I shift my face slightly, just to feel the weight of my mask and the sway of the bronze beads that dangle from it. To remind myself he can't see my face. Should we ever meet on the city streets, he'll have no clue he first met me here.

I'm safe.

Or as safe as I can be.

Shadowbanes are considered half Sinless. Sometimes called half-souls, because only half their soul has been saved. They are given a partial Absolution, but the reason why isn't public knowledge. Some say being partially stripped of sin allows them to carry out wretched tasks a true Sinless never could, such as killing Shades. Others insist it enables them to wield shadow monsters like weapons.

I haven't a clue if any of that is true, but it's clear the man in my audience is different from the Sinless lord. Where the other male appeared almost illuminated by his lack of shadow, the very air darkens around the Shadowbane. There is no effortless grace in his posture, no delicate perfection to his features. He looks to be a few years older than me, thirty at most. His shoulders are broad, his nose angled like it's been broken, his sharp jaw dusted with a short beard. His dark hair is overlong, falling in loose waves away from his forehead to the nape of his neck. His striking yet rugged appearance so greatly contrasts with the gentlemen in the room, with their perfect coiffures, expertly waxed mustaches, and vibrant frock coats. That doesn't mean he's unattractive, only that his beauty is unconventional. He's gorgeous the same way a lightning storm is—breathtaking despite its danger. Or maybe because of it.

Yet this beast of a man is the highest-ranking figure here. Shadowbanes serve directly under the royals and have more authority than the gentry. The sword at his back is evidence enough of that authority, for Shadowbanes are the only figures aside from the church's priests who are allowed to carry weapons. And theirs are made from coveted silver.

Gods above, seeing a Sinless lord at the Wretched Lair is already rare enough, but a Shadowbane? My palms grow slick with sweat. Shadowbanes don't tend to seek out entertainment like the Sinless lords occasionally do. Their purpose revolves around hunting down two things: Shades and bounties.

And since this is a Sacred City devoid of the former, that leaves only the latter.

Which is a big fucking problem for me, considering I undoubtedly have a bounty on my head. Not for the daisies I sewed on silk at the textile mill. That was a petty enough crime that the proprietress simply sold me off to Rockefeller. No, my previous crime is much graver than that.

The crime of escaping a Sinless.

I clench my fingers into fists, anchoring myself to some physical sensation that isn't my racing heart, and suck in a steadying breath. Then, forcing words from my lips that just might seal my doom, I tell my story again.

I fumble my performance. And the next. And the next. My threads get tangled in the second round, and my heart refuses to stitch correctly together. By the start of the third, I don't even bother with my props. And not once do I reveal my scar again.

It doesn't matter that the Shadowbane only stayed for half my story and I haven't seen him since. He shook my confidence, and it's probably for the best. A talentless storyteller like me couldn't be of interest to him, right?

By my fifth and final performance, my nerves settle to a dull hum. I finish my ending line and curtsy, though my audience is so deep in their cups they hardly notice. It's always like this at the Wretched Lair, since it's one of the few places such upstanding citizens as these can imbibe so unrestrained. Gluttony may be a sin, and would normally attract Shades, but in walled cities like Nalheim, the monsters aren't a threat. Such acts simply need to be kept from the public eye. Otherwise, the common citizens who keep pious lives would know their utopian city is a sham.

Mr. Rockefeller returns to the center of the room to thank his guests and conclude the evening's festivities. While a handful of patrons linger to finish their drinks, many others clear out at once, hungry for their next forbidden fare at the brothels and gambling dens. Such an honorable lot, the gentry. At least they know better than to seek further—and more private—entertainment from us, thanks to the rules of Rockefeller's club. We are not to be touched or spoken to. We are only to be looked at as we wait upon our stages until the last guest leaves. Only then, when no one is left to witness our exit, can we lower our guard and return to the barracks we call home.

Now that sleep is in sight, an entire week of fatigue catches up to me. Rockefeller's performers do more than entertain at the Wretched Lair. Some work in pleasure houses, while others, like me, serve as cleaning maids at various establishments Rockefeller owns. I let my gaze wander to my colleagues, who seem to share my exhaustion. The Bard's thick shoulders droop, his mandolin dwarfed by his enormous frame, his wolflike mask partly askew. The Lover's fingers flinch at his sides, and I wonder if he's yearning to rub his aching feet like I am. After spending the evening dancing, spinning an invisible partner upon his stage, I wouldn't blame him. The Blade flips one of her knives, always in motion, while the Harlot—

"Seamstress, is it?" The voice is male and chillingly soft.

My spine stiffens as a man saunters toward me through the sparse crowd. A man with no shadow. A man with golden hair and the harpist's blood still staining his lips.

I blink at him, hoping the Sinless lord might be a hallucination of my fatigue, but I should know by now the futility of hope.

He stops before my stage, expression empty as he stares up at me. "Step down," he says, his voice a honeyed drawl. The tips of his sharp canines peek from behind his lips when he speaks. "I don't like to crane my neck."

Fuck. This can't be happening. What did I do to draw his attention? I may have disregarded him as a threat after my close call with the Shadowbane, but my botched performances should have made me *less* interesting. My pulse beats a staccato rhythm. Where is Rockefeller?

A quick glance around the room shows no sign of my master, but what could he even do? The rules of the Wretched Lair don't apply to the Sinless. This man can touch, talk, and take all he wants, and no one can stop him. Not me, not my master, and not my companions, who now watch in frozen terror. Is this what happened on the last night the harpist played here? If so, I wasn't there to witness it. Nor am I close enough to the other performers to have been included in such gossip. The remaining guests stop to watch too, but it's only out of amusement, not pity or worry.

The Sinless's eyes narrow. "I won't repeat myself, sinner."

I bite the inside of my cheek, reminding myself of the command he gave me. On trembling legs, I descend from my marble block. He's tall, but so am I, bringing us eye to eye. I'd give anything to shrink down, to fold in on myself, though maybe it would be worse if he towered over me.

"How . . . can I be of service . . . my lord?" My words are stilted, jagged.

"Are you afraid of me?" The first hint of emotion crosses his face, a dash of cruel mirth. "Fear is only a virtue if it is reserved for that which is evil. To fear the Sinless is to be greatly wicked."

I purse my lips, for I have no answer that would please him. The truth is I've never feared evil things like the Shades and darkness as much as I've feared the Sinless. Shades never tried to cut open my chest.

"Here I thought you would be expecting me," he says. "I saw the way you were looking at me before the performances began. Were you envious of your friend?" He waves a hand toward the edge of the room, and I glance to where he's gesturing—the wingback chair he spent the evening in. Slumped on the ground before it is the motionless body of the harpist, eyes open and unblinking, skin a sickly blue.

Very fucking dead, then.

"Envy is a sin, you know," he says, drawing my attention back to him.

Hatred sparks in my chest, burning into rage. Wrath may be another grave sin, but I've always been helpless against its pull.

His lips curl as he speaks again. "I heard your performance was a vulgar one. You bared your breasts, I'm told. What kind of art do you call that? It sounds like fare unsuitable for a social club that serves the purehearted. Wouldn't you be more at home in a brothel?"

It takes all my restraint to keep my retort at bay, but as he arches a haughty brow, I realize his words weren't meant to taunt. He's serious.

"Answer me," he barks, making me jump.

"I had props under my robe, my lord," I rush to say. "I undid my robe to retrieve them, not to bare myself."

His eyes flick to my chest. "Show me."

My breath catches. "My lord?"

"Show me what you flaunted to everyone else, sinner."

I bring a hand to my chest, but not to obey. All I want is to hide all evidence of what I so stupidly revealed. Before now, it felt thematic to show my scar while reciting my tale, a hint of truth, a minuscule act of rebellion. It's not like anyone would know what it's from, especially not the average aristocrat who's spent their entire life behind these walls, ignorant of what happens in the unprotected villages, to criminals, to those who are sacrificed to the Sinless. No one would recognize the cause of such a scar. Not unless they've been on either end of the blade. Only the dukes and princes know what it takes to light their Holy Braziers.

But now that I've seen the Shadowbane, the one person whose job it is to know of crimes committed across the continent, my scar feels like a confession of treason.

For it is treason to have escaped a Sinless duke like I did two years ago.

Treason to have survived his attempt to devour my heart.

The Sinless lord moves faster than I can blink, suddenly close. He bares his teeth and closes his fingers over my wrist in another too-fast motion. His hand is uncomfortably warm, his grip so much stronger than I expected. I cry out as he wrenches my hand away from my robe. Before I can react, he tugs loose the top ribbon closure at the base of my throat. Then the next. Then—

A shadow falls over us. The Sinless halts his efforts, though it isn't of his own volition. His fingers loosen from my wrist, his other hand forcibly removed from my robe by the last person I expect. I launch back as the Shadowbane steps between us.

I thought he left hours ago. Did he . . .

Did he just fucking rescue me?

"I apologize for the disappointment, Lord Wheaton," the Shadowbane growls. His voice is so low and deadly it reverberates down my spine like the Bard's deep baritone when he sings. His hand remains clenched around the other man's wrist, much like how Lord Wheaton handled me mere moments ago. "But this one is mine."

Hearing him claim me as *his* sets my teeth on edge, but I don't dare argue.

The Sinless lord pales, but his eyes flash with defiance. I expect Lord Wheaton to fight the Shadowbane's authority, maybe even physically. Should they come to blows, I'm not certain who would win. The Sinless are said to be immortal, but what of the half-Sinless Shadowbanes? Who is stronger, a foppish immortal lord who spent most of his life fed from the proverbial silver spoon? Or the brutish halfsoul who deals in death and violence as his way of life? After a few tense moments, the Sinless's expression shifts into a mask of boredom, and he shrugs out of the other man's grip.

"As you wish, Shadowbane," Lord Wheaton says, a hint of disgust in his tone. Without a second glance, he strides away. The Shadowbane doesn't follow, but he pins his gaze on Lord Wheaton's every step until he exits the club.

Freed from both their attentions, I skirt to the side, finally catching sight of Mr. Rockefeller. He stands near the only other door in the room, the one reserved for his performers and servants. His stiff posture suggests he witnessed what transpired and knows his party needs to end. Now. With a nod, he opens the private door, lets in several servants—who will have to bear the burden of disposing of the dead harpist—and signals for his performers to retreat to the dressing room.

Thank the gods.

I make a beeline for the door.

The Shadowbane steps into my path. "Are you all right?" His voice is clipped, with an edge of exasperation. He rakes a rough hand through his hair, pushing back the dark, shoulder-length strands from his forehead. The veins on his hand bulge with the motion, as if he's fighting not to follow Lord Wheaton and pummel him. Or maybe it's me he wants to pummel. Perhaps voicing concern for someone so far beneath him is physically painful.

Well, he need not feign worry on my part. I'd rather he took the fucking hint Rockefeller is giving and left. Same goes for the other straggling guests, who don't even bother with the pretense of finishing their drinks and instead watch with unabashed amusement.

I gather enough composure to answer. "I'm fine . . . sir." I tack on the last part, unsure what honorific to use for someone of his status. My eyes flash back toward the door where Rockefeller still stands, ushering my companions down the dark hallway toward the dressing room. Though he watches me and the Shadowbane sidelong, his back is half turned toward us. This is yet another situation he has no authority over. If the hunter wants to feel like a godsdamned hero, it's up to me to ensure he does.

I dip into an uneven curtsy. "I am grateful for your aid, sir. You have my heartfelt gratitude, but I must bid you a good evening." As I straighten, I take my chance to sidestep him.

He mirrors my motions, blocking me again. Desperation claws at my chest. I just want out of here. I want my stiff bed in the barracks. I want to forget I ever caught the attention of not one but two dangerous men tonight. I want my heart to stop fucking racing like it's going to burst from my chest in a gruesome pantomime of my performance.

I curl my fingers, fighting to maintain a hold on my nerves. "You were very kind to help me," I say through my teeth, "but I must now join the others."

"You mistake my actions for kindness," he says, and I lift my eyes to his. He gives me a humorless grin that might as well be a snarl. "I meant what I said to Lord Wheaton. You belong to me now"—

I open my mouth to protest, but he seals his claim with the two words that brook no further argument. The name I left behind in a bloodstained cell. A name not even Mr. Rockefeller knows.

—"Inana Westwood."

CHAPTER FOUR

Inana

He knows. Fuck. He knows who I am.

Echoes of my name reverberate through my ears. Even though he said it quietly enough for only me to hear, I still hazard a glance at the guests who linger, necks craning for a better view of what's happening. And what exactly *is* happening? Is this the end for me? If he's discovered my identity, he'll seek to claim my bounty, which can only end in my execution. I'll be put to death the same way I was meant to die the first time: my chest flayed open, my heart fed to a Sinless royal.

Two years on the run wasted. All my plans for funding my escape from the continent gone.

Anger flares inside me like a stubborn flame.

I will not give in so easily.

Lifting my chin, I remind myself that I am still masked, and even if I weren't, he may not know what Inana Westwood looks like. My likeness has never been captured, for portraiture is a forbidden art. Even if my appearance was conveyed for the sake of my bounty, that's hardly definitive. He has no proof of who I am. He hasn't even seen my scar, thanks to his intervening with Lord Wheaton. With the top two closures of my robe undone, only the base of my collarbone shows.

With as much controlled ease as I can muster, I say, "I haven't a clue what you mean, Shadowbane. My name isn't—"

"Try it," he says, a threat in his tone and a maniacal hunger in his dark eyes. A dare. "Lie to me, sinner. They like the way it tastes."

Who does he mean by *they*? Our audience?

Just then, I feel something whisper-soft alight upon the side of my neck, then brush up the column of my throat. I fling my fingers toward the sensation, but there's nothing there. Nothing to brush away. Nothing to cling to. Yet it remains pressed over my skin, the feeling of a hand splaying open and giving my throat a light squeeze. Panic courses through me and I open my mouth to cry out—

"Make a scene, and this will end poorly," he whispers, stepping in close. He doesn't move as quickly as Lord Wheaton did, but his proximity holds equal threat. So badly I want to pull away, but the pressure on my throat only increases. "Obey, and I'll make this easy for you. But do not fucking lie to me."

He holds my gaze for a few tense seconds, then the pressure eases. The invisible touch slides away. From the corner of my eye, I note a slithering darkness receding into the hunter. When I try to look at it straight on, it's invisible. Then it's gone completely.

Was that . . . a Shade? A godsdamned shadow monster, here in the heart of a Sacred City? It shouldn't be possible, not with the blindingly bright chandeliers or the metallic walls, floor, and ceiling. The Shade shouldn't have been able to enter the city's silver gates. And yet . . . this man is a Shadowbane. Maybe the rumors about his kind wielding Shades like weapons were true.

They like the way it tastes. He meant his shadows. He can prove I'm lying by testing their attraction to me.

This is bad. This is really fucking bad.

"Come," he says and tugs me forward by the upper arm. I don't wrench myself from his grip, for he's taking me in the only direction I want to go. Toward Rockefeller. Toward the hallway. Toward a slim chance to escape.

My master doesn't meet my eyes as we brush past him, but he enters the corridor behind us, closing the door. Darkness envelops us, alleviated by spots of dim illumination from the sconce lamps along the walls. The Shadowbane halts me in place while Rockefeller continues past.

"Master," I call out, but he pays me no heed. Instead, he stops outside the dressing room and leans against the wall, arms crossed. His rigid posture is the only outward sign of discomfort over what's happening, but he is not my ally in this. Not that I expected him to be. It's more that I needed an excuse to glance down the hall, to calculate how quickly I might make it to the end if I run at full speed. That's my one fighting chance to reach the city streets, and then . . .

What fucking then?

"He isn't your master anymore," the Shadowbane says. He releases his hold on my arm, but that chilling *other* touch returns, bracing my cheek beneath my mask before tugging my chin forward until I meet the hunter's eyes. "I purchased your contract, which means your fate is now in my hands."

My stomach drops. If Mr. Rockefeller sold me to the Shadowbane, I no longer have a home in his barracks. No job cleaning tavern floors and laundering sheets at brothels. No glimmer of joy in my dreary weeks as I express my art upon a stage among enemies. No road map to earning my freedom.

I have . . . nothing.

Nothing . . .

Except my life.

And as long as I have that, I will fight. I refuse to face death while holding still. I will dance with it like a fucking lady until it strangles the breath from my lungs.

The Shadowbane opens his mouth to speak again, but I surge forward, thrust an elbow into his gut, and take off running. Rockefeller straightens in alarm as I rush past him but makes no move to intercept me. The door at the end of the hall is in sight as I pump my legs faster, faster—

Something hard collides with my back, and the next thing I know, I'm pressed face-first against the carpeted floor, one arm wrenched behind me while the other is pinned over my head. My jaw aches where it's crushed against my mask. That slithering touch returns, caressing the crimson veil that covers my hair with strokes so featherlight they make me shiver in revulsion.

Then comes a voice, a sultry yet masculine whisper almost too ethereal to hear. "*I bet she's pretty under there. Can I unmask her yet? See what those filthy lips look like when they tell lies?*"

"*She's pathetic,*" says a second voice, this one cold and haughty. "*Not worth our time.*"

"*She smells good.*" The third voice is slower, deeper, and comes from directly beside my head, along with a phantom breath that huffs against my ear. Terror climbs up my throat as I envision some toothy beast preparing to make me its meal.

"Control yourselves." The Shadowbane speaks under his breath, but it sounds like a shout compared to those eerie whispers. The soft touches retreat. I release a whimper of relief, but it's replaced with a cry as my arm is pulled tighter against my back. The hunter brings his face close to my ear. "I didn't say you could run, sinner."

I bare my teeth, fighting his hold to no avail while the beads on my mask clatter with my struggle. If only I could free one hand, remove my mask, and send one of those sunbeam spikes into his eye, his throat, anything. But his hold is relentless. "Fuck you," I grind out.

"*Oh, I'd take you up on that,*" says the first whispered voice. "*I like it rough, love.*"

"Enough," says the Shadowbane, though whether he's talking to me or to the voice, I know not. "Stop struggling, Seamstress, or I will rescind my offer to make this easy for you."

I huff out an exhale and cease my efforts, if only to save my energy for my next chance to escape. There *will* be another chance. There has to be.

"You clearly want to live," he says, "and I'm not here to take that from you, but I will if you make yourself my enemy. So you have two options, Inana Westwood."

I shudder at the sound of my name leaving his lips for the second time.

"Both options start the same. I'll get off you, and you will get changed with your companions. When you exit the dressing room, you will make one of two choices. Your first is to run, though I suggest you start by walking unless you want to give yourself away at once. Unmasked, I won't recognize you. Not at first, and not among your peers. When you reach the city streets, you can start running as fast as you wish, but I will follow. I may not know your face, but my shadows will know your taste. I will track you down."

The snuffling breaths return to the side of my face, and I get the distinct sense of a muzzle nudging my ear, followed by the swipe of something warm and wet.

A tongue.

That was a Shade's fucking tongue. I didn't even know they *had* tongues. Or voices, for that matter.

I can't stop the whimper that climbs from my throat as his threat is made clear. Run, and his shadows will hunt me down. Easily.

The Shadowbane speaks again. "Your second option is the one I suggest. Leave the dressing room and stand before me. Meet my gaze with your unmasked face. You will leave the city with me willingly."

Leave . . . the city? So he won't turn me over to Nalheim's prince, but to another Sinless? Dread opens a hollow pit in my gut as I consider facing the duke I already escaped.

My former fiancé.

The love of my life.

Until he became my enemy.

How cruel a fate would it be to let him finish the job of taking my heart? I'd sooner die by any other hand, even the Sinless King's.

"I'm not taking you to your death." His grip doesn't lessen, but his voice loses its harshest edge. "Not in this option. You won't be coming with me as my captive but as my Summoner."

My mind stumbles over the last part. "What the fuck is a Summoner?" I manage to mutter, my words muffled against my crooked mask.

"An artist. *My* artist." That doesn't explain shit, but he continues on as if it does. "Give me six months of service, no more and no less. Afterward, I promise I'll put you on a ship myself, see to it that you leave the Holy Continent a free woman."

Shock ripples through me at his words. Not only is he admitting there's a way off the continent, a prospect only spoken of in whispers by those of us with nothing left to lose, but his choice of words has my pulse hammering. *Leave the Holy Continent. Free woman.* He probably used those terms deliberately to stir my hope, but I must admit, it's working. Gods, it's working.

Normally when people talk about what lies across the sea, they use words like *exile, damned,* or *warmongering devils.* For regular citizens, leaving the Holy Continent would be a punishment, as this is the only land protected by the Sinless. But for outlaws, we know we're living on borrowed time. Hiding under false names can only take us so far. We can never rise beyond the bottom rungs of society without risking discovery for who we really are. I've never heard of anyone surviving as an outlaw for more than ten years, and those are the luckiest ones. Sooner or later, death catches us, by the hands of the law, the Sinless, or the Shades.

The Shadowbane speaks again. "Cross me and I'll kill you. I have no need for your bounty, but I do require a Summoner. Take my offer or run, but if you choose the latter, know it will be your last time running from me. I will not give you this chance again."

With that, he releases my hand, my arm, and eases what must be his knee from my back.

Every instinct screams at me to flee, but I'm still reeling from his threats and his offer of freedom. Plus, I don't doubt what he said; he won't let me go again, and should I choose to run now, he'll have me pinned down in a matter of seconds. If I want to escape him, I'll have to play along with his first option. Retreat to the dressing room. Doff my robe and mask. Leave with the other performers. Then flee the city and run until he catches me, led by that snuffling shadow monster he commands.

I blow out a heavy breath, fighting that incessant urge to dart down the hall at once. Instead, I rise unsteadily to my feet, straightening my mask to ensure my face is still covered.

The Shadowbane lifts both hands, palms forward, and steps back until several feet of space stretch between us. The light from the nearest sconce brightens half his face. His dark gaze remains locked on mine, but there's no threat there. No cruelty. Only curt demand. "Make your choice."

I can hardly process the mess in my mind to make a choice right now, but at least my first step has already been decided for me. The promise of a respite from the Shadowbane propels me toward the dressing room.

As Rockefeller opens the door for me, he places a hand on my shoulder. Keeping his voice low, he says, "Whatever you do, please don't run." I meet his eyes to find a flicker of pleading in them. Is he pleading for his own safety or mine?

The dressing room is silent as I enter, all eyes trained on me. With slow steps, I make my way to the rack of robes, which is already full of everyone else's attire. It seems I'm the last to get changed. Wary looks follow my every step, as do half-hearted sentiments.

"Are you . . ."

"Did he . . ."

"Does he know who . . ."

No one can finish their questions, because no one can afford to truly care. There's a reason none of us are friends, only cold acquaintances. When one of us fucks up, the rest risk being guilty by association. I've been on their side of this scenario before. Each time, I averted my gaze, held my tongue, and thanked the gods I was spared.

I'm not so lucky this time.

Or am I?

My instinct to flee remains strong, every muscle poised to obey as soon as I give the command.

But what about my second option? In exchange for six months of service as the shadow hunter's Summoner, he'll give me freedom. He promised. Sinless supposedly can't lie—being Absolved of sin and all that—so does the same go for Shadowbanes?

I can't imagine serving that asshole, not after how he pinned me to the ground and threatened me with his Shades.

Still . . .

If I accept his offer, I could be on a ship off this continent in six months' time. The mere thought has me shivering with a mix of terror and elation. No one knows what's out there, only that there is at least one other land that hasn't completely fallen to lawlessness and Shades. Our only evidence is Port Belfair, the sole port city on the Holy Continent, the sole source of outside trade. Rumors say there you can buy passage on a homebound trade ship if you speak to the right person and offer the right price. What happens after is a mystery. Maybe the other lands are brimming with war and sin and Shades. Maybe my chances of survival won't be any better there than they are here. But I'll take danger and mystery if it means freedom. I'll face war and shadow monsters if it means liberation from the Sinless.

I can ally with a dangerous man, play along with his rules, and serve him as he demands. It doesn't mean I have to trust him. I don't know what exactly a Summoner does, but I am an artist, just like he said. And what do artists do? They attract Shades. The very monsters he hunts. If his promise proves false, I will draw every Shade to me and laugh as they pick the meat from his bones. Even if it's the last thing I do. Even if they devour me next.

The medley of hope and violence steadies my nerves, enough that I manage to finish changing with only the mildest of tremors. Dressed in my common garb—an olive-green bodice and a brown skirt with a patched hem—I nod to my companions that I'm ready. They may have surmised my time with them is at an end, but routine kept them from leaving me just yet. We always return to the barracks as a group on performance nights. Safety in numbers until the bitter end.

The Lover raps his knuckles on the door, and Rockefeller opens it, allowing us to file from the room. My heart slams against my ribs as I trail at the back of our retinue.

I reach where the Shadowbane waits; my last chance to change my mind.

With a slow exhale, I halt in place. Shift to face the towering male while the other performers continue down the hall. Leaving me behind.

I lift my eyes to the Shadowbane's, finding his are already roving me from head to toe, as if memorizing every stitch of my drab clothing, every freckle that dots my upper chest and face, every strand of my strawberry-blond hair spilling loose over my shoulders. His attention sears me to the bone, an unspoken reminder that if he couldn't hunt me down by sight before, he can now. His dark eyes lock on mine, studying my gray irises now, and it's all I can do not to avert my gaze, not to shrink from his scrutiny—

A subtle shift of movement steals my focus, and I glance to the side. That's when I notice two figures standing farther down the corridor, half hidden in shadows. I recognize them both, the towering middle-aged man with the scarred face and the petite young woman with hard eyes. Fellow performers, Bard and Harlot. But what are they doing here? Only a fool would have stayed behind out of solidarity, which means . . .

"You weren't hoping it would just be the two of us, were you, Seamstress?" The Shadowbane's tone is dry, a corner of his mouth lifting in a taunting grin. My eyes track the angle of his lips, the way his dark lashes cast shadows over his cheekbones as his gaze burrows deeper into me. For whatever asinine reason, my stomach flips in response. Before I can compel my eyes away from that smirk that has my body doing traitorous things, he pushes off the wall and brushes past us. "Welcome to my crew, sinners."

CHAPTER FIVE

Inana

The tension in the air is as thick as the silence that blankets the streets of Nalheim, punctuated only by the rhythmic beat of horse hooves and wagon wheels on cobblestones. The Shadowbane manages the reins at the fore of the wagon, while Bard, Harlot, and I sit in the back. The vehicle is no different from those used in rural villages like the one I grew up in, with an uncovered bed, a wooden perch for the driver, and two horses hitched to the front. Not the grand hunting carriage I pictured someone of his rank owning. Since the Shadowbane commanded us to leave the city with him at once, we're the only souls on the road. Anyone seeking evening amusement knows better than to use the main streets. All to keep up appearances that Nalheim is home solely to saints.

I lean against the inner wall of the wagon bed, legs pulled to my chest, head tilted back as I watch empty storefronts and grand manors give way to clustered row houses, then factories. Night has fallen, but our surroundings are almost as bright as day. The astrotheurgical dome of light blazes from every angle overhead, leaving hardly a sliver of shadow between buildings or beneath the manicured greenery. My eyes glide to the center of the city, where Nalheim Palace towers from the summit. Its silver turrets shrink farther and farther into the distance, yet the glow that emanates from the tallest spire remains undimmed, the Holy Brazier an ever-shining beacon of safety. During the day, the dome cast by the brazier is invisible beneath the sun's rays, but at night, it maintains a twilight haze over the city, regardless of how dark the sky is beyond it.

I scowl at the blinding pinprick of light shining from that far-off tower. The brazier's secrets may be unknown to most citizens, but not to me. I know the price of its safety: a human heart. It isn't just in Nalheim. Every brazier in every protected city, whether walled or not, requires such a price. And now I know the secrets of the Sacred Cities too. They aren't the perfect havens I was raised to believe they were. The royals may reward those who prove themselves devout by inviting them into these walled cities, but once inside the silver gates where Shades can no longer follow, there's nothing to keep citizens from reverting to sin. Not if they hide it well enough.

It's that dichotomy that makes a Sacred City such an ideal environment for an outlaw. It's the one place we aren't supposed to exist.

When Rockefeller purchased me from the textile mill's proprietress, I thought he'd drop me off at a labor mine at best. When I realized he was taking me to a Sacred City, I imagined being fed to a prince. Gods, the dread I felt when I considered that my master maybe *did* know who I was. That he'd purchased me knowing I was a bigger investment than the proprietress had surmised. But that wasn't the case. If he'd known I was guilty of far worse than telling stories while sewing daisies on stolen silk, he wouldn't have given me a bed in his barracks, a job, and a clear path to buy back my freedom. Not to say I'm fond of having been bought and sold like property, but laws against human trafficking don't apply to criminals. So for me, twice convicted of forbidden art and lucky to be alive, my situation in Nalheim was as good as I could hope for. I had a plan. An outlet for my art.

Now . . . I don't know what I have, aside from the Shadowbane's promise of freedom in exchange for six months of service. But can I trust him? Can I even trust Bard and Harlot?

"Get some sleep if you can," comes the Shadowbane's voice over his shoulder. "We reach the city gates in an hour, and we'll remain on the road until daybreak."

None of us answer, nor do we ask where we're headed once we leave Nalheim. I posed a similar question when he first loaded us into the wagon, and all he said was "Somewhere else." A fucking wordsmith, this one.

My gaze flicks across the wagon to Harlot, who picks at her nails, a glower on her pretty face. She can't be older than seventeen, with ash-brown hair and blue eyes that hold too haunted a look for someone so young. Bard sits closest to the front of the wagon, his broad back facing our new master. The way he positioned himself between us and the Shadowbane feels almost protective, though there's nothing to suggest Bard is alert. His gaze is hollow, distant, strands of thin salt-and-pepper hair hanging over his forehead. One hand rests on the cloth-wrapped mandolin tucked close to his side while the other strums absently over strings that aren't there. Everywhere from his face to his hands bears deep scars, which makes me wonder about his story. What's the truth behind the sorrowful songs he sang at the Wretched Lair? And what about Harlot? What led her to choose such a moniker, to draw caricatures of her patrons living out their sexual fantasies with her while she gripped her pen like she was strangling it?

I know nothing about these two whose fate I now share. Or the mysterious hunter who calls us his crew.

My lashes flutter open to the most beautiful sight—the night sky.

I rub sleep from my eyes and tilt my head back, drinking in the inky black expanse speckled with glittering stars, and the moon at the center of it all. It's been a whole year since I've seen night. Not just darkness, but the true night sky. It's a comfort I didn't think I'd miss so dearly. No decent person would take comfort in the dark, in leaving the safety of one of the eight Sacred Cities. But I'm not a decent person, and perhaps I never was.

Even my mother called me a cursed child. Born on winter solstice—the longest night of the year, and a new moon at that—I entered this world a bad omen. The way Mother told it, Shades were clawing at the door despite the silver-lined walls of the midwife's birthing room for all forty-six hours she labored. And after I was born, they continued to screech and claw the remaining hours until sunrise. Were she not such a devout woman, I'd think maybe she had her own knack for storytelling.

But her tale isn't a unique one. No mother wants to give birth at night, for the Shades are drawn to new life almost as much as art. Scripture claims it's a mockery of our deities to procreate before we've earned our gods' forgiveness. It is therefore a sin, hence the Shades' attraction. Funny how it's the one so-called sin that isn't forbidden. Almost makes you wonder if it's bullshit. Or if there's a reason the church wants us to keep populating the continent to perhaps—oh, I don't know—replace all the people who are sacrificed to the Sinless?

I lower my eyes to the horizon, spotting the faintest beam of light above a silhouette of hills and trees. That must be Nalheim, far behind us. I slept through our exit from the gates, but based on the pitch-blackness surrounding us and our proximity to the city, I didn't sleep for more than a few hours.

A cool breeze dances over my arms, reminding me of another thing I've missed during my time in Nalheim—cold. The Holy Brazier not only illuminated the city but maintained the perfect temperature year-round. Not once did I need a cloak while walking home at night, or extra blankets on my bunk despite it now being late into fall. That may sound ideal to some, but I love experiencing seasons, from shivering before the hearth in the winter to wiping sweat from my brow beneath the relentless summer sun. It makes me feel alive.

I shift to the side, muscles aching from the half-sitting position I slept in, and search for the wool cloaks the Shadowbane pointed out when he loaded us into the wagon. Only . . . there's already one covering me like a blanket. I frown down at the warm weight on my lap, the corner of the cloak slipping down my torso. Maybe it was the chill that woke me, the cloak having come down from over my shoulders. But how did it get there? Did either of my companions drape it over me after I fell asleep? I doubt I have the Shadowbane to thank for such a kindness.

A glance at Harlot and Bard shows they too are tucked under cloaks, eyes closed. Bard still sits with his back facing the Shadowbane, but his head is lowered, bouncing with the movement of the wagon. Harlot is slumped on her side, using her sketchbook as a pillow. I'm about to tug my cloak back over my arms when I note the warm weight in my lap is from more than just the fabric. There's something heavier pressing down on my legs.

My heart stutters as I stare down at myself, noticing a thickening of shadows that form the mass of some large beast.

With its head in my godsdamned lap.

Terror courses through me as I recall the snuffling breaths by my ear, the tongue that slid over my cheek. Is this . . . a Shade? *That* Shade? The monster the Shadowbane threatened me with? What the fuck is it doing on me?

As if alerted to my rising panic, the shadow beast lifts its head, meets my eyes with two onyx orbs, and scrambles back on four paws. Then, with canine grace, it darts for the raised driver's seat and plants itself beside the Shadowbane.

"*She's awake.*" The voice slithers from the Shade, just as slow, deep, and ethereal as it sounded in the hallway. Sharp breaths strangle my lungs as I stare at the creature. It's semitransparent with a body like rippling black smoke, its silhouette so like a wolfhound. Most Shades manifest in vaguely humanoid shapes, with too-long limbs and featureless faces, their edges forever wavering and shifting. Some, though, appear as beasts like this one. "*She was warm.*"

"*I don't know about warm, but she is pretty,*" says a second voice, familiar in its seductive, lilting tone. One of the other Shades that spoke in the hall. Even though I can hear it, I see no sign of it.

"You think anything with a face is pretty," the Shadowbane mutters under his breath.

"*The brunette is pretty too.*"

"She's a child, Lust. Not even eighteen."

Lust. Is that the Shade's name? Or its . . . origin? Everyone knows the monsters are born from the seven human sins. They coalesced from mankind's wickedness during One Hundred Days of Darkness, and more continue to be born on dark nights or in shadowed places. It never occurred to me each Shade might embody a singular sin. It also never occurred to me a Shade could talk, yet here we are.

"I didn't say I wanted to fuck her, you godsdamned pervert. I just said she was pretty. I wouldn't fuck the big one either . . . though I might let him fuck me."

The Shadowbane heaves a grumbling breath. "I'm sure you would."

"I can't believe you let her *join us without offering a single apology."* That's another voice I recognize, the sternest one. *"She should have gotten on her knees and begged forgiveness for the disrespect she showed."*

"I didn't know you liked them on their knees." Lust's voice again. *"So do I."*

"Of course I do. It's the sincerest show of respect."

A chuckle. *"That's not at all why I like it."*

"Gods, enough," the Shadowbane says.

"Do you find it as strange as I do that our new master talks to himself?" Harlot's whisper is so unexpected, I nearly jump from my skin. Pulling my gaze away from . . . whatever the hell is going on in the driver's seat, I find the young woman is awake and has shifted closer to me.

Keeping my voice low, I say, "Almost as strange as the voices that talk back."

She furrows her brow. "What do you mean?"

"The other voices." When she looks only more perplexed, I add, "You can't hear them? You see them at least, right? His shadows?"

Harlot glances to the front of the wagon. The Shadowbane's posture has stiffened. He knows we're awake and can probably make out our conversation. She gives a wary nod. "I can see them. Or . . . one, at least."

"Shadowbanes cast abnormal shadows." This time it's Bard who speaks. His head is still lowered, but he stretches his legs and tugs his mandolin tighter to his barrel chest. "That's how you can tell you're in one's presence."

"I'm not talking about actual shadows," I say. "I'm talking about the Shades he controls." Bard says nothing, and Harlot only shrugs. Why don't they seem as disturbed as I feel? "Are the two of you fine with this arrangement? How'd you even get wrapped up in it? You aren't the ones who inadvertently attracted attention to yourselves."

Harlot pulls her head back. "What do you mean, how did we get wrapped up in this? We were chosen first. He spoke to Bard and me between performances and made us an offer to buy out our contracts. Freedom after six months of service? That's better than Rockefeller's terms."

I blink at her. "You agreed, just like that? You didn't feel . . . threatened?"

"Not any more than usual. *You're* the only one of us who made a scene."

"Yes, well, he didn't mention anything about service or freedom until after he'd already pinned me to the floor and promised to hunt me down if I ran from him."

A corner of her lips quirks. "And you didn't beg him for more? Honestly, Seamstress, if you wanted to brag, you could have just said so."

I level a look at her. "I didn't get some civilized offer between performances like the two of you."

"Probably because he knew you'd be the hardest to convince."

"Why do you say that?"

She gives a derisive snort of laughter. "We're not like you, Seamstress. I don't know your story, but it's safe to assume we're all fugitives. Our options are limited. We can be beggars, servants, or dead. For Bard and me, it matters not whom we serve or how we do it. I don't care about art, aside from the opportunity it gave me to work at the Wretched Lair, and now as a Summoner. You and Bard may share a similar passion for your craft, but he plays for himself, while you play for your audience. You relish being seen."

I'd argue that the masks we wore during performances say otherwise, but that's not what she means. And she's right. I crave the attention and love witnessing the effect my art has on others. Were it any other way, I never would have been caught the first time. I would have kept my storytelling private instead of sharing my secrets between bedsheets, my head resting on the chest of the man I loved while I spoke treason like a lullaby.

Still . . .

"Aren't you at all concerned about what he'll have us do?" I ask. "What duties does a Summoner perform? It's clear we'll use our art to attract the Shades he hunts, but to what extent? What if we're merely bait?"

"I've been bait my whole life," Harlot says, tone empty. "I'm not too concerned about what fucking flavor I am now."

"Language, Mary." Bard's sharp tone rings out through the quiet night.

Harlot's eyes snap to him, her expression volleying between startled and amused. Then it softens. When she speaks, her words are laced with pity. "My name isn't Mary, Bard."

Slowly, he lifts his head and stares at his surroundings as if seeing them for the first time. He runs a scarred hand over his face, clearing the daze from his eyes and replacing it with a haunted look. "Sorry," he grunts out, voice muffled against his palm. "Mary was . . ."

He doesn't finish, and he doesn't need to. Mary must have been someone dear to him. Perhaps around Harlot's age. Maybe someone he lost the day he received all those scars. I wonder how often he finds himself tangled in the past, how often he relives whatever nightmare he came from. I've found myself in such dazed states before, haunted by blood, piecing together broken shards of memories I've still to fully recall—

"Speaking of names," the Shadowbane says, his voice an unwelcome intrusion. My spine stiffens at the deep resonance of his tone. "It's time for your first training exercise as my new Summoners. Exchange your real names. Going forward, we'll be frequenting places populated by Shades, and the fewer lies we tell each other, the better."

I scoff. "You want us to go by our real names. Names associated with . . ." I can't bring myself to say it out loud. Names associated with our past deeds. Past crimes.

"That isn't something you need to be concerned about anymore," he says. "Shadowbanes can appoint whomever they wish as their Summoners, and those who serve them are above reproach. So long as you remain loyal to me, you need not fear persecution. Besides, I'm not asking you to share your surnames or to flaunt your identities before outsiders. Just share this piece of truth with each other."

I bristle, and I'm not the only one. Bard, Harlot, and I exchange wary glances. Bard clutches his mandolin tighter while Harlot's lips curl. "What if I prefer the name I went by at the Wretched Lair?" she says archly.

"I'm not fucking calling anyone on my crew Harlot."

I glare at the Shade hunter's back. "Maybe you should go first, Shadowbane. Trust and truth go both ways. You already know our names, and you've promised us a dream of freedom. Sounds too good to be true, especially when we don't know a damn thing about you or what it means to be your *crew*."

He heaves a begrudging sigh. Then, shifting to look over his shoulder, he says, "Dominic." His eyes sweep over us one at a time before lingering on me for too long. Moonlight glints over his face, and in that moment, three dark shadows stand out stark against the night: two humanoid Shades clustered close to one side of him, the wolfhound shadow on the other. All three stare at me with the deep, dark pits that serve as their eyes. These aren't just vague imitations with featureless faces. They have mouths, noses, hair. The wolfhound has a muzzle and a tongue that lolls from it. What's most unsettling, however, is the striking resemblance the humanoid Shades bear to the Shadowbane. They have his bone structure, his lips, his hair.

My blood goes cold. Everyone knows that if you ever see a Shade that bears your face, it's time to fucking run. Because that Shade is out for your blood. And if it consumes its victim . . .

It becomes the worst kind of Shade.

An Incarnate.

I've never seen such a monster, but I've heard stories of them. Shades who consume the humans they've imitated become corporeal. They copy their victim's bodies, to the best of their abilities, and become flesh and blood upon assimilating their prey. They're less sensitive to sunlight. They can enter homes, no matter how well lit, and always leave a trail of carnage until they're killed—something only a Shadowbane can do.

I don't know how this hunter has taken control of Shades that came so close to becoming Incarnate, nor do I know if I should be impressed or terrified. All I know is I do not like the way they're looking at me. To my relief, the sliver of moonlight retreats behind the trees, blanketing them in shadow once more.

I swallow hard, unsure if I should ask the question poised on the tip of my tongue. It leaves my lips despite my efforts to resist. "And your . . . friends? Do they have names?"

The Shadowbane—Dominic—goes rigid. The three Shades break into whispers, their voices layering over one another.

"*She wants to know our names.*"

"*I think she likes me.*"

"*Don't tell her a fucking thing.*"

Dominic's jaw tics, and he faces forward. Silence stretches so long I assume he won't answer. I'm surprised when he finally says, "Sloth, Lust, and Pride."

So I was right; his Shades are named after the human sins they were born from. I already know Lust is the lilting voice, and I assume the stern one is Pride. That leaves Sloth as the wolfhound. There's so much more I want to know. How does he control them? Are they a threat to us? Can he control *any* Shade, or only specific ones? Does he force them to hunt down their own kind?

"Your turn," Dominic says, reminding me this isn't the time to ask him questions, when we still haven't completed his supposed training exercise.

The three of us continue to eye one another warily, none of us eager to volunteer, until Bard speaks. "Rykar." His hands tremble, and he rushes to add, "But do not call me that. Bard will do, and if that feels like a lie, then don't address me by name at all."

No one argues with that, not even Dominic.

Harlot blows out a breath. "Harlow," she mutters.

I give her a withering look. "Really? You chose a stage name so close to your real one?"

She shrugs. "I'm not the creative type."

I disagree. She may claim she doesn't care about art, but I've seen her drawings. They're lewd and fantastic.

"Well, don't leave us in suspense," Harlow deadpans.

Right. It's my turn to bare my truth. My heart races, and not just with fear. There's a sliver of rebellious excitement there too. The thrill of not having to hide. The same thrill I felt every time I told my story at the Wretched Lair, knowing how much truth I'd layered in. With equal parts trepidation and elation, I state my name out loud for the first time since fleeing my hometown. "Inana."

"Great," Dominic says, tone flat. "Now no more fucking talking until daybreak, unless you want to start your Summoner duties as corpses."

I sneer at his back, though I belatedly realize his threat might not have been a personal one. Rather, he was reminding us of the Shades who freely stalk the night. Shades whose pitch-black eyes I can almost feel, watching us from the trees that line the road.

CHAPTER SIX

INANA

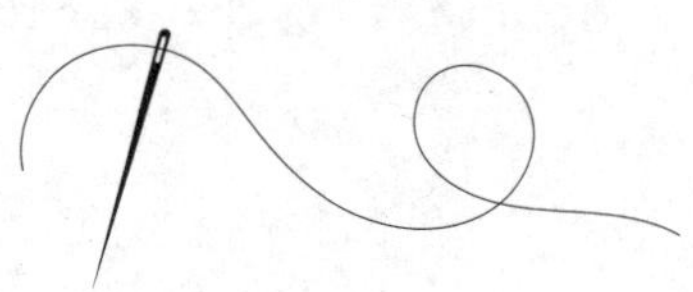

If Dominic was looking for a way to shut us up, he certainly found it. After his reminder about the wild Shades, Bard, Harlow, and I exchange not a word more, nor do we sleep. Instead, we cast haunted looks outside the wagon. I can't help but startle at every subtle movement, every sound of twigs snapping or leaves rustling in the ever-thickening forest. I see the monsters now and then, when the moon peeks out from behind the clouds and bathes our surroundings in the one kind of light Shades don't fear. Their wavering silhouettes stand out starkly between the trees. Humanoid, mostly, yet with very few distinct features save for long limbs, dark pits for eyes, and wavering ovals for heads. Their spindly fingertips cling to tree trunks as they watch our wagon pass by. At one point, a beastly Shade crosses the road behind us, its shape like a mountain lion, its dark eyes staring after us until distance swallows it.

Fucking hell, the night sky may be beautiful, but it's a terrifying time to be outdoors. I haven't lived outside the Sacred City's protection in a year; I nearly forgot how I used to spend my time after sundown before—silent or sleeping, safely tucked in rooms lit with an abundance of lamps and candles while reflective bronze disks hung from the rafters to amplify the light. Never did I or any other villager leave the safety of our homes at night, and we certainly didn't travel.

I glare at Dominic's back, enraged that he'd put us in such danger. Is this another one of his training exercises? Does he see this as some essential initiation, like sharing our names was?

I know Shades rarely attack unless provoked. Still, I'm not amused Dominic sought to press our luck and drive us straight through shadow-monster territory in the middle of the godsdamned night.

It's a relief when the sun peeks over the horizon, painting the sky in the first shades of rosy pink, gold, and blue. Once dawn fully rises and the forest road is illuminated, I break the silence with my poorly concealed ire.

"Why the hell did we travel at night, Shadowbane?"

He doesn't so much as look over his shoulder. "You know my name, Inana. Use it."

Annoyance flares hotter at the sound of my name on his lips. Especially since he didn't even need to look at me to know I was the one who spoke. I force my reply through my teeth, refusing to humor his demand. "Why did we travel at night?"

"I'd like to know as well," Harlow says, her glare almost as dark as mine. "Are you trying to get us killed straightaway?"

"Careful," Bard whispers. He's seated closer to us now and his voice is meant only for us. "He's our master, and much higher ranking than Rockefeller was."

He's right. Yet there's something about Dominic that makes it impossible to choose humility. Maybe the fact that he tackled me to the ground and let his shadow dog lick my face. Thankfully, there's no sign of any of his Shades now that the sun has risen.

"Shadowbanes work at night," Dominic says. "When we're assigned to protect villages, our most important work begins after sundown. Hence, I sleep during the day, and either work or travel at night. We were perfectly safe. Shades find quiet travelers uninteresting. You'll need to get used to resting before sundown from now on, as my Summoners work when I do."

I hate that what he's saying makes sense. Gods, of course we'll have to work at night. Shadowbanes can track down criminals and claim bounties whenever, but hunting Shades is something that can be done only under the cloak of darkness. That's why it's rare to meet a Shadowbane. I never came face-to-face with one in my village, despite a few having been assigned over the years to take care of particularly aggressive Shades.

"Are you ever going to tell us what exactly we'll be doing as your Summoners?" Harlow asks, brow arched. "Are we just bait, like our lovely Seamstress suggested last night, or do we have a chance at surviving six months in service to you?"

"Your survival depends on you," he says. "Listen to me, obey, and don't fucking betray me, and you'll survive. I'll train you as best as I can before we take up our first post together at Thornfal village. First, there's a final member of our crew to pick up."

Not long after, Dominic navigates our wagon off the main road and down a narrow forest path. We reach a wide, sunlit clearing beside a rushing stream. At the center of the clearing are the remains of what must have once been a stone cottage. All that's left is a foundation, three crumbling outer walls, and a partially collapsed thatched roof. Even though the architectural style is similar to those in rural villages, it must be centuries old. No one would have dared to live so deep in the woods after One Hundred Days of Darkness. The forest has been a breeding ground for Shades ever since.

A male figure darts out from the ruined cottage, heaving a sigh of relief at the sight of the wagon. "Thank the gods," he says as Dominic tugs the reins to bring the horses to a halt. He's dressed in brown britches, a tan tunic, and a vest that's unbuttoned and possibly inside out. He looks to be around Harlow's age, perhaps a couple years older, with pale blond hair, blue eyes, and soft features despite a subtle gauntness about him. Even in his drab clothing, he's as lovely as the boys who work in Nalheim's brothels. Which is to say pretty but a touch underfed.

"What happened?" An edge of concern laces Dominic's voice as he descends from the box seat. The three of us in the back of the wagon make no move to exit, instead exchanging a wary glance before turning our attention to the two men.

The young man stops before Dominic, wringing his trembling

hands, one of which is bandaged. Now that he's closer, I note a sheen of sweat on his forehead and a greenish tint to his skin. "I fucked up."

"Don't tell me . . ." Dominic's worry shifts into what looks like annoyance as he runs a hand over his face. "I left you a full vial. That should have been plenty for three days."

"It should have been, but a fucking Shade, Dom. It nearly stopped my godsdamned heart. I took a mere swig and suddenly there it was, creeping around the corner with long, spindly fingers. Startled me so bad I dropped the vial, shattering the whole thing. Then of course I cut myself on the glass. It couldn't have gone worse."

"Damn it, Calvin."

"Damn me, I know," he says, eyes pleading. "I wasted your blood, and no one is more sorry about that than me. As you can see"—he lifts his hands, which tremble harder—"I'm barely hanging on to my sanity. I'm too cold. I'm too hot. A fucking spider dropped on my head just five minutes ago and I haven't a clue if it was real."

A chill seeps into my veins. I know what this is. He's addicted . . . to Sinless blood, and he's currently going through withdrawal. I've only ever witnessed this once, when one of the Wretched Lair's part-time performers turned up shaking and sweating and hardly able to hold her lute. She'd been claimed as a Sinless's blood source the weekend before, and he in turn fed her his blood, only to discard her by the end of the week. A luckier fate than the harpist from last night, but I haven't a clue how long she went through withdrawal. I never saw her again.

What's most concerning, however, was that the man named Calvin said *your blood*, which means Dominic has made this man his thrall.

"When did you drop the vial?" Dominic asks.

"Like an hour after you left. I'm telling you, mate, this has been a nightmare three days."

"Fuck." Dominic reaches under his cloak and extracts a dark vial. It's barely out of his hands before the other man uncorks it and downs a sip.

"Oh, gods," Calvin says with a moan, eyes closed as he tips his head back. His tremors cease and his greenish pallor is replaced with a rosy flush. "Fuck me sideways and reverse it, that's good."

Dominic casts a glance at the back of the wagon. There's something like an apology on his face, but his tone is flat as he says, "Crew, meet Calvin."

Calvin corks his vial, eyes widening as his attention shifts to us for the first time. His pupils are blown wide, his expression overly cheerful. With a sheepish grin, he wipes the back of his unbandaged hand over his mouth, smearing a speck of blood over his bottom lip. "Shit, sorry. That's not the first impression I wanted to make."

His sweet yet bloodstained smile so greatly contrasts with the terror building inside me. I grip the side of the wagon until my knuckles turn white, my gaze volleying between Dominic and Calvin. Gods, it never occurred to me Shadowbanes had the same potent blood as the Sinless, being that they're only halfsouls. Does that mean . . .

"Do you thrall all of your crew?" Harlow asks, speaking the question that's trapped in my throat. Though her voice is level, her posture is as tense as mine.

Bard clenches his hand tighter around his cloth-wrapped mandolin, a murderous glare in his eyes. It might be the most animated I've ever seen him, and bloody hell, it's frightening.

"I do not," Dominic says.

"He really doesn't." Calvin waves a placating hand. "I'm a special case, I assure you, and I'm not thralled. What we have is an arrangement of equals. I give him my blood when he needs to feed—"

My eyes flash to Dominic. "You feed on blood. Just like the other Sinless."

He holds my gaze but doesn't answer.

"Not as often," Calvin says. "Never for pleasure, like those overly thirsty fucks in the Sacred Cities. He feeds when he needs to, and in exchange, he lets me live."

"He lets you live," I echo.

Dominic closes his eyes and speaks through his teeth. "You're making it sound worse, Cal."

"Sorry," he says with a chuckle. "What I mean is, well . . ." He begins unwrapping the bandage and steps closer to the wagon. The cloth over his palm is stained crimson, but when he holds his hand out to us, there's only the smallest of cuts at the base of his thumb. "I have a rare disease that prevents my blood from properly clotting. Sinless blood aids healing. See? That's why he gives me his blood. So I don't fucking die from a paper cut, or in this case, a tiny piece of glass."

Some of the tension eases from my muscles. I've heard about the healing power of Sinless blood, a miraculous albeit dangerous commodity. A scarce one too. Since acquiring it would rely on the generosity of the blessed ones who care little for common citizens, it's hard to come by, even for those willing to pay the price of addiction.

"I may be addicted to this surly bastard's blood," Calvin says, "but I'd be dead were it not for him."

I expect at least a verbal lashing for having just called his master a surly bastard, but Dominic merely shakes his head and approaches the back of the wagon. "We're off to a fine fucking start, aren't we?" he mutters under his breath as he unlatches the locks securing the endgate. He lowers it and waves us forward, unfazed by our distrustful expressions. "We'll be on the road again tonight. Stretch your legs. Eat. Rest."

Bard makes the first move to exit the wagon, then Harlow.

"I made stew," Calvin says, tilting his head toward the ruins. "I can almost assure you it's edible."

Dominic remains at the foot of the wagon as I prepare to descend. I hesitate, staring down at him, arms crossed. "Are you going to feed from us like you feed from him?"

He holds my gaze without falter. "Calvin is my dedicated source, and I have no plans to feed from anyone else."

"What if something were to happen to him?"

"Then yes," he says, jaw tight, "I would need a new source."

Nausea turns my stomach, though I suppose I should be grateful he didn't lie. I still don't know if he *can* lie.

Arching a brow, he holds out a hand.

What a godsdamned gentleman. I scoff and descend from the wagon without his aid. But as my feet hit the ground, he steps in close, chest almost brushing mine as my backside slams against the lowered endgate. "Careful, Seamstress. Flaunt your ire so boldly, and I might start to think you have it out for me. Remember what I said were your keys to surviving the next six months?"

I glare up at him, annoyed that I have to tilt my head to meet someone's eyes for once. Of course I recall what he said. Listen, obey, and don't betray him. I'm about to say as much, but whatever was going to leave my lips dries on my tongue, my mind halting as my eyes lock on his face. This is the first time I've been so close to the Shadowbane during daylight. It's a shock to find his eyes so near mine, each of his thick black lashes on display. While I first noted his eyes were a dark brown, I now see they're flecked with green. His tanned skin is decorated with slender scars, one of which runs beneath his cheekbone along the line of his bearded jaw. It's so thin, I'd only be able to see it from this close. My gaze lifts to his forehead, where bronze strands highlight his dark hair where the sunlight hits just right—

His brows lower into a questioning look, which reminds me I'm staring.

Fucking staring like some youthful maiden who's never seen a handsome face before. Which, yes, he *is* handsome. I'd be a fool to pretend otherwise, even though it fills me with no small amount of rage. I can't find a man who pinned me to the ground and threatened me attractive. I can't find a *Sinless* attractive, not even a halfsoul like him. Because even though I'll never admit such a treasonous thought out loud, I despise the Sinless. All of them. Protectors of mankind or no, I hate them, and he's one of them.

I could never have feelings for this man. Not good ones, at least.

A corner of his mouth quirks up, just like how he smirked when he welcomed us to his crew in the hall outside the Wretched Lair. For the first time, I catch a glint of his canines. They don't appear to be as elongated as a pure Sinless's, but they're sharp nonetheless. "Did you mean to get lost in my eyes?" he says, a note of taunting in his voice.

"Hardly," I bite out, stepping back. "I was . . . surprised you had a face, that's all, after seeing nothing but your back for hours straight."

"Are you saying you missed my face?"

"Absolutely not. It's hardly distinguishable from your ass."

"Because they're both so nice to look at?"

My cheeks burn hot. What the hell is he playing at? Is he . . . flirting with me? This bastard has been nothing but curt and cold since we met. A man of few expressions and even fewer words. I'm stuck gaping before I can form a coherent reply. "Neither is nice to look at."

"Careful," he says, his smirk deepening until a dimple pops just above the line of his beard. "You may not be able to see them during daylight, but they're there. And they can still tell me when you're lying, sinner."

The whisper of a phantom touch grazes my chin, but it's gone before I can attempt to swat it away. With that, Dominic turns his back and saunters toward the cottage.

With my heart pounding faster than I care to admit, I follow, all the while seething over the words we just exchanged. They replay through my mind again and again until my eyes drop down to his ass, seeking an answer to whether it really is as nice as his face.

Just as quickly, I snap my gaze away and scold myself for my curiosity.

Because, fucking hell, it's a nice ass indeed.

CHAPTER SEVEN

Dominic

Inana Westwood is going to be a problem. I suspected as much when she elbowed me in the gut and ran from me at the Wretched Lair. Now I'm certain of it, thanks to . . . whatever just happened between us.

"Was that you, Lust?" I whisper as I stride toward the cottage, my heart thudding heavily. Which, for a Shadowbane, is an anomaly. My heart should be slow and steady, an occasional beat hardly worth my notice. "Did you . . . possess me somehow?"

"*That was all you, lover boy,*" Lust says into my mind. "*Though I admit I enjoyed it almost as much as you did.*"

Did I enjoy that? Was joy the fiery heat I felt when I saw the petulant expression on her face? I'd sooner think it was annoyance, and I'm sure that's what it was at first. But when she looked at me up close, her ire wiped clean as she studied my face, something flared in my chest. I wanted to see her hatred all over again, and I wanted to be the cause. Me. Nothing else. Not our situation or preconceived notions or generalized suspicion. Just me. My voice. My words. I wanted to be the flint that sparked her fire, and fuck if it didn't feel good in the moment.

But that's the anomaly. I shouldn't feel like that for even moments at a time. Because it almost made me feel like *before.*

Ever since my partial Absolution six years ago, my emotions have dulled. An expected result of the astrotheurgical ritual that strips one's lunar energy—humankind's darkest aspects—from their soul. Had it been a full Absolution, I'd feel an even lesser range of emotion.

In a logical sense, I remember what it was like to feel everything to extremes, rising or falling in vicious spikes or hollow valleys. Anger, fear, joy, attraction. I remember flirting and fucking and being lost in the throes of pleasure. I remember how it felt to stir someone's desire or have them stir mine. To lock eyes with someone I found beautiful across the room, beginning a dance of seduction with words, looks, and small touches that culminated, whether an hour or a month later, in sweat-soaked bodies and breathless voices that screamed each other's names. I remember the games of sex and courtship. Not that I participated seriously in the latter, for I knew I could never be a husband, only a temporary lover. My fate was sealed from birth, and my upbringing ensured I never forgot, each day dedicated to my studies. Fighting. Sword forms. History. Scripture. All to prepare me for my chance at becoming a Shadowbane.

Inana catches up to me and brushes past, pulling me from my thoughts. Her shoulders are stiff, her entire being radiating with rage. My eyes fall on her tangled red-blond hair, a windswept strand whipping me in the cheek as she enters the cottage before me. I suck in a breath, scenting apples and honey. I'm struck with the urge to catch that tendril between my fingers, tug it—

I halt in place, my hand halfway to reaching for her hair. Curling my fingers, I fist my hand until my nails dig into my palms. What the fuck is wrong with me?

Keeping to the wall and as far away from Inana as I can manage in this crumbling shack, I watch as she joins the other three around an old stove. Thank the gods Calvin has managed to light it and cook an entire meal without burning the whole place down, though it remains unknown whether his fare is fit for human consumption. He's a shit cook at the best of times, and that's when he isn't fiending for my blood or collapsing from blood loss.

He stirs the pot as he learns his new companions' names, then ladles stew into copper bowls. His is the only posture that's relaxed, but he's currently high as all hell and very much used to this routine. After two years serving as my blood source, he knows new Summoners are always like this—on edge, one foot yearning for the freedom I promised while the other seeks the first chance to run.

"I didn't expect three of you," Calvin says, handing a bowl to Harlow, Bard, then Inana. "We normally only work with two."

Inana scoffs, her gaze shooting to mine. She knows from her conversation with Harlow last night that I approached Harlow and Bard first. "Was I just an afterthought?"

I fold my arms and lean my back more firmly against the wall. "You were a liability," I say, tone even. Normal. Thank fuck. "You almost became a Sinless's pet, maybe worse. Marcus asked me to intervene."

"Marcus?" Harlow echoes.

"Ah, Rockefeller," Calvin says. "How's the bloke?"

Inana's suspicion deepens. "You were already acquainted with Rockefeller?"

I clench my jaw. Of course my business partnership with Marcus Rockefeller would feel like a betrayal to her. Despite the outwardly aloof relationship he has with his performers, Rockefeller provides them with the kind of hope few outlaws are given. And he always makes good on his word. Unless, of course, I'm in the market for new Summoners. "He and I have an arrangement. One he can't refuse even if he wants to. I did him—and you—a favor when I claimed you as my Summoner."

"Are you suggesting I thank you after you gave me very little choice but to serve you?"

"Indeed I am. Would you rather I let Lord Wheaton drink you dry? Make you his pet and force you to do his bidding as his mindless thrall?"

She pales, but doesn't back down. "You admitted you'd sooner have let him have his way with me. You didn't intervene because you wanted to."

"You're fucking welcome," I say with a mocking wink. On the inside, annoyance writhes in my gut, yet another emotion I shouldn't feel. Doesn't she get that I didn't have to do a damn thing? I could have refused Rockefeller's plea to help her. I *should* have. I can't save everyone, and I can't afford distractions. There's a reason I didn't want her from the start. I knew she was trouble the moment I saw her at the Wretched Lair, when my shadows stirred in an undeniable pull toward her. Her every word entranced them, made them so *alive* with interest. I watched her first performance from far across the room. Her words were too distant to hear, but I saw her motions. Her crafted hearts. I tried to watch her second performance up close, but I had to step away just to keep my shadows from reaching out to her—whether to strangle or embrace her, I know not.

While it's essential my Summoners are effective enough to attract wild Shades, they can't be so talented that my own act unruly.

"What happened to your previous Summoners?" Bard says, one of the few times he's spoken directly to me. His voice is a slow, deep monotone, and his scarred face provides a welcome distraction from Inana. Though his question isn't the most pleasant to answer.

Noticing my hesitation, Harlow adds, "Did you send them off on a ship across the sea like you promised you'll do for us?"

"Some," I say.

"And the others?"

I heave a sigh, my silver blade suddenly heavy against my back. "Dead."

The three Summoners assess me with narrowed eyes.

"Look, what we're doing isn't any more dangerous than what you were doing in Nalheim. You know that, right? That you were flirting with danger at the Wretched Lair? Inana is proof of that. Your work as Summoners will be dangerous too, but I will do everything in my power to protect you."

Their distrusting expressions only deepen.

I don't exactly mind it. Their suspicion is healthy; it proves I chose them well, for I need Summoners with fire in their blood and darkness in their hearts. The overly compliant ones don't have the drive to survive the danger I'll put them in. The fervent ones who admire Shadowbanes too greatly will turn on me when I prove to be different from what they expect. And the ones who are too clever, too hateful of me and my kind . . .

Those relationships tend to end in bloodshed.

My eyes slide back to Inana, and I wonder where her fate lies.

"Well," Calvin says, his mouth full of stew, "we're becoming fast friends, aren't we? Don't be shy. Eat up."

That reminds the others of the bowls in their hands. They exchange cautious looks before Harlow takes a spoonful. Her lips pull into a grimace as soon as they close over the spoon.

"How is it?" Calvin asks, eyes glittering as he studies her.

Her throat bobs, and it takes her several moments to answer. "I've definitely had worse in my mouth. And better. A lot better."

Calvin chuckles. "I only promised edible."

I exit the ruins, my appetite gone, and make my way to the firepit. Sundown won't be for several more hours, but it's cold this deep in the woods. My body temperature has run warmer than a regular human's ever since my partial Absolution, but I remember how uncomfortable winter felt on my skin before. That's why I draped my Summoners' sleeping forms in their cloaks before we left the city.

Footsteps approach as I stoke the embers of the fire, and I'm relieved it's only Calvin. I need to get my fucking head under control before I stand anywhere close to Inana again.

Crouching beside me, he speaks low to keep his voice from carrying to the cottage, where the other three remain. "Something good came from spilling the vial. The Shade that startled me . . . It was drawn to your blood."

My eyes snap to his, and he gives me a knowing look.

One of the final Shades I've been seeking is *here.* I run my hand along the leather holster at my waist, where a dozen glass vials are stashed, some empty, some filled with blood, others filled with shadows.

"Tonight," I say. "We'll catch it after sundown, but not in front of them. They aren't ready for that yet."

Calvin gives a sharp nod.

Finally, some good fucking news. While it may not be the most important Shade I'm hunting, this is a much-needed win after the shitstorm these last few weeks have been. I still have to locate two vital Shades, ones that have eluded me to no end, and I only have six months to find them. Six months until I'm up for consideration to become a full-fledged Sinless. Six months until I have a chance to stand before King Kaelum. Six months until everything I've been trained for my entire life will either come to fruition or burn to ash.

CHAPTER EIGHT

INANA

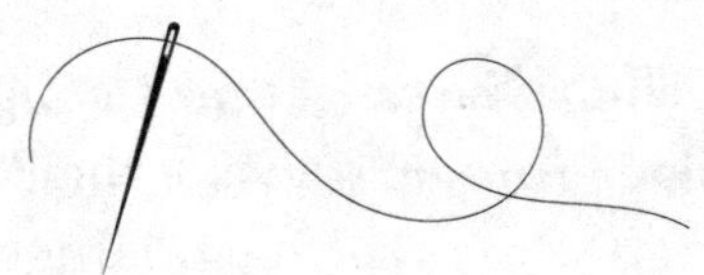

It turns out the Shadowbane does sleep during the day, though not in the way I expected. Instead of making a bed in the ruins, he's sprawled beside the stream, a rolled-up cloak beneath his head. His sword is propped against a boulder beside him, but his belt of vials and knives remains around his waist. His arm rests over his eyes to block out the afternoon light, but that's his main defense against the elements, save for his dark clothing. Shadowbanes must run hotter than mortals, because even under the sun, the air possesses an unmistakable bite. And the nerve he has to bare his roped forearms like it isn't cold at all, his black linen sleeves rolled to his elbows. Meanwhile, the rest of us are huddled around the fire with our cloaks wrapped tight around us, mugs of watered-down coffee in our hands.

I shift my gaze away from Dominic to take a sip of my drink. I grimace, finding it somehow bitter and bland at the same time. Turns out Calvin is just as bad at brewing coffee as he is at making stew. At least the man himself has proved to be far more tolerable than his fare. While none of us are eager to let our guard down—it's still only been half a day since we were dragged into this arrangement—Calvin makes it impossible to dislike him, with his easy manner and abundant smiles. I'm not sure how much of his friendly personality is influenced by Dominic's blood. It's true Calvin is nothing like the listless harpist, and the fact that the blood eases the symptoms of his medical condition makes it sound like an exchange between equals. But still . . .

I eye Calvin across the fire as he takes a small sip of blood from his vial. It's the second time he's drunk from it since Dominic gave it to him.

Calvin meets my gaze as he replaces the cork, then rubs a hand over his newly flushed cheeks. "What? Do I have something on my face?"

I'm slightly abashed that he caught me staring, but I might as well ask what's on my mind. "Are you truly not thralled?"

Harlow lifts her eyes from her mug, intrigued by the question. Bard, on the other hand, shows no interest as he stares with unfocused eyes into the fire.

Calvin tucks his vial into his vest and trades it for his mug of coffee. After a hearty drink, he says, "Fuck, that's disgusting. And no, I'm not thralled. Shadowbane blood is addictive, but it doesn't have the ability to control me or take away my free will the way Sinless blood does."

"How do you know?" Harlow asks. "What if you only think you aren't his thrall because he's convinced you otherwise?"

He meets her eyes with a sad smile. "I was a Sinless's thrall for six years. I think I'd know the difference."

There's no reproach in his tone, but Harlow's expression falls with a mixture of surprise and pity.

"I might as well tell you my sordid tale," he says. Thank the gods, because I'm burning with curiosity now. "As you know, I have a rare blood condition. It doesn't clot properly, so even the slightest lesions are dangerous. Excessive blood loss, anemia, infection. I've had a lot to fear from any injury, yet I never expected my downfall to be so pretty. Her name was Lady Gertrude. A Sinless, and one of the most respected aristocrats in the city of Tarun. I was twelve when she happened upon me and my family in the market square."

"You lived in Tarun?" I say. Tarun is one of the eight Sacred Cities. To live in one, you have to either be born there or be invited as a reward for piety. People like me, Harlow, and Bard were only allowed to live in Nalheim as servants, and only at Mr. Rockefeller's behest. We weren't true residents. Even those who finish their terms and earn their freedom maintain the rank of servant and can be forced to leave the city at any time. Or forced to serve the Sinless as their blood source.

"I was born there," Calvin says. "My family was middle class, desperate to rise to the gentry. If they'd known their chance would come courtesy of my scraped knee, I think they would have shoved me onto the sidewalk themselves rather than wait for a newsboy to do it by accident. For the relentless flow of my blood caught the eye of Lady Gertrude. Between stanching my wound, scolding me for causing a scene, and begging Lady Gertrude's forgiveness for inconveniencing her day with my appalling display, it took them a while to note the woman wasn't upset; she was fascinated. One financial transaction later, I was hers.

"Gertrude took me to her manor, introduced me to her other dedicated blood sources—all young boys—and told me to call her Mother from then on. For six years she fed from me, then healed my wounds with a sip of her blood. She was my addiction, my master, and my mother. A more loving parent than either of mine had been. Until I came of age."

Calvin's eyes go unfocused. "Lady Gertrude didn't like when her sources aged, and I'd already outlasted many who'd come before me. As quickly as she'd brought me into her home, the woman I'd called Mother for six years discarded me on the streets of Tarun the day I turned eighteen."

My stomach turns with rage. Who takes in a mistreated young boy, cares for him, then discards him for such a petty reason as aging? That's our perfect Sinless for you. Paragons of virtue. Incapable of sin. If that kind of cruelty isn't a sin, what the hell is it? My fingers curl into fists as Calvin continues.

"My parents didn't want me back. They'd been living pampered lives, thanks to Gertrude's generous compensation. If I'd lost her favor, it was my fault, and they wanted nothing to do with me, fearing any association might send them back to the middle class. I wish I could say I was heartbroken, but I was more preoccupied with my craving for Mother's blood. I returned to her manor, cried at the gates. I cut my palm and begged her to drink from me. The rest is hazy in my mind, as I was far from lucid by then. All I know is I eventually made my way to the fringes of the city and tried my luck at the brothels. No one wanted a discarded thrall, especially one in the throes of withdrawal, and the last person to reject me threw me physically from the premises.

"I sustained an internal injury, something that greatly surpassed a small cut or anything that could be treated by normal means. Even surgery would have been too great a risk, and none of the passersby were keen on summoning a healer. Then Dominic found me. His blood saved my life and helped release me from the call of Mother's blood. Not every discarded thrall is so lucky. Even those without serious medical conditions like me wind up dead from withdrawal. Dom saved my life, and I've been by his side ever since, about two years now."

My eyes flick toward Dominic's sleeping form, something softening in my chest. I still don't fully trust him or his promise, but his arrangement with Calvin seems genuine after all. That doesn't change what he is. A Shadowbane's sole objective, aside from hunting Shades and claiming bounties, is proving himself worthy of being made full Sinless. Regardless of whatever good he's done, he seeks to be one of them. Seeks to be among the ranks of cruel immortals whose every wicked action is vindicated by having been Absolved of sin and turned into living gods.

"What about you?" Calvin says, gaze landing on each of us in turn. "How did you end up as performers at the Wretched Lair? I'm not privy to the finer workings of Dom's business partnerships, but I know what kind of people Rockefeller recruits."

"You mean purchases from jailhouses," I deadpan.

Calvin shrugs. "Sure. How did you become, you know . . . outlaws?" Excitement flashes in his eyes as he says the last part.

I'm surprised when Harlow answers without hesitation. "Murder."

"Murder," Bard echoes.

Calvin nods along as if we're discussing our favorite colors before turning an expectant look to me.

"Treason," I finally say.

"Nice, nice," Calvin says, nodding more. He glances at each of us again, then flourishes his hand. "And . . . ?"

"And what?" I say.

"I want to know more about the murder, murder, and treason. I didn't ask what you were accused of. I asked how you *became* outlaws."

Harlow scoffs. "Why would we tell you?"

"I just bared my soul," he says, placing a hand over his heart in an exaggerated manner. "I won't demand the same in return, but wouldn't it feel nice to tell the truth and have someone listen for once? Someone who will believe your side of the story?"

"How do you know my side is any better than the other?" Harlow says.

"I don't." Calvin's lips peel into a crooked grin. "And it's just as good if it isn't, love."

They hold each other's stare for a moment. Harlow's expression is cold, while Calvin's borders on flirtatious. I almost feel like I should excuse myself and let them finish this conversation on their own, but the thought of stepping away from the fire eliminates that idea.

"Fine." Harlow speaks in a dry, dismissive tone. "I was sold off in marriage to a respected lord in my village. He was in line to eventually be made Sinless after a few more years of proving his devoutness. Better yet, he was recently widowed, which made him the ultimate prospect for every family seeking connections. I was fifteen and too young for marriage, but my family didn't give a shit. In his benevolence, he promised he wouldn't lay a hand on me until I came of age. What he failed to promise, however, was that his sons wouldn't touch me either, or that he'd care if they did. Earlier this year, I decided I'd had enough and laced every meal, every drink, with a sedative. Then I ordered the servants out of the manor and drenched every doorway in oil. I struck a match and watched that manor burn until dawn."

Calvin's jaw is slack while his eyes dance with fascination.

She tilts her head with an innocent smile. "Whenever I smell roasting meat, I remember that night with great fondness."

It seems to take Calvin no small amount of effort to tear his eyes away from Harlow to address Bard next. "How about you?"

Bard doesn't look up from the fire or utter a word. The slow shake of his head paired with his somber expression says enough. Whatever he's been through, he doesn't want to talk about it. Calvin takes the hint, giving him an understanding nod.

Which, unfortunately, means I'm next.

"Inana," Calvin says. "Lady of high treason, how might you have gotten that dreadful scar?"

My hand reflexively moves to my chest, where my cloak has parted to reveal the puckered line of flesh above my bodice. I open my mouth, but Harlow speaks first.

"Gods, she's going to talk forever. You know she's a storyteller, right? She relishes this kind of thing."

I cut her a glare but am surprised at the wry smile on her lips, the ease of her posture. Maybe she's only humoring Calvin by playing along. Or maybe telling her story offered a sense of liberation. Whatever the case, I must admit it sort of feels good, having a casual conversation for once. Not only that, but one where we exchange dark truths without fear of condemnation.

"At least leave the props," she says.

"I wasn't planning on using them." I roll my eyes, but I realize how close my fingers were to reaching for them, my two cloth hearts tucked in my bodice. Not for any other reason but comfort. I always feel most comfortable telling stories while my hands are busy, hence the trouble I once found myself in while decorating stolen silk. But I'm not going to speak fiction this time; it would feel disingenuous after what Harlow and Calvin confessed. And while it is daytime, we are nonetheless in the woods. Shades may be relegated to the shadows beyond the clearing, but I'd rather not draw one anywhere near me with art and lies.

That doesn't mean I can't add a little flourish.

"Mine is a story of a woman who lost her heart," I say, grinning as Harlow throws her head back with a grumble. "Mine is a tale of the treachery of love."

CHAPTER NINE

INANA

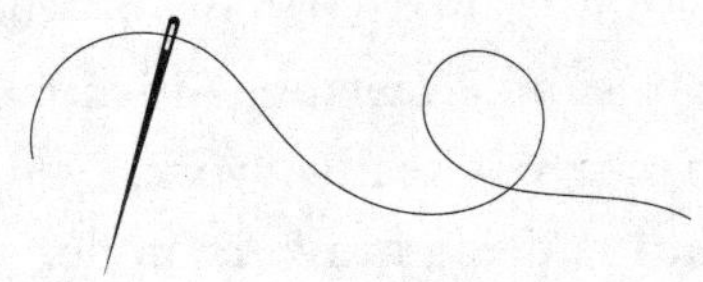

"It was a day for celebration when the villagers of Dunway learned we would soon receive a Holy Brazier," I say. "While everyone else anticipated protection from the Shades, I celebrated for a different reason. For the day we received our brazier, my fiancé would come home."

Calvin's eyes drop to my hands, perhaps seeking a wedding band. He won't find one. Not even the ghost of an indent from a ring now lost graces my finger, for our engagement never culminated in an exchange of rings. Ours was a secret affair, one my love insisted on keeping to ourselves until he finished military service at the capital.

"Four years he'd been gone," I say. "Four years in service to King Kaelum and hardly a word between us. I'd received a few letters during the first year, but they grew more sporadic after that. I held tight to the promises he'd made, reminding myself he was doing this for us. You see, he wanted to make a name for himself before we made our engagement public. That isn't to say I was always full of faith. Sometimes, in my loneliest hours, I wondered if he was ashamed of me. Perhaps he'd been ashamed of me all along, and that was why he wanted to make a name for himself first, so that no one would dare question his choice of bride."

"Why do you think he was ashamed of you?" Harlow asks, her prior teasing gone.

"I was the village seamstress, an already dubious occupation for its ties to art. But as you know, so long as artisans stick to time-honored patterns and keep from straying into creativity, we don't attract Shades." I don't mention how stifled I felt by this. It was tedious sewing the same patterns day in and day out, in the same bland shades. Only the Sacred Cities see a vast array of fashion and architecture, which I didn't know until I first set foot in Nalheim. Outside those silver walls, we live in simple dwellings identical to those that were built hundreds of years ago. Creative work, even the most innocuous kind, is done only during daylight hours, under strict regulations.

"Seamstress," Calvin says with a grimace. "Might as well have been a witch as far as your neighbors were concerned, eh?"

He's exaggerating, but he's not exactly wrong. Magic falls under the same umbrella as art, but it's perhaps even more taboo. While astrotheurgy was commonplace before One Hundred Days of Darkness, it's now forbidden to everyone except the highest-ranking Sinless and the church. Not much is made public about magic, but I've gleaned that it once was used in harmony with the gods. Practitioners would invoke divine energies by drawing astrotheurgical diagrams, ritual circles intricately adorned with elemental shapes and the gods' planetary symbols. After One Hundred Days of Darkness, magic in unholy hands was named a sin.

As a child, I craved a peek at a diagram, desperate to know what one looked like. Two years ago, I saw one. The day my story takes place.

"My village saw me as a witch, indeed," I say. "I lived alone, separate from my parents even though I was unmarried. I worked in what was considered a tainted field. But when we received the news that Dunway was deemed devout enough to be rewarded with a Holy Brazier, I was certain my neighbors would see I was just as pious as the rest of them, just as deserving of the good fortune King Kaelum had chosen to bestow upon us. Four years of missing my beloved were finally coming to an end, in the most spectacular way. Our newly appointed duke would escort home our men who'd left for the military. My fiancé would return at last and we'd have nothing standing in the way of our love."

I drop my gaze to the crackling flames roaring in the firepit. My voice takes on a bitter edge as I explain the next part.

"I was on my way to the celebratory procession to welcome our new duke when the guards ambushed me. They were unfamiliar men, their uniforms too fine for common citizens. They marched me through town, away from the main road where the procession would be held, and toward our run-down jail. I called out to my neighbors, fellow villagers I'd known my whole life, but they refused to look my way. I was locked in a cell, my wrists tied with rope and affixed to the wall behind me. The guards shut me in without a word of explanation. Hours passed, and not even my parents came to look for me. I lost track of time. The sun was still bright when—*finally*—my fiancé came."

Calvin and Harlow watch me with eager expressions. Even Bard lifts his head to assess me through the straggly black-and-silver strands that hang over his forehead.

For once I'm not lost in the joy of enchanting my audience. There's a sliver of delight in my heart, but the shadows of my past are too thick to allow it to grow. Telling my story like this, baring the truth, is so different from the tale I spun at the Wretched Lair. It isn't a bittersweet story of heartache and hope. Only rage. Regret. Hatred.

I continue. "When my beloved entered my cell, I wept with joy. He'd come to save me and he'd wrap me in his arms before my next breath. Yet breathe I did, and never did I feel those arms come around me. I forced my tears to abate so I could clear my eyes. Perhaps I'd merely hallucinated his presence, seen what I wanted to see. But there he was, the same man who'd left me with a passionate kiss and a promise of a dazzling future together four years prior. He was dressed in a fine suit of white and gold. His military uniform, I assumed. So why didn't he close the distance between us? Why did he merely stand there with a gold bowl in his gloved hands and such a cold look on his face? Why didn't he reach for me?"

My throat tightens at the memory. The way terror crept upon me as I studied him with new eyes. He set down the wide, shallow bowl, and

I realized what it was. Saw the astrotheurgical diagram etched inside it. It was even more beautiful and more intricate than I ever could have imagined, and I couldn't feel an ounce of joy about that.

"He didn't reach for me," I say, a harsh tremble in my voice, "because he hadn't come to rescue me. He came to . . ."

I swallow hard, partly to steady my voice but also to take a moment to select my words carefully. Some truths, like the cost of lighting the Holy Braziers, are considered treason to confess. Everyone knows Sinless of all ranks consume human blood, but what they don't know is what sets the dukes and royals apart from the Sinless gentry. It's more than the fact that the former can perform solar astrotheurgy; it's how they gain access to that magic.

"The man I once loved no longer cast a shadow," I say, "and his canines were as sharp as knives. I was chosen as a sacrifice for our new duke."

Harlow's eyes widen in realization. "Your fiancé was turned Sinless?"

"Your new duke . . . was Henry Berkham." Calvin says the name under his breath.

I stiffen, rage bristling up my spine. So he knows of the Duke of Dunway. I haven't heard a damn thing about my hometown since I escaped, and I've had no desire to. I doubt I could contain my revulsion at hearing how well my former fiancé is doing. But there's another reason I've avoided all news about my village . . .

The only way Henry could have formalized his appointment as Duke of Dunway is if he succeeded in taking a sacrifice. I thwarted his first attempt in my escape. My survival means someone else died in my stead.

I can't afford to feel guilty about that.

"You were chosen as his blood source?" Harlow says.

"Worse." I rub my scar, recalling my horror as he unsheathed a silver blade. He still hadn't said a word to me, hadn't responded to my tears, my pleas for an explanation. "He pressed a dagger to my sternum and spoke to me for the first time in four years, his voice soft and cold, yet strangled by the slightest tremble. 'Don't move, and this will all be over soon.' Like a fool, I obeyed, thinking this had to be some misunderstanding. Maybe he had to do this. To feed. Maybe he was in a frenzy for blood and couldn't bear to drink from anyone but his beloved." I scoff. "It's funny the excuses we'll make for a lover, even as they're hurting us.

"I held as still as I could as he pressed the tip of the knife into my skin. I cried out and his hands began to shake. The knife slipped from his gloved hands, and his composure fell with it. Cursing, he tore off his gloves and gathered the knife more firmly. That's when I saw the gold band on his ring finger.

"'Henry,' I said. 'Why are you wearing a wedding ring?'

"He met my eyes then, and there was no love in them, only annoyance. It sparked my own, burning into hatred as everything became clear. Henry must have impressed the king greatly during his military service, for he was not only turned Sinless but gifted a fucking wife. I, his secret former lover, was chosen as a sacrifice to keep his shame in the past.

"I said as much, shouting the truth at the top of my lungs. He covered my mouth so the guards outside the jail couldn't hear and brought his face close to mine. 'Yes, I'm ashamed of you,' he said. 'I'm ashamed I ever loved a sinner like you. But your sacrifice will save Dunway. This has to happen. I must . . .' He stuttered then, gagging on his own words. 'I must consume a human heart. It's the only way I can light the brazier. The only way I can *keep* it lit. And the first sacrifice must be you. You're the reason Shades claw at doors at night. You're the sinner who draws them here.'

"'With my sewing?' I said against his hand.

"'With your storytelling.'

"My heart fell to my feet at those words. My body shook from the betrayal of it all. 'Those stories were for you,' I said. 'Only you.'"

I close my lips, keeping his next words to the confines of my memory. *Don't lie to me. I saw you. I saw you talking to them. Whispering tales to things that moved in the dark. You were never afraid of them. You were always a sinner.*

I shudder now, the same way I shuddered then. I hadn't known he'd seen me speaking stories to Shades. Never to dangerous ones, and never at night. Only a few times did I dare utter tales to the helpless monsters I'd found trapped in pools of shadow. I can't even say why I did it, only that I couldn't help it. I was overcome with the same urge I felt when I spoke my first story as a girl, that same hunger for validation. I wanted to see if my stories were truly wicked, if art was really a sin. So why not test it on Shades who couldn't come after me even if they wanted? During the day, they were relegated to slivers of shadow. By evening, the villagers and I would be safely indoors surrounded by lantern light.

Harlow *tsk*s, shaking her head, but her lips are curled in a devious grin. "Wicked woman. I take it your argument did you no favors."

"No favors, indeed. If anything, it only steeled his resolve. He pressed me hard against the wall. He was so much stronger than he'd been before Absolution, and he pinned me in place despite my struggle and proceeded to open my chest. So I did the only thing I could think to do. I started telling a story."

Harlow barks a laugh. "You're fucking crazy."

"It startled him enough to halt his efforts, and he clamped a hand over my mouth once more. So instead of speaking, I hummed. I sang against his palm and watched his temples pulse. They say Absolution strips a person of the seven human sins, but there was wrath in his eyes then, and I used it as fuel to distract him. He was so busy muttering prayers to counteract my sins that he didn't notice the sewing needle in my hand."

Calvin arches a brow. "A sewing needle? You just . . . happened to have one?"

"I always had spare needles. Not intentionally, but I often tucked them into my clothing when I got distracted in the middle of my tasks, and I'd forget where I put them until they poked out from my hems hours or days later. This time, though, I remembered. I had two in my cuff. The first I used to pick at the rope until I freed one of my wrists. The second I used to slash open his neck."

"Is that how you escaped?" Calvin asks.

I open my mouth to confirm his intuition, but my mind stutters. I blink a few times, brief snatches of memory flashing behind my eyes. My recollection of what came after has always been hazy. With blood loss paired with the trauma of my experience, it's no surprise my mind has stifled some of my memories. Still, I owe my companions an end to my story, so I focus on what remains clear.

I envision slashing Henry's neck with the tip of my needle and put words to the vague images in my mind. "Blood welled for only a second before the wound sealed before my eyes. His teeth pulled back from his lips, and then . . ."

I blink hard, willing my memories to clear. "Pain, sharp and piercing. And blood. So much blood. I slashed him again . . .

"More blood.

"And . . .

"And shadows writhing in the corner of my cell . . .

"Blood soaking my dress, dripping to the floor, my head dizzy. Then there was . . . screaming. Shouting—"

"Inana." Dominic's voice shatters my thoughts, cleaving through my jagged, patchwork memories with a tone of warning. I snap my mouth shut and lift my gaze. Only then do I realize I've been staring at my hands, both of which are trembling. Harlow, Bard, and Calvin watch me with unblinking eyes. But as Dominic comes up beside me, jaw tight, gaze fixed on the trees surrounding the clearing, their expressions turn to terror.

I follow Dominic's line of sight.

All around us are Shades.

CHAPTER TEN

Dominic

This isn't at all how I wanted to wake up. It was bad enough when I was rudely pulled from slumber by my shadows tugging away from me, a physical discomfort that turns painful if they try to stretch too far. Of course it was Inana's voice that had drawn them. Even I was intrigued by her story as my mind cleared from the dregs of sleep. Then came the second interruption. A missive appeared before my eyes in a flash of astrotheurgical light, the parchment hovering in midair before dropping onto my face.

I had all of three seconds to read the damn thing before I saw them. Shades all around the clearing.

I've seen thousands by now, but the sight of so many gathered in one place sends a chill deep down to my bones. Dozens of them fill the spaces between trees, their slender, semitransparent bodies watching us with hollow eyes. One has managed to get so close that it's crouched beneath the wagon, peering from behind one of the wheels. What's even more unsettling is that they're acting so bold during daylight hours. True, the sky has grown overcast as day turned to afternoon, but there remains a distinction between the brightness of the clearing and the darkness beneath the trees. And these Shades are clustered as close as they can get to the edge of protective shadow.

"*This isn't ideal,*" Pride says. "*One would think they'd have the sense to behave for at least an hour.*"

I ignore him and speak to my Summoners, voice low and level. "First lesson of being a Summoner. Stay calm. Don't react. Breathe."

No one says a word, though I think that's more out of shock than obedience. Still, to my new crew's credit, they don't panic. I turn in a slow circle to assess where any other Shades might be. Sure enough, there are a few behind the trees across the stream too. Thankfully, Shades can't cross bodies of running water, so those pose no threat. My fingers flinch, eager for the sword I left by the boulder where I napped, but unsheathing my weapon would do more harm than good. Displaying any threatening behavior could send them into a frenzy. The best we can do is stay quiet and wait until they lose interest.

"Second lesson," I say, "raise your fucking hoods."

Calvin's hood is already raised, of course, for he's used to this. The other three belatedly follow, understanding dawning in their eyes. Though it's rare, Shades who take too great an interest in a specific person, usually because of their art, might seek to Incarnate. It starts with a Shade mimicking its target by appearance, its formerly featureless face shifting to mirror the human's. It escalates when the Shade consumes its victim, assimilating their flesh until their new form turns solid. It ends with a blade of fire severing the Incarnate's neck. There is no other way to kill an Incarnate, and neither the original Shade nor the person it consumed can survive.

"What about you?" Inana asks, her eyes flicking briefly to mine from under her hood. "You're not wearing a cloak."

"Don't worry about me. I'm not an artist, and Shades aren't interested in imitating my kind."

My heart thuds rapidly in my chest, which is when I realize I'm standing too close to Inana. Once again, being near her has made my emotions spike—fear this time. I take three steps away until familiar apathy returns. What doesn't change is our situation. My pinch of fear may have abated, but the Shades remain as intrigued as ever, showing no sign of losing interest. If anything, they're growing agitated, reflecting Inana's state as she was struggling to finish her story. Even my shadows buzz with disquiet, rippling against my skin as they huddle around me.

"Dom," Calvin says, and as I meet his gaze, he tilts his head toward the Shade beneath the wagon. It has peered farther out from behind the wheel, its spindly fingers clinging like spider legs. Its face, however, is a reflection of mine.

Fuck.

It's the Shade Calvin accidentally attracted while I was gone.

I wanted to wait until nightfall to capture it, but after the missive I received, I no longer have the luxury of time. If I'm going to capture the Shade, it must be now.

"Change of plans," I say with a sigh. "We're moving on to our first active training session. How to calm unsettled Shades."

"What?" Inana bites out in an angry whisper. "We're going to perform Summoner duties? Right now? Without knowing fucking how?"

"You're about to learn. Just trust me."

"Trust you?" Harlow lifts her head to glare at me from under her hood.

"You'll do great, love," Calvin says with a wink. She turns her scowl to him instead.

"Eyes down." The demand in my tone has all four heads lowering. "Now, Inana, tell a story. But not the one you were telling just before."

"That wasn't a *story,*" she says, an edge of panic in her voice. "That was . . . I wasn't lying."

"I'm not accusing you," I say, though I'm not sure how else to explain how she drew so many Shades if she was speaking truth. It's like her very voice is art to them. "What I mean is, your words left them restless and unnerved. A Summoner's duty involves knowing how your art influences the Shades and using that to get them to do what you want. In this case, we need to calm them so they'll wander away after your performance. Tell something false yet mundane."

"False yet mundane," she mutters. After a few more beats of silence, she begins. "There once was . . . a squirrel."

"*Oh, this one is boring already,*" Lust says.

Sloth, however, leans toward her. "*I like squirrels.*"

Inana darts a glance at me, a furrow between her brows. For a moment, I wonder if she can hear them. But . . . no, that can't be possible.

I nod at her to keep going, along with a stern "Eyes down."

She clenches her jaw before lowering her head once more. "There once was a squirrel who . . . lived in a tree burrow. He was small and . . . and cute. He collected . . . acorns."

I'd be amused if this situation wasn't so dire. It seems Inana does not excel at telling stories unrehearsed. Yet the Shades give her their full attention. Even Pride, who refuses to acknowledge interest in anyone or anything, is reluctant to follow as I slowly make my way toward the wagon.

"He loved all kinds of acorns," Inana says, "but the blue ones were his favorite. Yes, in this magical forest there were acorns of all shapes, colors, and sizes." She's hitting her stride now, her pacing more even.

From the corner of my eye, I see the Shade shift under the wagon, edging away from me to keep the campfire in sight. With unhurried motions, I reach into the wagon bed and retrieve Bard's mandolin and Harlow's sketching supplies. Then, just as carefully, I return to my crew.

"Every color of acorn had a different meaning," Inana says. "The pink ones could lead one to love."

I stop beside Bard and hand him the cloth-wrapped instrument, half expecting him to lash out at me for touching it. But he takes it from me with only the faintest of grumbles, then gingerly unwraps it. "Play something soft. Quiet. We don't want to draw more Shades than we already have, but this will divide the attention between you so Inana isn't bearing it all. There's a reason Shadowbanes work with more than one Summoner."

Bard begins to play, a simple yet playful tune.

I hand Harlow her sketchbook next, as well as her satchel with her ink and quills. "Draw pleasant images."

"They can't see what I'm drawing from where they are. What if that makes them want to get closer?" The worry in her voice makes her sound younger, closer to her seventeen years of age than the cynical, world-weary persona she's displayed thus far.

"It doesn't matter if they can't see what you're drawing. It's the act of creating that matters. And if you're infusing your work with calm, they'll feel it. Draw something that evokes your own feelings of safety."

With trembling hands, she opens her sketchbook, then sets out her inkpot and quill. I was impressed the first time I saw her ink drawings and am equally so now as she proceeds to set fine lines to her paper, starting at the center of the blank page.

I step back toward the wagon.

"*You won't let me watch?*" Lust says. "*What if she draws those sexy positions again?*"

"We have a job to do," I say under my breath, halting once I'm on the other side of the wagon. Its bed is between me and the campfire now, but I can still hear Inana's story, her words weaving seamlessly into Bard's tune. The Shade wearing my face remains beneath the wagon, fully entranced by my Summoners.

I unsheathe one of my knives and crouch down. Keeping my breathing steady, I press the tip to the earth and draw a circle. From there, I bisect it with a horizontal line. A hundred and eighty degrees, to represent the ground. Then I press the tip to the bottom of the circle and carve a diagonal line. I mirror that on the other side. Then I connect the lines, making them intersect at specific points.

Every line is precise yet second nature; I've drawn many ritual circles since I became a Shadowbane. We may be taught only a single astrotheurgical diagram, but it's more than most Sinless know. The Sinless gentry aren't allowed even the barest knowledge of astrotheurgy. The princes and dukes use solar magic—with a diagram almost identical to the one I'm drawing now—but they don't cast their own circles. Instead, they perform a ritual using a predrawn diagram etched into the Holy Braziers. The only people who know the full scope of astrotheurgy are the priests, for the church serves directly under King Kaelum. Their knowledge makes them the most powerful humans on the continent, and they guard it with their lives.

My diagram grows more and more complex with every line, but it isn't cluttered. It's orderly. Symmetrical. A mathematical equation of elements, angles, and planetary symbols, meant to call down divine energies from the heavens to reflect back on mortal earth in specific outcomes.

I complete the diagram by drawing the glyph for Bastien, God of the Sun. Then I retrieve a vial from my holster. One nearly empty, save for a single drop of blood. My blood.

". . . the purple acorns, however, taste the best," Inana says, continuing her story, "as everyone in the magical forest knows."

The Shade beneath the wagon remains perfectly still.

"Creatures come from miles to the violet tree . . ."

I place the vial at the center of my circle.

Uncork it.

". . . just to collect the purple acorns before sundown."

The Shade scuttles to the side, then whips around.

I take a few slow steps away. My shadows, meanwhile, stretch before me, splaying across the dirt in black puddles to darken the path from the wagon to the circle.

The Shade sniffs. Once. Twice. Then it begins to crawl.

I ease another vial out of my holster, Calvin's blood this time. Uncorking it, I bring a sip to my lips. The blood coats my tongue in a sickly-sweet richness with an iron tang, and I despise how pleasurable I find that taste. Heat rushes through my body, reacting to the flavor. The blood is an offering to my Sinless half, the half that was stripped of sin and filled with Bastien's divine light. My very soul hums with euphoria, for in this moment, I am a sliver of a god.

The Shade extends a hand from under the wagon, then another. Inch by inch, it crawls toward the vial at the center of my diagram, the monster with my face drawn away from the campfire performance by the scent of my blood.

I press my thumb over my vial. Tip it until a dab of Calvin's blood stains the pad of my finger.

The Shade now inches toward the center of the circle, its body wavering at the edges, losing its humanoid likeness until it's a mass of dark smoke.

I cork my vial. Return it to my holster.

The Shade stretches into a wisp of shadow, then reaches into the container—

I lunge for the edge of the circle. My shadows retreat just as I press my thumb to Bastien's glyph, painting it with the drop of Calvin's blood. The hum of my soul intensifies as the offering I gave to the circle resonates with the one that still lingers on my tongue.

Bastien's solar magic imbues the circle, creating a dome of light four feet wide and six feet tall. Exactly to the specifications in my diagram. It's so bright, it's almost blinding. Only my half-Sinless nature enables me to look at it head-on.

An unearthly squeal comes from inside the dome, the Shade trapped with nowhere else to go but inside the vial.

I wait one second. Two.

Then I reach inside the dome, slam down the cork, and wipe my hand across the circle. The dome of light goes out at once, as does the pleasurable hum in my soul. My hand trembles in the aftermath of such powerful astrotheurgy. The vial within is full, the Shade captured. I tuck it into my holster, catch my breath, and use my boot to wipe away all remaining evidence of the diagram. Then I round the wagon toward the campfire.

Not a single Shade remains, all having fled at the burst of light.

Four sets of eyes stare at me. Calvin wears a grimace, while the rest emanate trepidation. Bard's hands have gone still over his strings. Harlow's quill has frozen on her paper. And Inana burns me with a glare, chest heaving. She speaks through her teeth. "What the fuck was that?"

CHAPTER ELEVEN

Inana

Dominic holds my gaze, jaw tense, before facing the wagon. "We need to go. Now. Calvin, hitch the horses. We're leaving."

Calvin obeys, striding across the clearing to where the horses were tethered to graze. The rest of us exchange looks. None of us are keen to argue with his decision to leave after having been surrounded by Shades, but I don't fully understand his haste. Until I saw that flash of light, I wasn't afraid. Just like Dominic had said, our art calmed the monsters. Their postures slackened. Some had begun to drift away. What we were doing was working.

He's the one who interrupted us with that . . . that light. It wasn't a burst of flame or anything natural. It was solar astrotheurgy. The same kind of light used to ignite the Holy Braziers. The kind of magic that requires a heart sacrifice.

I narrow my eyes at him as he approaches us with a cloth sack, but what he extracts steals all my attention.

"Keep these with you from now on," he says, handing Bard the same bronze mask he wore at the Wretched Lair, its shape reminiscent of a wolf's face. Then he gives Harlow hers, an elegant oval decorated in roses and twining snakes. Finally he hands me mine. I stare wide-eyed at the floral filigree, the sunbeam spikes at the top, the trailing beads.

"Where did you get these?" I ask.

"Rockefeller. Before we left Nalheim. It's essential that Summoners work masked. Keep yours hidden beneath your cloaks unless you're doing anything that could draw Shades. So next time you engage in story time, make sure you protect your fucking faces."

"Why didn't you give these to us from the start?" I say as I tuck my mask into one of the padded pockets on the inside of my cloak.

"I didn't think you were going to do something so reckless before we'd even begun to train."

I scoff. "We were conversing during daylight. I already told you I wasn't lying. Furthermore, why didn't you give us these instead of telling us to raise our hoods?"

"You had your cloaks on your person."

"When you gave us our things," Bard says, accusation lacing his normally empty tone, "you could have handed them over."

Dominic rubs a hand along the sharp line of his bearded jaw, brow furrowed as if he's debating telling us something. He seems to think better of it and stalks toward his sword and whatever other belongings he left by the stream.

I shadow his steps. "Could it be you were hoping we wouldn't see your little display if we had our heads lowered?"

"Whatever do you mean." His voice is flat, devoid of question. He straps on his sword, gathers the cloak he used as a pillow during his nap, then strolls back toward the wagon, where Calvin is still hitching the horses.

I match my pace to Dominic's. "What were you doing with that Shade? The one under the wagon?"

"Shadowbane business." He climbs into the driver's seat, and Calvin hands him the reins.

He's delusional if he thinks that's the end of this conversation. Grinding my teeth, I hitch up my skirts and climb right up beside him.

His eyes widen as I plant myself on the seat, our arms pressed together. He fumbles the reins, and once he reclaims his hold on them, he pins me with a hard look. "What are you doing?"

"You etched an astrotheurgical diagram into the ground," I say, angling myself toward him. "You made a dome of light, just like the dukes and royals do."

"I saw it too," Harlow says. She climbs into the wagon bed and stands behind us with her arms crossed. Bard climbs up next, cradling his mandolin. Harlow's eyes jump to mine. "When you told us about your past, about being a heart sacrifice . . ."

I nod, then swivel my gaze back to Dominic. "My piece-of-shit ex-lover said he had to consume my heart. That it was the only way he could light the brazier. Does the same go for you?"

Dominic rubs his jaw again, and his defensive walls seem to crumble as he heaves a sigh. "I don't use solar astrotheurgy to the same degree as full Sinless do," he says. "I use a blood sacrifice, but it isn't any worse than what you already know about me. I use Calvin's blood, from vials we've stockpiled for that specific purpose. Drinking blood activates my ability to use solar magic, but only briefly. The Holy Brazier requires a greater sacrifice because of its powerful and constant use of astrotheurgy. That's why the dukes and royals need a heart sacrifice, and they need one at regular intervals."

Calvin snaps his fingers, eyes on me. "That's why you're guilty of treason. You know royal secrets. It's all coming together now." He taps the side of his head, lips quirked in a grin, then returns to hitching the horses.

"What was the light for?" Harlow asks. "Were you . . . killing the Shade? I thought that's what your silver sword is for."

"Shades in their common form can't be killed, only calmed and diverted away from villages," Dominic says. "My blade can temporarily disperse one, as Shades are sensitive to the brightness of silver, the same way they're sensitive to sunlight, but it will quickly re-form, and any act of violence against it will send it into a greater frenzy. The only kind of Shade that can be killed is an Incarnate, which is where my blade matters most. My sword is etched with a diagram like the one I drew in the soil." He reaches over his shoulder and grips the hilt of his sword. He lifts it from its scabbard to reveal an astrotheurgical diagram just below the hilt, almost identical to the one I saw at the bottom of the Holy Brazier two years ago. "I place a drop of blood on my tongue and another on the circle. That imbues my sword with fire, the combination of silver and flame allowing me to kill an Incarnate."

"You still haven't told us what you were doing," I say. "You did something with one of the Shades. I heard it scream."

Dominic frowns. "You heard it scream?"

I glance at Bard and Harlow, expecting them to say they too heard that deathly cry. Instead, they wear frowns that mirror Dominic's.

I bristle, unsettled by the way they're looking at me. "Can you just answer the question?"

His jaw shifts side to side. "I was capturing a Shade."

"Because it was wearing your face?"

"Yes."

The tension in my shoulders eases, his answer calming my anxiety. If Shades can't be killed, it makes sense he'd at least capture ones that have taken a step closer to becoming Incarnate. It's better than leaving yourself open to their bloodlust. But didn't he say Shades aren't interested in imitating Shadowbanes? Was that . . . a lie? Maybe I shouldn't be surprised he can lie; he's still half human.

"Can we go?" he says, a growl in his voice.

"Horses ready," Calvin says, giving them each an affectionate pat before rounding the wagon to climb into the back.

I bat my lashes at Dominic. "That wasn't so hard, now, was it? Maybe next time we ask you to explain something, just fucking answer."

His eyes darken, and he leans in closer. "You aren't the only one with trust issues. Or the only one fighting for something important."

"You mean being made full Sinless? How noble."

"You know nothing about me."

"I wonder why that is?"

He leans even closer, teeth bared. My eyes flick to his pointed canines, slightly sharper than a human's should be. A phantom touch wraps around my throat, not with pressure but a threat nonetheless. I see no sign of his Shades with it still being so bright out, but of course one of them is responsible. Unlike wild Shades, Lust, Sloth, and Pride seem capable of enduring sunlight; it only makes them invisible. Dominic's eyes volley between my own. "If you want my trust, earn it, sinner."

Rage sparks in my chest. My first instinct is to pull away, to shove at the shadow monster's invisible grip, but something bolder takes over. Instead of flinching back, I lean into the touch until our faces are mere inches apart. His pupils narrow to pinpricks as I speak with unfettered anger. "Same to you."

"For the love of the gods," comes Harlow's voice. She sits with a thud. "If you're going to fuck, just do it already."

"Language, Ma—" Bard cuts his words off, blinking hard, then aggressively shaking his head. He sits down across from Harlow.

My cheeks blaze as I reassess what I'm doing. How close my face is to Dominic's. How tightly my hands are balled.

Harlow gives Bard an apologetic smile, then says in a saccharine voice, "If you're going to *fornicate,* do it already."

"*Oh, I like her idea,*" whispers a voice I recognize as Lust's. The grip on my throat shifts into a caress.

"*Can we go?*" Pride says with a grumble. "*This bickering is getting tedious.*"

"*I want my seat back,*" says Sloth. Just then I feel something like an enormous paw land on my thigh. "*Can I at least climb in her lap?*"

I rise in a rush, the phantom touch releasing me just as quickly. I don't give Dominic a second glance as I climb over the back of the seat and drop down into the wagon bed. As soon as I'm seated, Dominic flicks the reins and the wagon lurches into motion. Harlow's eyes burn into the side of my face, an annoying smirk on her lips. I whip my gaze to her and point from me to the Shadowbane. "That's not what's happening here."

She shrugs. "If you say so."

Calvin takes a swig of his vial before saying, "He's not usually like that."

"Ooh," Harlow says. "So he only wants to hate-fuck Inana?"

"He does not—" I bite the inside of my cheek to keep from repeating her words. Not that I'm shy about sex. It's just that her words are ludicrous. I divert the topic away from me and lower my voice to a whisper. "Aren't Shadowbanes celibate? They take a vow, right?"

"I am not celibate." The voice that answers is Dominic's, setting me on edge all over again. "Shadowbanes vow to keep their naked bodies from being seen in full."

I choke on a laugh. "Do you fuck your lovers through a curtain, then?"

"No." He angles his head over his shoulder to meet my eyes. There's a darkness in his smile. A devious glint in his eyes. "I fuck my lovers while they're blindfolded."

That takes the breath from my lungs. The cruel curve of his lips has me picturing things I have no right to imagine. A woman in a blindfold, crying out in ecstasy as Dominic caresses her skin with his vile tongue. Him gripping her hips as he slams into her from behind. Or maybe she'd straddle him, and his hands would rove over her breasts. Maybe that dark hair of his would be soaked with sweat. Maybe he'd bite his lip with those sharp canines as he comes—

"Inana." Dominic's voice is rough. It pulls me out of my fantasy and makes my cheeks burn hot. There's no way he knew what I was thinking, right? He's no longer looking at me, his face forward, his posture stiff. A shadow passes over us as we cross beneath a large tree, and I catch sight of his three Shades, all staring down at me with those dark pits for eyes. "Move to the back of the wagon."

"Excuse me?"

"You're too close. Move to the back."

I'm almost of a mind to argue, for who the hell is he to lord it over where I can sit? But the flush coursing through me finds relief at the idea of widening the distance between us. So I rise on unsteady legs, blaming it on the motion of the wagon, and sit at the rear of the bed. I don't let myself look at Dominic again. Don't give myself any reason to return to such vulgar imaginings.

It's then that I realize just how long it's been since I've been aroused. After my fiancé's betrayal, I lost all interest in romance, and living on the run made even emotionless sex a low priority. Yet that spark I felt as my imagination took over, that sensual heat that pooled low in my belly . . . I can't say I hated it. It was almost as tempting as art.

CHAPTER TWELVE

Inana

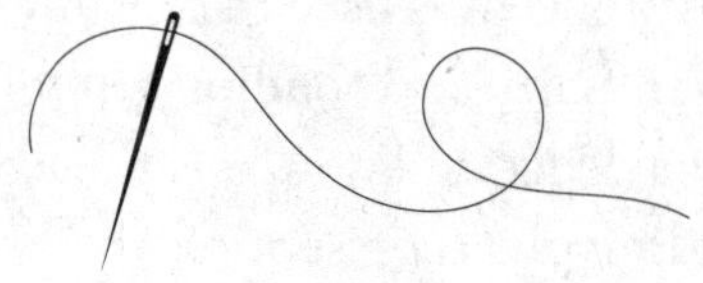

Once we're back on the main road, we discover the true nature of our hurry.

"Are we trying to get to Thornfal by sunset?" Calvin calls out to Dominic as he tugs his cloak tight to his body.

It's late afternoon, and now that we've picked up speed, the air rushes over us in an icy current. I pull my own cloak tighter around me and tuck my hand into the pocket that holds my mask. I run my fingers along the smooth filigree. I recognize the name Thornfal as the village where we'll be taking up our first post. Didn't Dominic say he'd train us as much as possible before going there? I wouldn't call the impromptu exercise we just did thorough training. Surely he meant to teach us more than that.

"We won't make it by sunset," the Shadowbane says, "but hopefully before sunrise."

"What's the hurry?" Harlow asks, her question aimed at Calvin rather than Dominic. "I thought we left the clearing because the location was compromised by Shades."

"He must have received a missive," Calvin says.

I frown. "A missive. But when? And from . . . whom? I saw no rider bearing a message."

"The church nearest to Thornfal would have sent it." At our blank looks, Calvin proceeds to explain. "Priests are the only ones who can quickly communicate with Shadowbanes while they're traveling, for they have access to common astrotheurgy."

My interest is piqued at that. I know the church hoards all knowledge of astrotheurgy. Even the Sinless are privy to just a singular branch—solar astrotheurgy—and that's reserved for the dukes and royals who light the Holy Braziers. And the Shadowbanes too, I suppose, after what Dominic said about his use of magic. I've heard rumors that astrotheurgy once was used in common ways, from infusing tonics with healing properties to sending letters in an instant across any distance. All one needed to know was the exact diagram set with angles, numbers, and glyphs representing the gods to effect the desired outcome. If the church still has that knowledge, it makes sense they'd use it when needed. They're the ones who perform the Absolution ritual on the Sinless, after all.

"We were due in Thornfal three days ago," Calvin says, "but had to take a little detour for"—he gestures toward the three of us—"you."

Harlow arches a brow. "Because you found yourselves with a sudden lack of Summoners?"

"Precisely," he says, oblivious to how ominous that sounds. "So it makes sense the mayor would seek us out if the situation has escalated."

"It has," Dominic confirms. "The missive didn't say how badly, only that the Shade targeting the village has grown more aggressive. Furthermore, if I don't arrive within twenty-four hours, my post will be given to another Shadowbane."

"Is that such a bad thing?" I ask.

Perhaps I'm imagining it, but his back seems to stiffen at my voice. It takes him a few moments to answer. "I would never endanger a village for my own ambition, but Shadowbanes earn accolades for defending their posts. The faster they de-escalate an active Shade attack—either by putting an end to an ongoing nightly threat or by dispatching an Incarnate—the more posts they're given. The more posts they defend, the more accolades they earn, and the higher the chances are that they will be chosen to complete their Absolution."

My stomach sours at that. Another reminder of what he seeks to become.

"But the most important accolades," he says, "are those earned in the months leading up to the summer solstice celebration in the Year of Bastien."

"That's next year," Harlow says. She's right, and with it already being twelfthmonth, the Year of Bastien begins in just a few short weeks.

Still, I don't know what's significant about that. An annual celebration occurs at the capital city nine out of every ten years for the god-of-the-year's holiday. Since next year belongs to the God of the Sun, that's summer solstice.

Every decade has one year dedicated to each of the nine gods, and a tenth dedicated to atonement. During each annual celebration, King Kaelum performs a ritual sacrifice of convicted criminals. He offers their souls to the patron god of the year to demonstrate that the criminals are but a small fraction of mankind and do not represent humanity. Then he tests his thirst. If he sets the sacrifices free, it means his thirst has ended; the gods have forgiven us, and the Shades are no more. However, if he drinks from them, it means we've yet to earn forgiveness. For five hundred years, the ritual has ended the same way—the sacrifices dead and drained of blood at the king's feet.

At least that's what I've heard. It's not like I've witnessed one of the annual rites. The capital is even more exclusive to residents and visitors than the other Sacred Cities are.

Dominic speaks again. "Shadowbanes are guaranteed to be turned full Sinless when they retire, usually after three decades of service. Rarely are they allowed to retire and complete their Absolution earlier than that. However, during the Year of Bastien, one Shadowbane is selected from a pool of nominees to be turned on summer solstice, regardless of how long they've served. These nominees are chosen by their patron princes."

"Each prince can only nominate one Shadowbane," Calvin adds. "Dom's patron, Prince Leeran, employs about a dozen shadow hunters. So the competition is fierce. Being late to our post already looks bad enough, but having to relinquish the post to another team . . ." He lets out a low whistle.

"You want to complete your Absolution that badly?" I say, glowering at Dominic's back.

He shifts his head to the side and eyes me from his peripheral vision. His jaw is tense as he speaks. "I always finish what I begin."

I'm not one to complain about sleeping arrangements, seeing as I've had no true home of my own for two years, but sleeping in a moving wagon next to three other people is fucking awful. It's almost as bad as waking up with a shadow monster invading my space. Again.

At first I think it's Harlow, as the body snuggled into my chest is smaller than me, but not by too much. Then I shift, preparing to push the girl over a few inches so I can gain some space between her and the endgate behind me, but instead of a solid body, my hand falls on something light and soft and just a little wiry. Like fur.

I open my eyes, blinking into the dark. It takes me a few moments to make out the shape, but sure enough, Sloth the shadow dog is lying next to me, his back pressed against my belly. Biting back a yelp, I launch backward, but the endgate gives me nowhere else to go. And where my alarm startled the creature awake last time, now he merely shifts to the side, stretches out, and rests his face on his enormous paws.

The sight does something strange to my chest. For a moment, it makes me forget he's a Shade. Under the blanket of night, where everything is bathed in shadow, he looks so much like a real wolfhound. Same long legs, giant paws, enormous head. Same wiry fur, same small ears.

I had a dog when I was a child, for a few short months. I fell in love with the beast, named her Butterscotch, but Mother couldn't stand the way she'd bark at night to alert us of Shades wandering outside. Not only was it disruptive to sleep, but Mother feared it would provoke the monsters to attack. I didn't mind the barking, and I'd never heard of a Shade attacking because of provocation from an animal. Yet one day I came home from running an errand for Mother at the market, and Butterscotch was gone. Mother said she ran away. That may have been true, or she may have let her out on purpose or sold her to one of the farms. Whatever the case, the sense of loss was too deep. I never sought the companionship of a pet again, not even after I took up the trade of a seamstress and moved to my own home.

Looking at Sloth now brings back that same tender feeling from when I had Butterscotch, and it opens a deep well of longing and nostalgia in my heart.

I reach out a tentative hand, half expecting it to fall through the creature. He was solid when I attempted to nudge him away, thinking he was Harlow, and there have been plenty of times where I've felt the pressure of the Shades' touch. But there have also been times where I've reached out to shove the touch away only for my fingers to close on air. So I'm surprised when my palm splays over fur again. Sloth doesn't stir or startle, so I let myself pet him, just out of curiosity. It's a strange sensation. Fur-like, but lighter. Like the texture is only a dream of fur. And he's warm too, at least somewhat, his belly rising and falling in a pantomime of breathing, his body pulsing with a slow yet steady heartbeat.

Maybe I'm being reckless. Maybe I'm just delirious from poor sleep and too much change these last couple days. But in the end, I decide not to push Sloth away. Instead, I close my eyes and continue to stroke the shadow monster's fur.

The next time I wake, it's to screaming.

CHAPTER THIRTEEN

INANA

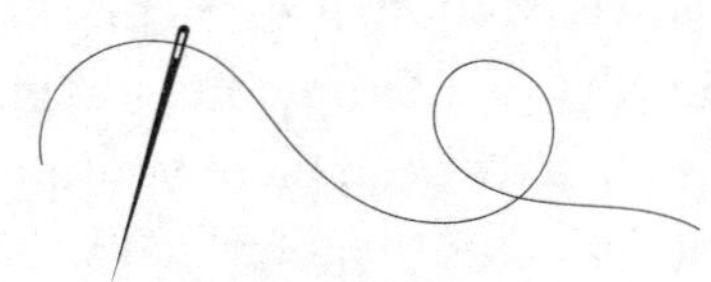

As we drive down Thornfal's main thoroughfare, a single word leaves Dominic's lips in an impressive display of extending a single syllable into a self-contained sentence. "Fuuuuuuck."

"Fuck indeed," I say behind my mask, only now understanding the cause of the screams I woke up to. We were still up the road from the village when Dominic roused us from sleep and had us don our masks in preparation to get to work.

"You've got to be kidding me," Harlow mutters, her hand covering her mask's mouth slit.

Calvin, who only has the hood of his cloak to obscure his face, peers from beneath it. "Is that . . ."

"Dragon," Bard says.

The fact that none of us question what he just said shows none of us had righteous upbringings. For dragons are a thing of fiction, lost to centuries-old tales that no one is supposed to tell. Yet it's hard to stop children—so unfamiliar with the concept of sin and so drawn to awe and whimsy—from exchanging fantastical stories or sharing myths.

And here it stands before us now, myth made nightmare. A gods-damned shadow dragon screeching in the center of town.

Its body, though composed of black shadow, is clearly reptilian in nature. Its neck is sinuous like a snake's, but its head, limbs, and tail are reminiscent of the little golden lizards I used to find sunbathing on rocks by the creek in the summer. Unlike any reptile I've seen, it has enormous membranous wings sprouting from its back. There's a constant shifting and wavering of its outline that keeps it from looking real. It's almost as if it isn't quite sure what it's supposed to look like. Probably because dragons are fucking fiction.

The most chilling aspect of all, however, is its size, taller than the houses that line the street and at least twice as long as our wagon. It's the largest Shade I've ever seen.

Dominic tugs the reins to bring the wagon to a halt. The horses skitter back slightly, unnerved by the monster up ahead. They didn't so much as balk when the Shades surrounded the clearing, which is further proof that what we're seeing isn't ordinary.

"It must be multiple Shades in one," Dominic says, his voice devoid of its usual coldness. There's real concern in his tone now. "I've never seen this before, not a Shade of this size. It shouldn't be possible."

"A dragon shouldn't be possible," Calvin says. "Shades take on humanoid forms, or sometimes creatures found in nature. The only time one would adopt a mythical appearance . . ."

"Is if it was imitating art," Dominic finishes for him.

"An artist did this?" I stand, gripping the back of his seat to anchor my nerves. The villagers have created a barricade of fire around what looks like the market square. With this being an unprotected village—no silver walls or Holy Brazier—Shades can enter Thornfal at will. My hometown was the same, yet never did a Shade of this magnitude attack. Never did we seek to create makeshift walls of fire to protect ourselves. Even with this defense, the flames only reach the base of the Shade's neck. The monster doesn't cross the blaze, but it snaps and screeches at the dozens of figures that are gathered in the square. In turn, the villagers cry out at every gnash of the monster's teeth, every shift of its enormous body. I'm not sure whether they're there for protection or to keep the Shade occupied until sunrise. Now that our wagon has stopped, I take in our immediate surroundings. Roofs have collapsed here and there, and windows have been smashed in.

And blood. A gruesome red smear paints the side of one of the buildings, and there's a dark silhouette in the adjacent alley that looks like half a body.

The dragon has done more than stalk the market square. It has killed.

My stomach turns. I knew this job would be dangerous. Only now is that starting to feel real.

"If they'd just stayed in their houses," Dominic says, running a hand over his face.

I gesture around us. "The houses aren't any safer."

"Probably because they ran and screamed. Shades don't go into a frenzy unprovoked. The best thing one can do during a Shade attack is stay inside. Keep the lamps burning. Don't fucking panic and don't look out the godsdamned windows."

"Easier said than done," I say, remembering such Shade attacks in my village. There was always someone who stayed by their window and screamed when they caught sight of a monster in the streets. That person rarely made it until morning.

I understand their compulsion to peek. Some people feel safer knowing what danger looks like and when it's coming. I felt that same instinct on several nights, especially as a child. Though my need to look out the window stemmed more from morbid curiosity than a need to put a face to fear. And I never made a sound when I saw the monsters.

"Time to work." Dominic urges our agitated horses to turn the wagon so the bed is facing the dragon.

My heart leaps into my throat. Even though the Shade hasn't noticed us yet, there was a layer of comfort when Dominic and the horses stood between us and the dragon. "What do we do?"

"First," Dominic says, shifting to face us, "we need to draw it away from the village. Bard, you will take the lead in this. We must offer it fare more tempting than the villagers, which means we must match its current energy. It's in a frenzy, which means you need to play something that calls to that state. Something dark. A rapid and chaotic tempo. As soon as we have its attention, I'll snap the reins."

"Are you saying . . ." Harlow's throat bobs beneath her mask. "It's going to chase us?"

"It is. And when it does, you and Inana need to craft your parts. Once we're deep enough into the woods, we'll stop. That's when we'll attempt to shift the Shade's energetic state, just like you did in the clearing. Even though the dragon is many Shades in one, the process is the same as it was then. You will calm it with your art. Your only additional objective will be to convince it to take on a new form. Something smaller. Less dangerous."

"How the hell do we do that?" I ask.

"You're the creative minds here," he says, but there's encouragement in his tone. "Harlow will draw a new form for it to take. I suggest an animal, something small. Inana will tell a story that conveys the details. Encourage it to adopt the new form with tantalizing words."

The weight of responsibility settles over my shoulders, making my stomach drop. "And what will you do?" I can't keep the edge of hysteria from my voice. "If we're doing all the work, what's a Shadowbane for?"

"I will protect you," he says, eyes locking on mine, even though he can't possibly see my irises through the openings in my mask. "A silver blade may not be able to kill it, but I can keep it from getting too close. If all our efforts fail, I can cut through it and disperse its form. Only temporarily, of course. It will re-form and return to the village tomorrow night, and we'll have to try this all over again."

It's a comfort knowing he can temporarily dispatch the monster, but I'm not at all keen on fighting this thing more than once. We haven't even begun and I'm already dreading the moment its attention shifts to us.

Which, turns out, is right fucking now.

The shadow dragon swivels its head on its long neck, and its pitch-black eyes find us.

"Bard," Dominic says with a sharp nod, and the musician strums a discordant sound on his mandolin.

I crouch down, my legs giving out beneath the empty stare of the dragon, and cling to the side of the wagon. Harlow does the same. Meanwhile, Bard settles as close as he can to the endgate and strums another harsh chord.

The Shade turns fully around to face us.

"Play." Dominic flicks the reins and the horses take off. Bard breaks into a tune in harmony with our wagon's pace, his fingers flying over the strings in a beautiful yet eerie melody. The dragon takes the bait, snapping its shadowed maw before launching after us.

I hardly dare to blink as the Shade gains on us. I imagine it could close the distance in an instant. Surely it doesn't need to run on its reptilian legs, for it's an incorporeal being unrestrained by the laws of physics. So perhaps it likes the chase. Or . . . the music.

Bard doesn't balk, doesn't slip up as his song draws the monster after us, back up the road we came down mere minutes before, weaving along the moonlit road far faster than we've driven before. Only then do I recall I'm supposed to be plotting my tale, coming up with something to convince the Shade to change shape. I angle myself toward Harlow. "What creature should it be?"

"I . . . I'm not creative," she says, voice trembling. "I told you this."

"We have to work together. My story must coincide with what you're drawing."

"Then you take the lead. I'll draw what you describe, that's all I'm good at. Please." The pleading in her tone sends a pinch to my chest, reminding me that despite her frequent bravado, she's a seventeen-year-old girl who only took up art to survive after murdering her abusers. And while I saw evidence of her creativity when she drew in the clearing, what I recall of her drawing only deepens that pit of sympathy. When Dominic told her to draw something that made her feel safe, it was a girl alone in a field. No houses, no people. Just a field and a girl with her face hidden beneath her hair.

"Fuck, I . . ." I heave out a heavy sigh. "I'll take the lead."

"Hold on," Dominic calls out, just as the wagon swerves to the side at a fork in the road. The path is just wide enough for our wagon, but far bumpier than the main road. The Shade follows us, slithering beneath the tree boughs, snapping off branches in its wake. "It's almost time."

My heart lurches into my throat. I still don't know what I'm going to say, what story I can tell the Shade to convince it to calm down. Still gripping tight to the ledge, I turn my head to see where we're going. All I can see is dark, the lanterns that flank the driver's seat illuminating only a sliver of the narrow road.

"Calvin," Dominic says, and the younger man springs into action, climbing into the front seat and taking the reins from the Shadowbane. Dominic steps down into the wagon bed, feet spread to maintain his balance, then takes a vial from his belt. With his gaze locked on the ever-approaching dragon, he uncorks the vial and takes a swallow of its contents. "Get ready," he says, unsheathing his sword with one hand while the other turns the vial over, thumb pressed to the opening. Moonlight glints off the silver blade. "Now."

Calvin brings the wagon to a halt, the horses whinnying as they stomp against the soil, eager to flee.

"Inana. Harlow." Dominic doesn't meet our gazes as he strides to the back of the wagon. He presses his thumb to the base of his sword, near the hilt, gifting the blood from his vial to the astrotheurgical diagram he showed us earlier. As he runs the same finger down the length of the blade, it illuminates with flame. Just then, the Shade reaches our wagon, its head whipping back at the sight of the burning sword. "Story time, sinners."

"Fuck." I'm even less prepared than when I told myself to start preparing. Bard rises to his feet, his frantic tune slowing the slightest bit. Dominic maintains a fighting stance, sword held steady toward the Shade, but makes no move to attack, only to keep it from lunging. The dragon shies away, then takes a tentative step to the side, jaw snapping in irritation. Dominic shifts with it, ever so slowly. Carefully.

"Speak, Inana," Harlow says, voice pitched high. Her sketchbook lies before her, bathed in the light from Dominic's sword. Her quill shakes in her hand, dripping ink. "Tell me what to draw."

I step between Bard and Dominic, fingers fisted at my sides. I'm half tempted to take my cloth hearts from my bodice to busy my fingers, but I'm not sure I could hold anything in this state. I swallow hard and speak a hesitant first line. "In the darkest, quietest forest . . ."

My voice is weak and not at all in harmony with the pace of Bard's melody, but the dragon whips its gaze to me.

I clear my throat and try again. "In the darkest, quietest forest, beneath the light of Vanna's pale moon, there lived . . . a squirrel."

"Really?" Harlow says from behind me.

The Shade lashes out with a foreclaw, gouging a deep gash in the side of the wagon before Dominic angles his sword to ward the dragon back. The wagon rocks from the momentum of the attack.

"I don't think it wants to be a squirrel," Dominic says, voice calm and oddly soothing.

"What the hell does it want to be?" I mutter, and the Shade lunges to the side. Dominic leaps to mirror its moves, keeping it from lashing out at us again.

Something firm and heavy presses against my legs. I know what it is at once, the distinct feel of a canine body. This time, I'm not alarmed by Sloth's presence. I'm comforted. Not that Dominic's Shades have proved to do anything particularly helpful, and right now Lust and Pride are nothing but twin pools of darkness at the Shadowbane's feet.

All right, all right. I can do this. I just have to meet its current state before I can convince it to become smaller.

Bard repeats the same measure as I gather my composure.

"In the darkest, quietest forest, beneath the light of Vanna's pale moon, there lived a majestic salamander. As tall as a mountain, with flesh made from blood-red jewels, it was the most beautiful creature around."

The dragon's form ripples, its silhouette wavering in time with the song. It tilts its head to the side in what I assume is fascination. I force more words from my lips, drawing its interest with mundane details about the magical forest and the other creatures who live there. About the sentient trees who greet the salamander as it makes slow progress across the land every night, exploring the world. Little by little, both my story and Bard's tune slow. Soften. So does my own energy. My voice no longer shakes, nor do my limbs. The monster's interest inspires a flicker of the same pride I felt at the Wretched Lair when my art enchanted my audience. I know this is a joint effort, but witnessing the Shade's subtle shift from aggressive to captivated feeds my artist's longing.

Harlow approaches with shaking hands and holds out her sketchbook. Upon it are several drawings representing scenes from the story.

Dominic takes a slow step back to allow the Shade a closer look. But not too close.

"You've calmed it," Dominic whispers. "Now try to offer it a different shape. Slowly. Weave it into your tale."

I infuse my tone with the same longing I feel now, the same I've always felt for that which is forbidden. Beautiful. Sinful. I turn myself over to my tale, no longer worrying over the right words to say. "The salamander wandered for an era, seeing every beautiful thing his forest offered. He was the king of beasts, and the most majestic of creatures. Yet he yearned for something he didn't have."

The dragon lowers its head, level with my face. A phantom tongue flicks out as it inches closer. There's no threat in its posture. No frenzy. And as its onyx eyes lock on mine, my nerves are soothed further. Or perhaps the Shade is the one that is soothed. Whatever the case, my fictional salamander's yearning echoes in the monster before me. I can almost feel its desperation to know more. To learn what it yearned for.

"What the salamander wanted . . ." My voice trails off as I lose myself deeper in the monster's eyes. Deeper in Bard's soulful tune. Deeper in the rhythmic scratch of Harlow's pen on paper. *What is it you truly want? What is it you crave?* I wonder.

The dragon's head swivels closer again, and I lift my hand in response.

"Inana," Dominic rasps and steps closer, prepared to ward the monster away with his burning sword. "What are you doing?"

"Wait," I whisper back, though not even I know why I'm reaching out to the Shade. Only that it feels . . . natural. The dragon's form continues to undulate with every strum of Bard's strings, and I know in my bones, in the pulse of my heart that beats to that same tune, that we three artists are fully in control. We have the Shade under our influence like a thrall to a Sinless's blood. If only I could understand it a little more. Give it a little more of what it craves.

I keep my hand outstretched and let it inch closer yet again.

What do you want to be?

My eyes drift over its dark body, slender neck, barrel chest, and dangerously long claws. Then to the wings folded against its back. Wings it hasn't tried to use. Wings it doesn't fully comprehend.

Warmth floods my chest, my blood, my soul. The shape of my story forms in my mind so quickly it almost makes me dizzy. "For so long, the salamander waited and wondered what he was missing. He was so lost in thought he nearly stepped off the edge of a cliff and tumbled into a glassy lake below. He stopped himself in time, his own reflection startling him. That's when it dawned on him, as he met his own face on the surface of the lake, crowned by the crescent moon shining in the sky above. He realized then, he wasn't a salamander at all."

The Shade goes still, its form frozen. No, not frozen, but radiating faster and almost too subtly to see. Its form on the brink of change.

"Didn't you know," I whisper, "that your wings were made to fly?"

It leans closer again, its snout mere inches from my hand. Bard's song takes on a hopeful tune, one so agonizingly sweet it brings tears to my eyes. I match my tone to it, weave my words into the dance of his strings. "Didn't you know . . . at the top of the tallest tree in the darkest and quietest forest, there lived a colony of squirrels? *Flying* squirrels, the moon's most sacred demons, beloved by Goddess Vanna."

Harlow's quill ceases scratching over her paper. "What the hell is a flying squirrel?"

My lips curl as I recall the few I spotted in the woods outside Dunway, on days where I strayed outdoors close enough to sunset to catch sight of the nocturnal creatures.

"As tiny as my fist," I say to the dragon—and for Harlow's sake—curling my outstretched hand before it, "with a long fluffy tail and whiskers that frame their noses. Their eyes glittered like jewels of the night, and their ears were small and rounded. From fore- to hindpaw stretched a fleshy, soft membrane, a wing unlike any other. They ruled the dark, gathering acorns of shadow and stashing their treasures in meadows. They'd climb to the tip of the tallest tree, singing songs to Vanna in trilling voices. Then they'd spread their limbs, reach for the stars . . ."

I open my palm again, and the Shade touches its snout to my skin. The dragon shatters at my touch into a dozen tiny shadows, flying squirrels with crescent moons on their brows.

". . . and fly to the constellations."

CHAPTER FOURTEEN

Dominic

I don't know where my fascination ends and my three shadows' begins. I don't know why I obeyed Inana when she told me to wait, why I let her reach out to touch a Shade instead of swinging down my sword like I normally would when one has gotten too close. I don't know why a single tear trails from my eye in the wake of my Summoners' art. All I know is that I'm *feeling* again. Fear and awe and . . . this strange fluttering hope that tightens my lungs as I watch the flying squirrels glide from tree to tree, testing out their new means of flight with palpable glee.

"They fucking did it," Calvin says, climbing down to the bed from the driver's seat.

"They did," I say under my breath. I didn't exactly doubt them, for they performed well in the clearing, adapting to the threat. But this . . . this was something else. I've never faced a Shade composed of many shadows, and a fucking mythical creature at that. I was prepared to end our first attempt with the swing of my sword and face it again the next night with an actual plan.

I don't know if I should feel proud or terrified of my Summoners' effectiveness. Or perhaps simply mesmerized by their talents—talents that would have enchanted the world five centuries ago but are now branded as sins, forcing them to express themselves only in the darkest and most dangerous—

I suck in a breath, realizing my emotions have gotten the better of me again. My eyes move to Inana. What is it about being physically near her that does this to me? I take a step away, then another, much to my shadows' protests. Even Pride has dropped his indifference, grumbling as I pull them away. Sloth refuses to budge, staring up at Inana with canine adoration. "Heel," I whisper, and he reluctantly obeys. Once all three have pooled back into me, I feel some relief from that overwhelming surge of emotion.

With a slow exhale, I run my thumb over the etched diagram at the base of my blade, smearing the blood until the flame extinguishes. Perhaps it would be wiser to keep it burning in case other aggressive Shades are near, but it takes a lot of energy to hold the power of a god. If I let it burn any longer, I'll need more blood. And I've never been one to waste what Calvin so generously provides.

Fatigue digs deep in my bones. I sheathe my sword and sit on the edge of the wagon bed, arms propped on my knees. It almost feels too quiet without Bard's tune or Harlow's rapid inking. Or Inana's melodious voice.

Calvin crouches beside me, holding out his wrist. "Need a fresh bite?"

"You know the answer." I level a dark look at him. He knows I won't take fresh blood unless I'm out of other options. Storing small amounts in vials feels more like a medical procedure and less like the curse of what I am. It may not be much, but it sets me apart from the Sinless who drink from their sources without restraint.

"Suit yourself." He takes his wrist back and leans against the wall beside me. We watch the three Summoners gathered on the opposite end of the wagon. Harlow hugs her sketchbook to her chest, posture tense as she studies the shadow squirrels playing in the night. Bard tilts his masked face to the sky, though it's hard to tell if he's watching the Shades or is lost in whatever dark memories he carries. Then there's Inana. She leans over the wagon wall, the beads dangling from her mask and swaying with her every move as she points at one flying squirrel that soars in a graceful arc from one bough to another.

"Almost makes Shades seem cute, huh?" Calvin says.

"Almost," I say. "Until you remember what they really are."

By the time we return to Thornfal, dawn has broken over the horizon. Our news that we've defeated the dragon isn't met with celebration. It never is when I've dispatched a serious threat. Because a serious threat means dead to mourn. Furthermore, there's always the chance the threat could return, in cases where a resident is responsible for attracting it. The three nights following the de-escalation of a Shade attack are the most important, for that is the most likely window of time in which a Shade would regain its frenzied state and return, drawn to whoever attracted it, either by a repeat of their sin, or by their guilt over having been responsible. The caveat is that the resident must be aware that they were the cause and feel guilty about it.

Regardless, a repeat attack never bodes well for the village, even when the perpetrator has been caught. Even if a town was next in line to receive a Holy Brazier, having a known sinner discovered in their midst can set them back to zero in the eyes of King Kaelum. Supplies like oil, wicks, and lamps will suddenly become unavailable to those villages. The nearest churches will withhold their support in requesting aid from Shadowbanes.

Fear is a powerful motivator in garnering obedience. And there's nothing more terrifying than seeing an entire village razed to the ground by Shades.

As the morning sun illuminates more of the damage done to Thornfal, the bodies being collected in the market square, the somber faces of those either busying themselves with cleaning or hunched in mourning, I can't help but cast a prayer to the gods that this is the worst they'll see. Whether that's more for the village's benefit or mine—to assuage my guilt for having been late to my post—I know not. But I'm about to find out whether I deserve blame or mercy.

"When did the dragon first appear?" I ask the mayor of Thornfal. My crew has been escorted to the inn, where rooms had already been prepared in anticipation of our arrival. As much as my body begs me to rest too, my duties aren't yet done.

The mayor rubs his brow. He's a middle-aged man with wire-rimmed spectacles, his nightshirt stained with soot and blood. "Last night."

His answer surprises me. "Last night as in . . . nightfall twelve hours ago?"

"Approximately," he says with an uneven nod.

I furrow my brow. I received the missive before then. All the letter stated was that the situation at my post had escalated from a routine service to emergency status and that my post would be given to another Shadowbane if I didn't promptly arrive. Routine posts are regularly assigned at villages, whether they see nightly Shade activity or not, whereas emergency posts are assigned when there are active attacks on homes or people. My post in Thornfal was meant to be a routine assignment, which is why I thought we had time to rest and train before arriving. So was it merely a coincidence that the threat level escalated during my tardiness? Or was my post mislabeled from the start?

"What was the reason for your plea to the church to alter the level of threat?" I ask. "What was the situation like before last night?"

"We'd seen an average amount of Shades," he says, voice tired, "but nothing worth fretting about. Then, three days ago, their visits grew more active, with some scratching at doors or even entering dark rooms in houses. One of my citizens was attacked when their lamp went out, so I sent my plea to the church. We had no idea our situation would worsen so quickly."

"Do you suspect anyone?" I hate this question. Hate the witch hunts it can inspire, just to shift the blame onto someone and cast the accuser in a holy light. But the mayor seems an honest man.

"No, Thornfal's residents are pious. We beg for mercy when we sin, and we cast out the unrepentant."

My eye twitches at this. He's perhaps too honest.

"Still, we receive our share of travelers. We can't vouch for those who aren't our own."

"No one reported suspicious activity when the first deadly attack occurred?"

"No, there was nothing."

I nod, letting myself be satisfied with that. He returns to his efforts helping the villagers clean up the market square, sweeping up soot and debris and scrubbing blood from cobblestones. My eyes snag on a deep gash carved into one of the stone houses. The Shade may have been calmed and encouraged to shift into harmless flying squirrels, but there's no forgetting what it was. What it did. The damage it caused. The people it killed.

And there's no pretending the dozen Shades took that singular shape of their own accord. Only an artist could have tempted them to become a dragon.

The next three nights will tell whether said artist is still in our midst.

CHAPTER FIFTEEN

Inana

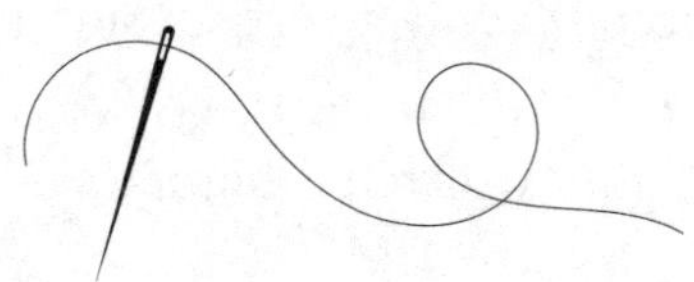

Thornfal feels so much like my hometown it makes my heart ache. Not that my life in Dunway was enviable, and after everything that happened there, even my happy memories are tainted. Still, an inadequate home is still a home if you've never found a place to call your own elsewhere.

Under the light of day, Thornfal is almost identical to Dunway. Same stone houses, same thatched or tiled roofs, same unobtrusive storefronts with the same bland wares. There are no trees or shrubs, offering as few places as possible for Shades to linger. There's even a dress shop that looks just like mine did: a simple brick building with militant-looking dress forms cluttering the window, boasting the most austere skirts and bodices made from the same patterns I traced and sewed day in and day out for the five years I was a seamstress.

I note all of this from the window of our loft room at the inn. We haven't left the loft since we retired here yesterday at dawn, our every need attended to by the servants who bring our food and drink. We even received gifts from the mayor: new cloaks and boots lined with fur to get us through the approaching winter, an assortment of wool clothing, clean vials for Dominic and Calvin.

The room itself is a gift, a grand suite compared to the barracks where I slept in Nalheim, and probably the finest accommodations this town has to offer. It's a large space with a sloped ceiling, wood-paneled walls, four beds, and an abundance of oil lamps, candles, and reflective disks hanging from the rafters to protect us come nightfall. After the makeshift barricade of flame we saw the night of the attack, I'm surprised the town has anything left to burn.

I shudder.

That night feels like a dream. A nightmare, more like, but one where I awoke not from terror but from victory. A strange, unearthly victory tinged with the sorrow that comes from knowing we were too late to prevent casualties. Yet that happens in every unprotected town; fatalities come with the territory of being plagued by monsters. That doesn't stop the conflict in my heart. The dragon Shade was terrifying. Deadly. It left enough destruction in its wake that the villagers are still cleaning up outside, from what little I can see of the market square from my window.

And yet . . .

What we did with our art, mesmerizing the Shade and convincing it to divide into flying squirrels . . .

I can't pretend that wasn't enchanting, for it was. But what kind of person finds any interaction with a Shade enchanting?

The kind that whispered stories to them when she thought no one was looking, I suppose. Or the kind that stroked Sloth's shadowy fur instead of pushing him away in the wagon the other night.

Speaking of Sloth . . .

"Where the hell has the Shadowbane been?" I ask, turning from the window.

"Sleeping, probably," Calvin says as he sorts through the new clothing we've received, placing them in different piles on his bed. I've already selected my chosen articles: a wool skirt in green plaid, a thick chemise, a brown leather bodice, and a fur-lined cloak.

"Is he too good for our company?" Harlow says in between bites of cream-dolloped scones. Every meal we've received, she's scarfed it down like it's the last food she'll ever have. Good for her. Might as well fill our bellies before we're forced to sustain ourselves on Calvin's cooking again.

"His room is next door," Calvin says. "He always sleeps alone."

"Always?" Harlow smirks. "How ordinary. What about all that talk about blindfolds—"

I choke on my own breath as I realize what she's getting at. My eyes whip to Calvin, though I'm not sure if I'm more desperate for him to answer or not to.

"Oh, that," he says. "Can't say I've seen him take a lover for a night, but if we're visiting a place that offers *that* kind of frivolity, I'm the first in bed with . . ." He snaps his mouth shut, eyes flicking to Harlow.

She stares at him through slitted lids.

Calvin dons an unconvincingly innocent expression. "I'm . . . in bed with perfectly angelic behavior."

Harlow scoffs, and even I chuckle at that. I'm sure wherever Calvin goes, he has no shortage of lovers. He isn't my type and is six years younger than I am, but I can see the appeal of his lovely face, his messy blond hair, and even his slender figure. Not to mention his flirtatious manner. He looks like a boy who can be easily broken yet knows his way around a lover's body. There's probably great satisfaction in being sexually obliterated by such a fragile thing. Or sexually obliterated at all . . .

Not that I'm contemplating sex. At least not with Calvin.

That, of course, begs the question: Who *am* I contemplating sex with? Dominic's face floods my mind at once. I recall the weight of his gaze after I finished my story for the flying squirrels. When our eyes locked, he didn't look away. Didn't try to hide his fascination, or the open vulnerability on his face. Our gazes snagged and tangled for what felt like an endless moment. I was still wrapped up in the awe of what we'd accomplished, in the awareness of our power as artists, and Dominic's expression compounded that tenfold. I felt powerful. Beautiful. In control. And the memory of that now sends a pool of heat to my core, a sizzling fire between my legs—

I shake the thoughts from my head. "How long will we be here?" I ask, changing the subject.

Harlow's expression turns eager. Even Bard, who has spent much of the last two days either sleeping or silent, lifts his gaze. Though neither has complained about their chance to rest in comfort, I imagine the idle time is getting to them as badly as it's gotten to me. For two years my days have been filled with manual labor, first at the textile mill, then working for Rockefeller. The sudden inertia is unsettling. Yet there's nothing for us to do here. There's no such thing as leisure time in small towns. Days are dedicated to work, whether at home, for an employer, or for a certain trade. There are no specialty shops, no books to read save for the holy texts, no gardens to stroll. I didn't even know such things existed until I lived in Nalheim, and even then I never engaged in such pastimes, for those were reserved for the elite, not servants.

"Two weeks is the minimum for a Shadowbane's post," Calvin says. "Whether we'll only be here for the minimum duration depends on the next couple of nights. If the dragon re-forms or nightly Shade activity is higher than average, we'll work to draw the threat away until it settles down. Dominic said last night was quiet, so if tonight and tomorrow prove the same, we'll move on to our next post at the end of next week."

"He's been keeping watch at night?" I ask. "Doesn't he need us with him in case there's an attack?"

"He'll wake us if there is," Calvin says.

I turn back to the window, my lips tugging down. I don't know why I'm annoyed to hear Dominic has been keeping watch without us, but I am. I may have felt powerful the other night, but I'm reminded we're only tools. What else could we be to him? He calls us his crew, yet he keeps a separate room and hasn't said a damn word to us in two days. I'm starting to understand why no one ever mentions Summoners, only Shadowbanes. We're just their dirty little secret—artists who get to use their forbidden craft, unbeknownst to the public—to take out when needed and put away when done. We do all the fucking work in drawing the Shades away, yet the Shadowbanes take the glory.

It's a wonder no one has revealed this secret.

Then I remember. We're outlaws. What fucking reason would we have to out the truth? We'd only be outing ourselves. Our crimes. Losing our slim chance to gain safe passage off this continent.

My lips curl in a cold, humorless grin. What a flawless system.

After nightfall, sleep eludes me. Perhaps my body has had all it can take of resting, for I can't stop tossing and turning, the light from the many lamps and candles blazing against the backs of my eyelids. I'm all for keeping rooms bright enough to prevent Shades from entering, but it's a godsdamned nuisance when I'm already struggling to sleep.

I roll onto my back and assess my companions. All three are snug in their beds, their steady breaths filling the room, their chests rising and falling in a gentle rhythm.

A thud sounds overhead. I lift my gaze to the ceiling, and it sounds again. Then again. It's soft and steady, moving from one end of the ceiling to the other. No one else stirs, for it isn't loud enough to interrupt anyone's slumber. It's only because I'm awake that I take notice. Still, the cadence is very much like footsteps, not the skittering of an animal.

The sound stops at the far end of the room.

Someone's on the roof.

And there's one person I expect to be awake at this hour.

My curiosity piqued, I rise from my bed, don my boots, and wrap my new cloak around my chemise. Then, on silent feet, I cross the loft to the window and pry it open. Chill air bites at my cheeks and I hear Harlow mutter a complaint in her sleep. I glance back at the room to ensure I still haven't woken anyone, then hoist myself onto the window's ledge. It's a dormer window, set midway through the pitched roof. I scoot from the ledge to the roof, securing my feet firmly on the tiles before closing the window behind me. Then, clinging to the ledge above the window, I stand as quietly as I can.

The night is beautifully dark, the sky clear and speckled with stars. I spot Dominic's silhouette farther down, limned by moonlight. He's half turned away from me, but I notice the open vial in his hand, extended like an offering. Then I smell it. The sickly-sweet tang of blood.

Something about the scent sets me on edge. It's not like I haven't smelled blood before, and I should be used to it from how often Calvin drinks from his vials, but the rotten scent hits the back of my throat, making me gag. A sudden spike of rage funnels through me, and I curl my hands into fists—

Dominic whirls around and caps his vial.

The scent disappears, and my muscles relax. My anger cools to a simmer, but what lingers serves as a reminder of what Dominic is. A half Sinless with secrets he refuses to share. Well, I won't make it easy for him to treat me like a tool, discarding me when he's done.

"What are you doing here?" Dominic's voice is sharp. Cold.

I climb the roof toward him, each step careful despite my ire. "I could ask you the same." My eyes drop to the hand that holds the vial. "What were you doing with that?"

"It's dangerous out here."

"Were you trying to catch another Shade?"

"I'm keeping watch," he says through his teeth. "Go back to your room."

I scoff. "Why? Hiding something?"

He strides toward me, his balance effortless despite the precarious terrain. "What I'm doing is none of your concern. You can't be out here."

"Looks like I'm out here just fine."

He reaches for my arm, but I lift it before he can make contact. He grabs for it again, and this time his fingers close around my wrist. He tugs me a step closer, expression dark. "Go back on your own or I'll haul you inside myself."

I hold his gaze with a glower and lean into his threatening pull. "I'd like to see you try."

"*Ah, so would I, love,*" comes Lust's deep and sultry voice. His dark shape coalesces beside the Shadowbane, his visage an impersonation of Dominic's. "*So would I.*"

Dominic closes his eyes, teeth bared in irritation. His hand opens at once, and I lower my arm. In taking a step away, my foot slips on one of the tiles. Dominic reaches for me, but at the same time, a heavy weight presses against my thigh. I regain my footing, thanks to Sloth, who now stands between me and the roof's decline. Dominic stopped himself before he could touch me and now closes his fingers into a fist. "You see? This is why I didn't want you out here. It's fucking dangerous."

"I was perfectly fine until you got handsy."

"Handsy," he echoes.

"*I like getting handsy,*" Lust says.

"*We fucking know, you prick,*" says Pride. His form wavers on the Shadowbane's other side. He too wears Dominic's face, but his expression is haughty where Lust's is flippant. "*The more you brag about your lecherous proclivities, the more pathetic it makes you look.*"

Lust scoffs. "*Stop trying to stir up my shame, Pride. You know I don't have any.*"

"*Clearly.*"

"*Gods, it must be exhausting for you, always looking down on everyone. I, on the other hand, prefer* going *down. You should try it sometime.*"

"*I don't need to try,*" Pride says. "*I either do something, and do it right the first time, or I don't.*"

Lust rolls his eyes. "*Just say it, Pride. You don't know where the clitoris is, do you?*"

"*Just say it, Lust. You've never lasted longer than three seconds, have you?*"

"*Was that a premature-ejaculation joke? Am I supposed to take offense? Sounds lovely to me.*"

Sloth's eyes volley between the bantering Shades. "*Can everyone just sit down where it's safe?*"

Dominic puts his hands on his hips and heaves a long-suffering sigh. Meanwhile, I'm left baffled. I never could have imagined I'd one day witness two Shades verbally sparring in a figurative dick-measuring contest. Do Shades even have dicks? Lust and Pride may wear Dominic's face, but below their necks, their bodies undulate in wisps of black and only a hint of clothing. An open shirt and loosened cravat for Lust. A crisp jacket and starched collar for Pride.

Dominic shakes his head, drawing my attention back to him. He seems annoyed by his Shades, but how much more annoyed would he be if he knew I'd heard every word? I'm almost of a mind to confess, just to see how he'd react. But I dismiss the notion when I recall the argument we were in the middle of when his Shades decided to have their own. As he stalks a few steps up the roof, I wonder if he'll tell me to go back inside again. Then, without meeting my eyes, he pauses and extends a hand back toward me. "Come on," he says, tone begrudging. "If you're going to linger like a thorn in my side, at least do it where you won't break your fucking neck."

I purse my lips but take his proffered hand, letting him aid my climb while Sloth stays close behind me. I settle onto the wide ridge at the roof's peak, Sloth lying at my feet while Dominic sits not too far away. Pride and Lust are now giving each other the silent treatment, hovering just behind the Shadowbane.

Tipping my head back, I take a moment to admire the quiet night, the canopy of stars, the silver glow of the moon, before I assess our surroundings. The streets are quiet, empty, the windows aglow with lamplight. There's not a single Shade to be seen. Reluctantly, I return my attention to my prickly companion. "Why are you so determined to keep us at a distance? You never answer questions plainly. You always put up a fight."

"I could say the latter about you," he says tonelessly.

"And there he goes," I whisper to Sloth, reaching to pat his head, "dodging another question."

Dominic rolls his eyes. "We can't have this conversation at night. The Shades—"

"Are only attracted to lies," I say.

"Except one of us seems to attract Shades even when she isn't lying."

"Is this about what happened in the clearing— Damn the gods. You're doing it again. You are so frustrating I could . . ."

"*You could what?*" Lust appears between us, his imitation of Dominic's features clearer than before. I imagine even his voice is like Dominic's, if the Shadowbane would speak in anything but his dry tone. "*Tell me what you want to do to me, and make it dirty.*"

"Leave her alone, Lust," Dominic says under his breath.

Lust pouts but retreats into the Shadowbane, leaving Pride to smirk, chin lifted in triumph.

"You want to know why I'm reluctant to answer certain questions?" he says. "Then let me ask you this. How did it feel to learn the truth of the Holy Braziers?"

I frown, considering his question. "I felt . . . betrayed. By my fiancé and by all Sinless."

"And why don't you spout the truth to everyone you meet?"

"Some wouldn't believe me," I say. "Others would arrest me for treason. The rest might fall into hysterics." I imagine what would happen if everyone suddenly knew that the Sinless feast on human hearts to light the braziers. It's one thing to know the Sinless feed from people. As far as the average citizen believes, a Sinless's blood source is kept alive. And if they die, what does it matter? They're only criminals. Or, in cases like Calvin's, the family of the chosen blood source has been fairly compensated in exchange for what appears to be a position of honor.

It's another thing to know the Sinless kill, claiming sacrifices without warning, without trial.

"Then imagine how much more I know than you," Dominic says. His voice adopts a gentle, almost pleading quality. "How many more secrets I carry. You only hypothesize what might happen if you share what you know. I, on the other hand, have firsthand experience. A Shadowbane's work brings us close to royal secrets that are kept from the public, and many don't pass these truths on to their Summoners. I do intend to share valuable intel, but I will do so only after we've established trust. In the meantime, know that I meant it when I said I've sent many of my retired crew across the sea, alive and well. I genuinely want that for you. Hate me and my kind all you want, but I am not your enemy."

I'm not fully convinced by the last part, but I'm most concerned about a pointed omission. "What about the Summoners you didn't send across the sea? You said before some have died, but how? You promised to protect us. Did your previous Summoners die under that promised protection? Or by a deliberate lack of it?"

He holds my gaze without falter. "My burdens are heavy, Seamstress."

I let him leave it at that, for I doubt he'd elaborate if I prodded more. It's obvious he's been betrayed by his crew—something I considered doing when he first gave me his ultimatum—and he's made it clear he won't hesitate to kill us if we take that path. Aside from being what he is, a Shadowbane hell-bent on becoming full Sinless plus an all-around asshole, he hasn't done anything to make me seriously ponder that option again. Especially if his promise proves true. If we can survive these next six months and he can get us off this continent,

I can put up with everything I hate about him. The promise of freedom, of not having to hide who I am or what I do, of not being labeled a sinner or an outlaw . . . it's enough to keep me at his side.

Of course, no one knows if the lands across the sea are any better than here.

I lower my eyes to the dark horizon and the hulking shapes of the nearby mountains.

"Do you know what's out there?" I whisper. "Across the sea? Are the other civilizations as damned as we're told?"

The history books say the Holy Continent was the only land blessed by Bastien. No other continent's king was turned Sinless or taught the Absolution ritual. The other lands live and die at the mercy of Shades, and the survivors are warmongering devils, continuing the same vile acts that angered the gods five centuries ago and plunged the world into One Hundred Days of Darkness. We have so little interaction with other continents, we can only believe it's true. Otherwise, wouldn't we have more than one open port? More trade? Perhaps limiting trade is a safety measure, to keep outsiders away from this pretend paradise.

Maybe it's to make it harder for us to leave.

Dominic shakes his head. "No one really knows what it's like, only that there are no Sinless. No Shadowbanes."

No protection from Shades, is what he means. All they have are natural means. Silver and light. It could be a thousand times worse than it is here, but that doesn't dissuade me from holding on to my goal. The alternative is running until the day I die, and outlaws don't tend to live long on the Holy Continent.

Sloth rolls onto his side, his head resting on my foot. I pet him again, this time stroking his soft ears. "What do you use them for?" I ask. "The Shades you catch. Sloth, Pride, and Lust didn't help us with the dragon. And where is the new one?"

"The new one is staying in the vial," Dominic says. "And I don't use my shadows to fight other Shades. The most they do against their own kind is darken my shadow or move it, allowing me to tempt the Shades I hunt close enough to catch. They do help me with other people, though."

My stomach sours as I revisit the few times his shadows have touched me. I may have warmed up to Sloth, but I'll never forget how invasive it felt when he licked my face when I was pressed to the ground, or the terror I felt when one of them had his hand at the base of my throat.

The reminder makes me reconsider petting the shadow dog, but I can't bring myself to pull away. Not with how real his fur feels, how warm and heavy his belly is beneath my hand. In this moment, he's just so doglike. I scratch him under the ears.

Dominic makes a strange sound, almost like a moan, and my eyes dart to him. He shifts it into a cough that he hides behind his fist.

I eye him beneath a furrowed brow and resume petting the Shade. "Why doesn't Sloth wear your face like the others?"

He glances down at the monster with a wry grin. "He may not wear my face, but he's still a reflection of me."

"How so?"

"I think we all have a primal, animal aspect to us. Don't you?"

I'm taken aback. I've heard such an analogy stated a time or two, but normally it's in reference to a wolf or a lion. Something proud and strong. "Your inner animal . . . is a dog."

His lips pull into a grin so wide and unexpected it makes my heart stutter. His posture is easier now, one hand planted on the ridge between us as he slumps slightly to the side. He holds my gaze with that smile, and I'm struck by how young he looks. How delicately the corners of his eyes crinkle. "A lazy, useless dog," he says, "who just wants to eat and sleep and be petted by a pair of skilled hands. Call me a good boy, and I'll be happy forever."

My mouth falls open. That was probably the most carefree thing he's ever said to me, and . . . I'm shocked by how much I liked it. By how warm it makes my stomach feel, how my heartbeat quickens in response. And maybe that's what emboldens me to do what I do next.

Lifting my hand, I reach for him, letting it fall on his hair. His dark strands are softer than I imagined they would be, despite being mussed by the breeze. "Good boy," I say, patting his head in what's supposed to be a taunting gesture.

Yet . . . it doesn't feel taunting. Nor does my voice hold an ounce of the ridicule I intended. Instead, my words are soft, almost breathless. And the way his pupils blow wide, the way his chest lifts with a hitch of breath, tells me he doesn't feel patronized at all.

We freeze like that, eyes locked, my hand still splayed over his hair. My cheeks heat, and before I can recall my inhibitions, my mind takes another path. I imagine what it would be like if we weren't master and crew. If he wasn't someone I hate. If we weren't on this rooftop keeping watch for monsters, but just a man and a woman enjoying a late autumn night. If we were just that, I'd find him . . . tolerable. More than tolerable. Handsome. Desirable, even.

Dominic leans closer, an almost imperceptible distance. In the same moment, his eyes dip to my mouth. In answer, my lips part, and I too find myself leaning closer—

Dominic's expression shutters, and he pulls back. With stiff motions, he rises to his feet. "You should go," he says, all traces of his lighthearted mood gone. The hand that had been planted between us opens and closes at his side.

"I . . . should go, yes," I say, too startled by what almost happened to argue. Yet I can't ignore the way my heart races. It's a traitorous rhythm, one it has no right to drum. Not for Dominic. A Shadowbane. A man who will someday be fully Sinless. Maybe even become a duke who will proceed to consume hearts.

I don't look back as I descend the roof and enter the window once more. And as I settle into my blankets, I try to ignore the way my lips tingle, pulsing in the wake of a kiss that never happened. Or the sound of Dominic's steps crossing the roof, stopping just over my bed.

CHAPTER SIXTEEN

Dominic

After three nights and only the tamest of Shade sightings, I feel like I can breathe again. Especially since the third night passed without any interruptions from Inana. Gods, she's a problem. Too curious. Too stubborn. And too damn effective at getting under my skin. Not to mention the surges of emotion I keep feeling. I almost kissed her, for fuck's sake. As much as I might have wanted to, and as hot as my blood roared as she stroked my hair and called me a good boy, I can't let anything like that happen between us. She's my Summoner and I'm her master. Anything more is a distraction I can't afford. Besides, romantic relationships are taboo for my kind, especially with a subordinate. A Shadowbane's duty is to his king, his patron prince, and the church. Everything else comes second until we're granted full Absolution.

No pious Shadowbane would ever romance a sinner.

Which means being alone with Inana is a bad idea. But trying to keep her at bay with curt words and a cold demeanor doesn't fucking work. It only makes her more riled up. More intrigued. More verbally combative. More attractive. More enticing in the way she lifts her chin, licks her lips, and—

I shake the thoughts from my head.

Inana meets my eyes across the rough-hewn table in the dining room of the inn. She gives me a perplexed look, which makes me realize I've been staring. Like an idiot, I glance away and pretend to have been scanning our surroundings. The dining room is brightly lit, with lamps on each table and wooden chandeliers that hang from the rafters. The buzz of quiet conversation fills the air, along with scents of meat, fresh bread, and watered-down ale.

This is the first time I've been with my crew since we returned from dispatching the dragon. Until now, my hours have been spent resting, interviewing villagers for potential leads regarding the artist responsible for the Shade, or keeping watch from dusk to dawn. With the threat officially de-escalated, I invited my crew to dine at the inn's tavern. The mayor was generous in his compensation, and even after the cut owed to Prince Leeran and the church, I still have ample coin left. What better way to spend it than by rewarding those who did the most important work to earn it?

My crew seems to be enjoying their prize. Bard savors the largest bowl of stew I've seen while Harlow works on her second plate of pork belly and eggs. Calvin's appetite is always on the weaker end, but even he splurged on herb-crusted lamb chops. My eyes glide back to Inana, who tears into a buttery roll. She seems to have a fondness for bread, which makes me inexplicably envious of the rolls she hoards. My eyes move from her lips, glistening with butter, to her clothing. It's different today, thanks to the mayor's other gifts. Her bodice is brown leather, lacing up the front, the cut low enough to reveal the tip of her scar. It juts through her delicately freckled skin, cutting diagonally across the modest swell of her—

I snap my eyes away again. Why the fuck was I looking at her . . . scar?

"*Is that what we're calling it?*" Lust whispers. It's too bright for him to be anything more than a pool of shadow on my chair. Unlike Sloth, who hides under the table, nudging Calvin for pets. He tried to do the same to Inana, but I tugged him away. "*I thought for certain you were ogling her tits. I don't blame you. They're nice.*"

Inana chokes on her bite of bread, then washes it down with a sip of ale. Did she . . . hear Lust? That isn't the first time I've questioned whether she can hear my shadows. On the roof, she watched Lust and

Pride with too much fascination for someone who couldn't hear their argument.

So why not test my theory?

I lean back in my chair, posture bored. "They can't be any nicer than all the others I've seen," I mutter.

"Huh?" Calvin says, brow arched.

Harlow too casts a questioning glance, while Bard briefly looks up from his stew.

Inana is the only one who doesn't look at all confused by what should seem a non sequitur. From her flushed cheeks to her seething glare, I can't think of any other explanation. She heard him. While anyone can see my shadows—mostly invisible during the day aside from the pools of darkness they cast—no one but me should be able to hear their voices.

She sets down her half-eaten roll and mirrors my posture, leaning back in her chair and folding her arms. However, instead of crossing them over her chest, she folds them . . . beneath it. Lifting certain assets until distinct swells rise above her bodice. Bloody hell.

"Are you going to eat or are you going to keep staring at my fucking tits, pervert?"

My first instinct is to say something cold and dismissive. Then I recall how well that went for me on the roof. She'll only argue or bait me to argue back. The only times I've left her at a loss for words are when I'm unintentionally flirting with her. Pushing her boundaries. Normally I try my best to resist the pull to do so, but what if I give in for my own benefit? Not so much that I almost kiss her again. No, that was a different kind of giving in. That was more letting my guard down. Allowing her to get too close. This time I'll give in just enough to startle her. Embarrass her. Make her want to shut that tempting mouth and keep her eyes from straying to mine.

I lean forward, lips lifted at one corner as my gaze sweeps from her face to her chest. "Why should I have to choose? I can eat and look at the same time. Might as well make a fucking feast of it, right, sinner?" Still looking at her chest, I spear a piece of venison with my fork and bring it to my lips, emitting a sound of deep satisfaction as I chew.

As intended, by the time my attention returns to her face, her mouth is pursed tight, her cheeks blazing.

Victory floods me in a dizzying rush. Is that really all I have to do?

"Oh, my gods," Harlow says, her voice strangled with laughter. She looks from me to Inana, covering her mouth. And that's when I remember we have a bloody audience. "Have the two of you still not fucked?"

"No," Inana says, but her tone sounds more like she's scolding an unruly puppy than answering the question. "It's not like that. There's nothing between us."

"Sure about that?" I say before I can think better of it. Now that I've let myself give in, I can't stop. My blood thrums in a sensation that is both strange and familiar. In this moment, I am the man I was six years ago, before my emotions were stripped along with half my sins. It shouldn't be possible. There's only one way a Sinless or halfsoul can experience a reversal in Absolution—one of the deepest, darkest secrets I keep—and this isn't it.

And yet . . .

Gods above, it feels fucking good.

"I'm sure," she says through her teeth.

I'm about to quip back about lying to my shadows, but an uncomfortable sensation skitters up the base of my spine. "Not the ass, Cal. You know it's weird."

That, of course, has my three Summoners going still.

"Excuse me?" Harlow's amusement grows tenfold. "What were you doing to his ass, Calvin?"

Calvin lifts his hands, an innocent grin on his face. "I was just petting Sloth. He likes butt scratches."

"Yes, well, I don't. Not from you." I take a deep swallow of ale, as if that will wash the sensation down.

The screech of chair legs against flagstones nearly has me spitting my drink. Because it's Inana who rises to her feet. The daggers she shoots with her eyes make me realize my mistake.

"Are you suggesting," she says, voice quavering in her efforts to speak low, "you can feel when we touch your Shades?"

I lean back in my chair again, blowing out a heavy breath. "I can feel what they feel, to a degree," I say. "Now will you sit down before the barkeep tells us to get the fuck out?"

She glances around the dining room. Sure enough, several pairs of eyes look our way. Public acts of anger or frivolity are frowned upon, for no one wants to be accused of doing anything that might attract a Shade, even during daylight hours.

With a feigned smile for the onlookers, she settles back into her chair and leans toward the table. "Why haven't you mentioned that? And how is it possible? Are they . . . tethered to you? Is that how they can move about during the day, while regular Shades can't set foot outside of shadows?"

"They are partially tethered to me," I say, "and I didn't mention it . . ."

I haven't a clue how to finish that sentence. I should have mentioned it, but I didn't because . . .

Well, because I liked when she began to warm up to Sloth. Liked the way her hands felt when she petted his coat. I almost liked it too much on the roof, when she scratched him just beneath his ears.

"He didn't mention it because it's weird as fuck," Calvin says, coming to my rescue. "Long story short, don't give Lust a handjob."

"No one needs that warning," Harlow says, then her lips quirk into a devious grin. "Unless . . . Inana, why are you so flustered? Did you diddle Lust after all? Oh, wait. Did you . . . *pet his dog*? Oh, my gods, you did."

"*She did,*" Sloth says, whipping around excitedly under the table. "*She's so nice and her hands are so gentle.*"

"You're the worst," Inana hisses, to Harlow's tittering delight. Even Bard laughs, a single huff of mirth.

"No reason to feel awkward about it," Calvin says. "Sloth is great to pet. You should pet him too, Har. Everyone should pet him."

"Everyone should *not* pet him," I say.

Harlow ignores me, responding only to Cal. "Ew, don't call me Har." She then proceeds to pet Sloth as he nudges her legs. He bumps next into Bard, who idly pats his head.

I wince at the soft pressure that reaches me through Sloth while the asshole dog relishes the attention. Yet I don't tell my Summoners off, because there is a part of me that likes it almost as much as he does.

"At least now I know what to do to make you uncomfortable," Inana says, a triumphant grin on her lips.

"I never said it would feel uncomfortable coming from you," I volley back with a wink.

Her only reply is a muttered "Bastard."

My amusement sharply drains as someone approaches our table. I expect it to be the barkeep, scolding us for talking too much or being too carefree. One doesn't normally scold a Shadowbane, considering their unquestionable authority, but since I'm not wearing my sword, the barkeep might not know who I am. But as I lock eyes with the figure, I find a familiar male face. One that sours my stomach and dampens every good feeling I've had over the last several minutes.

"Dominic Graves," says a man who's been a fucking plague to me for the better part of a decade. "I was hoping I'd find you."

CHAPTER SEVENTEEN

INANA

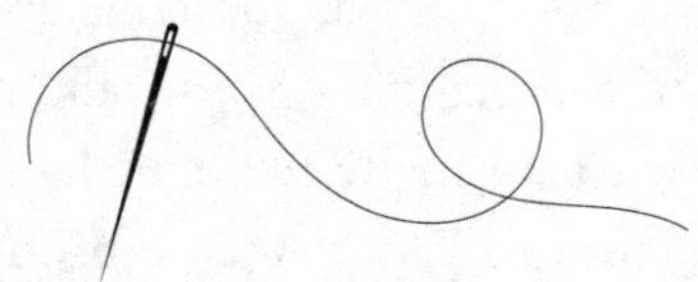

I'd be shocked at hearing Dominic's last name for the first time were it not for the shift in his expression. It shutters so fast it's hard to believe he wore a grin just a second before. It may have been a teasing smirk rather than the soft, open smile I glimpsed on the roof, but it was nothing like the dark look he wears now, his brows lowered, jaw tight, hands curled into fists. Whoever this stranger is, Dominic isn't happy to see him.

"Henderson," he bites out. "Why are you here?"

"Just passing through." The man named Henderson is forty perhaps, at least ten years older than Dominic, with combed-back russet hair and a slim mustache. Behind him stands a woman a decade or two older, her gray-brown hair pulled into an austere bun at the nape of her neck. Both are dressed in dark clothing: fine leather jerkins and wool greatcoats. Then I notice the hilt of the silver sword at Henderson's back, identical to Dominic's. He must be a Shadowbane, then. He looks down his nose at Dominic. "Almost had to save your ass, though."

"What the fuck are you talking about?" Dominic's fingers tighten around his fork.

"The mayor begged me to take your post if you didn't show."

"Are you suggesting you were here the whole time the village was being attacked and didn't come to their aid?"

Henderson gives a wry grin. "Being given your post is one thing, but poaching? I wouldn't soil my reputation just to make up for your failures, Graves. If the mayor was desperate, he could have taken a more extreme measure. There was one recourse that would have ensured my intervention."

Dominic's expression turns colder, and I glance from one man to the other. What does Henderson mean?

"You think he should have sacrificed a villager?" Dominic shakes his head and adds under his breath, "Of course you'd consider that a solution."

"One villager is nothing compared to the losses they sustained," Henderson says. "If an Incarnate appeared, I'd have had no choice but to dispatch it."

I puzzle over his words until they start to make sense. "You think they should have sacrificed a villager to tempt the Shade to Incarnate? So it could then be killed?"

Henderson turns his gaze to me but says nothing.

"The Shade we dispatched was a godsdamned dragon," Dominic says. "Comprising more than a dozen individual Shades. It would have required as many human sacrifices."

"Is that so?" Henderson's voice lacks any hint of surprise over the dragon or that it had been forged from multiple Shades. Is that because he already surmised as much when he witnessed the carnage without lifting a finger? Or . . .

I slide my gaze to the woman behind him. If Henderson is a Shadowbane, I assume she's his Summoner. As far as I know, Dominic never found any clue as to who may have created the dragon. All we know is that only an artist could have done it. Suspicion crawls up my spine, even more so when the woman's gaze locks with mine, a haughty glint in her eyes.

"Interesting new recruits," she says. Her voice is deeper than I expect, and not unpleasant despite her disinterested tone. It makes me wonder if singing is her talent.

Henderson's eyes sweep over all of us except for Calvin, which—along with the glower Calvin wears—tells me they're already acquainted. "Interesting indeed," Henderson says. "You wouldn't happen to have taken anything that belongs to me, would you? You certainly have made a habit of it in the past."

Dominic rises to his feet. "None of my Summoners belong to you."

"We might disagree, if their bounties are big enough."

A jolt of panic goes through me. Dominic assured us we wouldn't be prosecuted for any of our past crimes while we were in service to him. Was that a lie?

My fingers flinch, desperate to cover my scar, but such a sudden move would only bring attention to it. Instead, I hunch slightly forward, encouraging my cloak to fall closed over my shoulders but not daring to glance down to see if it was effective.

"We can disagree all we want," Dominic says, his voice edged in warning as he takes a step closer to Henderson, "but you would be in the wrong. You have no claim on my Summoners."

Henderson huffs a laugh, then scans the table. His eyes linger on Bard, narrowing with keen scrutiny. Only now do I notice how still Bard has gone. His normally distant stare is locked on the center of the table, his shoulders hunched, lips pursed tight.

Slowly, Bard lifts his head and pins Henderson with the most hateful expression I've seen him wear. He holds Henderson's gaze without falter. "Do I look familiar to you?"

Henderson's answering grin makes my blood go cold. "Interesting indeed," he whispers. Then he faces Dominic once more and holds out a slip of paper. "Speaking of what belongs to either of us, this is yours."

Dominic eyes Henderson warily before taking the paper from him. His jaw shifts side to side. "Why do you have this?"

"Your next post assignment was sent by messenger from the church," Henderson says. "Oh, don't look at me like that. Authenticate the letter with the church yourself. What do I care about your next post? I was in possession of the missive because the idiot messenger only knew to deliver it to the *Shadowbane at Thornfal.* See what happens when you spend so much time cleaning up after your own messes rather than performing your duties as Shadowbane? I could have had two of your posts, but I left both to you. Rather generous of me considering how close we are to the Year of Bastien, don't you think?"

"Generous? I thought you were more interested in collecting bounties anyway."

"Oh, that I am. Let's hope your current choice of . . . *company* doesn't conflict with my goals, or we'll find ourselves at an impasse."

"Threaten my Summoners," Dominic says, stepping up to Henderson and grabbing him by the collar of his greatcoat, "and you'll find yourself without a head."

Henderson only grins as Dominic hauls him closer. "Such sinful words from a halfsoul. Maybe I should send the church a letter of concern. Though it'd be a shame if you were stuck in an inquisition during such an important time."

Dominic bares his teeth but releases the other man. "Fuck off."

Henderson brushes off the front of his coat with irritating calm. "For now," he says. He gives our table a final glance before sauntering off, his Summoner trailing behind him. In their wake, the silence around us is deafening. I turn, finding all eyes from the other guests on us, including those of the barkeep, who wrings her hands before the kitchen door. We've made a scene, and now people are worried we might attract Shades.

Dominic must notice this as well, for he gives the room an apologetic bow of his head, then whispers to us, "We should go. We've overstayed our welcome."

I'm surprised by his reaction. A Shadowbane has the authority to do what he wants when he wants, just like the other Sinless. Yet his guilt over having caused a scene is written in his furrowed brow. Or maybe he dislikes the attention. Shadowbanes are rarely seen in public, and when they are, the general mood is tense. No one wants to draw the eye of the person hunting bounties or detecting the source of Shade attacks. Even the innocent can find themselves on the wrong side of justice if their neighbors are desperate to save themselves and label a scapegoat.

Without a word, we rise from the table. Dominic heads for the stairwell that leads upstairs to the inn, and the rest of us follow. I bring up the rear, only to think of the bread rolls I left behind. I turn back, reaching for the basket of yeasty goodness. It would be a crime not to finish them. Perhaps the butter too—

"They've all died. You know that, right?"

I freeze, finding Henderson's Summoner strolling toward our table. Her master is nowhere in sight, but that's not much of a comfort. I distinctly dislike this woman, even without knowing much about her. Ignoring her, I gather the bread and the butter dish and turn back around.

"All his previous Summoners," she says, "they're all dead. Why else do you think he needed you?"

My muscles tighten at the sound of her footsteps following me, but I pay her no heed as I proceed to the stairwell. As I climb, I see no sign of my companions.

The Summoner's voice follows me. "Your master isn't who you think he is."

I halt in the middle of the stairwell, not wanting to lead her any farther. The loft is located on the third floor, but she doesn't need to know where we're sleeping.

She takes a few steps closer. "He's been through more Summoners than any other Shadowbane under Prince Leeran."

I roll my eyes and face the woman. "Let me guess. Your master is also employed by Prince Leeran. He's competing with Dominic for the nomination to be turned Sinless."

"There's something wrong with the way he operates," she continues, as if I hadn't spoken. "He appoints outlaws instead of proper Summoners from the church. What is he offering you that's so tempting?"

"I can't see how it's any of your business."

"He doesn't even offer Absolution, does he?"

I pull my head back at that.

Her eyes brighten as if I've given her the answer she was looking for. She climbs another step. "He didn't even tell you that's an option? A Shadowbane who has been chosen for Absolution can request that his entire crew be made Sinless with him."

My stomach tangles itself in knots. Dominic could . . . request we be made Sinless too? None of us would want that, but shouldn't he have at least offered? Isn't that what his kind want—a world of Sinless? Instead, he offered us an escape from the continent.

Her lips pull into a pout that isn't even remotely convincing. "Why is he so cold to his Summoners? Why is he so cruel?"

I shake my head and proceed a few steps higher. "We're done here."

"Perhaps he wants to ensure none of you live long enough to tell his secrets," she says, stalling me yet again. "Is it true he captures Shades, keeps them in vials?"

I press my lips tight. I may not trust Dominic, but I trust this Summoner even less. And while I assumed capturing Shades was common practice for Shadowbanes—just not public knowledge—the way she says it makes me think her master does not do the same. But why?

As far as I've gleaned, Dominic only captures Shades that have imitated his appearance. Everyone knows that once a Shade wears your face, it will relentlessly hunt you until it consumes your body. What else could he do to prevent it from seeking to Incarnate?

Then I remember what Henderson said about the dragon. How he thought the mayor should have sacrificed villagers to tempt the Shade to Incarnate, after which the monster could be killed. Is that how most Shadowbanes handle Shade threats? Is that how they rid themselves of ones who've made them targets, by giving them someone else to copy instead? If Shades can only be calmed or temporarily dispersed, but Incarnates can be permanently killed . . .

Yes, of course that's what other Shadowbanes would do.

Does that mean Dominic captures Shades out of compassion?

If so, is that a good or bad thing?

A strange feeling writhes in my gut. I know I should hate the Shades. They kill people. They hunger for our flesh. Yet I've never been able to hate them the way I hate the Sinless. And the thought of Dominic treating both Shades and humans with care, valuing innocent lives rather than making a sacrifice for a faster kill . . . it makes me uneasy. And I don't know in what way.

"I'm not interested in whatever you're trying to stir up here," I say over my shoulder.

"Rykar Bodin," she says, an eager look on her face. "Is the older male in your party named Rykar Bodin?"

My pulse quickens. Though he only told us his name once, Bard did say it was Rykar. After which he begged us not to call him that. I deliver my lie with ease. "I haven't a clue who you're talking about."

Her expression darkens. "Lying is a sin."

"I'm an artist. I'm already a sinner."

"Summoner work is a holy path." Her voice trembles with fervor. "A path of atonement. If you seek Absolution, that is. What do Dominic Graves's Summoners seek?"

Survival, I want to say, but she doesn't deserve my honest answer. So I lift a roll from the basket, tear into it, and mutter a muffled "bread" before proceeding up the stairs. Thank the fucking gods she doesn't follow me again.

My anger grows in the wake of our conversation, and I chew my bite with a vengeance. As I reach the top of the stairs, I nearly leap out of my skin.

Dominic leans against the wall outside the stairwell, arms crossed, posture relaxed.

I toss the other half of my roll back in the basket. "What? Wanted to make sure I didn't sell you out?"

He pushes off the wall and heads for the stairs that lead to the loft. "I'm not the only person I was worried about."

I follow him. "You thought I would betray the others?"

"I worried her interest was in *you,* Inana." My stomach flips at the sound of my name on his lips. Even more so when he meets my eyes over his shoulder. "You'd do well to avoid her, Henderson, and any of his other Summoners."

I cut him a glare. "I wasn't trying to make friends. Do you think they did it? Did his crew create the dragon?"

"I'd be more surprised if it wasn't him," he says. We slowly climb the stairs, a step at a time. "Henderson and I . . . we have a tense history. This isn't the first time he's tried to sabotage me, but it's the first time he's put so many innocents at risk to do so."

"You can't report him to the church?"

"I have no proof that I can use against him. The only proof I have would incriminate me and give him the opportunity to open allegations of his own."

That reminds me of what the Summoner said about Dominic. How she thinks there's something wrong with the way he operates. "What did she mean, by the way?" I ask, unable to hide the trepidation in my tone. "About Shadowbanes nominating their crew to be turned Sinless with them?"

Dominic shakes his head. "I'm not going to nominate any of you. I specifically choose Summoners with no ambition to be made Sinless."

"Why?"

"An ambitious crew has never served me well in the past. I prefer to be the only one in my crew seeking Absolution."

"But . . . doesn't that go against your nature? Your ideals? Aren't you fueled by the belief that everyone should seek to become Sinless?" I can guess the real answer. I've suspected it for most of my life. Of course the Sinless don't actually give a shit about making the rest of the continent like them. For if there were no sinners, who the fuck would the Sinless feed from?

We stop outside the loft door. He hesitates, his fingers on the handle. He turns to me and answers in words almost too quiet to hear. The last words I expect. "Why would I wish what I am on anyone else?"

CHAPTER EIGHTEEN

Inana

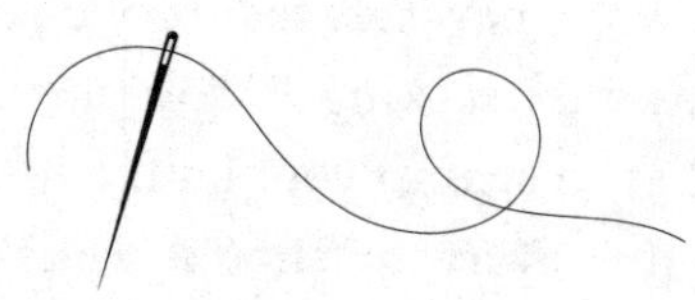

Snow falls by the end of our two-week stay in Thornfal. It isn't too surprising considering winter solstice is mere days away, not to mention our proximity to the mountains. And since we've seen no return of aggressive Shades, our post has officially been served.

Dominic was hesitant to trust the letter Henderson delivered, but after a few back-and-forth communications with the nearest church, he validated the missive as authentic. We have no choice but to trust it and go where we're needed next. Which is the village of Eldeen, a six-day journey north on the other side of the mountain pass. We've only been traveling for a day and I'm already restless.

I sit in the back of the wagon, unable to find sleep despite the abundance of blankets, the steady motion of the wagon, and the peaceful semidarkness, broken by a single lantern. Before we left Thornfal, we were gifted a cover for our wagon to keep out the winter elements. When I asked Dominic why he didn't have one before, he said he did, but it got destroyed by Shades. Not a comforting thing to hear, but all right. Regardless, even with such travel comforts, I can't keep my eyes closed. And I seem to be the only one.

Bard, Harlow, and Calvin sleep soundly beside me, their soft snores and rhythmic breaths filling our small space. Maybe that's why I can't sleep. Thornfal may have spoiled me by giving us such a large room and separate beds.

The last time I couldn't sleep was the night I found Dominic on the rooftop. Just like then, I emerge from my blankets, wrap my cloak around me, and join him under the night sky.

I don't meet his eyes as I climb through the canvas flap and onto the driver's perch. He doesn't seem surprised to see me. Maybe he could sense I was awake. Sloth greets me at once, a comforting weight on my lap as he lays his head on my thighs. I'm grateful for his shadowy warmth amid the chill in the air. Why did I come out here again? I blow hot breath into my hands, then pull my cloak closed around me. The forest road is quiet, coated in a dusting of snow that brightens the night. At least it isn't actively snowing, the starry sky only partially obscured by clouds. I spot a few Shades stalking by or peering out at us from the trees that flank the road. It isn't as unsettling as it was on our first journey, but I'm still not keen to draw their interest.

"Are you used to being awake at night now?" Dominic asks, voice low so as not to carry to the others. Or the Shades.

"Maybe that's it," I say, watching my breath form white puffs in the air. Every evening during our last week in Thornfal, Dominic had us join him for his nightly watches. We finally got to train in a way that felt like training, not merely adapting to a threat. We practiced drawing Shades away from the village, entrancing them with our art without triggering their aggression. It appears to be true that Shades only turn frenzied when provoked, either by violence against them or by frightened actions like screaming or running. So long as we stayed calm, made no hasty moves, and expressed tranquility in our art, they remained harmless.

He angles his head to look at me. "It's too cold for you to be out here."

I roll my eyes. It hasn't even been a minute and he's already trying to get me away from him. "Yes, well, I'm bored. If I stay back there, I'm going to wake them up with my tossing and turning."

His only reply is a grunt.

I assess him this time, realizing he's without a cloak or even riding gloves. His hair is half tied back, his dark sleeves pushed partway up his forearms. "Wait, what about you?"

"My body temperature runs warmer than yours."

"Really?" I remember assuming as much when I saw him napping in the clearing two weeks back without a blanket. I also recall how uncomfortably warm Lord Wheaton's hand was when he grabbed me at the Wretched Lair.

"Bastien's influence," Dominic says.

I'm surprised. Not by what he said, for I know the sun god is responsible for turning the first Sinless. He taught King Kaelum the Absolution ritual and showed him how to wield solar astrotheurgy to protect his chosen cities. What surprises me is that Dominic offered an explanation so easily, without me dragging it out of him.

It reminds me of what he said on the stairs back at the inn.

Why would I wish what I am on anyone else?

He didn't explain what he meant by that, and I've yet to find the right moment to ask. The way he said it, the edge of pain in his voice, told me he hadn't meant to say it at all. For now, it's a puzzle piece in the mystery that is Dominic Graves. I hadn't even realized he was a mystery until Henderson's Summoner confronted me. I'm starting to think she was right—there's something strange about the way Dominic operates. He collects Shades instead of encouraging them to Incarnate with a sacrifice so he can kill them. He offers his Summoners not Absolution but freedom. Yet he's been betrayed by his Summoners. And even though he supposedly wouldn't wish what he is on anyone else, he seeks to complete his Absolution.

A puzzle indeed. One I'll have to tread carefully to figure out.

My eyes drop to the side of his face, the scar that runs over his cheekbone, half hidden in his short beard.

He frowns, and I realize how intently I'm staring. "What?" he says.

Heat floods my cheeks, and my embarrassment shifts into a wicked impulse. Before I can think better of it, I reach from under my cloak and press my icy fingertips to his cheek. I expect him to flinch back, to hiss at my cold touch, but he doesn't. He freezes and then . . .

His lashes flutter shut.

A soft sound of contentment rumbles deep in his throat.

I snatch my hand back just as fast, my heart racing.

As he opens his eyes, a wry grin forms on his lips. He looks at me sidelong. "What? I thought you were warming your hands."

"I was . . . trying to bother you."

"You'll have to try harder than that, sinner."

I suppose the one benefit to my mortification is that I'm suddenly hot all over.

He angles his head, exposing his neck. "Go on. Warm yourself up."

I hate how tempted I am. He was warm indeed, in the brief moment I touched him. So, gingerly, I press my fingers to the crook of his neck, delighting in his warmth. I can't help wondering how much warmer his skin might be beneath his jerkin. How hard his muscles might feel under my palm. How far he'd let my hands roam beneath his shirt, over his abdomen, beneath his waistband—

Biting the inside of my cheek, I banish my imaginings and pull my hand away. Before I can get far, Dominic grabs my wrist. I don't know what he's about to do. Probably chastise me for having touched him, even though he's the one who told me to. But he doesn't. Instead, he gently tugs me closer until my hand is back where it was, palm splayed over the side of his throat, my fingertips tucked against his nape. It's how I'd hold someone while kissing them. How I'd pull a lover closer to deepen said kiss.

Dominic meets my gaze, his lids heavy with something that looks like want.

Like the way he looked at me on the roof.

"What are you doing?" I ask in a breathy whisper.

"Cooling myself down," he says. "Neither of us would like it if I got too hot."

My breath hitches and I get the feeling his words hold double meaning. Not just the warmth of his skin but also the fire that has sparked between us.

A dangerous fire.

One neither of us should touch.

Because he's a fucking Shadowbane. Loyal to the Sinless I hate, and one day fully one of them. And I am merely his servant.

Even after reminding myself of this, the heat between us doesn't cool. It only rises until a sizzling ember shapes my bold reply. "Is that so? What would happen if you . . . got too hot?"

His voice is thick as he answers. "We'd both catch fire."

My breaths turn shallow. I let my thumb drift over his neck, a subtle motion that has his skin prickling into gooseflesh beneath my touch. I watch with satisfaction as his throat bobs, and I get the sharpest urge to grab him by the collar and pull him into a kiss. A kiss of hatred and desire. We'd both be set aflame, just like he said. I'd be helpless to the burn, aching beneath those rising flames until I couldn't take it anymore. Until I *needed* more. Then I would throw one leg over his lap, straddling him, riding him until the need between my legs was finally sated—

A sound nearly escapes my lips. Whether a sigh or a moan I don't find out, instead shifting it into a cough. I clear the lust from my throat and the fantasies from my mind. When I remove my hand, he makes no move to pull me back to him. "You're right," I say. "Neither of us would want that."

"Neither of us," he agrees, and shifts his eyes back to the road. I dare not look at him, afraid of what I'll see; disappointment or relief would be equally unwelcome.

My hands feel chilly after the heat of Dominic's skin, so I tuck them beneath my cloak.

"*I'll keep you warm,*" Sloth says, his head once again in my lap, shadowy tail wagging off the edge of the footrest. He's a welcome distraction while I gather my composure.

"*I can too, love,*" Lust says as a phantom arm drapes over my shoulder. His form coalesces between me and Dominic, a seductive grin on his lips. His likeness to the Shadowbane is so convincing it compromises all my efforts to regain my senses.

"*I'm fine right where I am,*" says a grumpier voice. Pride appears on Dominic's other side, arms folded over his semitransparent chest. I'm grateful for his grounding presence, as haughty and aloof as he is. I can always count on him to keep his distance. "*Though I'll consider keeping you company if you ask nicely.*"

I huff a laugh, then realize my mistake as Dominic's eyes shoot to mine.

"You really can hear them," he says.

I sink down slightly, lips curled in a grimace. I've tried my best to hide it, knowing I'm the only one of us who seems able to hear his Shades. "Is that . . . rare?"

"It is," he says. "I can't hear any Shades but my own."

Sloth paws at my lap, so I pet the top of his head despite the icy air that nips my fingers. At least the cold air and soft fur keep me from thinking about how just a minute ago hot skin was beneath my hand. I hazard a glance at Dominic, ready to ask him more about his Shades, but he's gone rigid. Alert. Eyes narrowed on something beside the road.

I follow his line of sight.

There's a small clearing among the trees to the right, where three wagons like ours are parked. There's no sign of a campfire, no horses tethered nearby. It isn't the first time we've come across abandoned wagons left in shambles after a Shade attack. But at second glance, these aren't old and weathered or covered in moss and ivy. As we draw nearer, I see that despite the lack of a fire, there is a pit around which several bodies sit. No, not sit.

Slump.

Over logs, a stump, on a cot. Only one of the bodies remains upright, the bright snow illuminating their back, the subtle movement of their shoulders.

"Fuck," Dominic whispers.

"What is it?" I ask, dreading the answer.

"Wake the others. Don your masks."

"Is it . . ."

He gives a sharp nod. "Incarnate."

CHAPTER NINETEEN

DOMINIC

If there's one thing I wanted to protect my Summoners from, it's witnessing an Incarnate. The carnage created by a Shade is one thing. Incarnates are another. No one should have to face such a creature. And there's no doubt in my mind that's what awaits us. No living human would dare linger in the dead of night without a proper fire. Not to mention the gore that surrounds the sole moving body.

I stop our wagon just ahead of the clearing, ensuring the creature can't see us from where it sits. It will soon know of our approach, but I'd rather our option for a quick getaway isn't immediately visible. "Calvin," I say.

"On it." He climbs into the front seat and takes the reins. His hood is already raised, tugged low over his eyes, and his movements are quick and alert. He's used to these kinds of surprise interruptions to his sleep.

I round the wagon to where the other three emerge with their masks in place, the hoods of their cloaks up. "First of all," I whisper, "I'm giving you a choice here. You can come with me or stay with Calvin. To be honest, there's little a Summoner can do to aid with killing an Incarnate. They aren't as easy to calm with art, and it can often enrage them instead. But there may come a time in the future when you'll have no choice but to stand beside me and face one. If you want that time to be now, then come with me. If not, stay here."

Inana is the first to answer. "I'll go." Her voice trembles, but there's determination in it too. I didn't expect anything less.

Harlow shifts from foot to foot, gaze darting through her mask toward the dark campsite. "I . . . I'll stay with Cal."

Bard clutches his cloth-wrapped mandolin to his chest, then finally nods, dipping his bronze wolf mask. "I'll go."

"Sit next to Cal," I say to Harlow. "He doesn't have a mask, so he'll have to keep his head lowered most of the time. You can be his eyes. Keep watch. If any nearby Shades show signs of agitation, sketch calming images."

She gives a jerky nod before rushing to the front of the wagon and scrambling up beside Calvin.

To Inana and Bard, I say, "Many of the same rules we use for Shades apply to Incarnates. Stay calm. Don't react with fear. Don't make any sudden moves. The difference is that an Incarnate believes it's human. It has the memories of the body it consumed. Anything that reminds it that its identity is false will trigger its rage and make it attack. We will approach it as fellow travelers and speak to it as if it's human. The last thing we want is for the creature to suspect our intent and run. We can't afford to hunt the thing through the woods while getting chased by Shades. As soon as I attack, the Shades will feel threatened and turn aggressive. That's where you will come in."

"You just said we could have stayed back," Inana says. "How would you have gotten away without us?"

"My sword will be aflame," I say. "I'll be able to ward the Shades away. That doesn't mean I won't appreciate your aid. Yet you can still change your mind. You don't have to come with me."

Neither seems interested in reconsidering their choice.

"Come on, then. Follow my lead. Breathe." Slowly, we make our way from the wagon to the clearing. My steps are purposefully even, and the other two match their pace with mine. Our soles crunch over the snow-dusted road, loud enough to alert the Incarnate of our approach yet not so loud that we come across as a threat. This thing believes it's human, after all, and travelers are known to share their campsites with others on dark nights.

As we draw near, I notice furs in the back of one of the wagons and crates in another. The campers must have been trappers or traders. Finally, the campsite grows clearer: the bodies slumped around the firepit, the Incarnate perched on a log, hunched over something in its hand. I flex my fingers, craving the hilt of my sword but knowing now is not the time. Without any source of light in the clearing save for the moon above, igniting my sword from behind would draw the creature's eye at once and inform it of the threat.

Only calm, calculated attacks work on Incarnates. One chance. One swing of my sword.

Shadows shift in the dark, Shades creeping by with calm interest, keeping mostly near the trees. The Incarnate doesn't look at them or us as it continues to focus on whatever it holds. A scraping noise fills the air, in time with the creature's movements. "We've got visitors, Norm," comes a slow, feminine voice. There's something unnatural to it, a shift in pitch halfway through. A hollow rasp at the end.

The Incarnate halts its movements and looks to the side, toward one of the bodies. It's too dark to make out details, but it's obvious it's fucking dead.

"Norm, did you hear me? Are you going to greet them?"

Only silence answers, but the creature chuckles as if the dead had replied.

The scent of rot invades my nostrils, not at all the delectable aroma of fresh blood. This campsite must have been in this same state for at least a day, the cold preserving the bodies somewhat. It's a miracle the situation hasn't escalated, though this road doesn't see much traffic in the winter, and even if someone were to pass by, no one would be foolish enough to stop.

No one but a Shadowbane.

I glance back at my Summoners, give them an encouraging nod, and enter the ring of bodies. "Mind if we share your fire for the night?" I ask, infusing as much nonchalance into my voice as I can.

The Incarnate doesn't answer right away, instead resuming whatever it's doing with its hands. It's impossible to see more than a vaguely female form dressed in leathers, its face cast in shadow. The scraping sound returns. "Don't mind them," the creature says. Its voice cracks, shifts in pitch again. "They're wary of strangers. Take a seat. Soup's gone, but we've got plenty of company to go around."

"Thank you," Inana says, voice steady. I'm shocked she had the courage to say anything. She and Bard claim the only empty log while I position myself between them and the Incarnate, crouching by the firepit.

"Fire's out," I say. "Let me take care of that."

"Much obliged," says the Incarnate.

I shift to the side, where logs are stacked beside one of the bodies, probably the person who'd been tending the fire. My heart thuds in my chest, in time with the Incarnate's scraping sounds, as I arrange the logs and tinder in the pit. Then, with careful moves, I extract my tinderbox and strike the flint and steel until sparks catch.

Remaining crouched, I shift my gaze to the Incarnate. As the flames grow, our surroundings brighten a little at a time, reflecting off the snow on the ground. Inch by inch, the Incarnate's form is revealed. The person it consumed was likely in her forties, with brown hair tied back with a leather strap and a fox pelt draped over her shoulders. The Incarnate managed to replicate the clothing with precision, but its face is where its imitation struggles. Its skin is pale, its mouth too wide. Its eyes are as round as coins, blinking in disharmony. Its limbs are longer than they should be, wrists too steeply angled.

My eyes drop to its hands, and I finally discover the source of the scraping sound. It holds a steel carving tool that it scrapes against something long and . . . I swallow hard. It's a bone. A tibia, perhaps, based on the length, and still coated in flesh and sinew. But that's not the most unsettling thing. What's worse are the creature's fingers. It carves toward the hand that holds the bone, and with every too-aggressive scrape of the carving tool, the curved metal tip slides too fast and pierces the Incarnate's fingers. Fingers that no longer have tips, only shredded, bleeding nubs that drip.

Drip.

Drip.

To the crimson-stained snow at the creature's feet. Yet it continues to carve away, oblivious to its wounds or pain. It may have copied its victim's body, her memory, but the creature can't mimic her nimble moves or the craft the woman once partook in.

Bile rises in my throat, and my pulse quickens—

I suck in a breath, realizing the source of my spike in fear. It's my proximity to Inana, awakening my emotions at the most inconvenient time. A glance from my peripheral vision shows the terror in her eyes, the tremors that rack her frame. Bard manages to keep his calm somehow, but maybe he's not looking at the creature. Regardless, my fear combined with Inana's is too distracting. Yet I don't dare move away from her.

"Sloth," I whisper, and he knows exactly what I want him to do. He emerges from the shadows beneath me and settles in front of Inana, resting his head on her lap with a soft whine.

Inana lowers her masked face to Sloth and strokes his head with shaking hands. Through my connection to the dog, her touch is a ghost of a caress against me too, and we both relax, if only slightly.

I allow myself a brief glance at the bodies around us. All are dead, though some are in better condition than others. The one nearest me is female, a gash over her throat. On the other side of the growing fire is a male, his stomach flayed open, straight through his leathers. Then there's the one the Incarnate called Norm; he's missing a leg, an arm, and a head.

"Nice dog," says the Incarnate to Inana. "What breed?"

I open my mouth, but Inana manages to answer. "A wolfhound."

The creature chisels away at the bone.

Scrape.

Drip.

Scrape.

Drip.

"I used to have a bloodhound. Good for hunting." Its last words dip into a horrifying rasp, but the Incarnate doesn't seem to notice. "See, Norm? I told you we should have gotten another."

"Prepared for winter?" I ask, slowly reaching for the vials at my waist. My fingers linger between two different ones. The first is

Calvin's. The blood I need to ignite the flame on my sword. The other . . .

It would be fruitless to test the second vial of blood on the Incarnate. Even if I discovered this Shade is one of the two I seek, it wouldn't change a damn thing. Incarnates cannot shift back to their base form; they must be killed. For all I know, the remaining Shades I've spent years hunting have already become Incarnate and been killed by other Shadowbanes. It's impossible to know for certain, and I must keep looking until the very end. Even if it's hopeless.

Besides, any wrong move might trigger the Incarnate to attack. I can't risk my Summoners' lives just to answer a question that changes nothing.

I move my fingers back to Calvin's vial.

"We're more than prepared," says the Incarnate. Its voice continues to dip between octaves, between smooth and sinister. "Hunting may be scarce for the next few months, but we've got plenty of pelts to sell from our last hunt. Plus, I make and sell these."

It takes all my restraint not to flinch back as it extends the bone toward us, though none of us can bring ourselves to look closer. The creature's too-round eyes flick between us, eyelids blinking one at a time. Its lips pull back from its teeth, and for the briefest moment I fear I've fucked up.

But then it dons a smile. Too much teeth and too wide for comfort, but a smile nonetheless. "Ah, right. This one ain't finished. Not much to see." It places the bone in its lap and reaches for something by its feet. As it extends the new piece, I see it's an axe with an intricately carved handle. "Don't be scared. It's not art, it's just a tool. Nothing wrong with making tools."

My stomach sinks as understanding dawns. That's why this campsite was attacked. Whoever this woman was before she was copied and consumed by a Shade, she dabbled too close to creativity. While it's true that crafting tools is considered an essential trade and not close enough to art to draw a Shade's interest, the intricate whorls and patterns she carved made these something new. Beautiful. Imaginative. Something so impressive a Shade took too much interest and sought to become her.

The Incarnate reaches farther. "Here, take a look."

Bard accepts the tool, turning the bloodstained handle over in his lap.

"I'll sell it for a gold piece." The monster's grin widens as it picks up the bone again and resumes carving.

I remove the vial of Calvin's blood from my holster.

Uncap it.

Dab some onto my thumb.

"Though I'll be done with this one in a few more hours, if you'd prefer a custom piece. What do you say? How do you want this one to look?"

I bring my thumb between my lips and feel the rush of energy course through me as the iron tang melts over my tongue.

"Come on, tell me," the Incarnate says, demand in its voice. It lifts its gaze to Bard. "You want a wolf, like your face?"

"All right," Bard says. "A wolf, then."

The creature's round eyes grow larger, focusing on Bard's mask. Then Inana's. "You've got strange faces."

My pulse quickens all over again. Incarnates can't usually distinguish between human faces and masks. It's time to act. Carefully. Quickly.

I tip another smear of blood onto my thumb.

The Incarnate lowers its eyes back to the bone and carves again.

Scrape.

Drip.

Scrape.

Drip.

With my other hand, I reach behind me, gripping the hilt of my sword.

Scrape.

Drip.

Scrape.

Drip.

It halts, shadows streaming from the tips of its blunted, bleeding fingers. "This one doesn't look quite like that one." Its voice dips low, taking on a chilling edge, then rises to a shout. "This one doesn't *look* like that one *at all*."

I rise to my feet, unsheathing my sword, but the Incarnate mirrors my motions, hissing in its rage. Movement surges from the trees, Shades drawn to the outburst.

"Bard," I say, and press my bloodstained thumb to the diagram on my blade, then drag the finger down its length. It ignites at once. The Shades recoil, halting their progress, but the Incarnate isn't afraid of the light. It hisses again and launches toward me.

Bard rings out a beautiful chord just as I swing my burning blade.

Just as the Incarnate flings out a hand, sending a spear of shadow from its fingers.

Just as pain lances through my flesh, piercing beneath my collarbone.

Just as I send the creature's head tumbling from its stolen body.

CHAPTER TWENTY

Inana

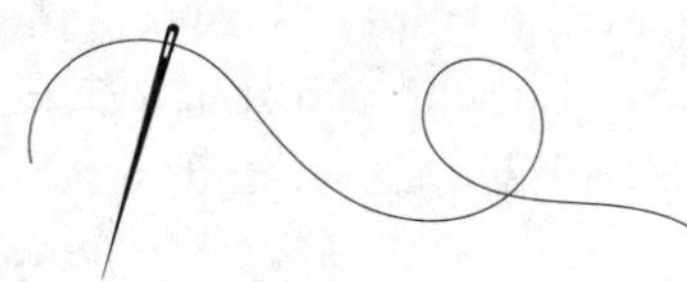

The corpse stands upright and headless for several seconds before it falls limp to the ground, blood and shadows streaming from its wound. I don't know when I rose to my feet. Maybe it was when Dominic did. Maybe I've been standing for minutes on end. All I know is the terror that courses through me. The disgust. I managed to keep my composure until now, my nerves steady despite the horrifying sight the fire revealed in the clearing.

Despite the Incarnate.

Its uncanny imitation of a living being.

The unsettling wrongness in all the aspects it couldn't mimic.

Now, as I watch the creature die, watch its skin char beneath its own shadows and melt from bone, every ounce of composure I kept fades away. My body shudders with tremors, my heart races like it will burst from my chest, and nausea churns in my—

My stomach lurches, and it takes all my restraint not to heave its contents beside the fire. If I did, I'd only make a mess of myself, masked as I am. I crouch down, no longer able to hold myself up. Sloth whines and nudges my cheek while a rough hand pulls me to my feet.

"We have to go, Inana." I belatedly realize it's Dominic's voice. It carries a note of concern, but it's gentle too. Shame sweeps over me.

Gods, I'm pathetic to react this way. "No," he says, and I realize I muttered the words out loud. He braces my shoulder with a palm, strong and firm. "Anyone would feel the way you do after seeing an Incarnate for the first time. I know I did."

I lift my eyes, take in Dominic's face. It's splattered with blood, which almost makes my stomach lurch all over again, but his dark gaze steadies me. My mind clears slightly, and I remember I'm not the only Summoner here. A melody weaves behind me, and I turn to find Bard, his hands shaking as he strums his mandolin. There's a harshness to every chord, like he too is struggling through the terror of what we just witnessed. Or perhaps it's due to the Shades that stalk us outside the firelight. One paces on four limbs, its arms longer than its legs. Others shift side to side, watching us with their hollow eyes. Another slinks along the edge of light, pulling itself across the snow on its belly.

"We've provoked the Shades," Dominic says. "They aren't calming down enough. We need to leave."

"What about the bodies? Shouldn't we turn them over so their faces—"

"We don't have time. Not while the Shades are restless. Besides, they're only interested in the living. They will neither mimic nor consume the dead."

I'm relieved. As much as I grieve for what happened to these people, I'd rather not look at them again, much less touch them.

Dominic must trust I've gathered some semblance of calm, for he releases my shoulder and takes a step back. His other hand is still gripped around the hilt of his flaming sword. "Let's go. Slowly. Calmly."

Another surge of fear tunnels through me at the thought of leaving the light of the campfire. Still, my feet obey as Dominic leads the way, a step at a time, away from the fire. Then to the edge of the firelight. Then a step outside it. The three of us huddle close together, Bard and Dominic circling me, Bard with his song and Dominic with his sword. I clench my jaw, hating that I feel so useless right now. I should be helping them. I'm a fucking Summoner. That's my job. But no matter how many times I try to bring some calming story to my tongue, no sound emerges. Nothing.

It's humbling, to say the least.

The farther we move from the campfire's light, the closer the Shades get. Thankfully, Dominic's flaming sword is just as bright as the campfire, if not brighter. Its range of light is merely smaller.

"Can't you just . . . cut them down?" I ask through chattering teeth.

"We've already upset them with the first act of violence, and that was against an Incarnate. Shades don't see Incarnates as one of their kind anymore, nor are they interested in them like they are in humans. If we attack one of their own, though, they will turn frenzied."

"This isn't a frenzy?" I ask, but I know the answer. The dragon was a frenzy. This . . . this is just aggressive interest.

Our progress feels painfully slow, even more so once our wagon comes into view. Probably because my legs yearn to run but I don't let them. Instead, I focus on my breath, the only imitation of calm I can conjure. Dominic hisses a sharp sound, and I fling my gaze to him. His sword arm has faltered and his free hand fumbles at his waist. He extracts a vial from his holster, thumbs open the cap, and downs its contents in full. His sword arm strengthens, as does the light of the flame.

Then I notice the hand that grips his hilt.

His fingers slick with blood.

The steady drip that falls from the sleeve of his jerkin.

My breath catches. I remember the moment Dominic swung his sword. I'd been so focused on the spray of blood, the sight of the Incarnate's head flying off its shoulders, that I barely gave mind to what else I saw: a spear of shadow shooting from the creature's hand and into Dominic.

"You're injured," I whisper, failing to keep the panic from my voice.

"I'll be fine," Dominic says.

I glance back at the wagon. Gods, we're close, but most of the Shades have followed us from the camp. A few have drifted away, but the ones with the keenest interest don't seem likely to let us go easily. If anything, they're growing more aggressive. The one on all fours darts around us in a circle, but when Dominic holds his sword toward it, it skitters back, hissing through its featureless face. At least there are no Shades up ahead, none eyeing the wagon or stalking the road.

"Quicken your pace," Dominic says, "but breathe. We're almost there."

I do as he says, walking more swiftly now. Calvin and Harlow peer at us from the front of the wagon, eyes wide.

Calvin's mouth forms a word I can't hear but can fully make out. *Fuck.* A second later, the wagon begins to move. Panic lances through me, but he isn't leaving us behind. He's only getting a head start so we'll already be in motion by the time we climb on.

"Bard to the front," Dominic says. "Play until we've lost them. Tell Harlow to draw if she can stay calm. Inana, in the back. And now . . . run."

We take off at a sprint, closing the short distance between us and the wagon in a matter of seconds, even with it moving. Dominic braces his free hand against my back, aiding my climb as I grab on to the back of the wagon.

Dominic steps up beside me, feet planted on the footboard, and releases me to grab hold of the canopy's frame. We're picking up pace now, and I fight against the momentum to pull myself through the flap. I'm halfway beneath the wagon's cover when something tugs my skirt and pulls me backward. It happens so fast, I don't even have time to scream.

First it's tugging my skirt. Then its phantom hand is around my calf and pulling me beneath the wagon, claws piercing my flesh. I tumble back, rushing toward the ground—

"Inana!" Dominic screams my name, and my fall is cushioned by a featherlight surface. Hands. Multiple hands.

"*You're all right, love.*" Lust. That's Lust's voice.

"*Get your fucking act together.*" And that's Pride.

A snarl sounds beneath the wagon, followed by a bark. Then the painful touch releases my calf, and a third presence lifts me. Shadowed hands pull me up, and I catch sight of Dominic swinging his sword, eyes dark, teeth bared in rage. I tumble into the wagon and peek back out just in time to see a Shade cleaved in two, its body dispersing into smoke. Five more give chase, closing in fast. Dominic disperses one, then another.

"Now is it a frenzy?" I shout over the sound of my racing heart, the wagon wheels speeding over the road.

"It's a fucking frenzy," he says, and cleaves through a third Shade. The light of his sword casts his face in hard lines of fury. Maybe it's the near-death experience and the fact that his Shades saved me from being dashed against the road, but my heart does strange things as I stare at the tightness of his jaw, the determination in his eyes, the strands of dark hair that whip free from where he'd tied half of it back, the expert way he swings his sword despite the blood that continues to drip down his arm.

He cleaves through the fourth Shade, then finally the fifth.

My gaze leaves his face to assess the road behind us. I expect more Shades to race after us, or perhaps creep from under the wagon like the one that grabbed me. But after several long moments pass and there's only the occasional Shade peering from the trees, indifferent to our passing, my heart rate slows. Dominic too must deem the threat gone, for he swipes the blade against his thigh, just above the hilt where the etched diagram is, and the flame goes out.

His limbs look heavy, his sword arm trembling. He locks eyes with me, his widening as if he hadn't expected me to be watching him, then heaves a sigh and sheathes his sword. I don't miss the way his features pull into a grimace or the way his arm falls limp at his side once he releases the hilt.

I move to give him room to climb through the flap and into the wagon. "Are you all right?" I ask as he stumbles inside.

He doesn't answer, but I can see it for myself. We left the lantern lit when we went to confront the Incarnate, and the light illuminates the blood on his face, dripping down his arm, his hand. There's a gash in his jerkin beneath his collarbone.

He slumps to his knees, shoulders drooping.

I hold out my hands to . . . I don't know. Help him? Steady him?

He falls on fucking top of me.

CHAPTER TWENTY-ONE

INANA

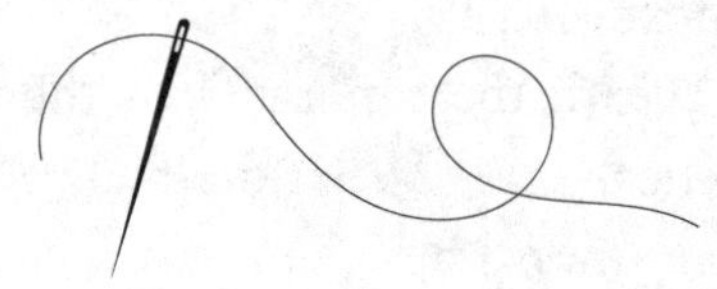

I lie still, crushed by his weight and shocked by the warmth of his body. And just . . . shocked. It's been years since I've had a man on top of me, and while this isn't exactly *that* kind of situation, it still makes my mind go blank for an embarrassingly long time.

"*I'm enjoying it too, don't worry.*"

I look to the side to find Lust sprawled casually beside us, facing me, cheek propped on his fist. He's only semi-visible, because of the lantern light, but his imitation of Dominic's visage is disturbingly accurate. Even that seductive grin, which I'm starting to glimpse more and more on the real thing. Sloth stands on our other side, whining softly as he sniffs his master's hair.

"*Pathetic,*" Pride says, staring down his nose at us with a pompous smirk.

My shock at being crushed by Dominic abates, especially when I remember how badly injured he is. I push off my mask, careful I don't stab Dominic with its sunbeam spikes. To think I fantasized about doing exactly that when we first met. Now I'm not even remotely tempted, even with him in such a vulnerable state. I still hate what he is and what he so desperately wants to become, and I'll be glad when we part ways in six months, but . . . I don't hate *him.* Not completely.

I don't fully trust him either. But there is more to him than I know, and I want to discover what that is.

As gently as I can, I edge out from beneath him, leaving him prone. The blood smeared on the front of my dress suggests he's still bleeding profusely, and when I assess his back, I see that the wound goes all the way through his shoulder.

Shit.

As I stand there staring at his unconscious form, I realize I'm at a loss for what to do next.

Harlow climbs beneath the canopy from the front of the wagon. "Calvin sent me to check on— What the fuck? Is he dead?"

"No, but . . ." I rush toward her, then part the canopy's opening.

Calvin's eyes fly to mine at once, lashes fluttering. He covers his mouth and passes the reins to Bard. "Ooooh, gods, that smell." His voice is almost euphoric.

I frown, then realize he's reacting to the scent of Dominic's blood. He's addicted to it, after all. And it's all over the front of me. I pull back slightly so only my head emerges from the opening. "Dominic is injured and unconscious, and I don't know what the hell to do. What do you normally do in these situations?"

Calvin slumps low in his seat but runs a hand over his face, as if fighting the lure of Dominic's blood. "Mm. Where was he injured? And with what?"

"Below his collarbone. And it was . . . the Incarnate. It sent some . . . shadow spear through him, I don't know. He'll heal though, right? Isn't he sort of immortal?"

Calvin scrubs his face again. "Damn. He normally heals quickly, but not from Shade wounds. If it punctured vital organs, his healing will focus on that first, but if he loses too much blood, his thirst will grow faster than he can heal, and . . . let's just say none of us want that."

My heart slams against my ribs. Just when I thought the threat was over for the night.

"The best thing we can do is clean his wound and stitch his flesh. His healing will do the rest. But it can't be me. I'll . . . hump his fucking leg or something if I go back there. It has to be someone else."

Harlow's voice is muffled beneath the canopy. "Sounds like a job for you, Seamstress."

I clench my teeth, but I suppose she's right.

"Strong spirits, thread, and needles are in the crate beside you," Calvin says.

I pull myself back beneath the canopy and riffle through the crate Calvin mentioned. I find a suture kit and the alcohol. Harlow ignites two more lanterns, knowing I'll need as much light as possible. She hangs them from the arched canopy, then helps me remove Dominic's scabbard. I stare at his jerkin, debating whether to cut it off him or try to remove it without destroying it completely. Reaching for one of his daggers, I choose destruction. I'm too worried that shifting him around will only make his wound worse. Besides, there's already a godsdamned hole in his clothing.

Carefully, I slice through the dark leather, then through his shirt. I gag at the sight of the wound, the ragged flesh, the blood that seeps freely from it. I'm not a fucking surgeon, so I haven't a clue what may have been punctured, but I wouldn't be surprised if it's his lungs. My hands tremble as I uncap the spirits and pour them over the gash. Dominic doesn't utter a sound, nor do his Shades, who've disappeared into the Shadowbane. Harlow hands me a curved needle, then catgut. I thread the gut through the eye of the needle and get to work.

At first, I flinch each time the needle pierces his flesh, but after a few stitches, I settle into the familiar routine. The materials may be different, but stitching wounds is so similar to sewing it makes me feel like I've done this before. Or perhaps it's because of my story, the one I used to tell at the Wretched Lair. I've imagined it so many times, stitching flesh. I can almost convince myself I really did stitch my chest wound back together myself. In truth, it healed on its own, for it wasn't deep enough to puncture vital organs. I've wondered time and again how Henry had planned to slice out my heart with such a shallow cut. I like to think my words unnerved him too much to truly give it his best effort. In my most generous imaginings, I consider whether there was a part of him that fought against what he was doing. I got away, after all. Did he let me go? Or did he flee after I cut him with my needle?

I complete the final stitch to seal Dominic's wound, but my mind is elsewhere as I try to remember what happened next. Like always, my memories are hazy. The blood loss was too great for me to have been lucid, and the trauma I endured lasted months. To be honest, I didn't start to feel like myself again until I got to Nalheim.

"Inana," Harlow whispers, pulling me from my thoughts. I realize my hands stopped moving. "Tie it off so you can stitch the front too. I don't want him waking up with raging thirst anytime soon."

She's right. This is no time to let my guard down. Work carefully, yes, but not slowly.

I tie off the row of stitches, then together we roll him onto his back. We tug off the severed halves of his jerkin and pull his shirt down to bare the wound. The rest of his shirt is trapped behind him, so I don't remove it all the way. I repeat the routine, cleaning the wound, then stitching it shut.

"Will you see if there are bandages in the crate?"

Harlow obeys and returns with several strips of cloth. I'll have to trust they're clean, for there's no way to boil and dry them now. She aids my efforts in wrapping the bandage around his shoulder, ensuring it's fully covered on both sides. Once finished, we release heavy exhales and sit back, saying nothing for a time. In the wake of our activity, it's painfully quiet, my blood no longer rushing in my ears. There's only Dominic's labored breathing and the rhythmic melody of the wagon's wheels.

"I'm going to check on Calvin," Harlow says. Once she leaves, I scoot closer to Dominic, looking him over and assessing what else I might be able to do to make him more comfortable. I unhook his belt of knives, his vials. Then I stare down at his torso, still half covered by his ruined shirt. I suppose I can use it to wipe the rest of the blood off him. Gingerly, I cut it away from the portion trapped behind him and lift it off his chest.

My eyes widen.

Not only because it's my first time seeing him shirtless, the expanse of rippling muscle, the deep V that disappears beneath his waistband. It isn't even the blood smeared over his side.

No, it's the mark on his chest.

At first, I take it for a tattoo, but the lines are too faint. Too pale.

It's a scar.

An intricate scar of countless lines that spans the front of his chest, from his upper abdomen to just a few inches beneath his wound.

An astrotheurgical diagram.

I shudder at how similar it looks to the one I glimpsed at the bottom of the Holy Brazier the day Henry came to take my heart. So similar to the one etched on Dominic's sword. I never imagined I'd see a ritual circle carved into flesh. It's repulsive, yet . . . beautiful somehow, or maybe that's just because it's on Dominic's skin.

With bated breath, I reach out a tentative hand, letting my fingertip graze one of the lines. I trace the raised skin, a chill creeping into my blood as I follow the angle from his sternum to above his pectoral. Much like the cut on my chest—

My hand goes still as something falls upon it. Dominic's fingers close over mine, halting my moves. I try to snatch my hand away, but his grip is stronger than it should be for someone who's been unconscious for the last several minutes. Though it's the hand on his unwounded side, so perhaps the bastard remains somewhat strong.

"You weren't supposed to see that." His voice comes out deep and raspy and his eyes remain closed. "No one is supposed to see."

Understanding dawns. An astrotheurgical diagram. Symbols and glyphs kept secret by the church, forbidden to the eyes of the public. "Is that why you said you blindfold your . . ." I almost say *lovers,* but the word gets tangled behind my lips. What's wrong with me? It's hardly a sexy word. Maybe it's the blindfold part that got me riled up. "Is that why you made a vow not to let anyone see you unclothed?"

He nods, a subtle motion.

"What happens if you break that vow?"

His mouth parts, and he runs his tongue over his bottom lip. I watch it with way more fascination than I'm willing to admit. "Blood," he says. "Hand me my vials."

I do as he asked. Normally I'd balk at such a curt demand, but I can't fault him for that sharp demeanor now. Besides, if he needs blood, I'm in no position to keep it from him. Not unless I want to witness what Calvin suggested could happen if Dominic doesn't get enough blood while wounded.

I hand him his holster of vials, and he selects one. With how much the wagon already smells like blood, I can't even make out the scent from the open vial. Just like he did when we fled the camp, he tips it back and downs the entire contents.

Finally, his lashes flutter open. His eyes find mine at once. "Cover me. Don't let anyone else see."

I return his scrap of shirt to his chest. Then I unhook my cloak and lay that over him too for good measure. "Are you going to answer my question? I've already seen it. What happens now?"

"I've vowed not to *show* my scar to anyone or *let* anyone see it. Your actions were all your own, and I was in no state to stop you. So if the church ever tests me with Shades to see if I'm lying about keeping my vows, I'll pass."

I'm surprised to hear the church uses Shades to test Shadowbanes, but I suppose it makes sense. I've heard criminal trials are handled in a similar way; I've just never known if it's true. Do the authorities truly use Shades in the name of justice? How? From what I've gleaned, it's taboo enough that Dominic catches Shades. Does the same not go for the church and inquisitors?

I want to ask, but there are more pressing questions on my mind. Especially while we're still alone. "What is it? The scar?"

He sighs, closing his eyes again. "There are some vows that are harder to get around."

"It has to do with your Absolution, doesn't it?"

"Smart woman."

I hate the way my stomach flips at his praise. It's the only conclusion that makes sense, though. Absolution is an astrotheurgical ritual that strips one's soul of sin, making it pure and incapable of attracting Shades. It's how humans become Sinless. The process of Absolution has been kept a secret by the church ever since it was performed on the very first man who was made Sinless—King Kaelum—five hundred years ago. Of course a ritual circle would be used. I just never imagined it was carved into the person's chest. No wonder he had to vow not to show his naked body to anyone. His very flesh is carved with secrets forbidden to common folk.

But why does Dominic bear a scar at all? I've seen other Sinless shirtless before, and they bore no such marks. They flaunted their bodies at the Wretched Lair as if they were the peak of beauty. And maybe they are, to some.

I gaze down at Dominic's covered chest, recalling every dip and rise of his chiseled torso. He isn't sleek and dazzling. He's rough. Broad. Hard. And for some reason, I find that so much more alluring than any other male form I've seen.

Will he still look the same after he completes his Absolution? Or will all those rough edges be smoothed away, leaving him like one of those too-perfect bastards I despise?

I harden my heart and push all thoughts of beauty and attraction to the back of my mind where I can pretend they don't exist. Without them, I can linger on logic instead. Another answer comes to me.

"Do you scar because you're only half Sinless? Because your healing isn't as strong as a pure Sinless's?"

He gives me the barest of nods. Gods, I wonder if part of the reason he keeps so much from us is that there are numerous things he *can't* tell us because of his vows.

"Put your cold hands on me." He must be delirious to say such a thing, and it reminds me of when I touched him earlier tonight, when we were together in the driver's seat.

"My hands aren't cold right now."

"They're cold enough," he says. "Please. I'll be burning up until my wound closes. Just touch my forehead at least."

I grimace, debating whether I should obey. This isn't at all part of my job description, so I can refuse. Yet there's something charming about how vulnerable he's being. I doubt he's fully lucid, which makes him slightly less insufferable than usual. Maybe I can use this to embarrass him later.

Giving in, I press my fingertips to Dominic's forehead. His skin is hot, making me realize my hands are in fact cold. I didn't notice when I was tracing the lines of his scar, but I was distracted by other thoughts then. Now all I notice is Dominic's warmth seeping into my fingers. Or maybe my coldness is melting into him. I turn my hand over, cooling him with the back of it. Then I do it all over again to his cheek. Then his neck.

His chest rises and falls, his breaths even, and I wonder if he's fallen asleep. I continue touching him, my mind wandering.

It drifts back to the camp, to the Incarnate. To its gory attempt at creating art with a bone taken from one of its victim's friends. Her husband, perhaps. My stomach turns, and my fingers go still in the crook of Dominic's neck, a comfort among the awful visions playing over and over and over in my mind.

I can't help but ponder who that woman was before. Crafting beautiful axes with what she thought was innocuous workmanship. Did she know she was attracting Shades with what she did? Did her companions know? Did she continue to create despite the risk?

My heart sinks with guilt as these same questions turn against me.

I've always been aware of my sin. Of how desperately I crave to tell stories despite knowing the dangers.

I always argued with myself, eager to prove that art wasn't truly a sin. It never felt like one. Fiction has never felt like a lie in the same way deliberate deceptions do. Yet I've seen the proof many times now. Shades are undoubtedly drawn to art. After getting caught twice, I was left jaded and uncertain whether I should hate myself or hate the world. I wasn't the only sinner, after all.

I've heard folk lying through their teeth during broad daylight. I've watched my neighbors leave their lovers' houses when their spouses were waiting for them to come home. I've seen innocents arrested by the church's priests and cruel Sinless positioned as gods. If I think too hard about the state of the world, it fills me with despair.

That's why I let myself sin again and again. Because art is often the one thing that feels pure, regardless of what the holy texts say.

But what I saw today . . .

My eyes well with tears.

"I'm not a good person," I whisper. Not to anyone but myself. I doubt Dominic can hear me through the haze of sleep. "I sin and sin again. Shades are born from our sins, which means I've made those creatures. I could have made the one that . . . that killed them." My voice breaks on the last part.

The silence that echoes grows as heavy as an accusation.

Then I realize Dominic's breaths aren't quite so labored anymore.

I stare down at him and find his eyes open.

He lifts his hand and brushes his warm fingers along my cheek, my jaw, swiping tears I didn't realize had fallen. "No, Inana. The only one of us who has ever sinned gravely enough to create Shades . . . is me."

I frown. He can't . . . he can't mean that.

"But the holy texts . . . they state that Shades are born from human sin." I don't know why I'm arguing with him. He can't possibly be lucid, to have said such a thing. Yet I can't stop the words that pour from me. "They say new ones are born every night from our sinful actions. They state nothing about the sins needing to be more or less grave, only that *all* human sin creates and attracts Shades. Everything we know about the Shades, the gods, One Hundred Days of Darkness . . . It's all there. Spoken *and* written by King Kaelum, a Sinless who can't lie. His words are validated by the church. So what the fuck do you mean?"

"Keep going," he says.

I wish he would just tell me, but my mind is spinning faster than I can control, drawing out the next thought. "If the texts contain omissions or falsehoods, then . . . then either they weren't written by King Kaelum, or . . ."

I swallow hard and utter treason.

"Or the Sinless can lie."

"And if that's the case?" Dominic says.

I curl my fingers into fists. "Then anything—everything—in the holy texts might be a godsdamned lie."

"Good girl," he whispers, his hand falling from my cheek as he sinks back into slumber.

CHAPTER TWENTY-TWO

INANA

I can't get my conversation with Dominic out of my head, but when the morning dawns and he wakes, I don't have the nerve to ask about it. Not with the others around. What he told me felt private. It *was* private. Because I'm the only one who's seen his scars.

At least the only one of his *Summoners.* I haven't a clue if Calvin has. From how long they've been traveling together, he must have seen Dominic shirtless at least once.

I watch the two of them across the small glade we've made camp in since daybreak. They're seated near the fire, engaged in an activity I purposefully positioned myself far away from. Since Dominic consumed all his remaining vials of blood, Calvin is filling new ones. I firmly avoid looking at the thin line of crimson on Calvin's forearm or the rivulet that fills the vial. You'd think I'd be desensitized to blood after last night, but what they're doing makes me particularly squeamish. Dominic is turned away, so I can't see his blood, but I know he's filling a vial for Calvin too. Apparently his healing has been stabilized and he's mostly back to normal, though when I changed his bandages this morning, his wound looked just as raw as it did last night.

Shadow wounds really must affect him far worse than regular ones. Yet cuts of any kind leave scars.

"Are you going to help, or are you going to keep staring and pretending you're not?"

Harlow's voice has my cheeks blazing. We're in the middle of pouring freshly purified water into skins after having gathered it from the river that runs along the road. Now that it's been boiled and cooled, it can replenish our dwindling stores. Meanwhile, Bard is rearranging the wagon, after having scrubbed Dominic's blood from it to save Calvin from whatever uncontrollable urges he experiences when surrounded by too much of his drug's scent.

"I wasn't staring," I mutter, and refocus on my task. We're on the opposite end of the glade, at least, so Dominic probably can't hear us.

"So you're going with pretending. All right," Harlow deadpans.

"I'm just . . . thinking." I purse my lips to keep from thinking *out loud,* no matter how desperate I am to share what Dominic said.

"Well, stop thinking. The sun is already beginning to set. We'll be back on the road in an hour, I bet."

Harlow's probably right. We've had all day to sleep and rest and recover from the horrors of last night. None of us could relax enough to sleep through the remainder of our journey, so we waited to sleep under the safety of sunlight. I think we've all come to understand why Dominic keeps a nocturnal schedule, even when traveling. As terrifying as it was to come across an Incarnate at night, or to travel through Shade-infested territory when they're most active, it's far more unsettling to consider *not* moving during such treacherous hours.

I do my best to stay focused on my task and not dwell on what Dominic said last night, but that only makes me aware of how cold my fingers are. My skin practically screams as I plunge the waterskin into the pot of water, which has more than cooled; it might as well be frozen. We haven't seen an increase in snowfall, but the air maintains a bite. Maybe I should take back what I said about loving all the seasons. Spending winter on the road is a far cry from the cozy days spent by the fireplace in Dunway.

Though I suppose it isn't officially winter yet. Solstice is . . .

I wrinkle my nose as I try to sort out today's date. Keeping track of the week is less vital now, unlike when I served Rockefeller.

I tilt my head at Harlow. "How many days until solstice?"

She shrugs. "Two? Or maybe it's tomorrow?"

"Huh. One or two days until my birthday, then."

"You were born on the winter solstice?"

"Much to my mother's displeasure," I say.

"Congrats on surviving another year as a sinner, I guess," Harlow says without even a hint of enthusiasm.

I huff a laugh, but her words remind me of Dominic's.

The only one of us who has ever sinned gravely enough to create Shades . . . is me.

I'm so desperate to ask what he meant by that. Last night I was more focused on the contradiction of his words versus the holy texts, but if he's right . . .

What grave sin was he talking about? What did he do that was so awful it created Shades? When he said *the only one of us,* did he mean of me and him? Or did he mean all of us as a crew? I can't imagine how he could be guilty of worse sins than us. We're outlaws running from crimes ranging from murder to treason. We're artists, whom the holy texts call the worst kind of sinners—

My mind stumbles. Stutters. Lingers.

If one thing in the holy texts is a lie, then anything else can be.

What if . . .

What if art isn't a sin?

Hope, vindication, and a dash of fury flood my chest for all of a second. Then I remind myself of all the proof I've seen. All the terrors I've witnessed. Despite what I want to believe, I know some things to be true.

Shades are attracted to lies.

Shades are also attracted to art.

Shades are attracted to violence.

Shades are attracted to crime.

Shades are also attracted to childbirth, I remind myself. But that is reasoned away by the holy texts, stating that procreation is a sin because of how it mocks our creators. Regardless, everything fits so seamlessly under the umbrella of sin when explained by scripture.

I clench my jaw. I've never liked the holy texts. How can I like something that calls me impure while positioning the Sinless as the epitome of perfection? Yet just because I dislike something doesn't make it false. When all I've seen is evidence supporting the texts, I've had no choice but to believe them while simultaneously hating them.

So . . .

Is it possible the texts contain numerous lies? Or is it just the part about how all sin creates Shades?

My mind spins to make sense of that. Even if it's the single deliberate falsehood in the texts, it's huge. If only the darkest kinds of sins create Shades, then humanity has been burdened with undue blame. Sure, it's clear even our most mundane sins *attract* Shades, but we've been blamed for *creating* them with those same actions all this time.

All.

This.

Time.

For five hundred years.

What the fuck does that mean, and why?

"What the hell, Inana?"

Harlow's voice snaps me out of my stupor all over again, and I realize I'm losing water from the skin I've filled, tipping it too far to the side while fumbling with the cork. I right the waterskin, but the cork slips from my frozen fingers and rolls across the snow-dusted glade.

"Damn it." I thrust the waterskin at Harlow so I can chase down the cork. It doesn't roll far, stopping beneath a cedar. The tree's wide boughs have created a shady space devoid of snow, and I crouch beneath them to reach for the cork. My fingers are about to close around it just as something catches my eye. I snatch my hand back and glance at the dark shape that stands out against the shadows cast by the tree. It's a squirrel, but . . .

Not just any squirrel.

It's a Shade.

I take in its small, semitransparent form, its pitch-black eyes, the flap of skin that extends from foreleg to hind leg on each side, the crescent moon perched on its brow.

My mouth falls open. It can't be. Can it?

It stands right beside the cork, tilting its head at me, tiny nose twitching. I can't imagine it's just a coincidence that this Shade looks exactly like the ones we convinced the dragon to shift into. It's either one of the very same Shades, or it's another that took shape based on one of them. Either way, it's all the way out here.

A chill runs through me, but I don't know if it's out of fear or awe.

Fear, I try to tell myself, especially after what I witnessed yesterday. I should fear them. I should hate them. I should reach for my mask and don it before the squirrel can seek to steal my face and become an Incarnate.

But even though I understand this to be the most suitable reaction, I can't bring myself to obey. At least logic is partly on my side. I need not make any sudden moves to whip out my mask; Shades seek to steal the faces only of those who enchant them with sin. Nor do I need to chastise myself for not succumbing to fear. Our jobs as Summoners depend on us staying calm and not reacting.

So I let myself be still for a few moments while the flying squirrel assesses me with what feels like benign interest. Then, slowly, I close my hand over the cork and prepare to rise—

The Shade moves, scurrying closer. I freeze, breathing slowly to control my instinct to flinch back. I may not be in the throes of fear, but I'd recoil from any creature who darted too quickly at me. The Shade takes a few hesitant steps closer, whiskers twitching as it watches me with those wide, dark orbs. Then it sits back on its haunches and brings its tiny paws to its fat little belly. Just like Sloth's, its fur looks so real, despite being made of wisps of shadow. And the way it's looking at me . . .

Holy shit. It's adorable.

My lips curve in unrestrained delight as I watch the squirrel bring a paw to its rounded ear, grooming itself. I can't take my eyes off it—

Something enormous bounds toward us under the tree. It brushes past me, throwing me off-balance, and I realize it's Sloth.

"Sloth, to me," Dominic says, his voice coming from behind me. How long has he been there?

The shadow dog pays his master no heed and charges for the squirrel, his jaws closing on air as the other Shade darts up the tree trunk. Sloth chases it in a circle, leaping up to snap at it while the squirrel jumps from branch to branch, squeaking in fright as it tries to evade the wolfhound.

"No, Sloth," I call out. "Leave it!"

Sloth, of course, doesn't listen to me either, and evades the laws of nature by padding straight up the damn tree trunk—because he's a fucking shadow and can do what he wants—and onto the bough where the squirrel has sought safety. His jaws snap above the branch, narrowly missing the squirrel, who leaps off just in time . . .

To land on my godsdamned shoulder.

My muscles seize at how close the Shade is to me. That it's *on* me. Maybe fear has begun to dawn after all, but I'd react the same no matter what wild creature leaped upon me, no matter how cute or evil said creature was. And that isn't the worst that happens.

As Sloth jumps down from the tree and barrels toward me, the squirrel squeaks in fright again and takes the opportunity to run down the length of my arm and up my fucking sleeve.

Now it's my turn to start squealing, as the rodent's shadowy body brushes up my arm, down my back, and . . .

Where now? Where the hell is it now?

In my panic, I've risen to my feet and darted out from under the tree, and now I spin, slapping at my clothing and trying to shake the rogue Shade out. I think I felt it dart down my leg, but it could have been my petticoats, so I shake out my skirts even more, jumping up and down as I unhook my cloak. Once my panic subsides and I'm fairly certain the squirrel is gone, I stop in place, panting.

All eyes are upon me, Dominic staring from a few feet away, the rest frozen in the middle of their tasks. Harlow still holds the waterskin, devoid of the cork I'm certain to have lost.

"What the hell was that?" Dominic says. There's no sign of Sloth, but of the three shadows he casts on the snowy ground, one wavers in agitation.

I smooth my skirts with all the grace I can muster. "There was a squirrel."

"A squirrel?" Dominic echoes.

"Inana and her squirrels," Harlow says, rolling her eyes as she tops the waterskin with a spare cork. Why didn't I do that?

I'm about to defend my honor, but I can't bring myself to describe what happened. What would they think if I confessed the squirrel was not just a Shade but *the* Shade, one of the ones we shaped with our art? What would Dominic say if I told him a Shade crawled inside my clothing? I have a feeling he'd make me strip down naked to ensure it wasn't still there, and—for the love of the gods—why is that thought making me hot and bothered?

No, it's the panic. The panic and the shaking of my skirts. If Dominic really wants to know, Sloth can tell him.

"It's . . . fine. I'm fine," I mutter, and stride back toward Harlow.

"*Why didn't you let me eat it?*" comes Sloth's voice, barely audible over the sound of my steps crunching through the snow. "*She was going to pet it! She was going to love it more than me.*"

"Enough," Dominic whispers. "You've got serious abandonment issues."

"*They're* your *abandonment issues,*" Sloth snipes back. It occurs to me, after I've already finished my waterskin chore and moved on to another, what a strange thing that was to say.

CHAPTER TWENTY-THREE

Dominic

Sloth has been sulking all evening, convinced Inana has fallen in love with a fucking squirrel. With my wound healed well enough—though still painful as all hell—I'm back at the reins when we set out. He's a pool of formless shadow at my feet, lifting his head to sigh every few minutes. His obsession with her is ridiculous. Though, when I think about what he said back at the glade . . .

They're your *abandonment issues.*

I don't like what that implies about said obsession. Obviously it's *not* mine.

Obviously.

Definitely.

Yet every time I shift my arm and wince at the resulting pain that sears through my still-healing tissue, I recall her beautifully cold fingers against my burning flesh, her tender ministrations as she stitched and bound my wound. My stomach tightens in a strange way when I consider that my skin bears threads she stitched inside me.

Like a piece of her, threaded through my—

"Godsdamnit," I mutter, grateful I'm driving alone tonight, the rest of my crew in back. "Is that you, Sloth? Are you romanticizing my wound?"

He answers with another sigh, then lifts his head. "*She considers us special, right? More than the others? I don't see her stitching the squirrel. She only sews things she loves, doesn't she? Like the cloth heart she keeps tucked in her dress?"*

"*Mm,*" Lust says in my ear, forming beside me. "*You mean tucked against those perky tits? When you put it that way, it does feel special, doesn't it?*"

I shift uncomfortably, praying to the gods that Inana is sitting too far in the back to overhear this conversation. The river that runs along the road should mask most of it, at least.

"*She's never told us a story,*" Pride says, and I'm shocked at his moody tone. "*Yet she told the squirrel one.*"

"What the hell are you on about?" I ask. "You've heard her tell stories plenty of times."

"*But none of them were just for us,*" Pride says. "*This one got a story all its own.*"

"When did she have time to tell this other Shade a story?"

Pride scoffs. "*Did you not see it? It was one of the moon squirrels, the flying ones from the dragon incident.*"

I didn't. I knew it was a Shade, mostly because Sloth sensed it and darted toward Inana. It's rare for my shadows to react aggressively to Shades, but luckily the squirrel wasn't provoked, only startled. So much so that it crawled inside her dress, apparently.

"*She never let us beneath her skirts,*" Lust says, and I fucking hate that he just stole my train of thought and twisted it down a path I had no intention of taking.

Yet now that he mentions it . . .

A spark of irrational envy courses through me at the thought of a Shade crawling beneath her skirts and over her bare skin.

"*Right?*" Sloth says, rising from his sullen puddle, encouraged by how tightly I grip the reins. "*It should be us. Only us. Ever.*"

I blow out a slow sigh, running a hand through my hair until my spike of emotion settles. Inana must be sitting too damn close indeed for me to be feeling this way. If I don't learn why her proximity does this to me—and fix it—I might just lose my mind well before our six months together are through.

Sloth whines, returning to a puddle, as if he too felt the subtle ache at the reminder that this arrangement is a temporary one. Before summer solstice, Inana will be safe across the sea. All my Summoners will be. Calvin too, if I can wean him off my blood in time and convince him to leave.

Whether I succeed at my mission or fail, I want all of them as far away from the Holy Continent as possible.

As the evening draws close to midnight, I realize my shadows aren't the only ones acting strange. There aren't as many this deep in the mountains as there are closer to more populated areas, so it isn't the fact that I notice so few, or that they pay our passing no heed. It's more the behavior of the ones I do see. They sprint past in wisps of darkness, all going the same direction we're headed.

My gut hollows out, an internal warning that something is amiss. "Why do I have a bad feeling about this?" I say, and my shadows form fully around me, abandoning their sulking.

"*I feel something ahead,*" Pride says. "*Something . . . drawing my attention. Not aggressively. Just attracting my interest. I don't like it.*"

I curse under my breath. It would be ideal if we could avoid yet another night of altercations, but I wouldn't be a Shadowbane if I weren't used to this kind of thing. A Shadowbane's travels aren't just for getting from one post to another. They're for handling any serious threats along the way, ensuring the roads are safe for travelers. Even if I wanted to stop for the night, we still have hours left before we reach our resting place. If we want to arrive at our next post before the snowfall worsens and makes the mountain pass treacherous, we must travel as long as we can every evening. Even if it means dealing with issues every damn night.

Leaning back, I reach for the opening in the canopy. My eyes find Inana's at once. So she was sitting close, just on the other side of the flap. Clearing my throat, I force my gaze from hers and say, "Masks on. Harlow, stay alert. If I call out or if you so much as sense trouble, start drawing. We don't want to attract Shades, just to calm any that might take interest in us. I don't know what it is, but we might have trouble ahead. Calvin—"

I don't even need to finish. He's already climbing into the seat beside me, ready to take the reins if needed. My Summoners act too, donning their masks. Bard and Harlow get their tools ready, Harlow opening her sketchbook and laying out her quill and ink, while Inana climbs halfway out the opening to perch on the edge of the wagon. She curls her fingers around the back of my seat. My pulse quickens at her closeness. I face forward again, but Sloth turns around and lays his face between her hands. She idly strokes his ears, which sends ripples of secondhand pleasure down my neck.

Focus, I order myself, and shift my attention to the road ahead. Snow has begun to fall again, though only a few inches blanket the ground. Still, it's enough to illuminate the darkness, the moonlight dancing over the glittering ivory. Another Shade races ahead, disappearing around the bend.

The roar of the river gets louder, which tells me we must be nearing the bridge that will take us east to the mountain pass.

We finally reach the bend in the road where the most recent Shade disappeared, and I catch my first glimpse of what awaits us. The bridge lies just ahead, a wooden structure wide enough for only a single wagon. I've seen this road congested during the summer when merchant travel is at its peak and several vehicles are awaiting their turn to cross, and it's certainly congested now. Yet in a way I've never seen.

Clustered before the bridge are over a dozen Shades, all facing the river. Not a single one sets foot onto the crossing, for Shades are wary of bridges. They can't pass through running water, and even though they can technically cross *over* it on something like a bridge or other walkway, they prefer to avoid such bodies of water altogether. Only a frenzy could get them to surge across, so their calm behavior should be a consolation.

Should being the operative term. I'm not comforted at all.

If the Shades are gathered in one place, calm or not, then something has attracted them. I can only hope it's an old piece of art—a small statue, perhaps—that was accidentally unearthed by a wild creature. Or perhaps a previous traveler built a cairn to mark a trail up ahead and made it a little too visually pleasing to avoid the admiration of Shades. Both have happened before.

"Harlow," I say.

"On it," she calls back, voice muffled through the canopy.

"What are they doing?" Inana's warm breath stirs the back of my hair. The beads dangling from her mask clatter in the wind, barely audible over the ever-increasing sound of the river.

"I don't know," I say. "Get back inside."

She, of course, doesn't listen. I only know because I can still feel her nearness, sparking my trepidation with every inch we close toward the group of Shades. We'll have to tread carefully if they don't part for us to pass. Driving through them could be seen as a threat, as could lighting my sword and forcing them to part. But if my Summoners can calm them, we'll be fine. They won't follow us onto the bridge unless we fully enrage them.

Thankfully, as we reach the rear of the group, they part for us to pass, as if they're only half interested in whatever snagged their attention. Perhaps it really is something minor. Yet that doesn't stop the hair from rising on the back of my neck as we proceed onto the bridge, the river's thunderous rhythm blaring all around us now.

"We're fine now, right?" Inana says. "It was nothing?"

"It's not nothing," I say. "Not until we discover the source."

"*It's still pulling me,*" Pride says. "*It let up momentarily, but it's growing stronger.*"

Sloth emits a canine whine. "*The river makes me nauseous.*"

"*Same here,*" Lust says. "*I couldn't get an erection right now if I tried.*"

"Not the fucking time," I say through my teeth. Their unease at being suspended over the river seeps into me. Even though my shadows can cross running water, unburdened by the restriction wild Shades have, they aren't fond of it. Perhaps that's what sets me on edge with every step the horses take, drawing us nearer to the middle of the bridge—

Movement comes from up ahead, emerging from the trees that flank the road. The snowfall has thickened in earnest, making it difficult to discern what comes our way. Soon I realize it isn't Shades that stride toward us.

It's people.

Moonlight illuminates five figures, four of which wear masks of featureless porcelain. The fifth is unmasked, revealing a familiar face with slicked-back russet hair and a slim mustache.

Henderson.

CHAPTER TWENTY-FOUR

Dominic

I clench my teeth, bristling at the sight of the other Shadowbane.

"What the fuck is he doing here?" Inana says, taking the words from my mouth.

"Get in the back," I shout, and pull the horses to a stop. "Please, Inana." She must be surprised by *please,* for she obeys without argument for once. "Calvin?"

"It's no good," he says, leaning to the side to peer around the wagon. He faces forward. "They're still behind us, but looking more agitated now."

Shit. That means I can't reverse the wagon without risking being caught in a frenzy sparked by Henderson's Summoners. Because of course this is a fucking trap.

My eyes fall on the hands of one of the Summoners, my gaze drawn to what they hold. I expect artistic tools, but . . . it's a bow nocked with an arrow. That can't be what fascinated the Shades, though it might be what's riling them up now. One of them, however, must be performing some art. Humming or singing or perhaps telling stories like Inana does. I can't see any of their lips moving behind their masks, but it makes the most sense. It's something we can't hear over the sound of the river but the Shades can sense. Something we can't see, to know whom to target should we seek to stop them.

I release a growling breath, having no choice but to humor whatever the hell this is. Henderson clearly planned this well. I should have known better when he gave me the letter concerning my next post, but I authenticated it with the church. Even if I suspected a trap, I had little choice but to obey my orders. So what is Henderson's goal tonight? Shadowbanes take vows not to directly harm one another, to prevent competition between Shadowbanes vying for their patron's nomination. Is he willing to risk breaking his vows, risk disqualification from next year's nomination? Does he hate me that much?

He stops several paces away. His armed Summoner keeps their arrow nocked but doesn't fully draw their bow. It's rare to see a Summoner armed. Most Shadowbanes don't trust their crew enough. Anger courses through me, but it's directed at myself. I've never armed my crew. Partly from lack of trust, but even those who've proved loyal . . . it just never occurred to me they'd be in a situation where I couldn't protect them. When our only foes are Shades, and regular weapons are useless for dispersing them, it never made sense before.

Now, as we're faced with an unmistakable threat from our own kind, I despise myself for not foreseeing such a possibility.

Henderson raises his hands, palms forward. The snow has begun to fall harder, creating a haze of fluttering white between us. "I'm here to talk, Graves, that's all."

"That's not what it looks like," I bite out.

"That's all it will be if you cooperate. I think you have some idea of what I want."

"I haven't a fucking clue."

"Come down here and have a chat, and I'll tell you my terms."

His terms. Like he's the one with the upper hand. I have the high ground with my wagon. If I wanted, I could snap the reins and run them down. The archer could shoot me or the horses first, and there's room for them to leap out of the way. Still, we could flee. But the violence could trigger a frenzy, and since I don't see any sign of Henderson's wagon, it's likely blocking the road ahead. Maybe with more Summoners.

Fuck.

Perhaps he does have the upper hand.

"Why should I humor your demands?" I ask, keeping my voice even to hide my growing unease. "You can't directly harm me without risking disqualification from Prince Leeran's nomination."

"True," Henderson says. "I may not be able to inflict violence upon you, but I can hurt *them.*" He angles his head, and I realize he means my crew. "See this?" He kicks something with the toe of his shoe, and a glass vial catches the moonlight. That's when I see the shapes drawn in the snow. No, not just the snow. On the bridge itself.

A ritual circle. He's carved a fucking astrotheurgical diagram into the godsdamned bridge. That's blasphemy. Shadowbanes are forbidden from drawing diagrams anywhere permanent, to prevent common folk from stumbling upon the sacred symbols. Only the church can etch the circles onto the Holy Braziers and our swords.

"Oh, don't look at me like that," Henderson says, his smile so amused I want to slice it off his face. "I'll clean up after myself. What's most pressing is what this means for you. If my Summoner shoots his arrow into that crowd of Shades, they'll stir into a frenzy and rush your wagon. Meanwhile, I will crush this vial of blood and light the circle, keeping us safe on this side. Understand we'll have to shoot anyone who crosses through the light, in case it's a Shade."

His threat has my teeth grinding. He seeks to strand us on the bridge, between dangerous Shades and his archer's arrows. His crew can't be blamed for anyone they *accidentally* harm during an active Shade attack. And it wouldn't count as Henderson directly harming me.

Henderson speaks again. "Think you can defend yourself and your crew against that many Shades? Or do you perhaps not give a shit? I'm interested to see how this plays out, since I'm partial to believing the latter. So many of your Summoners wind up dead. I had a nice talk with one of your last ones. Aelfred, I think it was? He told me some curious things about you."

My blood goes cold. I know all about what happened with Aelfred. I bear the burden of his life on the edge of my blade.

"That's what happens when you take outlaws as Summoners," Henderson says. "Aelfred said you offered him freedom from the continent instead of Absolution. I, on the other hand, offered him a place on my crew the next time we met if he gave me pertinent information.

And yet the next time I see you, you've got a whole new set of Summoners. Coincidence?"

Calvin's eyes burn into the side of my face. Not with accusation, for he too knows what happened with Aelfred. It's with worry. Henderson has discovered too much about me. Even without proof that what my former Summoner said is true, he could file a complaint with the church and have me tested. They'll use Shades to confirm if I lie.

I'll have to admit I promised my Summoners passage off the continent.

Something no Shadowbane should ever do.

Something I shouldn't even know is possible.

"It's all right," I whisper to Calvin, though I'm not certain it is. To Henderson, I say, "Is that why you endangered an entire village by having your Summoners forge Shades into a dragon? To punish me for interfering with your budding friendship?"

Henderson shrugs. "I wanted the information Aelfred promised me, and I figured that would hurry you along. If not, your failure would soil your reputation with Prince Leeran. A win either way."

So he admits it. He truly was responsible for the dragon. Rage courses through me, but I keep my voice nonchalant. "I think I know what this is really about. Still sore about what happened ten years ago?"

His eyes narrow at my change of subject, but he takes the bait.

"I knew back then there was something off about you," he says, eyes sparking with anger. "You failed your test to join the ranks of trainees, but then what? Lo and behold, you managed to capture the most wanted outlaw of the time. The man I'd spent three years hunting."

While he speaks, I reach one hand for my belt of vials, unhooking the buckle. I slip out one vial and tuck it up my gauntlet. "Guard this with your life," I mutter to Calvin, and slowly slide the holster to him.

Henderson scoffs. "You found the criminal where, again? In a tavern? How convenient."

"You just can't bear to face your own incompetence," I say with a wink.

"No, it was something else. You were given special treatment and invited to train as a Shadowbane while your mentor received Prince Leeran's nomination—an honor that should have been mine."

I roll my eyes. "You've been obsessed with me for way too long. Is this why you wanted to chat? To hash out old times?"

He thins his lips as if he only now realizes our conversation has veered far from where he wanted it. I'm ready to let him seize control again. I can't imagine this ending well unless I agree to our damn talk. One wrong move and he'll have the Shades behind us closing in. Even if I could manage to cut through the frenzy without endangering my crew, I'd still have to reverse the wagon off the bridge and flee back the way we came. Unless I deal with Henderson here and now, he'll follow us.

At least I have something like a plan.

He straightens, his expression darkening. "Come, Graves. Leave your sword and bring your Summoners."

I hand the reins over to Calvin, huffing a humorless laugh. "I'm not leaving my sword or bringing my Summoners. You're armed, and I don't believe for a minute that's your entire crew. You normally have five or six Summoners, and I don't see your favorite." I scan the four masked figures, finding none who resembles the older woman from the tavern. She's been his Summoner the longest, and if I recall, her name is Abigail.

"Leave the youngest, then," Henderson says. "I'm not interested in her anyway."

I bristle. That means he *is* interested in Inana and Bard.

"And if you insist on meeting as equals . . ." He unhooks his sword belt and passes it to one of his Summoners. At Henderson's nod, the Summoner sets it down in the snow behind them. "Satisfied?"

I'd feel better if we both kept our swords, but if he wants a farce, I'll play.

Besides, the diversion serves me well. While I unstrap my scabbard with one hand, I slide my hidden vial out from my gauntlet with the other. I uncork it, cover the opening with my thumb, and briefly tip it. As I set the sword to the side, I swipe my thumb over my tongue, the taste of blood filling my veins with a tingling hum of power. The pain from my wound disappears completely. By the time I climb down from the wagon, the vial is sealed and tucked back under my gauntlet.

"Order your Summoners out," Henderson says. "No artistic tools. Keep them four paces behind you."

"Bard. Inana." Under my breath, I add, "Sloth, tell Inana to hum. Tell her that she and Bard are to run back to the wagon when I give the signal. They'll know it when they see it."

Bard and Inana emerge from the wagon behind me. I sense Sloth pulling away, slithering in a pool over the snow and hiding beneath Inana's skirts. He passes on the message, his words hidden from everyone save for me and her. I feel the moment she obeys, my three shadows calming at once. Her voice is too quiet to catch over the roar of the river below us, but that's enough. So long as she hums and Harlow draws, we should be able to counteract whatever art Henderson's Summoner is performing. Until his archer fucking shoots, that is.

Slowly, I close the distance between us and Henderson, my fingers begging me to unsheathe one of the daggers at my waist. That bastard must not consider my knife skills much of a threat for him to have let me keep them. Though he too is strapped with a dagger, so I suppose we're even.

I stop on the other side of the diagram.

"What is this about, Henderson?" I shift my feet as I speak, letting the vial slide from my gauntlet to fall safely onto the snow before I fold my arms over my chest. "Why are you so godsdamned interested in my Summoners?"

"You know what they're guilty of, don't you? Murder. Of an unspeakable nature. Which makes their crimes treason too."

I sense the moment Inana stops humming, a heartbeat before I hear her cracked voice. "What?"

Henderson's eyes slide to her. "Ah, yes, you. The woman who destroyed an entire village with her actions."

Even from four paces behind me, her shock invades my senses. I mentally tug Sloth away from her, to free me from getting tangled in her emotions, but he won't budge. Damn that dog.

"Don't play coy," Henderson says. "I know you're a killer."

Her panic briefly abates. "You've got the wrong person. I didn't murder anyone or destroy a—"

"Dunway?" Henderson beams with satisfaction as she snaps her mouth shut. "I see you know what I'm talking about."

"I don't."

"Enough," I say, both to her and Henderson. She should fucking know better than to fall for his lure. "You have no right to interrogate them. As my Summoners, they can't be prosecuted for past crimes."

Henderson returns his gaze to me. "But a pious Shadowbane would dismiss his Summoners and turn them over to the crown if he found out they were guilty of treason. If you're not willing to do that, relinquish them into my custody. Let me turn them in. I'm willing to look away from your shortcomings and accept that they're due to a moral quandary you're having. Is that what it is? Do you feel guilty about condemning them to the crown's justice? Or . . ."

I shift slightly as his lips tilt in a devious grin. With subtle motions, I slide the vial forward with the tip of my shoe, hidden beneath the snow, until it reaches the edge of the circle. Then, without stepping fully down, I plant my foot over it.

"Or is it something more sinister?" Henderson says. "Do you perhaps dole out justice on your own, adopting these pitiful outlaws, using them, and then slitting their fucking—"

I bare my teeth and press my foot all the way down. Glass cracks beneath my boot, freeing the blood that hums in resonance with the iron tang still melting on my tongue. At once, light erupts before us, filling the diagram, as wide as the bridge and twice my height. Without hesitation, I dart through the pillar of light and come out the other side, charging straight for the armed Summoner. His hands tremble as he retrieves the arrow that must have fallen in the snow when he was startled by the unexpected light. He doesn't see me until my knife is already at his throat.

I whirl the man around, letting my blade dig into his skin. "Shoot him," I grate in his ear as we face Henderson, who scrambles on his knees. He manages to close his hands around the hilt of his sword but freezes when he sees me with his Summoner. The archer slams his head back, aiming for my nose, but I'm already angled away from him. His attempt does nothing but give me a reason to drag my blade across his throat. As I do, blood sprays from the wound.

The resistance of flesh against steel is so much stronger—so much more personal—than cleaving through a Shade or decapitating an Incarnate with my sword. Disgust writhes through me, but it's faint, as is the guilt and shame that always comes from taking a life, even with my blunted emotional range.

Two of the Summoners take off at a run, abandoning their master, while the third falls to my weapon, another clean slice to the throat. A quick death. Darkness stirs ahead, Shades drawn by violence. I feel only minor panic as I wonder if the same thing is happening on the other side of the bridge. The pillar of light should keep the other Shades from witnessing said violence, and if my Summoners obeyed the directive I left with Sloth and Inana, they should be doing their best to calm the Shades from whatever they may sense coming from here. My tether to Sloth is weak, stretched wide across the light, so I can't be sure.

All I can focus on is Henderson. The biggest problem here.

I push the corpse of his Summoner to the side and gather up the archer's weapon. It's been years since I've shot a bow, but muscle memory has me nocking the arrow with ease. I aim it at Henderson.

The man still hasn't managed to stand, and now he releases the hilt of his sword, rolling onto his back with his palms raised in surrender. "Graves—"

"Did you really think this was going to go your way?" I say, stalking a step closer. "Did you think I'd let you threaten my Summoners and not turn the threat back on you? Did you think *you'd* be the one to incite violence tonight?"

"You can't shoot me," he rushes to say. "You'll break your vow."

"No, I can't shoot you." My eyes flick to the shape that rushes toward us, mask askew, eyes wide. It's Henderson's favorite Summoner, and as Abigail dives over his body, shielding him from me, I let my arrow fly, piercing her in the back.

Henderson cries out, but I don't stay to see if the wound is fatal. With how many Shades swarm onto the bridge, finally coerced into enough of a frenzy to step upon it, his crew's chances of survival are now in their hands. I rush back through the pillar of light, nearly knocking Inana down in the process.

She stumbles back, and I hold out my arm to steady her. "What . . . what happened over there?" Her eyes rove my face. "Wait . . . That's a lot of blood."

"It isn't mine. Come. We can't go that way anymore." My eyes dart to the wagon. Relief uncoils in my chest as I find this side of the bridge far calmer. The Shades remain gathered at the edge, but they show no aggression. Bard strums his mandolin, his soothing tune in stark contrast to my racing heart. Calvin is already encouraging the horses, a step at a time, to reverse.

I take Inana by the wrist and pull her forward, desperate to get away from here as soon as we can. My mind spins as I mentally plan our next best route. Fuck, we'll have to take a godsdamned detour to the south—

"Dom," Inana says, tugging her hand from my grip. I'm about to tell her this is no time to argue, but I find her attention isn't on me or my momentary touch but the pillar of light. She holds a hand out to it, flinching back when her fingers make contact.

She turns her masked face to me. "Is it supposed to be this hot?"

"What do you mean?" I frown. It didn't feel any warmer than usual when I raced through it, though maybe that's because I'm a halfsoul. Heat doesn't affect me the same way. Domes of light aren't any warmer than the mildest rays of sunlight. Even the flames that light our swords are mild. Unless . . .

Dread fills my stomach as my eyes dip to the circle, glowing brightly beneath the pillar and illuminating every line, every glyph of the diagram. It looks the same as the one I draw to capture Shades, just with different symbols regarding the height and width.

No, not the same.

There's a different glyph.

One relating to heat.

The bridge shudders. Shakes. "Get back," I say, but it's already too late.

The circle splits in half, the wood cracking, splintering.

I lunge forward, reaching for Inana.

She reaches back, fingertips brushing mine . . .

Before the wood drops out from beneath her, plunging her down, down, into the river below.

CHAPTER TWENTY-FIVE

Inana

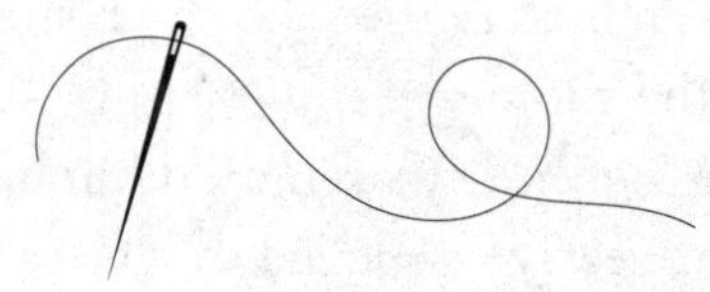

The first thing I feel is the cold.

The first thing I think is *Fuck, I'm going to die.*

Then the current takes me, churning my body in its violent pull and dragging me under before I can gather a full breath. Something slams into my side, a piece of the bridge, perhaps, and the remaining air leaves my lungs. *This is it,* I think. Even if I could swim, it would do me no good. I can't sense up from down, can't seek the surface—

Icy air slices over my cheek, bared where my mask is askew. I steal a breath, clawing for something, anything, to cling to. Another heavy weight slams into me, and I grab for it. It's a plank of wood from the bridge, and I lock my arms around it like my life depends on it. Bloody hell, it likely does. The plank keeps my head above water for the most part, though the current batters me, throwing me against rocks. Pain spears through my limbs, and I wouldn't be surprised if I've shattered every bone in my body.

I blink, trying to make out anything but the water rushing all around me, but no matter which direction the current turns me, all I see is water, darkness, or sky. I can't find the shore. Everything is moving too fast. Me, the water, the wood I cling to.

My knee crashes into something hard, but my limbs are too cold to feel it now. Then my back collides with another mass, this one jutting out from the river. My plank slips from my grasp, and I claw at the rock I've slammed against, hooking my arm over the top and hugging myself around it. The seconds of relative stillness feel like heaven, even as the river churns around me. I gather in heaving lungfuls of air, then try to lift myself higher. If I can just climb up on the rock, I can get a view of the shore, take a fighting chance at getting out of this fucking river. For a second, I see it. Only one eye remains uncovered by my sideways mask, but it's enough. A silhouette of trees bobs over the rapids. I heft myself an inch higher and catch sight of rocks. A snowy bank. Shore. That's the shore.

My arms begin to loosen, my strength draining with every breath I take. I cry out as I'm nearly wrenched off the rock. My godsdamned waterlogged cloak has caught on something, or perhaps it's been pulling downstream this whole time and I'm only now succumbing to its tug. I can't fall back into the current. I . . . I won't make it back out. I know this like I know my own heartbeat. My only option is to release one hand to unhook my cloak. But if I let go, even for a second, I'll lose my grip on the rock.

Gritting my teeth, I fight the weight dragging me down the river. Pull my arms tighter. Lift my body higher—

My strength gives out and I surrender to the current.

Surrender to death.

Surrender to . . . the strong arms that close around me. I don't know how it's possible, but I know it's him. Dominic. His arms are clamped around my waist, his legs braced against the rock. Then he shifts his grip, securing me in one arm. The rushing water batters us as he navigates us around the rock, to the side nearest the shore. We pause there, and I realize he's speaking to me, whispering into my hair.

"Breathe. You're going to be all right. Are you ready?"

I don't know what I'm supposed to be ready for, but I nod anyway.

The next thing I know, I'm moving again, dragged by the current. But I'm not alone this time. Dominic's hold doesn't let up, and there's something else here too. A canine face keeping my head above water. Paws paddling beside me. Two dark shadows filling the space between us. Dominic fights the current while somehow working with its pull until we're closer to the shore. Closer to safety.

My feet slam into the rocky riverbed, but it's a welcome sensation. I kick out, doing my best to gain purchase on them, to aid our progress, until—finally—I collapse on the riverbank, gathering shuddering breaths. Everything hurts now. No, it doesn't hurt. I can't feel anything. Sensations drift from pain to numbness, and I realize my eyes are no longer open.

My consciousness is fraying at the edges.

Maybe I'm dying, even after all of that.

Again, strong arms come around me, and I sense the world falling beneath me. Or perhaps it's only that I've been lifted up. My face feels lighter, and I realize I'm no longer burdened by my mask. Instead, something warm—so delightfully, deliciously warm—presses against my cheek. I whimper at the relief it brings.

Then a voice in my ear, so soft and kind, and I wish I could remember whose it is. "You're going to be all right, love. You hear me?" His lips graze my temple as he speaks again. "You're going to be all right."

That same warmth floods my hand; it must be pressed against the same surface my cheek is. I spread out my fingers and let that warmth soothe me, along with the heavy beat that thuds against my palm.

The next thing I think is *Dying isn't so bad.*

The holy texts are wrong. Hell isn't at all what we've been led to believe. It isn't some endless void crawling with Shades and demons. It isn't a pitch-black hole filled with the stench of rot and the perpetual burn of icy air. If anything, it's the opposite. It's warm, peaceful.

Come to think of it, maybe I'm not in hell.

Maybe I defied the odds and made it to heaven.

That would explain the glittering sunlight that wraps around me. I'm not sure when I opened my eyes, but my surroundings take shape, piece by piece. Honeyed sunlight, sheer curtains blowing on a wind I don't feel, an opulent bed beneath me—a bed unlike anything I've ever experienced, layered with pillows and the softest blankets my skin has ever felt. If this is to be my eternal grave, then perhaps the gods like me after all. The scent of cedar, snow, and smoke fills my senses, so at odds with my surroundings, but as I roll onto my side, I discover the source.

A man lies beside me, eyes closed, lips parted in slumber. His dark hair spills over his pillow, and I find myself entranced by his beauty.

Then I remember his name.

Dominic.

Confusion tangles the back of my mind, sending visions of cold water and a flash of terror, but it's gone before it can grow. I blink, then study him again, and I'm no longer confused by his presence. Of course he's here.

And . . . where is here again?

Dominic stirs before I can ponder the question too long, his eyes fluttering open, led by those long black lashes of his. He turns toward me and wraps a muscled arm around me. I'm shocked at first, by his touch and my realization that we're both fully naked—weren't we covered in blankets a moment ago?—until my mind slips back into contentment and I can no longer recall why I was surprised.

He pulls me into his chest, and I press my palm over his pectoral, luxuriating in his warmth, his heartbeat. He kisses the top of my head, and I nestle deeper into him.

"Tell me a story, love."

The voice is low, deep, and guttural, thrilling in its sleep-drunk beauty. But there's something about the words he said that sends a shock of fear through me. I pull back, expecting a different face to look down at me. Because Dominic has never said those words to me. It was someone else. Someone who . . .

Dominic meets my eyes with a frown, and I'm torn between the vision before me and the one that haunts the edges of my mind.

A man who pulled me to his chest long ago. *Tell me a story, Inana.*

A man who used those same stories against me later. *You were always a sinner.*

"What's wrong?" Dominic's warm hand comes to my cheek, and every thought flees my mind, drifting away until I can't recall what put the worried expression on his face.

"Nothing," I say, wrapping my arms around his waist. "How about I sing you a song instead?"

He pulls back and lifts my chin until our eyes meet. "Let's make it a duet."

The hunger in his eyes stokes a fire deep inside me. There's nothing I want more than to make music with our sighs. So I claim his lips with mine, and he meets them eagerly. I angle my head, deepening our kiss. When I part my lips, his tongue sweeps in, caressing mine in slow, seductive motions.

Want sparks between my legs, and I roll my hips.

Dominic smiles against my mouth, then breaks our kiss, rolling me onto my back. He pulls away slightly, his fingertips grazing my cheek, my bottom lip, then trailing down my neck. His eyes dip, drinking in the sight of my peaked nipples. I arch my back as his hand skates from my neck, down to my chest, circling the curve of my breast before cupping it fully. He watches my nipple harden between his fingers and I go slick with arousal at the sight of him biting his lower lip, his sharp canine nearly puncturing his skin.

Gods, I'm dizzy with desire as he continues to circle my nipple.

A soft whine leaves my lips when he releases my breast, but I'm satisfied with the direction his hand moves next, smoothing over my stomach and down, down, down, to the curls that dust my mound. I slowly part my knees in invitation, spreading myself wide for him. He releases an appreciative moan, then grips my knee, parting my legs farther. I rock my hips again, so ready for him to touch me, to sate the growing want that's burning hotter and hotter by the second.

"Such greed," he says with a wicked smirk, then lowers his lips to mine. Our kiss doesn't linger this time, and he soon leaves my mouth to glide his tongue over my other nipple. I cry out, panting as he draws slow circles with his fingers up the inside of my thigh, closer and closer to where I want him to be. I feel like I'll explode if he doesn't touch me soon. Like everything around us will burst into particles of golden dust and I'll be left on the brink of want for the rest of my existence.

Hell indeed.

"Touch me," I whine, shifting my hips as his hand finally trails to just outside my mound. He freezes, both the hand at my sex and the mouth over my breast. I open my eyes and stare down at him with a hateful glare. He holds my gaze as his tongue hovers just over the tip of my nipple. I arch my back, meeting his tongue the rest of the way, and he gives in, suckling me. "Bastard," I bite out. "Touch me already."

"What do you say, sinner?" He slides his fingers outside my entrance, painting my folds with my slick arousal without entering my aching core. Then he drags his thumb up and around my clit but doesn't give me the pressure I need.

I groan in my impatience, rolling my hips to meet his hand, to silently beg for the friction I want. Fuck, why can't I feel the friction?

"What do you say?" he repeats. "I want to hear you beg."

He presses down the slightest bit, rolling his thumb over my clit for all of a heartbeat. It isn't enough. Not nearly enough. Yet somehow pleasure courses through me. A frustrated, agonized pleasure that needs release. Friction. Gods, I hate this man.

Yet I want him.

Need him.

I give in to his demand. "Please," I say through strangled, panting breaths. "Touch me, please."

"Good girl." He slides his fingers down my sex. Fuck, it feels good.

But it still isn't enough. There's something . . . missing. Something I can't quite reach. Why is he holding back?

"Please," I cry out again. "Dominic!"

His name leaps from my throat in a way that feels different from every other word I've said. From every moan and whine I've made over the last several minutes. Maybe it's the way silence echoes in its wake that makes it so strange. Or the way my eyes fly open to find dark stone where a second ago there was golden light.

And that's how I find myself awake and grinding my ass against Dominic's rock-hard erection.

CHAPTER TWENTY-SIX

Inana

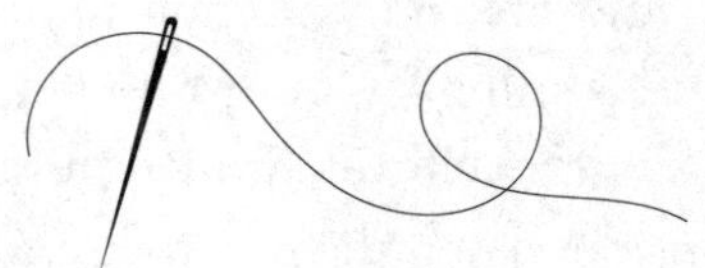

My heart races while I gather my bearings.

Several things dawn on me at once . . . and all of them are about Dominic.

He's naked.

His warm chest is pressed against my back.

His mouth is nestled in the crook of my neck.

His hand is cupped around my breast.

And he's awake.

I can tell by how still he holds, how soundless his breaths are, how stiff his arms are . . . as well as certain other things.

Then there's me.

Also naked.

My arm is extended behind me, my hand tangled in Dominic's hair.

My back is arched, my hips frozen mid-roll against Dominic's cock.

My thighs are slick with the same arousal I felt in the dream.

And I just moaned Dominic's name out loud.

Neither of us moves. Neither of us wants to be the first to break the silence, the awkwardness, the . . . strangeness of whatever just happened.

Yet I can't deny the heat that still burns at my core. Waking up hasn't lessened it, only caught me in the middle of sating my need. No wonder I couldn't find the friction I yearned for in my dream.

Visions of my sex-filled imaginings flood me, amplified by the reminder of where Dominic's hand is. He's cupping my breast, my nipple pebbled beneath his fingers, just like in the dream. It was his tongue grazing it, of course, but—

Oh, gods. The reminder of how dream-Dominic looked up at me when he teased me, told me to beg, sends another shock of warmth through me. My mind is still hazy. I don't quite know where we are or why we're here or how the hell we got into this situation, but for the briefest second, I consider being the first to break the moment. Not to end it, but to . . .

I don't know, maybe to finish what we started, for the sake of easing this tension. This burning heat that's so strong it's almost painful. From how hard Dominic is behind me, his cock pressed against my ass, I imagine it might do him some good too. We're already here. I'm already on the brink of an orgasm, and I sure as hell don't mind him finishing it for me. So what if I shifted slightly, parted my knees like I did in my dream, a subtle invitation that he can take or leave?

I gather in a shaky breath . . .

Dominic leaps up at once.

"What the fuck?" he mutters, running a hand over his face and taking several strides away.

I push up from . . . wherever I was lying. A makeshift bed? It's hardly more than a faded piece of canvas over several layers of something slightly squishy. Pine branches, maybe, based on the scent. I push back the blanket—which turns out to be my damp cloak—and look around us. We're in a cave. Daylight brightens the opening, but all I see is white outside it. Inside the cave, roots and branches climb over the walls in twining patterns. There's a roaring fire at the center of the cave floor and not much else.

Just me and Dominic.

Who's still naked.

"What the hell kind of dream was that?" he mutters under his breath. He runs his hand over his face one more time, then shakes his head. I watch him, brow furrowed, as he tugs his trousers from one of the roots overhead and pulls them on. I get an eyeful of his still very erect—and rather impressive, if I'm being honest—cock.

Snatches of the dream flood my mind again, but I force them away, force my eyes away from the low rise of Dominic's trousers, the wide expanse of his scarred chest, minimally obscured by the bandages I wrapped around his wound. I need to clear my head enough to consider what the hell we're doing here.

As I come down from the high of my dream, my arousal abates, and my rational mind makes its first appearance. It's about fucking time.

It all comes back to me. The bridge. The river. Dominic lifting me in his arms.

That's the last thing I recall, but . . . why are we here? Where are the others?

Why were we naked?

I must say the last part out loud, because Dominic blurts out, "I couldn't leave you in your icy clothes. Here." He tugs another article of clothing from the vines and throws it at me without looking. I realize it's my chemise. Embarrassment dawns in slow, mortifying waves.

I look from my naked chest to my chemise. Then at all the other pieces of clothing hanging to dry. I pull the chemise over my head and scramble to my feet. "You fucking undressed me?"

He rolls his eyes, still not looking at me as he pulls on his boots. "You're welcome."

The slickness between my thighs remains, and my embarrassment grows. Oh, my gods. I was *grinding* against him. It felt right during the dream. It even felt right afterward, when we first woke. But now . . .

"You . . . you got in bed with me? Naked?"

He plants his hands on his hips, jaw tight. "It wasn't like that," he says through his teeth. "You were fucking shivering. You needed heat. I gave you mine."

"By wrapping your arms around me and feeling me up?"

Finally, he looks at me with a seething glare. "I would never touch you like that"—

I scoff. Never say never, because he fucking *did*.

—"without your consent." His expression softens and his tone turns gentle. "I'm sorry, Inana. I wasn't aware of what I was doing . . . what *we* were doing. I was . . . dreaming."

The sincerity of his apology strikes me like a blow to the chest. I know I should yield. Give in to my mortification and admit I'm the one who was grinding against his cock. *I'm* the one who was dreaming about him—

Wait.

"What do you mean you were dreaming?" I ask. I may have been dreaming about him, but who was he dreaming about? And why does the thought of him touching me while dreaming about someone else—even a nonexistent dream-stranger—make me so enraged? "What kind of perverted dream were you having that had you groping me in your sleep?"

His expression darkens all over again. "I could ask you the same, sinner."

"I never said I was dreaming."

"Oh?" He takes a step closer, lips lifting in a taunting smirk. "Were you awake, then, rolling your hips against my cock of your own accord? Did you cry out my name because you wanted me inside you? Because you wanted my touch?"

Fuck. He heard me shouting his name. This can't get any more humiliating. My cheeks blaze as I fold my arms and feign nonchalance. "You think I'd ever *want* that kind of touch from you?"

He stalks closer now, and I take a step back. "Yes, I think you do. I think, the next time you want my touch, you're going to beg me for it, and you're going to do it out loud, not in a dream."

The blood leaves my face. Why does it seem like he knows what happened in my dream?

"You want to know what else I think?" he says. He holds my gaze as he takes another article of clothing hanging from the roots, then another, closing the distance between us with each step. "I think I wasn't alone in that dream. And I think you liked it just as much as I did."

"That's not possible," I say, huffing a shaky laugh. "How could we have the same dream?"

"It was *your* dream, and you should be grateful we shared yours and not mine. Because I don't dream; I have nightmares. Again, you're welcome for saving your damn life." He steps into my space, leaving only inches between us. I suddenly feel naked all over again, with his chest still bare and mine covered only in my thin chemise. His shirt and jerkin are draped over one arm, but he's made no move to don them. Meanwhile, my clothing remains hanging near the fire.

I smother the piece of me that wants to shy away and instead lift my chin, my chest, and step into *his* space. I bat my lashes. "Maybe you should be the one thanking me, then. We both know which one of us liked that dream more."

My attention drifts down his chest until it lands on his waistband. It takes all my effort to shift my features into a sneer, to pretend I wasn't impressed by what I saw.

As I return my gaze to his, I expect to see anger in his eyes. For his jaw to tighten. For him to be the one to make the first move to break the tension and walk away, just like he did when we awoke.

But he doesn't.

His eyes glitter with some blend of mirth and malice, and he bares his canines in a seductive grin. Then, before I can react, he takes my chin between his fingers, tilts my face to his, and lowers his head. He stops with his mouth an inch away from mine, and my breath catches, my lips parting involuntarily. My heart speeds, and my nipples harden against the fabric of my chemise. Just like that, slick heat returns to my core.

"Yeah, Inana," he whispers over my mouth, his breath skating over my lips. "You're right. We both know which one of us liked it more."

With that, he releases me and storms out the mouth of the cave.

CHAPTER TWENTY-SEVEN

Dominic

I stop outside the cave, surrounded at once by a blanket of falling snow. Each flake melts into a puff of steam as soon as it touches my skin, but at least it manages to cool me down. I need it after this morning. After that dream.

Gods, my cock still throbs with need, straining against my trousers. I gather the cool air in my lungs, willing some of that ice to flood my lower regions, but it's no good. The memories won't leave me. I can still feel the soft mound of her breast in my palm, the hardness of her nipple between my fingers. Can still feel the curve of her bare ass against my hips. And that's only what happened after we awoke.

The dream itself . . .

Now that was a fucking experience. I meant what I said when I told her I don't dream, for I rarely do. It's uncommon for Shadowbanes. When I do dream, I see nothing but blood and shadows, see the faces of Incarnates, of every person I've slain. When this happens, I tend to thrash in my sleep, which is why I take private quarters whenever we post up in a village. What I didn't tell her was that there was another reason I knew the dream undoubtedly belonged to her.

Because I saw that dream through her eyes.

It should have unsettled me, finding my own face staring back at me while my tongue painted circles over those spectacular tits. It should have felt like I was fucking myself. But it didn't. Because I was more focused on the fact that Inana's view of me—her fantasies about me—drew so much pleasure from her. That was enough to stir my own. To make me so half mad with desire when we awoke that I nearly rolled on top of her and finished what we started.

It was the shame of that thought that had me springing away from her. What kind of asshole can only think of fucking when he wakes up next to the girl he spent all night and half the morning caring for?

An asshole like me, that's who.

But only because it's *her*.

Blowing out a heavy breath, I finally don the rest of my clothing, pulling my shirt over my head, followed by my jerkin. The gods must be punishing me. Inana is the worst person I could be alone with. The worst person to be stuck with. But I can't regret it now. Even if I could choose again, I'd still jump into the river after her. When I saw her slip away from me, time stood still. My chest felt like it had collapsed with the bridge. I couldn't see her face behind her mask, but I could feel her terror. Her shock. I gave myself only the briefest moment to consider what to do. Just long enough to assess the situation on our side of the bridge once more. Just long enough to meet Calvin's eyes and exchange a knowing nod. Then my mind was consumed with saving her.

"*You're welcome,*" Pride says, reading my train of thought. Under the light of the sun and in the brightness of the snow, he and my other two shadows are relegated to pools of gray near my feet. "*What a fucking nightmare that was.*"

"*I can't believe you made us swim,*" Lust says.

Sloth is the only one whose commentary lacks disdain. "*Turns out I'm an excellent swimmer.*"

"Thank you," I whisper. I know they didn't like being submerged in running water. Our connection allows them to cross it just fine, but that doesn't mean they don't hold at least a fragment of the same fear wild Shades do. Yet they aided me, lending me their strength to hold Inana up and battle the current.

Footsteps approach, and I stiffen. Inana emerges out into the snow. She blinks profusely, snowflakes coating her hair and lashes at once. "Oh," she says, "it's awful out here."

It seems her mood has calmed as much as mine. Perhaps we can be civil now. She waves a hand before her to bat away the falling flakes, but it's no use. There's nothing but white and trees and flurry to be seen. She takes another step forward, and I thrust out an arm to bar her path.

She halts, then leaps back when she realizes she was about to walk off the edge of a cliff. It's only a five-foot drop, but I doubt she'd find it pleasant. "What the hell? Where are we?"

"Come," I say, ushering her back into the cave. Thankfully, she doesn't argue, and we step back under the shelter. I point to the left. "There's a short trail this way that leads to the river. I pulled you out not far from here."

She dusts snow from her cloak, then from her red-gold hair. "How did you find this place?"

"I was looking for a wide enough tree to take shelter under and found this instead. It was much easier to see before the snowstorm hit."

She looks out at the several inches built up outside the cave, weighing down the branches of the pines. It's a far cry from the mild dusting we traveled through the last few days. "This all happened overnight?"

"It did."

Silence falls between us, growing taut with every breath. I want to break it but I don't know how.

We turn to each other at the same time, but she's the one who speaks.

"Thank you," she says, her words flying from her mouth as if they escaped on their own. She keeps her eyes on my jerkin as if she can't bear to meet my gaze. "You saved me from the river and ensured I didn't catch my death from the cold. I . . . I probably owe you my life."

It takes me a few breaths to find my words. "You don't owe me anything. And I meant it when I said I'm sorry. For how you woke up. That was—"

"It's fine," she says, her eyes flicking briefly to mine. "I was confused, but . . . I didn't hate it. Being warm, that is. I know the logic of body heat and nudity. It was . . . smart."

Something brightens inside me, pride at having been called smart.

I force the feeling away. What am I, a fucking schoolboy? I clear my throat. "Are you injured? Lacerations? Broken bones?"

She arches a brow. "You mean you didn't get an eyeful when you were undressing me?"

I glower, but she merely grins.

"I'm fine," she says. "Bruised, but that's all. I felt like I was being dashed against a thousand rocks and broke every bone in my body, but that was probably just the cold."

Concern tightens my chest. "You weren't hurt the other night either? I wasn't in any state of mind to check on you, seeing as I had a hole punched through my fucking torso."

"Oh." She pulls her head back, surprised by my question. She shifts her leg, then lifts her skirt, looking down at her calf. "Honestly, I forgot to search myself for wounds the night I was tending yours, but no, I'm fine. The Shade grabbed my leg when it tried to pull me under the wagon, but it must not have broken the skin."

My concern eases. I'm glad I was the only one hurt that night.

"So . . . where exactly are we in relation to where we were? I take it we've been separated from the others. Are they safe?"

"We're at least two miles downstream from where we were, which is even farther by road. The others should be safe, though. The Shades on their side of the river were calm, even after the bridge collapsed."

Her expression turns wary. "What about the other side? What happened with Henderson and his crew?"

I thin my lips, debating whether I should tell her what I did. But there's no use keeping secrets like that, just to hide how coldly I ended lives last night. I'd do it again if I had to. "I killed two of his Summoners," I say. "Shot his favorite, Abigail, with an arrow, and fled while aggressive Shades were starting to cross the bridge. I don't know what happened to him, but he would have had to fight through the Shades to get to his wagon. He could be dead."

"Hopefully. What side of the river are we on?"

I release a grumble. "The wrong side. Well, the right side if we were still heading the direction we were going before, but there's no use continuing east just the two of us, without the wagon and our crew. We need to join the others on the opposite side and take the southern pass instead, but there isn't another bridge for several more miles south."

She furrows her brow. "Can't we . . . maybe cut down a tree or something? Use that as a makeshift bridge?"

I blink at her, impressed she had the same thought I did last night, when my mind spun to concoct a way out of this damn mess. If we can find a narrow enough portion of the river and a tall enough tree, I can cut it down so that it falls across to the opposite bank. "Yes, but there's one problem. I have no axe. Not even my sword, just my knives. The cave has been used as a camp before, but its previous visitors left nothing behind save for scraps of old sacks and a rusty mug with a hole in it."

She folds her arms and assesses the cave. Her gaze lingers on the fire. "What about what happened with the bridge? Can't you use your astrotheurgy to burn through the base of the tree instead of chopping it down?"

"I could," I say with a sigh, "but there's another problem. I left my vials with Calvin."

Her gaze shoots back to mine, her face paling as understanding dawns. Without my blood source, I can't use astrotheurgy. She idly rubs her neck, and I wonder if she's realizing what else that means.

If I'm struck by the thirst, I'll need her to be my source.

I curl my fingers into fists, fighting the way my mouth waters at the thought. No, I will not use her like that.

"So what do we do?" she asks, dropping her hand from her neck and folding her arms tighter against her chest. Maybe I'm imagining it, but her breaths seem shallower. Her posture tense. Is she worried I'm going to jump her? Sink my teeth into her throat like one of those fucking lords in the Sacred Cities?

I step away, just to demonstrate my control. Whether the demonstration is meant more for her or me, I'm uncertain. "We can't do anything until there's a break in the snow. It isn't safe to travel on foot in a blizzard, and Calvin knows what to do in these situations."

"Which is what?"

My fingers automatically move to my waist, seeking my holster, but of course it isn't there. "Calvin and I have a way of finding each other."

"How?"

I breathe deep, choosing my words carefully. "My vials contain the Shades I captured."

"The ones with your face?"

I nod. "If we're close enough in proximity, they could scent my blood. Their reaction will be subtle, but they will tug against their vials. Calvin can use that as a compass of sorts. Meanwhile, he has vials of my blood. Sloth, Lust, and Pride should be able to catch the scent if he opens one near enough. They will have made camp not far from the bridge. Calvin will begin his search once the blizzard calms. Once they find us, they can use the tools in the wagon to cut down a tree for us."

"So you're saying we have to wait here until they get close enough for this . . . makeshift Shade-compass theory to work?"

"Yes."

Her lips pull into a grimace, and she rubs her brow. When she meets my eyes, there's trepidation in them. "But our problems would be solved if you had a blood source to fuel your astrotheurgy and help you cut down a tree?"

My pulse quickens at what she's suggesting. Why did she have to say that? After all the energy I expended in the river, not to mention my still-healing wound, it's only a matter of time before I feel the strain of thirst. My gaze falls to her neck and my mind fills with a vision of my lips on her skin. Fuck, I bet she tastes divine.

I sink the tip of my canine into the inside of my lip, forcing my mind from such thoughts and focusing on that brief piercing of pain instead. It takes all my restraint to speak evenly. "If we choose to take that option—and we only will as our last resort—it's useless to consider it now. Once we leave the cave, we lose our most certain means of shelter. We can't risk that until we know the wagon is close."

"So we're stuck here for now?" Her voice trembles slightly. I watch her throat bob as she swallows hard. "Together?"

The word *together* has my britches tightening, has my blood roaring, and I need to get out of this cave again. I'm not even sure if I manage to answer her question before I stride away to find my belt on the cave floor. The familiar weight of my blades eases some of the vulnerability I feel without my sword and vials. I let my palm rest over the hilt of one while I rush back to the mouth of the cave.

"Where are you going now?" Inana asks, throwing her hands in the air.

"You need to eat," I say, pausing near the opening. I turn halfway to look back at her. "I'm going to take care of you. All right? I promise."

Her bewildered expression remains trapped in my mind as I march through the snow toward the river.

CHAPTER TWENTY-EIGHT

INANA

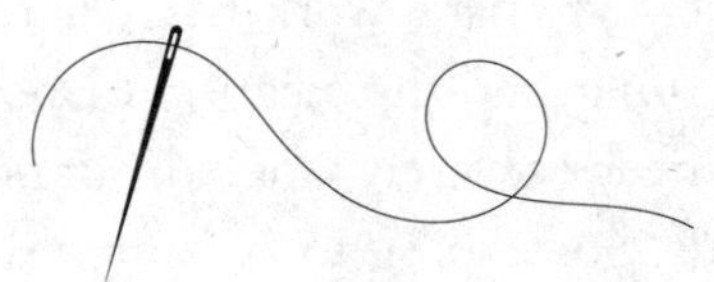

It's only after Dominic leaves that I realize how long it's been since I've been well and truly alone. When I lived in Nalheim, my hours were devoted to working, performing, or sleeping in the barracks. Always near others. Never a moment of complete silence, for even the lavatory was a shared space. The textile mill was similar, though most of my days were spent in a haze, still recovering from shock after escaping Henry.

I suppose the last time I was alone for an extended period . . . was back home.

Henderson's taunting words come back to me now, sending a chill through my blood.

The woman who destroyed an entire village with her actions.

What did he mean? Who does he think I murdered, and in what way did I destroy Dunway?

I pace around the fire, anxiety simmering in my chest with every step. Now I'm desperate for Dominic to return. If anyone knows what Henderson meant, it's him. He knew who I was at the Wretched Lair. He knows of my crimes. It was never a subject I wanted to discuss with him before, especially since he was giving us amnesty. A clean slate not as outlaws but as Summoners. But if there's some fabricated tale going around regarding what happened in Dunway, I need to know what it is.

And if it isn't fabricated . . .

What the hell happened to my village?

I curse under my breath and stalk over to a pile of pine branches, pushing them aside to reveal my mask and one of my fabric hearts. I found them here when I was getting dressed and nearly wept with relief that at least one of my creations wasn't lost or destroyed during my dunk in the river. My patchwork heart is the only one that remains, but it's something, and the creation I labored over the longest. It's still damp, the threads severely tangled, but now I have something to do with my hands. Something to take my mind off the questions swarming inside my head.

I take up the patchwork heart and begin brushing through the threads. It's daylight and the fire has brightened the cave well enough, so there shouldn't be much harm in working on this. I'm not making art; I'm fixing something. It's practical—

My hands go still over the damp crimson threads. The Incarnate's voice fills my mind, followed by a vision of its bloody fingers scraping against a bone.

It's not art, it's just a tool.

Shame burns molten in my gut. What the hell is wrong with me? I was feeling anxious and my first instinct was to handle art and call it mending? It's logic like that that got the carver killed. Just because it's daylight doesn't mean it's safe to flaunt my art. There's a reason Dominic hid my heart under the pine boughs.

With a sigh, I return it to where I found it and sit by the fire.

And wait. And wait. And wait.

Dominic returns what feels like hours later, though it's still daylight. The sky is as blinding white as it was when I awoke, the snowfall just as incessant. He marches in, trailing chunks of packed snow, then sets down an armful of cedar leaves and what looks like sprigs of wild rosemary, upon which he rests two filleted fish. I blink in surprise, all the anxious questions I'd been storing up in his absence now fleeing my mind. He caught fish in that horrifying, freezing river? With no pole or net? Perhaps he crafted a spear or sent Sloth out to snatch them up in his muzzle. Before I can ask, he storms back out.

When he returns, it's with an armload of thick branches that must be meant for firewood. Then he leaves again and returns with another armload. And another.

Gods, how much work did he do?

"We'll need to keep the fire burning during every hour of darkness," he says by way of explanation. He adds a log to the fire, then sets about carving several sticks, removing the bark and chiseling them into points. He then notches them together until they create a cross. I furrow my brow, unsure what it's for, until he drapes the two fillets on them.

"It's for cooking them," I say as he props them just outside the fire. I'm amazed by how quickly he worked, how expertly he set this up with minimal tools at his disposal. Now *this* is practical craft. Necessary art.

That dampens my mood, reminding me of what I want to ask him.

I open my mouth to ask, but when I turn toward him, his back is to me.

And his shirt is sliding over his head.

My cheeks heat. "What are you . . ."

He meets my eyes over his shoulder, and I quickly look away. "I need to dry my clothes again," he says.

Right. That's rational. Of course he does. He's been outside for hours and has probably gathered icicles in his clothing. He returns to the fire and sits on the other side. I note he kept his trousers on. His chest is bare, and I let myself look at it only to assess the state of the bandage I wrapped around his wound. There's no sign of blood, so at least he hasn't torn his stitches. I lift my gaze, taking in the moisture dripping from the ends of his dark hair, which he's pushed away from his forehead. The light of the fire dances across his face, over the bridge of his gorgeously crooked nose, that sharp jaw, that short dark beard.

I shut my eyes and remind myself to stop staring. This is no time to admire the Shadowbane. It's time to interrogate the bastard.

"What did Henderson mean about me?" I say in a rush.

Dominic meets my eyes but says nothing.

"He said I was a murderer. That I destroyed my village. What did he mean?"

His shoulders tense, and for a moment I wonder if I'll have to strangle the answers out of him. The thought of my hands around his throat is strangely intoxicating, so it's a relief when he says, "You truly don't know?"

"Which part? That I supposedly murdered someone, or that my village was destroyed? I know nothing about either."

"Two years ago," Dominic says, speaking slowly, carefully, "Dunway fell to a frenzy of Shades. Most died. The few survivors relocated to other towns."

Most died. Does that include . . . my parents? My neighbors? The people I grew up with? I may not have been anyone's favorite in my hometown, not even my parents', but I would never wish death upon them.

My heart thuds like a leaden weight in my chest. "How did it fall to a frenzy? The village should have been protected. The duke . . . Henry . . ." Gods, was Dunway attacked *because* I escaped? Because Henry didn't claim another victim and light the brazier in time? But why *then*? Dunway saw its share of Shades and even had to call in the help of a Shadowbane on occasion, but there was never a threat big enough to potentially erase our entire village. Did my escape itself draw the Shades? Did my sin in defying a Sinless stir a frenzy?

"Henry Berkham is dead." Dominic's words stall my thoughts. "Every survivor of the attack insists he never arrived in Dunway. Records state he was killed in a Shade attack on his way to the village. Before his Absolution ritual could happen."

I shake my head. "That . . . that's impossible. I saw him. He was Sinless—"

"I believe you, Inana. I believe you were the last person who saw Henry Berkham alive, and that he was already Sinless."

"Then what the hell does this all mean?"

"Think it through." His tone is gentle. Calming. "Henry Berkham is dead, that's a fact. Records state he was never given the Absolution ritual and died while he was still mortal. Yet you saw him alive and very much Sinless. Sometime after you escaped imprisonment, Dunway was attacked by Shades, leaving very few survivors. The only ones left alive confirmed they never saw their promised duke arrive. What do you think the truth is?"

I bite my bottom lip as I consider what he said. If the records contradict what I know to be factual—that Henry was without a doubt turned Sinless—then the records are lying. As are the survivors, unless they somehow missed the celebratory procession like I did and truly don't know Henry arrived in Dunway. But he did arrive, and he was already Sinless. And now he's . . . dead?

I shake my head. "How can a Sinless immortal be dead? The Sinless can't be killed . . ."

My voice trails off as understanding dawns cold and sharp.

"A Sinless . . . *can* be killed. Is that what this is all about?"

"If it's true that Sinless can be killed," Dominic says, "imagine what lengths to which the church and crown might go to keep that a secret."

A chill runs down my spine at what he's suggesting. "Are you saying Dunway was destroyed by Shades on purpose? Because if anyone discovered the truth—that Henry did arrive in Dunway, fully Sinless, and died right after—they'd know Sinless *can* die. And that . . ."

"That would make the Sinless vulnerable," he says.

"But . . . how? How can a Sinless be killed? How did Henry meet his end?"

"I thought if anyone knew," Dominic says, "it would be you."

I pull my head back. "Do you think I killed him?"

"Did you?" There's no accusation in his tone, but I bristle nonetheless.

I open my mouth to deny it, but my words don't come. The truth is, I don't remember what happened after I freed my wrist from my bindings and sliced Henry's neck with my needle. Could I have killed him? I don't think so. I'm sure if I did something so extreme, I'd remember. Right?

"It doesn't matter what you did or didn't do," Dominic says. "Even if you killed him, I wouldn't blame you."

I lift my eyes to meet his over the fire. His expression is fierce yet sincere. But isn't that contrary to who he is? What he stands for? Shouldn't he be terrified of me? If I knew how to kill a Sinless, I could kill him too. Yet he's never acted afraid of me. He's never flaunted the so-called virtues of his kind. And his peers—at least Henderson—resent him. Suspect him. He offers his Summoners freedom instead of Absolution. And the way he feels about himself . . .

Why would I wish what I am on anyone else?

"What are you?" I ask, my voice coming out quiet.

He runs his hand through his snow-slicked hair, sending droplets falling on his broad shoulders. A dark, humorless grin warps his lips. "Maybe it's time I told you everything. Maybe it's time I gave you the one weapon that could be my undoing."

Terror flits through me. Whatever truth he's hiding, it has convinced some of his previous Summoners to turn on him. Am I ready for the truth? Will my opinion of him change once he confesses his secrets?

Who will I see sitting on the other side of these flickering flames?

An ally? My master? A Shadowbane who doesn't seem as awful as I first thought him to be?

Or an enemy?

I take a bracing breath. "Tell me."

CHAPTER TWENTY-NINE

Dominic

Several times now I've shared the truth with my Summoners, but never has it sparked so much fear beforehand. Maybe it's because of Inana's proximity. The woman who forces me to feel in ways I'm not supposed to. Maybe it's because I can't bear the thought of how this could end.

There are two results I'm familiar with.

Looks of awe and admiration.

Or bloodshed.

I unsheathe one of my knives and flip it idly in my hand, just to steady my nerves. "Do you know the creation story?"

She frowns. "The holy texts say we were given life by the nine gods, but not much else."

"The full story has been lost to time," I say. "Or, more accurately, the church's interference. All the old stories are locked away, along with the knowledge of astrotheurgy. Regardless, I'll tell it."

She stiffens. "Is it safe to tell stories, even in daylight? You don't have your sword if Shades come around."

I shake my head. "This story is a true one. Besides, Shades aren't interested in what I have to say."

She doesn't look convinced, and I don't blame her. I've said Shades don't Incarnate off Shadowbanes, yet she's seen Shades wearing my face. Of course she'd be hesitant to believe me. But I have a perfectly reasonable explanation for the Shades who look like me. One she'll soon understand.

"Long ago," I say, "Bastien and Vanna were the only gods in the sky, the sun and moon forever in a dance of balance. Light and dark. Beginning and end. Eventually they sought to procreate. They had seven children and gave them dominion over their own planetary bodies. Herald, Serafina, Malen, Lilith, Sylas, Dian, and Kole. Each of these gods developed their own personality, but forged as they were from their parents' essences, there was always a balance, thanks to the influence of Bastien and Vanna. Light and dark. Beginning and end. Life and death.

"Soon the seven young gods were struck with the yearning to procreate, so they too chose to give birth to new forms, combining their divine energies to create humankind. Thus, we were born on this world, reflections of our creators. Our very souls are made of their divinity, our gods' unique essences woven together like a tapestry, spanning the whole of human potential. Not just human *perfection*, but the full spectrum. The balance of light and dark. The dance of the sun, moon, and all seven minor gods stitched into our very essence."

She stares, in awe of my story. "That's far more detail than we were given during weekly liturgy. I knew we were created by the gods, but to think our souls are composed entirely of divine energy. It makes sense now, some of the things we were taught yet never given a full explanation for." She pauses, brow furrowed as if she's piecing something together in her mind. "The seven young gods gave us the seven holy virtues, didn't they?"

"Not just the virtues," I say, flipping my blade again. "Remember, each of our parent gods is the child of Bastien and Vanna. They have both solar and lunar energy, a light side and dark side, which they passed on to us.

"Herald, God of Prosperity, gave us generosity and greed.

"Serafina, Goddess of Love, gave us compassion and lust.

"Malen, God of Wisdom, gave us humility and pride.

"Lilith, Goddess of Justice, gave us patience and wrath.

"Sylas, God of Harvest, gave us temperance and gluttony.

"Dian, Goddess of Beauty, gave us awe and envy.

"Kole, God of Purpose, gave us diligence and sloth."

The awe leaves her face. "You're saying the gods gave us not only the seven holy virtues but the seven human sins too?"

"Those aspects weren't always called sins," I say, "nor were they considered evil. Before One Hundred Days of Darkness, Vanna was just as respected as Bastien. Back then, darkness was seen as necessary, the way night is essential to balance out the day. Harvests must be reaped. Life must end. One must understand sadness to also know joy. Those darker aspects, those endings, it's simply lunar energy. Vanna's influence reflected on our planet and in our souls."

Inana shrugs. "If this story is meant to illustrate that sin isn't evil, then that means Shades aren't inherently evil either, which I suppose I can understand. They're more like . . . terrifying wild animals. But that doesn't change anything. Whether we call it sin or lunar energy, Shades are drawn to it. I hate that it's true. I hate that it includes art, but hating something doesn't make it false."

"It is false," I say. "Art isn't human darkness. It's a miracle of life."

"Why are Shades attracted to it, then?" There's desperation in her eyes, a war between wanting to believe what I'm saying and all the evidence she's witnessed. All that she's been taught to believe. Her expression falls. "How do you explain why Shades are so obsessed with art that they'd kill us for it?"

I know she's thinking of the Incarnate and its fruitless attempts at replicating art. She's right that the carver died because of her craft. The Shade was so obsessed, it killed the woman and her entire camp to try to become her. To try to do what she could do.

But not because art is a sin.

"Shades aren't what you've been led to believe they are," I say, my pulse quickening as I stumble dangerously close to words I shouldn't say out loud. But I can't keep it from her any longer. "We're all told that Shades are drawn to sin because they manifested from sin. That's partly true; they are attracted to lunar energy because they *are* lunar energy. Sin, if you will. But they're also attracted to that which makes them feel alive."

"So art . . . makes them feel alive?"

"Yes," I say. "The same way other mundane aspects of the human condition make them feel alive. The lies we tell for survival or wickedness or even just for amusement. The passion stirred between lovers. The violence between enemies. The miraculous act of procreation and childbirth. It's all brimming with life and humanity, and they're hungry for it."

I can practically feel how her heart races, how the wheels in her mind turn. She holds my gaze without blinking. "If they aren't what I think they are, then what are they? If they're merely lunar energy, what created them? Was it Vanna, like the holy texts say?"

I shake my head. "Shades may be made of lunar energy, but it was not the moon goddess's will for them to manifest as monsters."

"Then where do they come from?" She rises to her feet as if she can't bear to sit still any longer. Her eyes flash with accusation as she paces around her side of the fire. "You said so yourself: Your sin has created Shades. You said you were the *only* one of us who could have created a Shade."

"I meant that," I say, my voice quavering with anticipation. My chest hums with it, a blend of terror and excitement. She's getting so close to the truth now. So fucking close. I flip my blade once more. "In a sense."

"Then what did you do?"

I sit up straighter, my hand clenched around the hilt of my knife. "Not what I did. What I *am*."

Her brows lower to a glare as she asks me the same question she voiced earlier, her tone sharpened to a point. "What are you?"

Slowly, I rise to my feet, sheathing my dagger. I stride closer to her, but not too close. "I am a Shadowbane. A halfsoul. Not because half my soul has been cleansed of sin in a religious sense, or in any other intangible way. I am a halfsoul because half my soul has had its lunar energy physically *removed*."

She goes still, eyes wide.

"Four pieces were cut away entirely." I lift a tentative hand to my scarred chest and bring my index finger to the top half of the ritual circle carved there. I've never used my scar to convey the truth to a Summoner before. Inana is the only person aside from Calvin who's seen it. But I want her to know. Need her to fully understand.

I tap one glyph. "This means *cut*." I point out four places where *cut* is marked beneath the glyphs of four different gods, carved at the ends of four different lines. I tap on the glyphs for each of the gods' names. "Herald, Dian, Lilith, and Sylas. Their lunar aspects were cut from my soul. In other words, Greed, Envy, Wrath, and Gluttony."

I move my hand to the bottom half of the circle and the three lines there, with the glyph for *cut* midway through each line. Again, I tap the names of the gods, then voice their associated lunar aspects. Or what we now call sins. "Malen, Serafina, and Kole. Pride, Lust, and Sloth. These were only partially severed from me. Enough that I still feel through them and control them, but they can act as separate entities, no longer fused to the rest of my soul."

Her expression goes blank as she pieces together what I've told her. All the clues I gave her along the way. All the half-hidden truths I wasn't sure if I should share. She takes a step back. "Your Shades . . . they don't look like you because they tried to Incarnate from you. They look like you because they're . . . pieces of your soul?"

I nod.

"And the ones you catch in vials . . . those are the pieces that were cut away entirely?"

Another nod.

Her chest heaves with shocked, weighted breaths. "Does that mean some of the wild Shades might also be slivers of someone else's soul?"

My heart slams heavy against my ribs. "Not *some*."

Her throat bobs. Once. Twice. Her voice comes out in a whisper. "All of them?"

I speak treason with my answer. "Yes. Every last one. All created as a by-product of Absolution."

As her understanding deepens, her expression darkens. Her fists curl at her sides and her lips peel back from her teeth. "Do the Sinless know the truth? Does the church?"

"The church, yes," I say, "but only a select few Sinless. King Kaelum and some of the original princes."

Tremors rack her frame as she stares into the roaring fire. "The holy texts lie. The *king* lies. If Shades are created from Absolution alone, then the average citizen doesn't create them. Only the Sinless do, yet they blame us for it. They let their own fucking souls terrorize villages while staying safe beneath their domes of light."

"Yes." I'm torn between wanting to reach out to comfort her and bracing myself for her rage. Because it's coming. I can see it in the way her irises dart across the fire as she puts more and more pieces together. The way her body goes still.

The way her eyes slowly drag up to mine. "Did you know the truth before or after you became a Shadowbane?"

Ah, here it is. The answer that will draw her hatred. "Before."

In an instant, she charges at me, closing the distance between us in three quick strides. I don't shy away, don't step back. Not even when she wraps her hand around my dagger and pulls it from its sheath. Not even when she flicks the blade to my throat. "You fucking knew. You knew what the Absolution ritual would do. You knew it created Shades, yet you did it anyway. You wanted it. Is this why your Summoners turn on you? Because they find out you're part of the fucking problem? Because you knew the truth all along, yet so desperately want to complete the very ritual that creates *more* monsters? To become one of those lying, bloodsucking—"

"I don't," I say, my voice like a growl. I lean closer, letting the edge of my own dagger break my skin. I hold her eyes, the fury on my face matching hers. "I don't want to become one of them. I want to burn it all down."

CHAPTER THIRTY

INANA

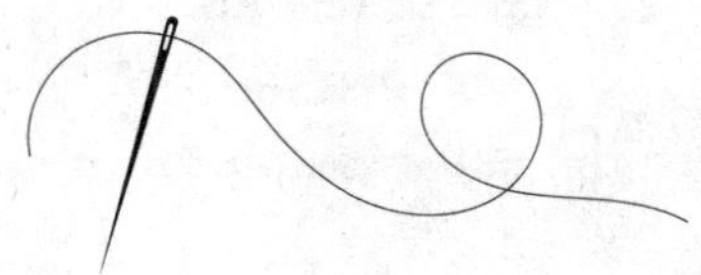

The fervor in his eyes, the darkness in his voice, has my grip slackening on the knife. Before I know it, he grabs my wrist and twists until I release the blade. He takes it from me and pivots us both to the side. My back collides with the cave wall, and he pins my hand over my head. I expect him to bring the knife up to my throat now, but his hand is empty, his palm slamming beside my head.

He presses the front of his body into mine, igniting a strange blend of fury and desire.

"What are you saying?" I ask when I manage to find my voice.

"I have a mission," he says. "I've been training for it my whole life. Keeping secrets my whole life. Playing a role for the eventual greater good."

"What is your mission?"

His jaw tightens, and I don't think he'll answer. Then he says, voice barely above a whisper, "I'm going to kill King Kaelum. That's why I need Prince Leeran's nomination: so I can attend the solstice ritual at the capital, end the life of a tyrant, and start a fucking war."

A shudder ripples through me, excitement dancing with my rage. My body reacts like he just serenaded me with the most seductive lullaby. One of violence instead of romance. One that has my core heating just the same. I relinquish my strength to the wall, letting it support me as my knees buckle beneath the weight of my conflicting reactions. "How? How will you do it?"

Again he hesitates before answering. "I collect more than just my own Shades."

I ponder his words until pieces connect in my mind. The way his Shades are attracted to his blood, strongly enough that Calvin can use them as a compass to find us. The vial he held open on the rooftop back in Thornfal and hid as soon as I saw it.

"The vials," I say. "You have some of the king's blood?"

He nods.

"You're looking for the cut-away pieces of his soul. But how will that help?"

"How do you think?"

I grit my teeth. I think we're well beyond him making me come to my own conclusions so he doesn't risk breaking his vows. But if he thinks I can find the answer on my own, then it must be staring me in the face. I revisit everything I learned.

Shades are the lunar energy—the sins—that are cut away in the process of turning a human Sinless during the Absolution ritual.

Shades are drawn to their original body's blood.

Dominic has a vial of the king's blood and seeks to collect his Shades.

All so he can kill King Kaelum, an immortal Sinless who can't be killed.

That's when I recall what started this conversation.

Sinless *can* be killed.

"Can a Sinless's Absolution be reversed?" I say. "Can they be made mortal again if you collect their Shades?"

Some of the tension leaves his face, and he slowly releases me, his fingers lingering over my wrist before fully pulling away. "Yes. And now you know the most dangerous, most treasonous secret I keep. The Sinless can be made mortal again if their lunar energy returns to their souls. I don't know how Henry Berkham died, and it seems neither do you, but it's only possible if he was made mortal again. Somehow, he regained the shadowed pieces of his soul and died. That's why Dunway was destroyed."

I remain propped against the wall and let my arms hang loose at my sides. "If these secrets are important, how did you find out the truth? Do all Shadowbanes know?"

"I only know the truth because it was instilled by the rebellion. I was raised on the truth. Raised keeping secrets."

The word *rebellion* sends a thrill through me. It isn't just Dominic at work here. There's a whole secret movement behind his plan.

He continues. "Some Shadowbanes discover bits and pieces of the truth due to the nature of our jobs. But we're trained to *want* to keep those secrets, regardless of our vows, for it spells our own undoing should they ever get out. We're trained to believe being Sinless is the highest anyone can aspire to, and Shadowbanes are promised the gift of Absolution upon retirement. Very few others are given that guarantee. Most humans, as you know, live and die mortal, lamenting that they were never deemed pure enough to become Sinless. So Shadowbanes have very little reason to question what we're taught or do anything that could risk our standing with the church and crown.

"Moreover, we have every reason to obey. Before our partial Absolution, the crown rewards newly appointed Shadowbanes by moving our closest relatives to the Sacred City of our patron prince. Outwardly, this is a blessing. The ultimate dream. Our families are kept safe and living in luxury, but there's a sinister side to that. If any Shadowbane steps out of line, rebels, or is caught for treason, they aren't the only ones who are punished. Our families are punished too."

I frown. "Does that mean your family is in danger?"

"My family is part of the rebellion, though not in the same way I am. They aren't even related to me by blood. They play their roles knowing it will likely end in their deaths."

A strange sensation washes over me. Of feeling too small in a much too large world. After I discovered the truth about the Holy Braziers, that a heart sacrifice is needed to light and sustain them, I felt like the only person who knew treasonous truths. The only person who'd seen the dark side of the Sinless. The only person who doubted the holy texts and everything we were taught to see as perfection. All along, there was so much more to it. And there are others who know the truth. Even darker and more shocking truths than the secrets I've carried the last two years.

It makes me dizzy just thinking about it.

"How did things get this way?" I ask, my voice as small as I feel. "If Vanna didn't create the Shades, then is Bastien's role a lie too? Did he not bless humanity?"

"He did not," Dominic says. "Bastien did not teach humankind Absolution; it was invented by the king and the church. Some rebels believe King Kaelum had good intentions five hundred years ago and sought to create a world without sin. Others believe he wanted to win a war by inventing everlasting flame, a source of fire strong enough to wipe out his enemies in a single night. It's unclear whether he succeeded in doing so, but his attempt likely resulted in the Holy Braziers that are used today. Whatever the case, his priests warped common astrotheurgy for purposes the gods never intended. Common astrotheurgy was always meant to balance all the energies of the gods in small magical processes. Yet Absolution does the opposite. It creates imbalance. It strips lunar energy from one's soul and fills the void left behind with more solar energy. Our bodies were never meant to contain such an overabundance of life. That's the real reason my kind are overcome with the thirst for blood."

"What do you mean?"

"When our lunar energy is removed and replaced with solar energy, we have to make up for that imbalance. In other words, to counteract the overabundance of life coursing through our bodies, we must engage with death."

My stomach churns. Yet another thing humankind is blamed for when it isn't our fault. The Sinless don't crave blood as proof that humans have yet to earn the gods' forgiveness; they crave it because they tampered with their souls. That must also explain why the dukes and royals consume hearts to light the braziers—they need more death and darkness to harness the energy of light and life. No wonder there's a difference between common astrotheurgy and solar astrotheurgy. One honored all the gods and resulted in small magics. The other takes energy from a single god to perform massive feats.

I heave a tired sigh. "Why didn't you tell us all of this from the start? Why did you let us believe you're one of them?"

He takes a step back. "Because I *am* one of them. I may not want to be, but the things I've done in the name of my mission, in the name of being a Shadowbane, have forever stained my hands with blood. I don't deserve your admiration or respect. Can you imagine how many other villages there have been like Dunway? How many towns I didn't save? Why do you think Shadowbanes are sent to serve two-week posts instead of permanently appointing a Shade hunter in each unprotected village? To give the illusion of safety while allowing fear to control the population. My only salvation is that I've never been ordered to make my Summoners stir a frenzy of Shades to punish a village. The church knows to appoint teams like Henderson's for tasks like that. But if I was given the order . . . what do you think my choice would be? Obey like I'm expected to and sacrifice a village, or defy orders and sacrifice my mission?"

My heart collapses to my feet, but his reasoning makes sense in a twisted way.

He must see the disgust in my eyes, for he turns around and stalks toward the fire. Crouching down, he turns the spits of fish to cook the other sides. "Another reason I didn't tell you right away," he says, "is because this knowledge is dangerous, for me and you. The less you know, the less you can be held guilty for, should assholes like Henderson get the better of us."

"I'm already guilty of treason," I say, my shoulders slumped as I too return to the fire. I don't add that I'm supposedly guilty of murder too, because that's still up for debate. It may be a fact that Henry is dead, but neither I nor Dominic knows how he died.

"Yes, but now you can use the intel you've gathered on me to save your own skin. Previous Summoners have done so—or at least intended to—and I didn't blame them. Not even as I cleaved their heads from their shoulders and buried their corpses."

I settle on the opposite side of the fire and meet his gaze with narrowed eyes. "Is that a threat?"

"That depends. Are you with me or against me? I meant what I said all along. I will free you from this fucking place. You once asked what was across the sea, and I said there were no Sinless and no Shadowbanes. You understand what that means now, right? Maybe the other continents are full of warmongering devils. We don't know for certain. But there sure as hell aren't any Shades."

His words strike me in the gut with the combined force of betrayal and hope. Another lie we've been led to believe—that the Holy Continent is the only place that's even remotely safe from Shades, thanks to the Sinless and braziers. Now I know that's a lie. It's the only place where Shades exist. And since Shades can't cross bodies of running water, then across the sea . . . lies safety.

"Continue to aid my mission for what remains of our six-month term," he says, "and I will see that you survive."

I rub my brow. "I've already agreed, haven't I? Knowing the truth doesn't change that."

Something relaxes in his expression.

"Why six months, though?" I ask. "You could have demanded a much longer term, and we wouldn't have had a choice in the matter."

"That's all the time I have left," he says. "I'm almost out of the king's blood, and getting more is no simple task. Rebels lost their lives to procure just the small amount I was given. Which means I have to make this count. The king only meets Shadowbanes in person during the solstice ritual—in other words, once every ten years—and only those who are nominated by their patron prince. You see why I've done everything I can to gain Leeran's favor. If I earn his nomination, I'll get the chance to stand before the king. And if I've collected all his Shades, I can make him mortal and end his life. Or I will die trying."

"You're willing to sacrifice your life?"

"I was born into this mission. It's all I've ever known. And yes, I see it as worth my life."

I don't know if the heaviness I suddenly feel is grief or respect. My feelings regarding this man have never been more complicated. He's more than what I thought he was. More righteous, but maybe more dangerous too. Before, he was easy to hate. Now I understand him but still hate parts of him. Particularly the part that has been able to turn a blind eye and obey orders just to get closer to his goal. A goal that could light the first spark of a rebellion against the lying Sinless, but will he even live to see it? Can I fully trust someone whose focus is so sharply homed in on his mission that everything else takes second place? He may have promised my survival, but he could never place his crew over that which he was born to do.

My gaze drifts to his hands, his knuckles scarred from countless battles with Shades. Then to the bandaged wound, stitched by my very fingers. Then down to his chest, marked with that dizzying array of lines and glyphs, so beautiful and repulsive now that I know what that ritual circle did. He knew the truth before he was a Shadowbane, which means he bore each cut aware of what it would do. I can't say whether that kind of dedication makes him deranged or . . . or really godsdamned attractive.

"It's getting late," he says, drawing my attention to his face. "Dark will fall soon. We'll have to stay quiet until morning."

Disappointment makes my shoulders sink, but I could probably use the silence. I have a lot to think about. A lot to process. I'll certainly have all the time I need, what with the nights being at their longest. In fact, tonight just might be . . .

"Oh," I say. "Is it winter solstice?"

He frowns, as if giving it some thought. "I believe so."

"It's my birthday, then."

His mouth curls into a sideways smile. "Happy birthday, Inana."

I return his grin, a truce after our tense conversation. Meanwhile, I bury down the racing of my heart, the traitorous pulse that quickened at the sound of my name spoken so tenderly on his lips.

CHAPTER THIRTY-ONE

INANA

It is the longest night of the godsdamned year, in more ways than one.

Dominic offers to keep watch so I can sleep, but I couldn't sleep if I tried. Once dark falls, a Shade decides to share our cave, creeping through the shadows wherever the fire's light fails to hit. It does nothing but watch us with its hollow eyes, tilting its featureless face as it huddles down in the farthest corner, wrapping its too-long arms around its spindly legs. I don my mask for good measure, which seems to intrigue it more, but at least it can't copy my face.

That's one thing that hasn't changed in my mind since learning the truth; Incarnates are still just as terrifying a threat as they were before. The only difference is now I know why Shades seek to Incarnate. They yearn to be whole again. To be alive. And now I understand what Dominic meant when he said Shades aren't interested in copying Shadowbanes. They're only interested in Incarnating off humans, those who are truly alive with their souls intact. The only time they're interested in Sinless or Shadowbanes is when they smell the blood of their original bodies. The Shades who wear Dominic's face didn't copy him; they *are* him. The wild Shades of his that he caught probably matched his appearance only after smelling his blood.

As soon as the Shade gets bored and finally leaves, something else consumes my focus: the heavy strain in the air of the cave, the tension taut like a bowstring, stretched between me and Dominic. It's pulled tighter by the silence punctuated by our breaths, the wordless stares we accidentally share throughout the endless night. I'm so aware of him, so conscious of every inch of space that separates us, and I can't tell whether I want it to grow or shrink.

No wonder people have gone mad during winter solstice.

I nearly weep with relief once the first blush of sun blooms over the horizon. I'm not amused to find the snowfall as heavy as it was yesterday, and Dominic doesn't look pleased either. Outside the mouth of the cave, he cuts a thin slice over his palm and lets a few drops of blood fall into the snow. His posture is tense, the quiet words he exchanges with his Shades unhopeful.

I can't see much of them aside from a ripple of three pools of shadow on the ground. Still, it's strange to think of them as pieces of him. No wonder their ethereal voices sometimes sound like his. How Lust's seductive teasing is a little too spot-on. How Pride's haughty remarks could almost be mistaken for Dominic's. They came from the lunar energy in his soul. Shadowed reflections of the gods who made him. Who made all of us.

Dominic returns inside the cave only to inform me he's going to collect firewood again. He doesn't give me a moment to reply before he's gone. Is he avoiding me? Desperate to escape before I hound him with a thousand more questions? He doesn't need to bother. I'm still trying to wrap my mind around what I learned last night.

I pull my cloak tight around me and emerge from the cave, greeting the quiet morning and immediately regretting it. The temperature is miserable and I'm quickly dusted in white. So desperately I want to stretch my legs, to walk, but there's no way in hell I'm taking a stroll in this. Which means another day stuck in a cave. Another day hardly able to walk more than twelve paces one way, then the other. Frustration ripples through me, a palpable current that moves through my body. I release my annoyance with a grumbling huff and whirl back toward the cave. But when I do, a subtle weight alights upon my shoulder. I pause, expecting to find a chunk of snow has fallen on me from one of the trees above the cave, but . . .

My breath catches.

It's a Shade.

The creature is barely visible beneath the sliver of shadow provided by the boughs overhead, but I can make out its tiny squirrel body, its round eyes, the crescent moon perched on its brow. It's the same little bastard that crawled up my dress a couple days ago.

With a yelp, I step back and brush my palm over my cloak, sending up a flurry of dislodged snowflakes. Another step back, to move out from beneath the shadow of the tree and fully into the light—

My heel slips, meeting air where I expected there to be more ground, and the next thing I know, my breath has been knocked from my lungs. I'm on my back in a bed of snow, blinking rapidly, my mind too shocked to understand what just happened. Then I see the edge of the cliff above me. I recall Dominic holding me back to keep me from stepping off it yesterday. It isn't a steep cliff, so I felt no qualms about standing so close today, but . . . fuck, turns out a five-foot fall still feels like shit when it takes you by surprise.

I move my arms and legs, finding them cold but not injured. At least there was plenty of snow to cushion my fall. Gingerly, I push up on my forearms.

That's when the troublesome little asshole reappears.

The squirrel leaps onto my chest, its form more visible now thanks to the shadow cast by the cliff wall. Its whiskers twitch, face tilted in what almost looks like concern.

"Are you following me?" I mutter as I sit straighter. It moves to my shoulder, and for a moment, the interaction is almost amusing.

Until I remember what this squirrel is.

A sliver of a Sinless's soul.

If that wasn't enough to sober me, the reminder of what it means when a Shade takes too much interest in someone does.

Shades only stalk the people whose faces they want to steal.

Whose bodies they want to consume so they can become Incarnate.

The squirrel may be cute now, but that can change in an instant.

I tug my hood over my head and brush off my shoulders, hoping I've dislodged the troublemaker.

I'm soaked and freezing by the time I make it back inside the cave. I skirted around the ledge and climbed up a much milder incline. It was the longer way around, but it beat scaling a wall with my frozen fingers. Dominic still isn't back, so I make haste in removing my icy clothing, partially to dry it but also to ensure the Shade hasn't hidden anywhere. I see no sign that it followed me inside, so my muscles relax.

Once my clothing is hanging from vines around the fire, I cast a glance at the mouth of the cave, wondering how much time I have before Dominic comes back. Now that I'm naked, I have the distinct urge to wash myself. I saw Dominic do it this morning before sunrise, using the old cup left behind in the cave. He warmed melted snow and a sprig of the rosemary he'd harvested from nearby, tipping the cup slightly to the side to keep its contents from running through the hole punctured in it, and washed his face. He offered me the next cup, and while I enjoyed rubbing the warm water over my cheeks, I yearned to do the same with other parts of me.

I nibble my bottom lip before I decide—fuck it. Might as well take the opportunity now. As quickly as I can, I huddle by the fire, repeating the same motions Dominic made earlier, warming fresh snow with a sprig of rosemary. Once it melts, I pour it over my arm. Then repeat for the other arm. It's a tedious process, but soon I get lost in the routine, in the scent of rosemary that fills my nostrils, in the momentary warmth that coats my skin. The heat from the fire keeps the water from freezing on my skin, and now only my legs are left. I melt the next cup of snow, stand by the fire, and pour the cup of hot liquid down my thigh—

A clattering sound has me whirling toward the mouth of the cave.

We both freeze. Dominic's eyes go wide, his armful of firewood rolling at his feet. His gaze sweeps over me as if he can't understand what he's seeing. Then his eyes lock on mine, and his jaw tightens. His throat bobs as he works to find his voice. "I'll . . . go back out."

He starts to turn around, and my first reaction is relief.

But his look of startled surprise lingers in my mind. Gods, it was priceless. The way he dropped his armload. The way his eyes drank me in. I'm torn somewhere between pride that I could inspire such a reaction from him and amusement. I purse my lips to keep from laughing. "You don't have to leave," I rush to say. "Just . . . stay there."

He halts, back facing me. His rib cage expands with the weight of his heavy breaths. "Why are you . . ."

The fact that he can't finish the question amuses me more. He's truly flustered. While I'd rather not relate my embarrassing tumble from the cliff, I am enjoying his torment. "Why am I naked?" I say, enunciating the last word. "I thought I could use a bath."

"You should have waited until I returned. So I could give you proper privacy."

I smirk at his back. "It's not like it's something you haven't seen before."

He angles his head to speak over his shoulder, but keeps his eyes averted from me. "I assure you, I did not let my attention linger on your body when I took care of you."

"Why not?" I stand taller, hand on my hip, emboldened by the sudden surge of power I feel. Power over *him,* this strong and deadly man. He might not be looking at me, but there's something thrilling about standing so freely, so bare, in his presence. "Were you uninterested?" I ask, infusing my tone with a taunting lilt. "Does my body not do it for you, Dominic?"

The view of his profile reveals his tight jaw, the slight baring of his teeth. His fingers curl into fists at his sides. His tone dips so low, it sends a shiver through me. "I think we both know that isn't true."

His eyes drift ever so slightly toward me, just a glance from his peripheral vision. I hold his gaze without falter, and he quickly looks away, lashes fluttering as if he's been granted a moment of sweet euphoria. The veins in his hands bulge from how tightly he squeezes them.

Heat blossoms in my core, sparked by his reaction to me. He's struggling. With want. With desire. I can read it in the stiff lines of his muscles. In the tic at the corner of his jaw. This energy isn't new, and it filled the cave to the brim all night. Filled us both in the wake of that strange dream we shared. Even before that, when we rode at the front of the wagon together and I touched his skin while he used layered words to describe the heat between us, the burn we'd feel if we gave in. Before that it was the kiss we almost shared on the roof. This has been growing for weeks.

The memories set me aflame, and my nipples pebble where the warmth of the fire, the heat of my desire, and the ice in the air collide.

"You don't have to be a gentleman," I say. "I'm letting you look now."

A soft sound escapes him. The ghost of a groan. Still, he refuses to turn around. "You should get some sleep now that it's daylight."

I take a tentative step closer. Then another, keeping close to the fire. "Are you going to keep me warm, then? Just like you did yesterday?"

A beat of silence. Then, "Are you saying you want me naked beside you?"

"For the sake of warmth."

Another silence, and this one stretches long. Then the sound of my breaths growing heavier fills the air, and I know he can hear it too. Just like I can hear his, see the way his back expands and contracts with the force of them. The crackle of the fire weaves through them, conducting a melody at the crossroads we've reached. Which way will he choose to waltz?

He could take my bait.

Turn around.

And give in to my taunting and stoke the embers already burning between us.

Or he can draw a firm line. Tell me how important his mission is. That this kind of desire is a distraction and we should never entertain it again.

The thought of him taking the latter road already leaves me cold. Empty.

It's been so long since I've felt desire like this, and I don't want to let it go. Because on the other side of this growing need are all the things I don't want to think about. The truths I've learned. The answers I've yet to uncover. The uncertain future.

I still don't know if I can trust Dominic. I don't know if the things I've learned about him make me hate him more or less.

But this isn't about trust or even hate or like.

It's about *want.*

It's about arousal.

And I want mine fucking sated.

"Let's just get this out of our systems," I say, giving him one more nudge.

Slowly, he turns, and a spark of victory shoots through me. Then the weight of his hungry stare lands on me, and I'm no longer certain I'm the one with the power here. He locks his gaze on mine, pointedly keeping his eyes from straying to the rest of my body, even as I stand taller, even as I step closer, give him more to look at. It's maddening how he withholds his attention, refuses to drink me in with that same sweeping look he gave me when he entered the cave.

Like a hunter stalking his prey, he draws a few steps closer. "Then you know what needs to be done."

I give him a questioning look.

"I told you that the next time you wanted my touch, you were going to beg for it." He steps closer until he's just a foot away. He still doesn't let his eyes move lower down my body. Instead, his dark irises burn into mine as his lips curl into a cruel smile. "So beg, sinner."

The way he says *sinner* isn't an insult, and I wonder if it ever was. In this moment it's a seduction, and the demand in his tone has me salivating. The tingling warmth between my legs burns hotter. He's testing me now. Turning my taunting back on me and seeing how far I'm willing to go. Are we just baiting each other? Playing? Seeing which of us will break first? One of us always does.

Today it won't be me.

I close an inch of space, brushing my tangled hair off my shoulders to ensure every inch of my skin is in full view. "Please," I say, my tone soft and sweet and so unlike how I normally speak to him.

He lifts his chin, looking down at me in a way that should make me feel small but only makes me want to rise higher. "More," he grunts out.

I step closer again, still holding his eyes, and this time I reach for him. My fingers fall on the buckles of his jerkin. One at a time, I undo them. He lets me slide the cold leather off his chest, then down his arms. "Please."

"More."

I reach for the hem of his shirt now, slowly lifting it from his waistband. My palms skate up his chest as I tug it higher. He aids my efforts at the last minute, and as his shirt comes over his head, I step in to close the rest of the space between us. He sucks in a breath as my breasts press against his torso, and as he drops his shirt to the ground, he finally lets himself look at me, at the press of our bodies. He bites his bottom lip as I pull back slightly, letting him watch the way my nipples graze the raised lines of his scarred chest.

He lifts a hand, and I expect him to touch me at last, but he drops it before he can make contact. Closing his eyes, he tilts his head back, his tenuous hold on his control betrayed only by the smile that flicks over his lips. "This doesn't feel like begging," he says, voice thick.

He's a fucking liar, but I like this game. So I hook my fingers beneath his waistband and tug him along with me, one step at a time, until we reach our makeshift bed. I lower myself onto my knees upon the pine-stuffed fabric. Then, keeping the rest of my body upright, I stare up at him as I undo his trousers. His breaths come hard and fast with every button I unfasten. When I finally pull his waistband down, his cock springs out fully erect.

I let myself admire it up close, its massive length, its impressive girth, before returning my eyes to his. "Please?" I part my lips and flick out my tongue, closing in toward the head of his cock.

He crouches down, bringing his face before mine as he holds my chin between his fingers. There's something feral in his gaze as he bares his teeth, displaying his pointed canines. "You think I'm going to let you put your mouth on my cock before I've even kissed you?"

I scoff. "I told you not to be a gentleman." My words come out breathless. "This isn't about romance. It's about fucking."

His eyes fall to my mouth, and he runs his thumb over my bottom lip. That wicked grin returns to his face. "If you want to fuck my cock, then you'll fuck my tongue too, however I want it."

I nearly collapse at those words. The need burning in my core only grows, my thighs slick with it. "Fine."

"Say it, love. Beg."

I part my lips again. Lean forward an inch. "Please, Dominic."

He crushes his mouth to mine.

CHAPTER THIRTY-TWO

INANA

His kiss is hard and insistent as he works his mouth against mine. This isn't like the kiss we shared in my dream, where touch was only an imagined thing and friction was nonexistent. This is rough. Wet. And so fucking good. His beard scrapes against my chin and his tongue moves against mine, tangling with it. I've never had a kiss that felt so much like sex before any of our other parts came into play, but that's exactly what this feels like. Fucking with our lips. Seducing each other with our sighs.

I fall back, guided down by Dominic until I'm lying on the bed. Dominic's mouth leaves mine to drag kisses across my jaw, then down my neck. His hands explore me too, roving down my shoulders, my arms. Finally, one of his rough palms cups my breast, and I lean into it. He circles my nipple with his thumb, sending shock waves of pleasure through me. His mouth moves from my collarbone down to my other breast. He kisses all around it, teasing me. Then he looks up, eyes locked on mine, and lowers his tongue to my nipple without fully touching it, just like in my dream.

"How often have you dreamed of this, sinner?" he says, his breath caressing my skin.

"Not as much as you think, asshole," I say, and arch my back, lifting my chest until he has no other choice but to taste me. He grins as he does, then swirls his tongue over my hardened peak. I whine, my cries pitching higher as he fully takes my nipple into his mouth and sucks. My apex burns hotter, and I rock my hips, hooking a leg around him to lower him farther down.

His cock grazes the inside of my thigh but he refuses to lower himself any closer. Instead, he glides a hand between us, over my stomach, down my side, and around the curve of my ass. "You're so wet I can feel it all the way down here," he says, slicking his fingers through the moisture between my inner thigh and ass crease.

I groan, and he silences it with another kiss. As he pulls away, our gazes lock, and I'm startled by the tender look in his eyes. There's still a dark and heavy want in his expression, but there's a gentleness too. One that has my heart thudding faster. Deeper. My legs spreading wider.

He leans in to kiss me again, slower, sweeter, and his hand leaves my ass to trail down my outer thigh, then to my knee, then up the inside of my leg. He's finally close to where I want him to be, but there's something about the slow caress of his mouth I can't shake. The deepening emotions flooding my heart.

I pull back from the kiss, and his hand freezes on my thigh. "Blindfold me," I say before I can reconsider.

He frowns down at me, and I can't handle that expression. Such concern. Such care.

"Isn't that part of your vows?" I ask, my voice trembling.

"You've already seen my scar. I don't have to hide it from you."

"Do it anyway," I say. "I want you to."

What I really want is to smother this terrifying tenderness that feels inseparable from the lust and need burning inside me. I don't know which one of us is responsible for this feeling, and I don't want to know. I don't want this to be special. I want him to fuck me the way he's fucked everyone else who came before. This can't be anything more than that, and he knows it. I know it. I may understand him better than before, and I may want him more than I've ever wanted anyone, but that doesn't change what we are. He's a Shadowbane on a dangerous path, one that will likely end in his death. I'm an outlaw with her heart fixed on freedom.

Now that I know the other lands aren't damned by Shades like we're led to believe, my hope for a future is brighter than ever. I have no place in whatever revolution he's part of. I believe in his cause, but I'm a survivor. I could never risk my life the way he does, for a war that feels too daunting to fight. For a goal I might not live to see fulfilled.

Our relationship ends in less than six months.

This can't be anything more than sex.

His eyes volley between mine, and I fear I've spoiled the moment. That I've lost him, lost this delicious euphoria we were only starting to stir.

Then his crooked smirk returns. "What do you say to get what you want?"

My trepidation melts away, crashing beneath a tidal wave of seduction. "Please."

He pulls back, but there's a tangible pressure that lingers, curving around my wrists and pulling them overhead. I watch his impressive backside as he strolls toward the fire, perplexed by what's holding me down, when it dawns on me.

His Shades.

I can't see them, but I can feel their phantom touch, as solid as it was the first time they held me down in the hall outside the Wretched Lair. A similar shock courses through me now, but it's smoothed by my own intrigue. These shadows aren't random monsters he collected and subdued like I first thought. They're . . . pieces of his soul. They are separated yet still tethered. He can feel what they feel, direct them, control them. They are, by extension . . . him.

Dominic returns with one of my stockings that I'd hung to dry.

The Shades release me, and he pulls me to sitting, then crouches behind me. "You sure you want to do this?" he asks, draping the stocking over my eyes but not yet tying it behind my head.

"Yes, but . . . one question first." A blush heats my cheeks as I debate the best way to word my query. "Is . . . is Sloth going to . . . you know? I mean, I know he's *you,* but I can't think of him as anything other than a dog."

Dominic brings his lips to my neck, a deep chuckle rumbling in his throat. He grazes my flesh with his teeth. "No, love, Sloth will not be joining us. He isn't interested in these kinds of activities."

I relax at that, and he drags his tongue up my neck now too. Not being able to see him through the stocking that covers my eyes adds a layer of curiosity. Danger. Pleasure.

"What about the others?" he whispers as he finally ties the stocking behind my head. "They don't normally join in things like this, but . . . I can't fucking help it when I'm around you. I want to be around you. They are me, so they want to be around you too. Sometimes I can't tell whether it's me or their nature as Shades that wants you more. It drives me fucking mad."

A thrill moves through me, pooling between my legs. Then a light and teasing touch finds my knee, caressing up my thigh like Dominic did before I stopped him with my request to be blindfolded. Yet this touch is softer than his hand was. It's one of his Shades.

"Do you want me to stop?" His voice is hard and gravelly in my ear. "I can make them stop, but . . . fuck. I just want to touch you everywhere. With every hand I have."

This should be strange. It *is* strange. And yet . . .

"Don't stop," I say with a gasp.

Dominic tilts my head back, kissing me deep. Then I feel him lay me back down and move over me like he was before. This time, however, those *other* touches join too, pinning my wrists and cupping my breasts. With my eyes covered, I'm hyperaware of every touch, of the distinct difference between Dominic's firm flesh and his shadows. He gently parts my knees and settles between my thighs. His hand trails down my belly again, then sinks down, down, until his fingers find my folds. He swirls them through my slick arousal, giving me the first sense of the friction I've been longing for ever since I was teased with it in my dream.

I roll my hips against his touch, awaiting the firm press of his hips over mine, for the length of his cock to nudge my entrance, but that isn't what happens. Instead, he shifts lower, lower, dragging kisses down the front of me, over my abdomen, then across my inner thigh. I can't understand this torturous preamble until he kisses toward my center and his lips reach my outer folds.

Panic rushes through me as I realize what he's about to do. No one has ever kissed me . . . down there. I was more than happy to put my mouth on him, had he let me, but him doing the same to me feels different. Self-consciousness has me squeezing my thighs, tightening them around his shoulders.

"Do you not like this?" he asks, pausing before he can lower his mouth.

"I . . . I don't know," I breathe, two instincts at war within me. One side wants to urge him away. The other yearns to lift my hips, spread myself wider, and push that mouth right over my center. "It's just . . . I'm not one of the perfumed courtesans you're probably used to."

Another chuckle rumbles through him. "Did you not bathe just for me?"

"That was hardly a bath."

"Do you think I fucking care?" The darkness in his tone has my legs weakening, my core heating, and when he gently presses a palm on the inside of my thigh, I fully yield. "Last chance, love. Do you want me to stop?"

"No."

The first brush of his tongue has me crying out. The second has my eyes rolling to the back of my head. He drags his tongue up the center of me, then presses it over my clit. The euphoria that courses through me as he swirls his tongue over it is better than anything I've ever felt, and it grows tenfold as his shadows glide over my nipples, circling them in tandem with Dominic's tongue. I feel like my entire being will be torn apart by the force of my pleasure, and my whimpers turn to moans.

Dominic's hand joins his mouth, stroking my center until one finger dips ever so slightly into my slick core. I buck my hips, begging him to enter me deeper. He obeys my wordless command, thrusting his finger all the way in, then out. In then out. His tongue continues to work my clit, and a phantom mouth closes over my breast, suckling with the softest, most delectable pressure.

Fuck, this is too much.

And somehow not enough.

I want him inside me, filling me to the brim. I want him slamming into me with his full force.

As if he can read my yearnings, he satisfies my want by adding a second finger.

Gods, it's so good.

I struggle against the shadow hands pressing my wrists, and they let up, allowing my fingers to fall to Dominic's head. I weave my hands through his hair, pressing his face more firmly against me as my back arches off the ground. I'm losing control, unraveling in a way I never have before. His tongue works faster, dancing with the rocking of my hips. His fingers pump harder, curving to reach deep inside me.

One phantom hand cups my breast, while another joins Dominic between my thighs.

"Are you going to come for me, love?" Dominic asks, and two other voices join with his, but it's all the same. All *him.* All united in the coaxing of my pleasure.

My orgasm rises from deep within, surging with every thrust of Dominic's fingers, every flick of his tongue, every tightening grip of his shadows.

"You taste so fucking good," he says against my clit.

I fall over the edge, my climax coursing through me in mind-obliterating waves. Even if I weren't blindfolded, I think I'd see nothing but stars. I cry out with the undulating swells of pleasure, and Dominic guides me over every crest, shifting his momentum, his motions, until the last vestiges of my orgasm pulse around his fingers.

I'm a limp, spent puddle of satisfaction, mute in the wake of my moans. Now there's nothing but our panting breaths.

"Fuck," Dominic says, his body taut with restraint. "Inana, I have to come."

I'm shocked to hear he was brought so close just by pleasuring me. "Then come," I say, voice weak. I reach between us, fisting my hand around his length. I'm still quivering from my orgasm, yet hungry for more. I want him to fill me, to thrust inside me. But when I try to angle his cock toward my center, he stalls my hand.

"Not this time, love," he says. If he's trying to torment me and leave me aching for more to ensure there *is* a next time, I daresay it's working. I moan, half in frustration, half in appreciation of his girth. Gods, he's huge. I pump my hand up and down his shaft and his fingers join mine. He jerks suddenly, then again, and hot liquid spurts over my inner thigh. I gasp in surprise and perhaps a touch of pride at having made him come so fast. His hand guides my pace, emptying him completely until he goes still.

"I'm sorry," he says, slicking his hand through the mess he just made on me. "I should have asked before I came on you like that."

"No," I pant out. "I liked it. Besides, I told you not to be a gentleman."

I reach for the blindfold and shove it away from my eyes. There's a bashful grin on his face as he stares down at me. I mirror his expression, then drink in the sight of his sweat-slicked skin, his wet, swollen lips, his empty yet still-imposing cock. He takes my stocking the rest of the way off my head, then runs it over my thigh. A corner of his lips lifts as his gaze meets mine. "I'll wash this for you."

"What did I just say about being a gentleman?"

His expression turns serious. "This isn't being a gentleman," he says as he finishes cleaning me up. "This is what you deserve."

I don't know what to say to that, especially when I see that tender spark in his eyes again. So I say nothing and fall back on the bed, catching my breath. I say nothing as he lies beside me and covers us in my cloak.

"Sleep while you can," he says, folding his naked body around mine. "I'll keep watch and keep you warm. Since you begged so fucking nicely." He brings his lips to my earlobe, nipping it before settling back down.

Still, I say nothing as I let myself melt against him. As I envelop myself in his warmth. Knowing that if I let myself speak, I might accidentally admit that I'm ever so slowly—ever so certainly—falling for a man with a death wish.

CHAPTER THIRTY-THREE

Dominic

I don't expect to fall asleep. But I know I'm sleeping because I'm dreaming. And even though the dream is clearly a nightmare, it isn't mine.

It's hers.

The woman asleep in my arms.

My heart stutters as I see Inana's face etched in terror. She's in a rustic cell. Daylight filters in through the barred windows, while a lantern hung from the rafters illuminates the space around her. Her wrists are bound with rope and tied to iron bars affixed to the wall. Seeing her like that makes me want to scream. To race to her rescue. This time I'm not experiencing this dream through her eyes, but as a helpless spectator instead. I can't will my body to move.

A man steps into the light, blocking my view of Inana, and understanding dawns. I know what this nightmare represents.

This is the day Inana nearly lost her heart to a Sinless duke.

This man is that asshole, Henry Berkham.

He's dressed in a fine suit of white and gold, with a red cape affixed to his lapels. I can't see his face from where I stand in the corner of the cell, but my viewpoint shifts slightly to the side so that Henry is no longer blocking Inana. Her expression warps with a relief so sweet it makes my heart feel like it will split in two. For I know that relief won't last long. I know what happens next.

I try to scream, try to shake myself out of this nightmare to spare her from experiencing the terror of this day. But no matter how I try to fight free from my position, no matter how I try to open my mouth and scream, nothing works.

And that's when I stop fighting.

That's when I realize . . .

Maybe I should stay quiet and watch. This is all in the past, and I can't save Inana from this nightmare anyway. So why don't I try to glean what I can from this? She may not remember how this interaction ended, but what if her subconscious does? What if the answer to Henry Berkham's death is here, in this dream?

I've never cared about his death, and I still don't. But the mystery of his demise revolves around Inana. Knowing the truth might not help me protect her any better than I already can, but if she isn't responsible for killing him, then we'll have nothing to worry about if any other Shadowbanes seek Inana's bounty like Henderson did.

And if she *is* responsible for Henry's death . . .

Then I'll know everything I need to know to keep her crimes—and anyone who seeks to uncover them—buried.

My rage simmers into patience, and I watch the dream unfold with deadly calm. The newly appointed duke steps in close and unsheathes a knife. Inana's relief melts off her face, twisting into confusion, then to blank shock.

Henry slices open the front of her bodice, baring the center of her chest. Then he presses the tip of his blade to Inana's sternum, but drops the knife before he can make the first cut. With trembling hands, he removes his gloves and closes his fingers tighter around the hilt. That's when Inana notices his wedding ring. Her shock turns to fury, and my heart wells with pride when I see her lips pull back from her teeth. She spits words of vitriol, raging at him for what he's trying to do to her. For covering his shame with murder.

"Yes, I'm ashamed of you," Henry says, covering her shouts with his palm. I've never wanted to pummel someone to death with my bare fists so badly. "I'm ashamed I ever loved a sinner like you. But your sacrifice will save Dunway. This has to happen. I must . . ." For a single second he truly seems to struggle with the moral implications of what he seeks to do. "I must consume a human heart. It's the only way I can light the brazier. The only way I can *keep* it lit. And the first sacrifice must be you. You're the reason Shades claw at doors at night. You're the sinner who draws them here."

Inana scoffs against his hand. "With my sewing?"

"With your storytelling," he says, bringing his face close to hers.

Her eyes turn down at the corners, brimming with agony. "Those stories were for you. Only you."

Henry's tone darkens. "Don't lie to me. I saw you. I saw you talking to them. Whispering tales to things that moved in the dark. You were never afraid of them. You were always a sinner."

Inana's throat bobs, and she sags against the wall, defeated by his words. They must be true, then. I don't recall her mentioning that part when I overheard her story, but I can't blame her. How could I blame my beautiful little sinner for being exactly who she was always meant to be? An artist. A storyteller.

Henry tightens his jaw, recovering from his moment of hesitation. He presses his forearm over her shoulder, pinning her in place. Slowly, he drags the knife across her skin, an inch at a time. I grind my teeth at the sight of the blood running down her chest and soaking her bodice. She struggles against his hold, but it's no use. He has a Sinless's immortal strength now.

Yet Inana isn't fully defeated.

Her lashes flutter from the pain, but she gives him a dark smile. "You know what I did today, Henry?"

"Stop speaking or I'll slit your mouth open."

"I went to the market," she says, unfazed. "I went to the market and saw . . . now, you won't believe this . . . a teeny-tiny statue of a cock. Here's the best part: It had your name on it—"

He halts his cut and slams his palm over her mouth, smothering her words.

That's when I see movement stirring at the corners of the cell,

Shades coalescing in pools of shadow. Despite the daylight streaming through the barred windows of the cell, there is plenty of darkness, between that and the lantern light.

Inana begins to hum against Henry's hand, and the Shades grow even more interested, some standing at their full height and leaning as close to the lantern light as they dare. Henry growls in his anger but resumes his cut, muttering to drown out the sound of her song.

"Work quickly," he says to himself, "but carefully. Thirty degrees from horizon to Sylas. Shit, I should have carved the circle first. I'll carve it last. Thirty degrees from horizon to Sylas. Cut at ninety and one-eighty. Motion at seventy . . ."

My blood goes cold as his meaning dawns on me. When Inana told this story in the clearing, she said Henry began praying when she was humming, but her assumption was wrong. Because of course she couldn't have made sense of his muttered words. Only someone like me could know.

He isn't uttering nonsense; he's verbally rehearsing an astrotheurgical diagram. One that's different from the circle I use for light and flame. This one revolves around Sylas, God of Harvest.

Because . . .

He's harvesting her heart.

He isn't merely cutting it from her chest.

He's removing it while it's still beating.

My stomach churns. I may know much about the secrets of the Sinless, but there are many things I've yet to uncover. Not even the rebels who trained me, fed me secrets from as far back as I can remember, know all that is kept by the church and crown. This must be something only the dukes and royals know—that their heart sacrifices are taken using astrotheurgy. No one ever sees the bodies of the sacrifices once the ritual is complete. The hearts belong to outlaws and criminals, people without rights. People who can be discarded without a care, without honoring their families by sending a body back for burial.

I'm so disgusted I can hardly see straight, but this nightmare isn't over.

I force my gaze away from Henry's careful cut, to Inana's bound wrists. I recall what she said she did next, and I catch sight of the sewing needle fraying at the ropes until her arm swings down, freed from its bonds. Henry pulls back, startled by the sudden movement. Inana flicks her fingers toward her cuff, tugging a second needle free and slashing out at the duke. He winces, slapping a hand over the slice on his neck, but no sooner than he has removed his palm, the cut has sealed.

"Of all the idiotic things you could do," he says with a dark chuckle. "I can't be hurt by you. I can't be killed."

I hold my breath, even though I know I'm dreaming. Inana never finished her story after this part. She was interrupted by me and the Shades that surrounded the clearing.

This . . . what's happening now . . . is new.

I'm so entranced, I almost miss the Shades that have slithered through the cracks in the walls, coalescing in the corners. There are over a dozen now, and their hollow eyes are fixed on Inana and Henry. I can almost feel their hunger. Their fascination. A trio slinks across the faintest strips of shadow until they're pressed between the wall and the edge of the lantern light that encases Inana and the duke.

Henry shifts his grip on his knife, his hand now at his side. "Useless, Inana. Your attempts to escape me are utterly useless. *You* are useless."

She continues to hum, but her lips wobble and tears stream from the corners of her eyes.

"You're a sinner. A criminal. Do you know what I am? Do you know I am your better now?" His voice rises to a shout, and the Shades around the cell vibrate with the growing intensity of it. "I am a fucking duke. And *you*. Will. Submit. To. Me." He lunges for her, and her mouth opens in a heaving breath, her song cut short. It takes me several seconds to understand what has happened.

Then my viewpoint shifts to the side. Then closer. Closer. Another step closer. A crimson stain blooms over Inana's abdomen, the hilt of the knife protruding from her bodice.

Henry pulls out the blade and stares at the wound with wide eyes. He whirls around, running a hand through his hair. "I fucked up," he mutters, a frenzied look in his eyes. "I fucked up. I fucked up. Hurry. I need to hurry."

He whirls back toward Inana, knife raised toward her chest again, but she swings her hand toward him, slicing his cheek with her needle, once, twice, then pierces it through the side of his throat. He staggers back. The slices on his cheek are already healing, but blood seeps beneath the needle, a vein nicked open and unable to close around the foreign object.

The Shades hiss and clamor at the sight of the blood, clustering closer within that sliver of shadow.

Henry doesn't notice them. Doesn't notice anything but the needle he pulls from his neck as he steps to the side, his heel planted directly on the divide between shadow and light. Bridging it.

The Shades surge forward.

They slither up his ankle, beneath the leg of his trousers. He kicks out, whirling around and flailing his arm as bulges appear beneath his white-and-gold jacket. His hand strikes the lantern, sending it rocking side to side.

The light swivels across the room from the momentum of the lantern, casting Henry in shadow, then light. Shadow then light.

His bleeding neck falls under a faint beat of darkness.

The Shades funnel out from beneath his collar and into that still-open wound. Barely a pinprick, but they claw at it, opening it wider, slithering into that nicked vein one at a time.

I count the number of Shades that enter his flesh.

One.

Two.

Three.

My heart races. I know what's happening. I know what this means.

Four.

Five.

Six.

Seven.

Henry doubles over, screaming.

My eyes meet Inana's over his bent-over form. Her rage seeps into me. Or maybe it's my rage.

One thing is clear.

She wants Henry Berkham to die.

I want him to die.

Death. Vengeance. It's all I can think about. All I can taste.

It thrums through everything I am, everything I ever was.

And with his seven cut-away Shades back inside his body, Henry is mortal once more.

The man straightens and charges for Inana.

The light continues to sway.

Left.

Right.

Left.

Right.

I step along a path of shadow, my eyes locked on Inana's. Her wrath is mine and mine is hers.

Right.

Left.

I'm just behind Henry now, and all I can think is how I want to reach inside his body and tear out his heart. Claw it from between his ribs. Rip it to shreds.

Kill him.

I'm going to kill him.

I stretch out my hand, impossibly long in the narrow sliver of shadow. My fingers meet his back, and he freezes. Stiffening.

I glance at my hand.

My fingertips are made of shadow.

I suck in a breath and sit upright, a sound tearing through my throat that might have been a scream.

Or a hiss.

Or laughter.

What the fuck was that?

Visions from the nightmare flash in my mind's eye, vibrant at first but fading with every breath I catch. The end of the dream lingers the longest. Haunting me.

I blink several times to clear my eyes, my mind, my thoughts. The cave takes shape around me, replacing the jail cell. My eyes fall on the roaring fire, the fading daylight streaming through the mouth of the cave. Then Inana.

Gods, Inana.

She's still tucked in my arms, facing me, her face twisted in agony. Tears stream down her cheeks.

I lightly shake her shoulders, trying to snap her out of the nightmare. I call her name, shake her again, but she only whimpers.

I raise my voice to a shout. "Inana!"

Her eyes fly open, and her body goes still. For a few moments, she just lies there, staring up at me with wide eyes while she heaves sharp, strangled breaths. I pull her closer, staring down at this fierce and beautiful woman. How could I have let her experience that nightmare? Why didn't I fight harder to free myself—and her—from it earlier? Staying in that dream was useless. I learned nothing helpful, only confirmed what I already suspected: Henry Berkham was made mortal when his Shades entered his body, drawn by the blood that seeped from the wound Inana inflicted.

That's no surprise. Henry would have undergone his Absolution ritual after he arrived in Dunway, performed by the priests who escorted him there. Which means his cut-away Shades would have lingered nearby. The ritual only sends them away from their original body to the nearest, darkest sources of shadow. Which is why, in unprotected villages without silver walls, newly appointed dukes must light their braziers as soon as possible, to push their Shades even farther away and keep them from getting close enough to reverse the Absolution. The dukes may not know that's the reason, but it is behind the instructions they receive upon accepting their appointment. Regardless, that's how his Shades found him so quickly once they smelled his blood.

Yet I still don't know how Henry died. Or how much of the nightmare I can take as fact.

In the dream, Inana was stabbed in the abdomen, but she bears no scar. I would know. I worshipped every inch of her body this morning.

She sniffles, and I push away all thoughts but those of her. I take in her ruddy cheeks streaked with tears, then lift a fingertip, gently wiping away the trail of moisture.

Her lips quiver and pull into a sad smile. "Sorry," she whispers. "I . . . I don't know why I'm crying."

"You had a nightmare," I say, wiping another tear.

She shakes her head. "I don't remember it."

"I'm glad." I don't elaborate, don't tell her that I was there. That I remember it. That I wouldn't wish that memory on anyone. No wonder she forgot what happened that day. The trauma must be unbearable.

Her breathing evens out and she relaxes in my arms. My heart constricts, somehow soft and aching at the same time. How have I lived six years without feeling this range of emotion? Without the pleasure and pain that pierces my chest? How will I live without it again, after she's gone, safe across the sea? How can I risk her life for the duration of our agreement? How can I focus on anything *but* her?

She reaches a hand toward my face and caresses my cheek. That's when I realize I'm crying too. Or I was. What the hell is happening to me? Hot moisture drips down my face in trails I haven't felt in even longer than six years. Maybe it's from the nightmare. Maybe it's because of her.

Her thumb brushes a tear away, then moves across the line of my jaw. Then to my mouth. She lifts her head, and I lower mine to meet her lips, a taste of salt between us. Our kiss starts as a tender thing, then blooms into something more urgent. It heats my blood until I'm on fire, ready to take her in every way, ready to let her take me, mold me, shape me—

"*I smell it.*" Sloth's voice has us both going still. I reluctantly pull back from Inana and find Sloth huddled nearby in the shadows growing at the farthest corners of the cave. Daylight is waning, which means I need to get a hold of my fucking senses.

"You smell what?" I ask.

Sloth rises in a canine stretch. "*Your blood. The others are close.*"

CHAPTER THIRTY-FOUR

INANA

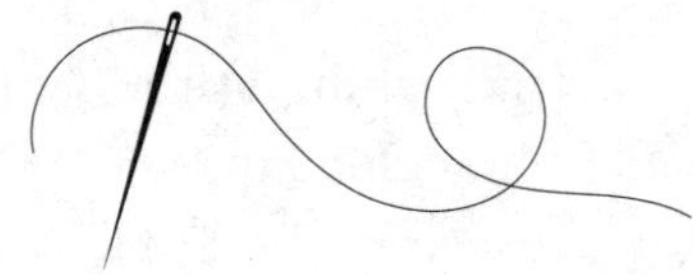

"Bite me," I say in a rush, before my nerves can falter. We stand on the snowy bank beside the rushing river. The opposite shore is in sight, across the narrowest and gentlest expanse we could find close by. Yet it isn't near enough. The water is still too treacherous to swim across.

Dominic's eyes darken, but he says nothing in reply.

"Just . . . just do it. It's fine. What if it's the only way?" Anxiety claws at my chest. As much as I've enjoyed . . . certain benefits from being stranded with Dominic, I'm eager to get back to the others. To ensure they're safe.

The sky is darkening toward evening, and this is the first break in snowfall we've seen. Yet even though Sloth insists he briefly sensed Dominic's blood coming from somewhere nearby, we still haven't seen any sign of the others. Dominic cut his palm and spilled his blood in the snow to aid Calvin's efforts in finding us, but that was at least half an hour ago. It doesn't help that we can't see the road from here.

Dominic heaves a sigh. "I said it would be a last resort. We haven't reached that level of desperation."

I roll my eyes. "I said it's fine. Besides, this is the perfect tree." I point at the old tree not far down the river. It's mossy and weathered, tall but not too thick, with hardly any lower branches left on it. And it looks tall enough to fall straight across the river, and then some. "If we're going to make our own bridge, this is how, right? What if the river is interfering with your captured Shades' senses? What if crossing will help us find them?"

He glances from the river to the tree, then back to me. His expression takes on a tormented edge. "I don't drink fresh blood if I can help it. It . . . it's how I separate myself from them."

"That's why you drink from vials? Does that mean you've never tasted fresh blood?"

"I wouldn't say never," he says, tone laced with regret. "The first thing we feel after regaining consciousness following the Absolution ritual is an intense thirst. The priests who perform the ritual sacrifice an acolyte, locking them in a room with us until we feed. The acolytes don't survive."

My heart aches, both for him and for all those sacrificed acolytes. Gods, how many humans have been sacrificed for the Sinless, between Absolution, lighting the braziers, and general feeding? How many Sinless even are there? I never realized quite how many there were until I lived in Nalheim, where Sinless lords and ladies could be seen on almost every street. There must be . . . thousands across the continent. Which means there are seven times that number of Shades, minus the ones that have been killed after becoming Incarnate.

Just when I'd gotten a respite from my swirling, nagging thoughts and questions, my anger sparks all over again.

But none of my anger is at Dominic.

I step closer to him and place one hand on his chest, over the cold leather of his jerkin. "I'm not offering myself as a sacrifice. I'm giving you my blood as your Summoner."

His breath hitches and he fists his hands at his sides as if to keep from reaching for me. "You don't understand. Fresh blood . . . It's different. And since it's been so long since I've fed, I could lose control, especially if it's coming from you."

"*Most definitely if it's you,*" Lust says. It isn't quite dark enough to see him clearly, but I feel a wispy touch running through my hair. "*And I like losing control.*"

Another caress, this one against my cheek. It seems his Shades are rebelling against Dominic's determination not to give in and touch me. "*It would be a godsdamned honor if you let me taste you,*" comes Pride's voice.

"*I'll be a good boy.*" This voice is far more innocent than the others, and it comes with a bump against my leg. I pat Sloth's head with my free hand.

"Will you three give her some space?" Dominic chastises. His Shades retreat, though I can feel their reluctance to obey in their lingering touches. "It's bad enough with just me fiending for her."

"Who said it was bad?" I step in closer, holding his gaze. His eyes flick down to my throat, and I can almost feel the thirst radiating through him, written in the arch of his upper lip, the slight baring of his canines. This is the first time I've considered how hard it might be for him to hold off his thirst for days on end. From what I've gleaned, he doesn't feel the need to feed as often as a true Sinless, but still.

A groan rumbles in his chest.

That's when I reach for his hip and unsheathe his dagger. "Bite me," I say, bringing the blade under his chin, "and if you drink too much, I'll stab you in the fucking face."

He blinks a few times, the hunger draining from his eyes and shifting to amusement. With a slow exhale, his posture relaxes. "Fine. Just not in the face."

I give him a coy smile. "Very well. I'm starting to like it, after all."

"Only now?"

"It has its merits. But this . . ." I sweep the blade down his neck, then lay the flat of it across his throat. He doesn't so much as flinch. "I could live without you talking for a day or two. So behave, all right?"

His answering smile is so warm, so godsdamned beautiful, it makes my breath catch. "All right. Let me prepare the tree first."

We proceed to the tree and I watch as Dominic gets to work. First he takes his second knife and slices off the outer bark for a smoother surface, then he begins to carve. His moves are precise, his cuts even. I'm surprised by how efficiently he works, drawing something so complex. Once it's finished, he turns to me and sheathes his knife. "Are you sure?"

"I'm sure," I say, though my words come out a little breathless. If someone had told me I'd one day offer my blood willingly to a Shadowbane, I'd never have believed them. But a lot has happened that I never would have predicted. The most pleasant of these surprises being Dominic. My feelings for him are more complicated than ever, but my attraction to him is undeniable. My respect for him is strong. And I do know one thing. "I trust you not to hurt me."

"Keep your trust in that blade instead," he says, nodding at the dagger still clenched in my hand. He motions me closer. "Where do you want it?"

"Oh," I say, the blood leaving my face. I shudder, remembering how woozy I got from watching Calvin and Dom with their vials. "Not anywhere sensitive, and not over a vein."

"Blood flows easier from the places you consider sensitive, and faster from a vein. It would be over sooner that way."

"Yeah, that's not happening."

He chuckles at my unease. "I suppose a tougher area would force me to drink slowly. It's up to you."

I can't keep the look of disgust off my face as I extend my arm and pull back my sleeve. Dominic slowly takes my hand and presses his lips over my knuckles, all while holding my gaze. Then he turns my hand over and kisses my palm, then my wrist. It's sweet, but now my panic is growing.

He trails kisses up my inner forearm.

"The other side," I rush to say, shifting so my outer forearm is toward his lips.

His mouth curls in a wicked smile. "Very well. Get your blade ready."

My heart races, my hand trembling as I press it to his throat. For all my earlier bravado, my nerves are fraying now. Just when I think I might give in to my panic completely, a familiar weight bumps against my leg again, steadying me. Then a light hand on my shoulder, bracing me. Another smoothing my hair, calming me. My lungs relax as Dominic's shadows wrap around me in exactly the way I need. My anxiety shifts into anticipation. I feel just as bold yet vulnerable as I did when I stood naked for him in the cave, daring him to look at me, quivering for his touch.

He holds my eyes again as he presses one more kiss to my outer forearm. He pauses, a question in his eyes, and I nod.

I don't let myself look away as he opens his mouth and presses his teeth against my skin. I see it before I feel it, the tips of his canines sinking into my flesh. Then there's the sting, a sharp pressure that has my breaths shortening.

"*You're doing so good,*" Lust whispers.

"*That's my fucking girl,*" Pride says.

A flutter of euphoria soars through me, pooling low in my belly. Dominic extracts his canines, then presses his mouth over the wound. Another sense of pressure, but this time it's from the mild suction of his mouth as he pulls blood from the lesion. He swallows once. Then another pull, another swallow.

Just as fear begins to darken the edges of my mind, he breaks away, lips glazed with my blood. With slow, gentle movements, he brushes his thumb over my puncture wounds, collecting a dab of my blood. His Shades remain close to me as he releases my arm and turns toward the tree, where he smears my blood over one of the lines of the diagram. The ritual circle sparks with light, but Dominic returns to me at once, cutting open his palm and painting my wound with his blood. His Shades whisper more comforting words, offer more tender touches, until the sting eases. The punctures close until there's nothing but smooth flesh smeared with blood.

Dominic kisses my knuckles again. "Are you all right?"

His Shades seem to know exactly when I've regained enough of my calm to allow me some space again. It takes me a few breaths to find my voice. "Yes. That was . . . fine." Fine might not be the best word for it. It was terrifying. Fascinating. And, based on the heat at the apex of my thighs, strangely erotic. I sure as hell am not telling him that.

He folds my hand in his and guides me a few steps away from the tree. The light is contained to the width of the diagram, and unlike the pillar on the bridge, it doesn't extend in height. Instead, it gently glows over the bark. The scent of charred wood fills my nostrils, and soon the tree begins to creak. When the diagram burns through enough to split the wood and send the tree tipping, we step back again. I squeeze my fingers tight around Dominic's as the tree falls cleanly across the river to the other side.

My mouth falls open. "It worked. It actually worked."

He winks. "Did you doubt me?"

Crossing the fallen tree is another ordeal all its own. I've never had anxiety around bridges, but that was before one collapsed out from under me and I got to be keenly acquainted with the terrifying river that now rushes beneath my too-narrow walkway. Dominic doesn't share my fears, even going so far as to walk backward across the tree so he can hold my hands and guide me along.

"You're showing off," I say, voice uneven.

"You aren't giving yourself enough credit," he says. "You're walking across a half-rotted tree that we just knocked down and is admittedly only precariously positioned on the other bank. Anyone would find this challenging."

"Anyone but you," I mutter.

"Anyone but me." Another wink.

Bastard. We're defying death and he's . . . flirting with me?

Once we reach the other side, I race for the first wide pine I see, collapsing to the ground beneath its shelter of boughs. "I am never doing that again."

Dominic crouches before me, rubbing my shoulder while a devilish smirk curls his lips. "You did great."

After a few steadying breaths, my nerves calm down, and he helps me rise to my feet. I meet his eyes, aware of how close we are. His hand remains on my shoulder while the other comes up to brush my cheek. Everything inside me yearns to lean into him, to claim his lips with mine, but logic sobers me. There's something we haven't talked about yet.

"When we find the others," I say, "this ends, doesn't it?"

His brows pull together. He brushes a strand of my hair away from my face and tucks it behind my ear. "Why should it?"

"That was supposed to be a one-time thing. I said we'd just get it out of our systems." My heart rails at my own words while my mind knows they need to be said. I remember the way he held me this afternoon, brushing tears from my cheeks after the nightmare I can't recall. I remember how tightly we held each other. It was the kind of tenderness I sought to avoid by having him blindfold me. It's the kind of tenderness we can't let grow. Not with where we're headed when my term as his Summoner ends. I'll be crossing the sea to where I can finally live freely. He'll be diving headfirst into a war he probably won't win.

"And have you, Seamstress?" His voice dips low and he brushes his thumb over my mouth. My lips part in response, my breaths quickening. "Did you fuck me out of your system yet? Get your fill of me?"

I part my lips wider until my teeth close over the tip of his thumb. I bite down just the slightest bit. "No," I say. "You barely took the edge off."

I don't know who kisses who first, but suddenly we're a tangle of lips and limbs. He backs me against the tree trunk and grinds his hips into mine. There's no satisfaction with so many layers of clothes between us, but we can take care of that. He's already unclasping my cloak, groping at my bodice. I arch into his touch as he frees one of my breasts, just enough to close his mouth over my nipple—

"Are we interrupting?"

Calvin's voice has us freezing in place. We jump apart to find two faces peering beneath the boughs. Calvin blinks with a look of feigned innocence while Harlow smirks, eyes locked on the hand Dominic uses to cover my bare tit. I swat his palm away and tug my bodice back in place.

"No," I say, and I've never heard a single syllable sound so unconvincing.

Harlow snorts a laugh, and she and Calvin stride away from the pine. "It's about time," Harlow mutters.

CHAPTER THIRTY-FIVE

Inana

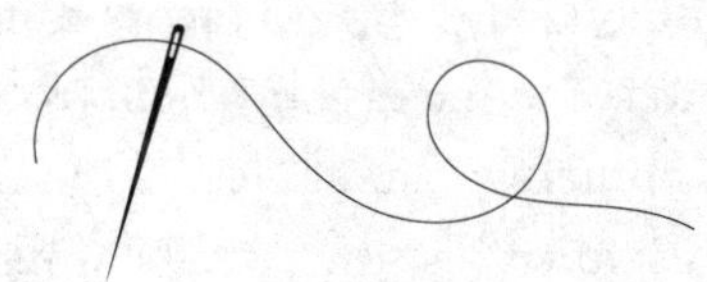

It feels good to be back with the others. It felt good to have Dominic grinding against me under that tree, and it could have felt a hell of a lot better if we hadn't been interrupted, but I can't regret that we were. We can't let this . . . *thing* between us grow into anything more than sex. And even though Dominic whispered that he has every intention of finishing what we started the next time we're alone, I think we could both use some space to cool off. To ensure we get our heads on straight, so when we do revisit our desire, it *stays* in the realm of just sex.

At least that's what I quickly tell Harlow when she begs me for details. It's night now, and even though the back of the wagon is lit with lanterns, I don't dare speak in more than a whisper or talk much at all. Dominic is at the reins, giving me that much-needed distance from him and our sexually charged energy, and we'll have to stop before dawn because of the road conditions and the horses' needs. That means it will be many hours before daylight makes it safe enough for a full conversation.

Once we do make camp, I'm pleased to see the snow isn't nearly as bad as it was closer to the bridge. Only a few flakes fall here, and a break in the clouds overhead reveals a pure blue sky, bright with rays of sunlight.

"We'll have to take the southern pass," Dominic explains. He's sharpening his knives while we warm ourselves around our campfire with mugs of bitter coffee and bland stew. For once, I can't complain about the food. After two days drinking melted snow from a leaky cup, this is heaven. "It will set us a week behind, but it's the fastest way to get to Eldeen with the bridge gone."

"Will you still have a post?" Harlow asks, wincing as she sips her coffee. It appears being stuck with only Calvin as a cook while they hunkered down in the blizzard did no favors to her perception of his fare. "They'll give it to someone else by then, won't they?"

"If it escalates to an active threat, yes," Dominic says. I hate how the mere sound of his voice has my core heating, even when he isn't speaking to me. He meets my gaze across the fire, and I force my eyes away. Still, I catch his crooked smirk as he returns to sharpening his blade.

"Do you think Henderson survived what happened on the bridge?" Calvin asks. His eyes are glazed over, his motions languid from downing half a fresh vial of Dominic's blood. From what Cal told us, he did his best to conserve his stash when we were separated, since he knew he'd need to keep some blood so Dominic's Shades could sense it. "The last thing I saw was him and one of his Summoners limping away from the collapse, but there were dozens of Shades swarming the road ahead of them and no sign of their wagon. We didn't wait to see what happened to them in case it riled up the Shades on our side of the bridge."

"If he survived," Dominic says, "I hope he knows better than to fuck with us again."

Bard slowly approaches the fire. He'd been chopping firewood but now settles on one of the logs beside Dominic. His eyes are unfocused, his posture tense, drawing all our attention to him. "I . . . I should come clean about something."

Dominic pauses sharpening long enough to say, "You don't have to tell us anything you don't want to. I don't give a shit what Henderson said."

Bard's jaw shifts side to side. "Still, it isn't fair to keep it to myself any longer. Not when it has already endangered the others." His gaze sweeps from Harlow, to me, then to Calvin. He flexes his scarred fingers and clears his throat. "What Henderson said about me is true. I murdered a Sinless."

My pulse quickens, in both shock and understanding. I recall what Henderson said at the bridge.

Murder. Of an unspeakable nature. Which makes their crimes treason too.

Now that I know Henderson thinks I killed Henry Berkham, it makes sense Bard has been accused of the same. Murdering a Sinless.

"Is that possible?" Harlow asks, voice small.

I note that Calvin doesn't look at all surprised. He likely knows even more secrets than I do, given how long he's been with Dominic.

"I didn't know it at the time," Bard says, "and it wasn't my intention. I wanted the Sinless to hurt, that's all."

Harlow's expression twists with a blend of sympathy and curiosity. Those same emotions resonate in me. "What happened?" she asks, tone gentle, encouraging.

The last time we told our stories, Bard clammed up, and I expect him to do the same now.

Instead, he heaves a sigh, one that unclouds his eyes, his face. "Three years ago," he says, "a Shadowbane came to my home with two of his Summoners. All were masked, even the Shadowbane, so I never saw their faces. They said they were investigating the source of Shade interest, due to an increase in Shade activity. He'd heard I descended from a family of renowned musicians, which is true. Music was once the pride of the Bodin name, long before One Hundred Days of Darkness. Talent was said to run in our blood. After art was outlawed, my ancestors continued to pass down the knowledge of music. Never to play; only to understand, so when the day came that we'd earned our gods' forgiveness and we no longer had to hide our craft, someone could carry on the Bodin legacy.

"I, like every Bodin before me, studied sheet music, practiced chords. I kept a five-hundred-year-old forbidden instrument in the basement. Once a month, I descended the stairs, lit the lanterns, and practiced the finger placements, never strumming. Never making a sound. It was supposed to be harmless.

"Then the Shadowbane came."

His voice shakes and my heart rate climbs. I know his story doesn't end well, and I'd be lying if I said I wasn't desperate to know his tale. It's the wicked artist in me.

No, not wicked.

Just an artist.

In a wicked, false world.

Dominic hasn't shared the truth with Harlow and Bard yet, but this is the first time we've been awake together in the daylight. Now is the safest time to tell stories.

"What happened?" Harlow asks. "What did they do?"

"They searched my home for evidence that someone in my family was guilty of attracting Shades," he says. "They went into the basement, found my hidden sheet music. Then they pried at my floorboards until one came loose. They uncovered my mandolin.

"I assured them I only held on to it as a keepsake, that I never played it. I begged for them to make an official arrest, to hold a trial and test if I was lying, and the Shadowbane seemed disappointed by that. He hauled me out of the house and ordered me imprisoned. I went along willingly, not fighting his Summoners when they wrenched my arms behind my back. But then my daughter came home.

"Mary . . . when she saw me like that, she demanded to know what happened. I begged her to go inside. To stay with her mother. I promised I'd sort this all out, that they'd give me a trial and discover I wasn't guilty of attracting Shades. Her eyes fell on the mandolin in the Shadowbane's hand, held between two fingers like it was a filthy thing. Mary wrested it from his grip, placed her fingers over the strings, and . . ."

A sob breaks from his throat and my eyes sting at the pain in his expression.

He lowers his head, shoulders quivering. When he sits upright, breathing a shaky sigh, his cheeks are bright with the trails of tears, a sad smile on his lips.

"Gods, she played so beautifully," he says. "I had no idea she'd discovered my secret and sought to carry her own, but the way she played made it clear. She'd practiced in silence even more than I did, which was astounding for a girl of only sixteen. So when she said, 'I'm the guilty one. I'm the musician in our family,' the Summoners released me at once and took her instead. I screamed. I pleaded. I cried for them to offer the same trial I'd begged for, because she couldn't be guilty of attracting the Shades. She may have known how to play, but she never would have played out loud."

My heart twists at his words. I can't tell whether he truly believed she wasn't guilty of attracting the Shades or if it was just a father's desperate wish, perhaps a father's desperate naïveté, but it doesn't matter to me if she played out loud or not. It doesn't fucking matter, because if I was in her place, I wouldn't have been able to resist hearing the beautiful, haunting music of those strings. I would have given in to the devil's call, just like I always have with storytelling and sewing.

Bard continues. "I rounded up every coin I could find. Sold everything of value. Just to offer something to the masked Shadowbane to keep him from turning my daughter over to the crown. To beg him to give her a local trial instead. Take her to the church and let them test her. But the Shadowbane was long gone by the time I filled my purse, and when I went to the jail, my daughter was gone too. Not dead. No, she was given to Lord Doan, the most respected Sinless in town, save for our duke."

"Duke," I echo. "You lived in a protected village."

He nods.

That makes me doubt the sincerity of the Shadowbane's hunt for a culprit. Door-to-door investigations are normally reserved for unprotected villages, where the threat level is higher. Sure, an increase in Shade activity can pose a threat to a protected village. Without silver walls, Shades can enter a town if they find a large enough patch of shadow to hide in. But even when Shades do enter protected towns, they never get far enough to cause any damage. The Holy Brazier makes it too bright, the shadows sparser the closer one gets to the heart of the village.

"I suspected then that the search had been a ploy," Bard says. "Lord Doan wanted a plaything, and the Shadowbane was hoping he'd find just enough evidence—even if it was fabricated—to arrest someone Doan would like. That's why the Shadowbane was so disappointed with me. Because I wasn't quite to Lord Doan's taste. Still, I fought. I pleaded with the duke, the aristocrats, the higher-ups. I at least wanted to know if my daughter was alive. During this time, my wife worked on our daughter's behalf too, unknown to me. One day, I came home to an empty house. My wife left a note that she was going to offer Lord Doan a trade."

He pauses for a few moments, eyes darting across the flames as if seeing his past in them. "The next time I saw my wife and daughter, one was dead and the other . . ."

Tears stream down his face, and I find my eyes are leaking too. Harlow watches him with a trembling hand over her mouth. Calvin's head hangs low, hidden from view. Only Dominic watches him without outward emotion.

No, that isn't true. I've studied that stoic face of his long enough to see the tells of his rage, written in the pulse at the corners of his jaw, the thinning of his lips, the paleness of his knuckles as he curls them around his knife and whetstone.

I cling to his rage, using it as an anchor to keep from getting swept away in the tide of Bard's sorrow.

"My wife . . . she'd been drained of blood until she died," Bard says, "while Mary had been fed from too, but it was so much worse than that. She'd been played with like a toy, made to bleed not for food but for entertainment. It was evident in the countless cuts that marred her body. They were everywhere. Everywhere. She was barefoot. Discarded at our doorstep only half conscious. I cleaned her up, called for the doctor, but it was too late. Half her cuts were infected. Her body was already shutting down from sepsis. She took her last breath in my arms. And I . . . I forfeited my life the same day."

His tone darkens, sending a chill through me. "I knew I could never atone for what had been done to Mary and my wife. It was my fault. I'm the one who kept the music. I'm the one who made forbidden art available to my child. I'm the one who couldn't stop the Shadowbane from taking her. So I opened my flesh, marking it with every cut that had been inflicted upon her, and I let them bleed."

I look at his scars with fresh understanding. All those cuts on his face, his hands, they were all . . . self-inflicted. Not only that, but they were first marked on his daughter.

My rage simmers beneath my skin.

"I stalked Lord Doan," Bard says with deadly calm. "For days. Weeks. Learned his habits. The places he liked to go, especially alone. Then, when I had my chance, I abducted him. A Sinless may be stronger than the average human, but I was much larger than him and used to manual labor on our farm. Lord Doan was weaker than me. So badly I wanted to crush his skull, but first, I wanted him to suffer. I took him outside the barrier of the brazier and hauled him deep into the forest. There I tied him to a tree and proceeded to open the same cuts I now bore. The same he carved into Mary. Once they sealed closed, I opened them again. Again. By the time night fell, I had an audience of Shades, but I didn't care. I'd die torturing the man who tortured my little girl, and I'd do it with a knife in my hand and his blood on my blade.

"What I didn't expect, as the night grew darker and the Shades drew closer, was for their interest to be in *him,* not me. Nor did I expect that when they clawed at me, it was only to get to him. Or, more accurately, inside him.

"Seven Shades entered his still-healing wounds, and that's when I saw his cuts could no longer close. That's when I held his head by his hair and opened his throat. That's when I learned the secret to ending the Sinless's immortality."

Silence stretches long and vast as the weight of Bard's story settles over us.

Harlow is the first to speak. "I . . . I don't understand. You're saying if Shades enter a Sinless through open wounds, they can be killed?"

Bard shrugs. "I don't know why, but yes."

I exchange a glance with Dominic. It's time they knew.

Dominic opens his mouth, but Bard rushes to say, "That's not all. There's more."

Dominic gives him a nod. "Go on."

"I joined your crew under false pretenses. I didn't agree to be your Summoner for the promise of freedom, but in the hopes that I'll find the Shadowbane who gave my daughter to Lord Doan. I know it isn't you, and I suspect it isn't Henderson either. The Shadowbane wore a mask, so I never saw his face, but he saw mine. He'll recognize me. And when he does, I am going to kill him, and anyone who tries to stop me." Bard gives Dominic a seething, pointed look.

Dominic doesn't blink away. He only says, "I won't stop you, so long as you remain loyal to me."

Bard's jaw tightens, then he uncurls his fists and gives a sharp nod.

"Besides," Dominic says, laying down his knife and whetstone and propping his elbows on his knees. "You aren't the only one who entered this partnership under false pretenses."

He glances at Calvin, then at me.

Then, with a deep breath, he says, "It's time you knew the truth."

CHAPTER THIRTY-SIX

INANA

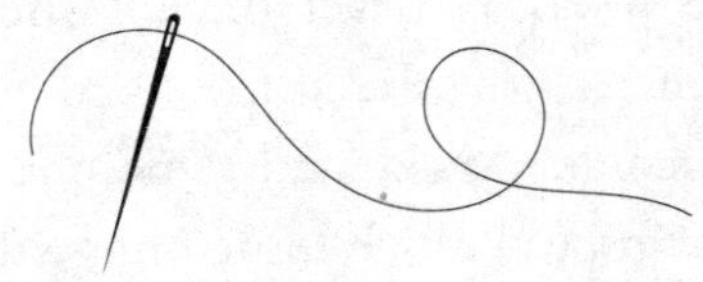

Nothing really changes once the others know the truth. Bard takes it all in with stoic silence, Harlow with a rare expression of fury. It casts a somber mood over our travels, but I know none of Dominic's fears of betrayal will transpire. Not with us. Because the truth doesn't change any of our plans. Bard wants revenge, regardless of who or what creates the Shades. Harlow wants off this continent for the same reasons I do. Her bounty may not be as impressive as mine or Bard's, as evidenced by Henderson's lack of interest in her, but she's still a fugitive. And now that we know the outside world isn't crawling with Shades like we once thought, the prospect of freedom is more alluring than ever.

It isn't until we reach Eldeen that I realize things *have* changed.

We're over a week late by the time we arrive. Word already spread to the village about the break in the bridge, from merchants and messengers who'd tried to traverse the pass from the other side, so we come with the perfect excuse. And since there were no active Shade attacks during our tardiness, we're able to claim our post without further delay. There's no surprise waiting for us from Henderson, no news of his survival or demise, so Dominic's reputation remains untainted by all that happened.

As the first night of our stay in Eldeen approaches, I expect things to be the same as they were in Thornfal. That Dominic will keep his distance and patrol the streets on his own.

But he doesn't.

He takes us with him this time. We keep watch from rooftops, then stalk the sleeping streets. Once Dominic deems the village clear, we assess the conditions in the outlying forest. We come across a few Shades, but they're benign. Still, we keep our distance when he opens his vial of King Kaelum's blood. He says it's too dangerous for us to stand close, in case it does attract one of the king's sought-after Shades, which may turn aggressive at the smell of their original body's blood. I don't mind staying back, for I remember the rotting scent of that vial from the rooftop, so much more pungent than Dominic's and Calvin's fresher blood. How long has he carried that vial? Is it even effective anymore?

If I think too much about it, his mission seems so fruitless. So impossible. Yet I keep that to myself. I may be keenly acquainted with the futility of hope, but it's a powerful drug. Sometimes the only thing that keeps you going.

When the sun rises after our first night, Dominic does the last thing I expect; he retires to the same suite as us. I don't know if I should be pleased or annoyed that he chose to stay with us, now of all times, or that he chose the bed the farthest away from mine. If he'd kept his own room like before, I could have snuck away for . . . certain activities.

With a huff, I riffle through the gifts that were left on my bed overnight. Clothing, mostly. A fresh pair of boots. It's not nearly as much as we were gifted in Thornfal, but we also aren't saving this village from a frenzied dragon Shade.

"Disappointed?" I stiffen as Dominic's voice is suddenly behind me, his breath caressing my ear.

I glance over my shoulder, finding him so close it makes my breath hitch. In my periphery, I catch movement behind him, the others arranging their own gifts on their beds. It's all that stops me from turning fully and pressing my lips to his then and there. We haven't had much alone time, and I'm divided on how I feel about that. My desire for him hasn't cooled, and I'm eager to know what else he can do with that tongue, those fingers, that cock, but . . . I'm so afraid I'll get carried away. That I'll get too invested.

Even if I didn't mind that our partnership has an expiration, I still know better than to be careless with my heart. It didn't work well for me before.

"Disappointed," I echo, as nonchalant as I can manage. "Why would I be disappointed?"

"Come outside with me," he says, angling his head toward the pair of carved wooden doors that lead to the balcony. He doesn't wait for me to agree before striding through those doors. I glance back at our companions, too distracted by their gifts to pay us any heed, and follow him out. As soon as I step over the threshold, he pushes the doors closed behind us. Then his hands find my waist and my back is pressed against the door. I manage only a startled gasp before his lips are on mine, his front flush against me.

Despite my initial surprise, I sink into the moment, parting my lips for his tongue, angling my head so he can kiss me deeper. Gods, I've been craving this. The taste of him. The feel of him. I wind my hands behind his neck and into his hair. He presses himself more firmly against me until I can feel his length straining his trousers, even through my skirt and petticoats. I don a devious grin as I slide one hand between us, cupping his impressive shape. He groans and rocks his hips as I stroke him over the thick material of his pants. I'm about two seconds away from lifting my skirts and freeing his cock when he suddenly pulls away.

He takes a single step back, releasing me to brace his palms against the door on either side of my head. His breaths come out uneven, his hair tickling my collarbone as he lowers his face next to mine. "I want you in my bed," he whispers.

I lean more fully against the door, then lift his chin with my forefinger until he meets my eyes. "And whose fault is it that I'm not? You chose now, of all times, to get chummy with your Summoners?"

"I didn't think it would be this hard."

My hand returns to his firm bulge. "You mean like this?"

He bites his lip and stifles another groan. "Gods, Inana, you have no idea how badly I want to fuck you right now on this balcony in broad daylight."

I lift my chin until our lips are just a breath apart. "Then why don't you? Why did you stop? I can be quiet. The others won't know."

He heaves a ragged sigh, then his eyes dart to the side of the balcony. "It's not our friends I'm concerned about."

I follow his line of sight, expecting him to be glancing at the windows that flank the balcony doors. Instead, he's looking at the street just two floors below, busy under the morning light. Eldeen's citizens are already going about their day, most too immersed in their activities to notice the couple on the balcony above, but I find at least one pair of judging eyes on us: a woman carrying a basket of vegetables. She scowls and averts her gaze.

Away from the sight of me cupping Dominic's cock for the entire town to see.

I snatch my hand back. My desire hasn't drained with the reminder that we're potentially being watched, but my rational mind has come to meet it halfway. Public signs of affection are considered taboo, since they could attract Shades, but now I know that isn't because such acts are sinful; it's because flirtation and lovemaking are signs of life, just like art and violence and other demonstrations of passion. Regardless, this isn't the time or place to sate the need that burns inside me. Daytime may be the safest for sexual acts, and under daylight even safer, but with nothing other than an awning overhead and a thin wooden railing around us, we're in plain sight.

"I can't fuck you the way I want to," Dominic says as he steps back, placing an agonizing amount of distance between us until he's leaning against the wooden railing. Despite his words, he continues to watch me like he means the opposite. His gaze sweeps over me, lingering on the rise and fall of my breasts, the curve of my hips, undressing me with his eyes.

"Then you should stop staring at my tits." I smooth out my skirts, as if that will convince the slick heat growing between my thighs to behave. It takes all my self-control to turn back toward the door, knowing that if I stay out here any longer with him, I'll throw caution to the wind and say *Fuck propriety and fuck me along with it.*

Just as my fingers reach the handle, a wisp of shadow coalesces beside me, only partially visible beneath the awning's meager shade. A strong, semitransparent hand splays against the door while an imitation of Dominic's face—no, a sliver of his actual soul—smirks down at me.

"*I didn't say we were done.*" It's Pride's voice, but there's an extra layer to it, a tone I know intimately as Dominic's.

I slowly turn back around and find Dominic still watching me with his heated gaze from where he leans against the balcony, arms crossed. His grin is wicked, his eyes dark and seductive.

A second shadow appears on my other side. Lust drags a featherlight finger over the swell of my breasts as he whispers in my ear. "*I may not be able to fuck you how I want, but that doesn't mean I can't get you off.*" Again the voice is doubled, even though Dominic's lips don't move. What I'm hearing isn't being carried across the balcony from where he stands. It's being delivered straight through his Shades.

"*Do you want that?*" Pride, Lust, and Dominic all say in unison. "*Do you want me to touch you where no one else can see?*"

My eyes return to the street below, but my logical mind has been defeated by my arousal. How could it stand a chance against those three filthy voices, the two sets of shadowed hands that skitter over my skin. I don't care that we have an audience. I don't care who watches me unravel. My answer comes out with a whimper. "Yes."

Lust and Pride close in around me, one bringing a set of lips to my neck, the other a tongue across my clavicle. Pride's hand cups my ass while Lust's slips under my bodice to squeeze my breast. There's hardly any room for a hand, not even a shadow one, but he still manages to tease my nipple, circling it with his light touch, making it scrape against the fabric of my chemise. My lashes flutter shut and a moan nearly climbs from my throat, but I bite my lip to stifle it.

"*Eyes open, sinner,*" Dominic says through Pride. "*Keep those eyes on me. I want you to know exactly who's pleasuring you.*"

I do as I'm told and meet Dominic's gaze across the balcony. He remains leaning against the balustrade, but his arms are no longer crossed. Now his hands are braced beside his hips, fingers gripping the railing so hard the veins on his hands and forearms stand out. There's a strange blend of desire and focus on his face, and I realize how much effort it must take him to act through his Shades like this. Especially as Pride's hand is suddenly no longer cradling my ass through my skirt and is now flush against my skin. Lust's fingers release my nipple, curving around my breast before skating down my ribs, my stomach. Which means his Shades are currently in two states at once, both fluid and solid—fluid enough to move through the fabric of my clothing, yet solid enough to interact with my flesh.

"How much of this can you feel?" I ask, my voice hitching as Lust's fingers reach the mound of curls at the apex of my thighs.

"*All of it,*" Dominic says, his voice tripled by Lust and Pride. "*This is all me, love.*"

His Shades grip me tighter, kissing up my neck, over my jaw, while Dominic's eyes grow heavier with desire. Lust's fingertips find my clit just as Pride's slide down the center of my ass until they reach my slick core. I'm dripping wet, and his fingers circle my opening, teasing my sensitive skin. Lust presses down on my clit. A squeak of pleasure erupts from my lips and I have to slap a palm over my mouth to keep from making another sound.

"I thought you said you could be quiet," Dominic says, this time speaking out loud, his voice carrying over the space between us.

"I—" My attempt to insist I can is cut off as Pride plunges his finger fully inside me. I arch my back against the door, then get control of myself. To onlookers, we may just look like two people conversing on a balcony, and maybe the awning casts me in enough shadow that I don't stand out, but if I writhe too much, I'll surely draw someone's attention.

Yet . . . for the strangest reason, that doesn't bother me. Not now, when stars are forming behind my eyes and Pride is pumping inside me faster. Not when Lust is expertly circling my clit, the way Dominic did in the cave. Not when the man before me pants heavily as if he really is touching me, feeling me. The intensity of his gaze has me convinced he could coax me to climax with the heat of his eyes alone.

"*You feel so good on my fingertips,*" Dominic says, his voice returned to a whisper carried through his Shades. "*You look so good when you whimper with my Shades inside you.*"

Pride slips in a second finger. The next sound that tries to crawl up my throat succeeds, muffled by the hand I still clamp over my lips. I can't keep my body from rocking, can't stop the subtle roll of my hips as I ride the fingertips that strum me, fill me. My pleasure builds, radiating through my entire body, ready to erupt.

"*That's it, love. Show me what you look like when you come.*"

Just like that, I unravel, my climax rolling through me like a tidal wave, pulsing against Pride's fingers, rolling with Lust's expert motions against my clit. The Shades surge with me, bring me down, down, down the wave of pleasure until I'm spent.

I heave a breath and turn my weight over to the door behind me, my legs like liquid. Dominic pushes off the railing and gathers me to him, framing my face in his hands, pressing a kiss to my lips. It's laughable how chaste we must look, just a gentle kiss in the daylight, when in reality my undergarments are soaked in the wake of the release I just had in public.

"Is that all we can do?" I ask as he pulls me into an equally chaste embrace, save for the rock-hard bulge between us. I wish I could give him what he just gave me, but without his rather convenient shadow-wielding ability, I can't get him off in any inconspicuous way. Gods, there's so much more of him I want to experience. I want to feel him deep inside me. I want to ride him to my heart's content in a bed of our own. I want to burn through my desire for him until I'm sick of it. "I want more of you. More than stolen moments and public orgasms."

"Inana fucking Westwood," he says, tone teasing as he smiles down at me. "Don't tell me you've been a romantic all this time. Is it an intimate date you're asking for?"

My heart flips, first with surprise that he mistook my lust-addled question for something sweeter, then with a flutter of joy. Though my mind is quick to recall that's more than what I want from him. More than what we can have. And yet . . . I don't correct him. Instead, I give in to that flutter of joy, squeezing him tighter. I can let myself have this for now. Can't I?

CHAPTER THIRTY-SEVEN

INANA

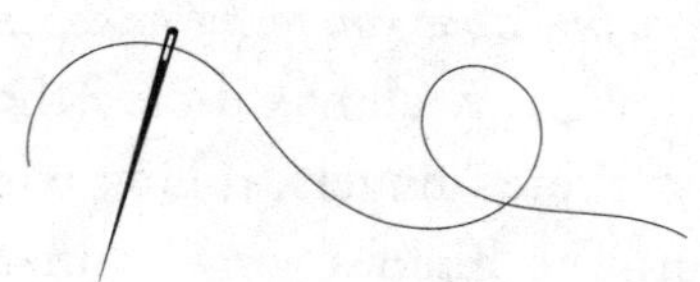

After five days of what becomes a beautifully mundane routine, five days of performing our duties together as a team, five days of sleeping on the opposite end of the room from Dominic, five days of him whispering filthy words in my ear and giving me fleeting, teasing touches with his Shades, he wakes us up from our daytime slumber when the sun is still high in the sky.

"Get dressed, sinners," he says as I rub sleep from my eyes. "We're going to the market."

I do a double take as my bleary eyes focus on him. For once, he isn't dressed in all black and strapped with weapons. He appears to have borrowed some of Calvin's clothes—or perhaps he was gifted common garb like the rest of us—and wears linen trousers, a cream shirt, and a brown waistcoat. His hair is tied back, and he finishes off his ensemble with a greatcoat. I stifle a laugh. Not because he looks odd, but because even without his dark leathers, knives, and vials, he still *looks* like a fucking Shadowbane. A confident, powerful man, at the very least. I don't know who the hell he's trying to fool, but I find it oddly charming.

"Why are we going to the market?" Harlow says with a yawn. Her ash-brown hair is a tangled halo around her head, and she absently smooths it with one hand.

Dominic tosses a small pouch on her bed, then one on Bard's, then Calvin's, then mine. As I catch it, I find it's heavier than it looks. Inside it, there's . . .

"You're giving us money?" Harlow says.

"Ah, I love money." Calvin shakes the purse's contents into his palm. "We should get cream puffs."

"What's this for?" mutters Bard, a glint of suspicion in his eyes. He's been more relaxed lately, as if telling his story freed him from at least a few demons of his past. Yet I can't blame him for not fully warming up to Dominic, after what he went through. It probably feels like he's being paid to keep silent about Dominic's secrets.

"We won't need many supplies for our next post," Dominic says, "since it's only twenty miles east. So we have some extra. Spend it or don't, but it's yours."

I stare down at my purse full of glittering coins. I doubt it amounts to much, but it's been a long time since I've had money of my own to spend, so it feels like a fortune. My eyes lift to Dominic's, and his are already on me. His mouth quirks, and I think I know what this is really about.

He's taking me on a date.

Dominic leads us through the streets of Eldeen until we reach the market square. There's no snow on the ground this side of the mountains, and the sky is clear. The air is still icy, but that doesn't stop the townsfolk from bustling about in the cold to enjoy market day.

The mood isn't nearly as boisterous as it was in Nalheim's marketplaces, where citizens shop and hawk wares with far less restraint than in unprotected villages, but it's still more lively than I'm used to. Numerous stalls line the road, some with food, others with clothing or household items. Calvin spots a stand for cream puffs and immediately takes Harlow by the hand and drags her along with him.

Bard makes a beeline for a stand with small knives.

As soon as I'm alone with Dominic, his fingertips slip between mine. My heart stutters at his warm touch, at the too-intimate gesture. Yet when he tightens his grip on my hand, I don't pull away. I like the feel of this too much.

Way too much.

"So you don't get lost," he says, leaning in close so I can hear him over the clamor of the crowd.

"I think you're just jealous of Calvin and Harlow," I say, catching sight of them at the pastry stand, their fingers still entwined. *See? It doesn't have to mean anything,* I tell myself.

Calvin and Harlow seem to have forged a bond lately, but I don't believe it's romantic. Not yet, at least. Harlow may speak flippantly about sex, but she's still young. Still haunted by what was done to her by the husband she murdered along with his despicable sons. When she draws pictures of calm and safety, she still only illustrates scenes where she's alone in nature with not a soul around her.

Gods, we're all so fucking broken. A patchwork crew, like the heart I stitched.

I never was able to unravel the threads of my crafted heart after my dunking in the river, and I may have shed a few tears when I cut them off. The heart itself remains intact, though, and I keep it tucked in my bodice like always.

"Call it what you want," Dominic says, drawing my attention back to him, "but until I let go, you're my hostage."

He leads me from stall to stall, admiring the wares. He releases my hand to purchase us small meat pies, and I take a moment to myself, waiting at the center of the market square. My eyes rove the stalls, then the surrounding buildings. It looks just like Thornfal.

No, just like Dunway.

My gaze floats above the thatched and tiled roofs to the snow-capped mountains beyond. The sight makes my blood go cold.

When I first learned we were passing the mountain range to reach Eldeen, I didn't think much of it. The Cassia Mountains are visible from almost anywhere in this region. I even spotted them from Nalheim once, when I ran an errand for Rockefeller in the heart of the city and reached one of the highest points, where I could see beyond the silver walls.

This view, though, is almost exactly how it looked from Dunway.

Which means . . .

I swallow hard. I don't want to think about how close we might be to my hometown.

A hometown that no longer exists because a Sinless lost his life there. I still don't understand how it happened or if I'm truly responsible.

Dominic's approach is a welcome distraction from my darker thoughts. His grin is wide and a touch wicked when he stops before me.

I extend my hand, eager to stuff my face with the meat pie and forget everything I don't want to consider. "Give me the goods," I say.

His lips spread wider. "In public? So shameless."

I roll my eyes, but I rather like his teasing. "Give me the damn meat. And don't you dare make another dick joke."

He chuckles, a deep and carefree sound that truly makes this feel like a date. Like something regular people get to experience. A beautiful illusion.

Finally, he places something in my waiting palm, but it isn't one of the meat pies. Instead, it's a simple rosewood hair comb. It has no artistic embellishments, no excess ornamentation. It's a practical accessory and perfectly suitable to be sold in a public market.

Yet my throat tightens at the sight.

"I saw you looking at it when we passed the stall earlier," he says.

I blink up at him. "You knew?"

"I knew." Without another word, he takes it from me and turns me around. I feel him tugging my hair, his strong hands surprisingly gentle as he sweeps messy tendrils away from my forehead on each side. He slides the comb in place, securing the top half of my hair, then turns me back around.

I can hardly see him with how my eyes glaze. Why is he doing this? Why is he making *us* about more than sex? Why is he stealing my fucking heart—

"Inana Westwood?"

I freeze at the voice. It's not exactly familiar, yet it brings about the faintest spark of recognition. Taking a step away from Dominic, I face the stranger.

No, not a stranger.

I can't place her face, but I know her.

Or at least I did. From home.

"Is that really you?" the woman says. She's a handful of years older than me, and her eyes look heavy. Haunted.

My mouth falls open, but I don't know what to say. Dominic places a firm hand on my back, a wordless offer that he can usher me away, should I wish it.

I don't budge.

"It's me," the woman says, "Tera Holmes. I was—"

"The tanner's daughter," I say, finally putting a memory to the name and face. My heart slams against my ribs. I should be relieved to see her, to see that someone truly did survive the attack on Dunway. But her presence feels more like an accusation somehow. "What are you doing here?"

"Eldeen was the closest place where I had family," she says, eyes turning down at the corners. "The only place I could go after . . . Well, you know."

"After Dunway was destroyed," I say, voice trembling. "You said this is the closest place where you had family. How far away is Dunway?"

She furrows her brow. "Maybe fifteen miles southeast. Did you not realize that when you came here?"

I shake my head.

"Gods, no wonder you're so surprised to see me. I'm surprised to see you too. Everything happened so fast, none of us were prepared. I had no idea you survived. So few of us made it out alive."

My stomach churns as my next question crawls up my throat. "My parents . . . did they . . ."

Tera's face falls. "No, hon. They were confirmed as casualties. Were you not aware?"

"I wasn't there when it happened," I say, my mind spinning. I may not have been close with my parents by then, and I could only assume they had died after Dominic told me what happened. But hearing their deaths confirmed is something else. It feels like a blow to the chest.

She puts a hand to her mouth. "Gods, that's . . . I'm so sorry. That must have been a horrible thing to come home to."

Her words blare in my ears, my mind.

Come home to . . .

Come home to . . .

Come home . . .

She has no clue I didn't come home. I didn't know. I didn't mourn.

And . . . and it's my fault.

Maybe I didn't kill Henry. Maybe I did.

But if I hadn't struggled, hadn't fought for my life, Dunway would still be whole. It would have a duke, a dome of light, and my parents would be alive. If only I'd let him—

"Inana," Dominic whispers, cutting through my thoughts. Something presses against my legs. Sloth, hidden in the shadows of my skirts, invisible in the daylight yet firm enough to feel. To comfort me. To help clear my head.

"It's fine," I bite out, my words meant for Dominic and Tera in equal measure. "I'm fine."

Tera gives me a sad smile, her teary eyes roving to Dominic before settling back on me. She heaves a sigh. "I'm glad to see you've moved on," she says. "That you were able to find happiness after such a tragedy."

Her tone is gentle and sounds so genuine to my ears, but my heart reacts with brambles and thorns, raging at the hidden accusation.

She sniffles, then tugs me into a sudden embrace. "I'm so glad I got to see you again, Inana Westwood," she says, voice strangled with emotion. Then it dips low, barely above a whisper. "We survivors know the truth."

I stiffen, and she pulls away, her sorrowful smile in place.

She's gone before I can stop her, before I can ask what she meant by that last part.

Was she referring to . . . the truth of the attack? That Dunway was destroyed on purpose?

Or did she mean the truth about me? That I'm at fault?

Was I included when she said *we*?

Or did she mean her and the other survivors . . . against me?

Anger and shame and confusion war in my mind, my heart. My feet start moving before I know it. I can hardly process Dominic's words as he asks if I'm all right, can hardly feel his touch when he tries to take my hand. I pull away, unable to bear his concern or focus on anything but the cacophony in my head.

What really happened to Henry?

What did I fucking do?

Do I deserve to be alive when so many died? Even though it's the Sinless who hold the highest fault?

I find myself back in our suite, not quite remembering how I got there. Dominic is still begging me to talk to him, but I'm not ready.

Not ready.

Not ready.

He relents when the others return, and I curl up on my bed, feigning fatigue. I roll onto my side, tucking my hands beneath my pillow.

My fingertips brush against something. It's thin, smooth.

I tug it out from beneath my pillow. It's a piece of parchment marked with a single line of writing, scrawled in black ink.

Turn yourself in. Don't you owe it to the ones who died?

My pulse quickens as I tuck the note back beneath my pillow before the others can take notice. My mind spins with even more questions. Did Tera leave this? Had she already known I was here? Did she ask a maid to deliver it?

I don't know the answer, and I sure as hell am not turning myself in.

Yet maybe I do owe it to the ones who died to at least take responsibility for my part in what happened.

Only one thing is certain.

I need to remember the truth.

CHAPTER THIRTY-EIGHT

Dominic

I hate seeing Inana in pain. I hate that I can *feel* her blaming herself, all because of what that woman said. Her innocent condolences followed by that sinister fucking whisper. I heard it. My Shades heard it. I don't know what Tera Holmes was playing at, but if I were a worse kind of man, I'd show up at her door and make her pay for upsetting Inana. Maybe she didn't mean for it to sound the way it did, but it doesn't matter. Inana took those words the worst possible way.

I hate that I can't reach her in this state.

She's stubborn and prideful, and I know she needs time to grieve. To process. Yet I hate it all the same.

The others notice too, and it makes our evening patrol a somber affair. I do my best to remind Inana that I'm here, I'm close, with small touches and lingering looks. I need her to know she can lean on me if she feels like she's breaking, yet all she gives me is "I'm fine. Really."

She's not fine.

She's not fucking fine.

I give her the space her body language demands.

When the sun rises and my crew retires to our suite, I file my daily report with the mayor. Another peaceful night. Another successful watch.

After that, I'm still on edge, still too awake, so I visit the bakery across the street from the inn. I may not be able to do much for Inana until she's ready to let me, but I might as well ensure my crew is fed when they wake this evening for our next patrol. The inn will provide dinner as usual, but their fare is almost as bland as Calvin's. The bakery, however, is known for serving even better meat pies than the ones at the market.

"A Shadowbane," the middle-aged baker says, blinking in surprise at my sword as I walk through the door. "I heard we had one posted up here, but it's still rare to see one of you, much less two."

She's right. Shadowbanes keep to themselves during their posts, rarely leaving their temporary residences aside from the occasional meal at a local tavern. Partly because of their nocturnal schedules, but also because my kind are often met with trepidation, especially when there are active attacks that result in inquisitions and arrests. But—

Wait.

My mind lingers on her words.

"What do you mean two?" I ask.

"Oh, there was another one, just a few days ago. Stayed at the inn across the street, probably. A friend of yours, yeah?"

It's an easy assumption, that all Shadowbanes are comrades. Friends. She would be wrong, especially regarding one man.

I clench my jaw. It takes all my restraint not to speak through my teeth. "What did the other Shadowbane look like?"

She pales, but delivers her description. My fingers curl into fists, tighter and tighter with every word. I'm out the door, my order abandoned, before she's even finished speaking. I rush back to the inn, up the stairs, and into our suite—

Inana is gone.

Her bed is empty.

My shadows thrum in echo of my rising panic. Sloth paws at her blankets, slithers beneath her covers. His low growl has me pushing the pillow aside.

My rage darkens as I read the note I find there.

I crush it in my fist.

CHAPTER THIRTY-NINE

Inana

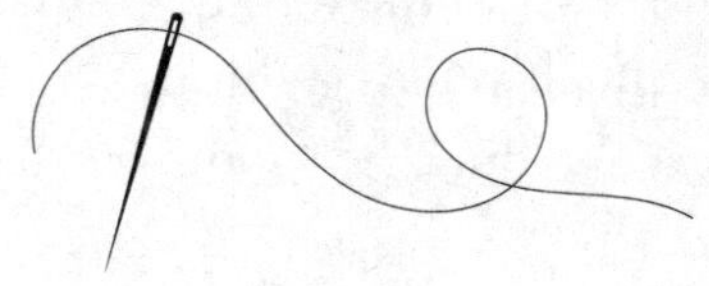

By late afternoon, I'm surrounded by ghosts.

Not spirits. Not even Shades. Just a tableau of the past, so hauntingly familiar.

Dunway is exactly as I remember it. Same main road, same forest in the distance. The way the sun dips toward the horizon, casting a golden glow slanting over the Cassia Mountains, looks just like it did every day in the hours between afternoon and evening.

The only difference is that Dunway is now empty.

Trembling, I dismount my borrowed horse and tether the palfrey to a broken fence outside one of the first houses along the main road. Not spending a single coin yesterday came in handy for procuring a horse this morning. That isn't to say it was easy. The stablemaster eyed me with suspicion, a stranger seeking a horse without an appointment. All it took was flourishing my mask, announcing myself as a Summoner in service to Eldeen's current Shadowbane, and asking if he wanted to be the one to tell the mayor he was obstructing Shadowbane business or if I should. After that, he took my coin without further question and even gave me directions to my destination.

That wasn't the end of my troubles. I still had to get here, and I haven't ridden a horse since I was a girl, much less traveled alone. Half the time, I wondered if I was even going in the right direction.

Then familiarity dawned and I knew I was close to home.

Now I'm here, and I can't fight the bone-deep chill that creeps into my blood, not from the cool air but from deep inside me. Was I right to come here?

I slowly make my way down the road, past empty houses with boarded-up windows and crumbling façades. Some buildings bear terrifying gouges carved down the walls, rents in the roofs, or doors hanging from their hinges. The only sound is my footsteps and the occasional caw of a raven from the woods. With each step I take, I see a younger version of myself walking ahead.

Six-year-old Inana, holding her mother's hand while they buy bread from the baker.

Ten-year-old Inana, climbing over the fence that lines the wheat fields, then striding to the other side, where she whispers her first words of fiction while gazing at the forest beyond.

Nineteen-year-old Inana, kissed by Henry for the first time, right here on the corner on Beltane Eve.

My teeth chatter as I approach the home I grew up in, a two-story abode of pale stone and a thatched roof, a withered garden outside. The front door is missing and the windows are shattered. I approach the walkway, but my feet refuse to move any farther. All I can see inside the house is darkness, perhaps a few pieces of overturned furniture, but I can't bear to see more. I already knew my parents didn't make it. Seeing how they may have suffered won't make this better.

I'm here for one thing.

My memories.

I choke on my short, sharp breaths as I leave my parents' house, quickening my pace as I proceed to the other side of town. I'm dizzy from all the destruction I pass. All the open, empty houses, the abandoned businesses. It seems like such a waste to have left Dunway like this. It could have been rebuilt. Salvaged.

But, no, of course it was left in this state.

Because it stands as a warning.

An example.

To most, it says: *This is what happens without the Sinless. This is why you need us.*

To the few who know the truth, it says: *This is what happens if you defy us.*

Finally, I reach my adult home. The dressmaker's shop. The only place I was allowed to participate in something like art and be only mildly condemned for it.

This is the last place I was before I was imprisoned.

I ball my shaking hands into fists as I follow the same path I did then, recalling how light my steps were, how bright my hope was, when I strode toward the main street where the duke's procession would be held. I follow those same steps now, my heart aching with memories of my own naïveté. Gods, how happy I was then, in those moments between stepping outside my door and getting captured by the guards.

Such a brief and beautiful slice of joy, where I was certain my life was going to be perfect. Dunway had a duke and Henry was home. I'd see my love at any moment. He'd sweep me into his arms, and in a matter of weeks, we'd marry. Of course we would, for how would he be able to stand waiting a moment longer?

Those were the thoughts of a woman who'd only lost her heart the gentle way.

I halt in place, right where I remember seeing those guards, how they blocked my path, stared down at me, then took hold of my arms. My heart collapses in an echo of how it did then, with the fear, the confusion, the sense that all the hope I had so stupidly built up was about to come crashing down.

My eyes are glazed as I whirl around, just like the guards turned me, marching me back toward my home. Then past it. I remember how I called out to my neighbors who passed us by. Most stopped, but none said a word in my defense. None asked what was happening. Some didn't even stop at all.

My feet slow to a halt as I recall the most painful memory of that horrific walk through town. One I didn't have the heart to relay when I shared this story with the others.

This is where I saw my parents.

This is where they locked eyes with me, brows lowering, not with concern.

With disdain.

Mother shook her head. "What did she do now?" she muttered.

And they just walked on by.

They let them take me.

They didn't fucking care.

I bite my bottom lip to keep it from wobbling. I can't even be angry now. I can't be hurt. Because even though my parents watched with disinterest as their cursed child—the girl born on the most inauspicious night of the year, the one who was always scolded for telling lies, the one they caught reading a novel she found buried in the woods—was dragged away toward the village jail, I can't blame them.

Because they died.

For my lies.

For my art.

For my freedom from death.

And I still don't know if I'm sorry. I still don't know if I wouldn't escape all over again, even if I knew what would happen to everyone else.

Swallowing back my tears, I resume my walk, remembering how weak my legs felt by this point. Not from fatigue but just . . . disappointment. Hurt.

I stop outside the jail, stomach churning as I assess its gated windows. Some of the bars have been pulled clean out and discarded on the ground. Then I see the half-broken front door, and the porch marred with dark stains I can only imagine are from blood. With a bracing breath, I enter, slowly walking past the sheriff's office, then down the hall to the cells. My breaths come faster now, sharper, as I approach the open cell at the far end.

This is it.

This is where I was held.

Where I escaped.

I stop outside it, closing my eyes for a few moments to gather my composure. Once I've gained some semblance of control over my breathing, I open my eyes and step inside.

It's just how I remember it. Stone walls, the farthest affixed with iron bars, two of which still bear the shredded ropes I cut myself free from. Moldy straw all over the floor.

And blood. So much blood, dark and discolored and . . . everywhere.

I smother my mouth with my hand and take a few more steadying breaths.

Everything inside me wants to run. How could I make myself relive this experience?

But I must relive it. Because already I can feel my memories stirring, sharpening, brightening. They're right there, waiting for me to pull them forward and confront them at last.

On trembling legs, I move to the far wall, press my back against it, and raise my arms, just like I was forced to then. Visions flash through my mind, of the guards tying me to the bars. My sobs and wails, unheard as I was left to wait alone for hours.

Hours.

Hours.

Then him.

Henry.

That hope and happiness that soured as I learned the truth of what he was. What he'd become.

Then the rage. Hatred. My steely resolve.

I angle my fingertips toward my wrist, recalling how I'd pulled a sewing needle from my cuff. The way I fought the pain of every inch of skin Henry sliced through while I worked my needle against my bindings, fraying every fiber of that rope until my hand came free. I remember the second needle I extracted from my cuff.

I slash out with my hand, just like I did when I cut his neck.

And then . . .

A chill moves through me as the next memory becomes clear. One that was only a blur until now.

I heave forward, recalling the searing pain that lanced through my gut when Henry . . .

He stabbed me.

I splay my palm over my abdomen. Over the wound I forgot. The wound I bear no scar from.

What the fuck?

My eyes glaze, partly from tears, partly from the memories that overlay my vision. Gods, I'm remembering it now.

I remember . . .

CHAPTER FORTY

Inana

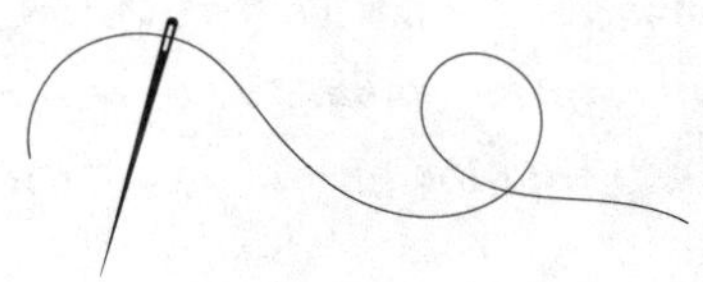

The pain is blinding. I've never felt anything like it, and I nearly lose consciousness. Henry pulls out the blade, eyes widening at the wound he inflicted upon me. He whirls around, muttering to himself, and my blurry eyes move from him to the edges of the room, where shadows are alive with movement.

I focus on that growing darkness, the Shades I attracted when I hummed against Henry's palm. Maybe I can't kill him. Maybe I can only wound him. But if this is my end, I will go out with violence. I will do whatever it takes to inflict as much pain as I can with my final breaths.

Henry turns back to me, knife raised, but I slash out with my needle again, opening a gash in his cheek before I stab him in the side of the throat. I lose my grip on my frail weapon, which means I no longer have anything to cut through the ropes binding my other wrist. He staggers back, and the Shades writhe with interest, hunger. His eyes lock on mine with a hateful glare. Never could I have imagined the man I loved would look at me like this.

Never could I have imagined love would turn so ugly.

So deadly.

I meet his hatred with a wicked smile as the Shades grab hold of his heel, the one planted at the edge of the lantern light. He flails as they climb up the leg of his trousers, and his motions jostle the light dangling above.

That's when I notice the Shade just off to the side. It isn't hungry like the others. It's quiet. Patient. Curious.

But as its hollow black eyes meet mine, something changes. I've earned its intrigue. I clear my throat, choking on the sobs that try to escape my lips. But instead of crying, I hum. Then I sing. I don't know what words I utter, but with them I convey my rage. My thirst, as deadly as any Shade's, is for vengeance. Death. Violence.

The Shade rises to its full height, a creature of gangly limbs and a blank, featureless face. It approaches Henry with its shadowy fingers outstretched. My eyes jump back to my former fiancé, who now claws at his neck where a wisp of shadow slithers into the wound I gave him. Tears stream down his face, eyes bulging.

The Shade behind him steps closer.

Henry freezes, and a squelching sound reaches my ears. Blood dribbles out of his parted lips.

Then several things happen at once.

A sliver of shadow, like an elongated claw, slices overhead, cracking the ceiling beam and sending the lantern tumbling into a pile of straw, casting half the cell in darkness. Another sliver leaps toward my remaining bound wrist. A minor slash of pain, and my wrist is free. Henry collapses to his knees. Then falls face-first on the floor.

The Shade stands behind his body, a human heart clenched in its fist.

I gasp, slumping down the wall, just like I did then.

What the hell was that?

What . . .

the hell . . .

was that?

The Shade killed Henry. I could say it wasn't my fault, but I remember now, the way I pleaded with my song. The way I wove rage into every note, every word, calling to the creature.

And the creature obeyed.

I catch my breath, staring at the bloodstained ground where Henry's body fell. My legs beg me to run, to scramble off this moldy pile of straw and not remember a single moment more, but . . .

I can't run.

I need to remember.

Slowly, I drag my eyes from the blood to where I recall the Shade standing, holding its gruesome prize.

"You . . . killed him," I say, voice hollow. With both hands free, I press them to my abdomen. Hot blood seeps between my fingers and my vision goes blurry at the edges.

The Shade drops Henry's heart to the floor and scampers closer. I try to sit up straighter, to stand, to run, but I can't move.

What's the point, anyway?

This wound . . . I won't survive it. Not without a healer, and who the hell would take me—the duke's disobedient sacrifice—to a surgeon? Especially once they see Henry dead before me. No, this can't end well. It can only end.

I'm just glad I took him out on the way.

I flinch as the Shade crouches before me. Its spidery fingers extend toward my chest, and I expect it to reach inside my rib cage and pull out my heart next. I wait for the shock of pain to come . . . but it doesn't.

The Shade presses its semitransparent palm over the cut across my breast, and I get the strangest sense of sorrow radiating from it.

"Are you showing me compassion right now?" I could laugh if I wasn't in so much pain. Here I was taught to fear the Shades, yet the man I loved, one of the Sinless I was taught to admire, was the real monster.

The creature rifles through the straw. I blink, my eyelids growing heavier. When I force my vision to focus, there's a glint of silver between the Shade's fingertips. One of my sewing needles. It holds it toward me, and I shake my head. "This isn't a wound I can sew shut," I say, but I wonder if it even notices my abdomen. Its attention seems fixed on my chest.

Something like frustration ripples through it, and in the next blink, I see my own face staring back at me. A perfect replica. A shadowed mirror.

Terror dawns, but it's short-lived.

What does it matter whether I'm killed by a knife wound or an Incarnate?

Still, it's uncanny to see my reflection made of shadow.

The Shade with my face flourishes the needle, then points to the matching wound on its chest. Just like I suspected, there's nothing on its abdomen. It doesn't understand that I've been stabbed.

It offers me the needle again, pointing from its chest to mine.

With a sigh, I accept the needle.

Its lips—my lips—pull into a satisfied smile, and it scampers back, mirroring my posture and sitting across from me.

It occurs to me now how intelligent this Shade seems to be. It knows what a sewing needle is and what it can do. And its replication of my face, my clothing, my body . . .

Something warm and sad and dreadful pools in my heart. "You've been watching me a long time, haven't you? Are you the one I've always whispered stories to?"

It doesn't respond, and I don't expect it to. Shades can't talk. They don't have voices.

The creature gives me an encouraging nod, eyes lowering to my chest wound again. Then it takes up Henry's discarded heart, plucks my other needle from the bloody ground, and threads a strand of shadow through it. My stomach lurches as it stabs the needle into the heart, pulling the thread through. Then again.

Again.

Again—

I'm pulled out of the memory with a lurch.

My body is racked with tremors as I reach inside my bodice and extract my patchwork heart.

I stare at the even stitches, the colorful array of fabrics. I constructed my hearts with so much passion, so much fervor, so much . . . familiarity. As if I'd done it before. As if a beating, pulsing patchwork heart was something I'd seen and felt, not just in the story I told at the Wretched Lair.

I remember—

"Stop," I say, unable to handle another moment of the macabre tapestry the Shade is making of Henry's heart. It's now threaded with veins of shadow and sinew, a patchwork monstrosity.

The Shade halts its efforts, cocking its head to the side. Tendrils of shadowy hair fall over the face that looks just like mine. I sense agitation wafting from it, so I soften my voice.

"Try something else," I say, choking on the last word. I can't tell if my wound has stopped bleeding or if I'm merely losing feeling. All I know is this isn't the last sight I want to see. I lift one hand, so heavy and weak, to my chest. "Try stitching that up first."

The Shade looks from me to its own cut. It gives me a pointed look, as if to say, "You too." The expression is so human, so real, I wonder if maybe I'm *the replica.*

I pretend to obey, bringing the needle to my chest and mimicking stitches.

Satisfied, the Shade copies me, but far more convincingly, threading shadows through the wound.

I don't know how much time passes. I think I might close my eyes for a while.

When next I open them, the Shade beams at me, pointing at its imperfect line of stitches.

"Look at that," I say, coughing. "You've created art. That's all it takes, you know. Even mending something broken is art. Whatever you mend becomes new."

I don't know what I'm saying.

Where even am I?

The Shade crawls back over to me, grinning with my lips. It holds out a hand as if it wants me to take it. As if we might entwine our fingers and skip through town like sisters. What the hell does it want from me? Can't it see I'm dying?

Yet beneath my irritation there's tenderness too. This monster killed my enemy. It tried to help me, in its own twisted way.

I slump farther down the wall, feeling a strange numbness settling over me.

"Are you going to eat my body when I die? Turn Incarnate with my face?"

The creature lowers its hand, its shoulders slumping. Finally, its eyes dip down to my abdomen. Shadowed hands frame my face, and my own eyes stare back at me, filled with terror.

"Are you grieving for me?" I let out a bark of laughter, and I realize this still isn't the last thing I want to see or feel. And I don't want it *to feel the way it feels now either. I don't want my apathy or its sympathy.*

I want fire and rage and victory.

The embers spark in my chest.

Infusing my final breath.

"Go ahead," I say. "Eat my body. Just promise me one thing."

A shadow tear trails down the Shade's face.

"Kill the guards on your way out."

The Shade presses its forehead to mine, its wrath rising to meet my own. And when I speak next, so does the creature.

Our voices are one.

"Get revenge."

The memory ends there. I stare down at my patchwork heart, my vision overlaid with that gruesome shadow-stitched heart held in the Shade's hands.

My hands.

The Shade's hands.

What does this mean?

It can't mean . . .

That I'm . . .

Footsteps sound on the floor, coming down the hall.

I don't stiffen. I'm not even surprised. I knew it would be a matter of time before Dominic found me. I didn't try to hide where I was going, for I only wanted a head start. I lift my eyes, my lower lip wobbling. "I was expecting you—"

My voice locks in my throat.

"Were you?" Henderson steps into the cell.

CHAPTER FORTY-ONE

Inana

I rise to my feet in a rush, but with my back to the wall, there's nowhere to go. All I can do is stare as Henderson stops just inside the cell. I hoped he and his crew had died while trying to flee the Shades after the bridge collapse, and I thought I'd gotten my wish when we heard no news of his arrival in Eldeen. Surely if he'd survived he would have tried to get there first, to make things as difficult for us as he could.

But I was wrong.

Because here he stands with his favorite Summoner at his side and two men dressed in white robes and silver gauntlets, their faces veiled. My gaze falls to the swords at the strangers' hips. I've never seen men like these before, but between their veils, their robes, and the gold crests on their lapels of a sun with seven sunbeams—King Kaelum's royal insignia—these must be holy men. Armed priests from the church.

I haven't set foot inside a church since I was a girl, and that was only for weekly liturgy. Dunway's chapel only had a pastor and a handful of acolytes. There were no guards. No holy soldiers.

They must be here for me.

This was a fucking trap.

"Did you leave the note?" I ask, my eyes darting back to Henderson.

On my periphery, I study the windows, all of which remain barred. Why couldn't this cell be one of the ones that had its windows clawed open?

"I did," the female Summoner says.

I assess her, finding no sign of the wound Dominic inflicted upon her. Maybe he didn't shoot her in a fatal spot. Or maybe Henderson healed her with his blood. Whatever the case, I am not at all pleased to see her smug face. "Did you arrange for Tera Holmes to guilt me as well?"

"I informed her an old friend was alive and in town," she says. "I expected her to seek you out before the end of your post, and you found each other."

"Abigail insisted you would do the right thing if prompted," Henderson says, his tone edged with impatience. "She said you were the sensible one, yet instead of heading straight to the church like Abigail predicted, you came here. Why?"

I scoff. "You really thought I was going to turn myself in? If that's the case, how the hell did you find me here?"

Henderson's expression darkens, but Abigail steps forward, tone placating. "We arrived in Eldeen well before you did, so we were already keeping watch on your party, ready for you to make your move after speaking with Miss Holmes. Besides, you left a trail for us, didn't you? You wanted to be found."

I bristle at her words. Partly because she's fucking right. I made no secret of where I was going or what I was doing, blatantly flaunting my identity as a Summoner to the stablemaster. But it was so Dominic would know where I went, not these assholes. Gods, why didn't I realize this was a trap?

Abigail speaks again in her annoyingly calm voice, like I'm some feral animal she's trying to save. "You came here to atone, didn't you? I could tell you were surprised when Henderson mentioned Dunway on the bridge. You were confused. You must not have known the consequences of your actions. Or perhaps it was only an accident. Whatever the case, you can repent."

I press my back closer to the wall. "By turning myself over to the fucking crown?"

"It doesn't have to be the crown," Henderson says. He gestures toward the veiled men flanking them. "If you are truly repentant, you can throw yourself on the mercy of the church."

I huff a cold laugh. Of course it doesn't matter to him who takes custody of me, so long as he gets my bounty and recognition for his good deeds as a Shadowbane. It makes me wonder how godsdamned high my bounty is to make him go to such lengths. Maybe he saw me as the easier target compared to Bard, but we both must be worth a lot to fuel his obsession.

"There is hope for you," Abigail says. "If you seek the church's forgiveness, just like I once did, you too can become a Holy Summoner—"

"I'm already a Summoner," I bite out.

"You're nothing but an outlaw," Henderson says. "You may have amnesty while you're in service to a Shadowbane, but I don't see Dominic Graves anywhere, do you? Who's to say he hasn't cut you loose already? I certainly can't take your word for it, and the priests are my witnesses. They too can only assume you are a lone outlaw and nothing more."

My pulse quickens at what he's suggesting. He can skirt around the rules. So long as he can say he thought I was no longer employed by a fellow Shadowbane, he can arrest me.

"Choose wisely," he says. "This can only end in your arrest, so decide whether you prefer the church's forgiveness or the crown's justice."

I glance from him to Abigail, then to the armed priests. They're blocking the doorway, my only means of escape. I step to the side, and my foot lands on something hard beneath the straw. A brief glance reveals a glint of metal, mostly buried. What could it . . .

A spark of hope blossoms inside me. I shift my foot again, assessing the shape just to be sure.

But it must be what I think it is.

The knife Henry dropped after he stabbed me. After the Shade pulled out his heart.

Abigail steps closer. "To repent, you must unburden yourself of your sins. Let them go, Miss Westwood."

I glance down at the knife again, just a brief flick of my eyes.

"Confess," she says, voice soft and melodious as she holds her palms toward me. "Tell us everything you know about Dominic Graves."

My blood goes cold. That's what this is about. It isn't just about my bounty; it's about taking down Dominic too.

"He isn't who you think he is," Henderson says. "He is not the kind of Shadowbane you want to associate with. There's something wrong with how he operates, and I will find out what that is if it's the last thing I do. If you tell me what you know about him, confess before our holy witnesses, you will be forgiven."

"You can do this," Abigail says. "I knew you were sensible when we first spoke in Thornfal. I knew you were just like me. You've sinned, but you were only trying to survive. You sinned again because you thought all hope was lost. You thought Absolution was only a distant dream of your past. But you're sorry now, and you can atone. Return to the path of righteousness, and you can regain everything you've lost. You could even be made Sinless."

I purse my lips, but I can't hide my smile. It isn't a grin of joy but of wicked amusement. "You thought I was the sensible one? You couldn't be more wrong about me. I'm nothing like you."

She frowns, her sympathy replaced with shock. "I refuse to believe you're wicked. Let me save—"

I crouch down, reach for the blade, and lunge for Abigail. Her eyes go wide as I grab her wrist and wrench it behind her back, my taller height an immediate advantage. Then I face her forward and press the knife—still stained with my dried blood from two years ago—to her throat. "Let me pass."

The priests' swords are already raised, and Henderson slowly unsheathes his. His expression is calm. Amused, even.

I press the knife's edge more firmly against Abigail's throat, and she cries out. "I mean it," I say. "I will slit her fucking throat if you don't let me pass."

"Do it," Henderson says, taking a slow step closer. He doesn't bother shifting into a fighting stance. His lack of fear is unnerving. "I can heal her. I can stab straight through her just to get to you. Meanwhile the priests can hack off your arms. My blood can heal your wounds just enough to keep you alive. Not that I need to. It's only that your bounty is worth more with your heart still beating."

The organ in question riots in response. This isn't going how I wanted.

"Slit her throat or drop the knife," he says. "This is the last choice I'm giving you."

My knife hand trembles. All it would take is one swipe of the blade, and I could spill Abigail's blood. Seize my chance. See if Henderson is bluffing about stabbing through her to get to me. Dominic said she's Henderson's favorite Summoner. Maybe they're more than just a professional partnership. Maybe they're like . . .

Like me and Dominic.

That thought has my hand shaking harder. As much as I despise these people, I can't bring myself to cut this woman's throat. Abigail is a pious, ignorant fool. Her reverence is for lies, but she doesn't know that. Or maybe she doesn't want to look too hard lest she discover the darkness creeping beneath everything she stands for. Either way, I can't kill her. I've never killed anyone—

The memory of Henry's heart in the Shade's hand flashes through my mind.

I hesitate too long.

The priests lunge forward and wrench my arms, forcing me to release the Summoner. One pulls my wrist behind my back, just like I did to Abigail, while the other attempts to wrest the knife from my fingers. I bare my teeth and tighten my grip, focusing all my rage on the veiled priest.

Hatred burns in my heart, a sickening, nauseating, beautiful fury.

It simmers in my blood.

Rises to the surface of my skin.

Radiates down my arms to my fingertips.

I cry out as the priest finally loosens my grip, but as the knife falls to the ground, darkness fills the space in its absence, a tiny wisp of shadow that grows against my palm.

There is no lantern light to brighten the cell.

Not this time.

A Shade coalesces in my hand, taking form as a flying squirrel. The priest gasps, but before he can react, the Shade leaps from my hand to his shoulder, then beneath his veil. The priest makes a choking sound and begins to convulse, slowly at first, but then harder. Harder.

His body goes still just as blotches of red splash against the other side of his veil, painting it in blood.

The squirrel flies out from beneath the veil, lifting it, and I catch sight of the man's bleeding eye sockets, nostrils, and mouth, spread wide in horror. As the Shade reaches my hand, it disappears.

Into my skin.

A tingle forms against my other hand, the one behind my back. The first priest barely hits the floor before the second spasms behind me. Another grunt, and this time something warm and wet strikes the back of my head.

The second priest falls.

Henderson cradles Abigail against his chest, his eyes wide as he takes in the dead men, my shadow-wreathed hands.

I can't help but follow his line of sight to my palms, shocked by what just happened.

What I just did.

Because . . . that was me.

That was the result of my rage. My will.

"What the hell are you?" Henderson's voice quavers, and now he has the good sense to raise his sword in earnest.

"Let me pass," I say through my teeth.

"You're . . ." His expression twists with disgust, and he lowers his mouth to Abigail's throat. She cries out as he sinks his teeth in, and I take advantage of his momentary preoccupation to run past him. My feet fly beneath me, as fast as my racing pulse. I charge out of the jail, down the street, my mind whirling to comprehend the chaos in my head, my heart, my . . . my fucking body.

I don't get far before pain strikes my lower back. My legs give out, and I tumble to the ground. I roll onto my side, twisting one arm behind me to wrench the blade out. It's the same knife I threatened Abigail with. The same Henry stabbed me with. My hand shakes too hard to keep hold of it, and it slides from my grip.

I scramble back as Henderson closes in, his sword blazing with astrotheurgical light.

Abigail follows just behind, her legs unsteady, her palm pressed to her puncture wounds. Her expression burns with scorn as her eyes lock on mine.

Too soon, Henderson stops before me, the tip of his sword mere inches away. I freeze. Everything inside me blares with warning. Deadly. Deadly. Deadly.

So why doesn't he cleave his weapon through my neck?

"There's never been one like you," he says, voice trembling with terror and awe. "You . . . you're worth more than I thought."

Abigail reaches us and gathers the knife off the ground before leaping a few steps back. She brandishes the blade. "We have to kill her. There's no hope for her now."

"No," Henderson says, eyes alight with fire and greed. "This is something the church will want to study. Carve apart. See what it's capable of."

Abigail looks at him like he's lost his mind. "We can't—"

"Carve a diagram," he says in a rush. "We'll trap it in light and surround it in silver. We have silver bricks in the wagon. We'll line the perimeter of the diagram with that. Then we'll send for the church."

Trap it . . .

Trap me . . .

In light and silver?

There's no doubt now what they think I am.

What *I* think I am.

Abigail reluctantly obeys, crouching on the ground and tracing lines on the dirt road. I'd be surprised Henderson taught his Summoner an astrotheurgical diagram if I wasn't so focused on what he said.

He thinks he can trap me in silver and light?

Me?

He's probably right about what I am, but he's wrong about his plan. It won't work. Twice I've proceeded through the silver gates of Nalheim. I lived within its perimeter for an entire year. Almost every week I was surrounded by the silver walls of the Wretched Lair, blindingly bright from the glow of the chandeliers.

Bright enough to give me a headache.

But nothing worse.

Henderson frowns down at me as a bark of laughter escapes my lips. With sunlight overhead, he can't see the darkness that tingles against my palms, but I can feel it. It tingles all around me, through me, surging out in every direction and begging to be free. It cowers at the sight of the flaming sword, knowing how quickly it could kill me, but it awaits my command just the same. Waits for me to give it permission to illustrate my wrath in whatever deadly shape I desire.

My gaze shifts from Henderson to Abigail, and cold resolve fills my blood.

Inana Westwood has never killed anyone.

But I have.

I blow out a breath and free my wrath, and every dark emotion it's tangled with. Shadows leap from my palms, my legs, my heart. One spears Henderson through the chest while the other pierces Abigail's throat. They both go still, but my shadows don't. They continue to slash and rage, spraying me, the ground, and the air with blood.

I don't know how long it lasts. All I know is when it's over, I'm bathed in scarlet.

My shadows dance around me, humming with voices I'm in no state to hear, caressing my shoulders in soothing motions.

I pull myself up, sitting back on my heels, and stare down at my hands.

Hands that aren't mine.

Hands that aren't fucking mine.

And I scream.

CHAPTER FORTY-TWO

Dominic

I sense her before I see her and dismount my horse to run the rest of the way. Sloth howls, tugging at me as he races ahead. The sky has darkened with the last rays of sunset, and panic sears my chest. It took me too long to get here, even on the stablemaster's fastest horse. Why the fuck did I leave her alone? Why didn't I bring her with me when I made my report to the mayor? I don't know what happened to her, but it can't be good.

Not if Henderson is involved.

Fury has my legs flying faster, a sure sign that she's close.

Her absence gave me a slight respite from my emotions, a blanketing numbness despite the logical frenzy in my mind. But now that I can feel her, my emotions rise like a tidal wave, crashing over me and sending my heart colliding with my rib cage.

"*There,*" Sloth, Pride, and Lust say all at once.

I see her now, but I don't understand all that I'm witnessing.

She's folded over in the middle of the abandoned road, blood and gore splattered all around her. Severed limbs and bits of flesh are scattered about. My eyes fall on a glint of silver, a Shadowbane's sword, and I sure as fuck hope it's Henderson's, and that it's his body parts that litter the road. But I can't concern myself with his fate now. It's Inana who absorbs all my attention with every step I draw closer. As she sobs into her hands, shadows writhe all around her, but they're shapeless, undulating with her overflowing emotions. How can this be? How can Shades be surrounding her when night has yet to fully fall?

Then I realize I'm not seeing them with my eyes but sensing them through my Shades.

These ones are invisible in the daylight.

Just like mine.

And that makes even less sense.

Dozens more Shades creep between buildings, safe in the long stretches of shadow left by the waning sun. As soon as darkness falls completely, these wild Shades will pile on Inana too.

No. This can't be happening. I can't lose her. I can't fucking lose her.

I close the distance between us. "Inana!"

She stiffens, and a tendril of shadow slices out at me. I dodge back, avoiding a deep cut, but pain sears my skin in a line from my abdomen to my thigh.

Inana whirls around, and the shadows disappear. Her eyes are wide, her face and hair coated in blood, but she scrambles to her feet with a sob. "Dominic."

I start toward her, still not understanding what the fuck just happened, but I don't care.

She's whole.

She's safe.

She's alive.

Inana takes one step forward before she launches back, her voice pitched with sudden rage. "What is that?"

I pull up short. Gods, she's so close. Just three paces away. Why is she suddenly angry? Or is she . . . terrified?

Her chest heaves with panting breaths as her eyes lock on my thigh. I follow her line of sight and find blood coursing down my dark trousers. But it isn't mine. Not most of it, anyway. The cut is shallow; the Shade merely nicked my—

Dread carves a hollow in my gut as I stare at my holster of vials. Three were cracked open by the attack. Two bearing Calvin's blood.

The third . . .

No. No. No.

Not the king's blood. Any vial but that.

"What the fuck is that smell?" Inana says, voice ragged. She shakes her head, backing away from me. Her gaze won't leave the leaking blood. "I won't. I won't go back. I won't go back."

I assess her, my mind scrambling to make sense of this.

Inana stands at her full height and the cloak of Shades returns, wavering around her like a pitch-black aura. They're still invisible to my body's eyes, but my Shades can see them. Yet mine don't react. Sloth doesn't growl. Pride doesn't shout. They just . . . watch. Entranced. "I'll never go back," she says through her teeth, her voice pitched low. "He cut me away, he doesn't deserve me, he—"

"Inana," I say, making her jump.

She relaxes the slightest bit. The shadows disappear, but her voice maintains its haunted edge. "That blood. It belongs to . . ."

"King Kaelum," I say, the words cold on my tongue. "Why did you react to it?"

"The smell," she says, hugging her arms around herself and shrinking back. "I can't stand it, and yet . . . I want to devour it, claw at it, kill it, become it."

Shadows dance over her shoulders, humming, vibrating, growing more and more visible in the waning light. My heart falls to my feet. Suddenly everything I'm seeing makes such cruel sense. "How long?" I swallow the lump in my throat. "How long . . . have you been Incarnate?"

She shudders at the word, and so do I.

I hold my breath for the answer. Did it happen here? Just now? Because I was too late?

Was this . . . my fault?

"Since the day I killed Henry Berkham," she says, voice empty. Slowly, she drags her eyes away from the blood leaking down my thigh to my face. She tenses as soon as our eyes meet, her own widening. She hugs her arms tighter around herself and takes a step back. "What are you going to do to me?"

Only then do I realize my automatic response. One hand is already on the hilt of my sword, the other hovering over my vials.

"You're going to kill me," she says.

I open my mouth, but I don't know what to say. Nor can I force my hands to move. I may not be the most devout Shadowbane, but killing Incarnates is what I've been trained to do. Incarnates are inarguably dangerous. They consume their victims. Slaughter those who once were their victims' friends and lovers. Incarnates can't live like real people. They can only act out an imitation of the life they stole. The only fate for an Incarnate is death, and I've never balked at that. Never been tempted to let one live.

But if what she says is true, it . . . *she* . . . Inana has been Incarnate since the day I met her. Living. Breathing. Smiling.

How is that possible? She showed no sign of being like the Incarnates I've slain. None are as sensitive to sunlight as Shades are, but it never occurred to me an Incarnate could walk past silver gates or be surrounded by silver walls without so much as flinching. And she's so much more than *just* an Incarnate. She's one of the king's elusive Shades. Her reaction to his blood makes that plain, though why is she reacting like this now? She's been near when I've held the open vial—no, I suppose that isn't true. She's never been *this* close to it, and never for this long. The closest she ever came to it was on the rooftop in Thornfal, which was only for a moment before I capped the vial. Ever since, I've kept my Summoners at a distance when I test the blood. The amount that drips down my thigh is prolonging her exposure. Even I can smell it, clouding the air with its sickly-sweet aroma.

Still, how did I not know what she was? How did my *shadows* not know? Sloth whines beside me while Lust and Pride are as dumbstruck as I am.

My own voice echoes in my mind, words I relayed to my Summoners.

Shades don't see Incarnates as one of their kind anymore, nor are they interested in them like they are in humans.

Then why . . . how . . .

I shift my attention to the wild Shades drawing closer, closer in the fading light. They watch Inana with hunger and fascination.

My mind fills with the memory of her voice weaving stories. The anatomical hearts she crafted with her own hands. She isn't like any

Incarnate I've seen. She isn't like the ones that try so desperately to feel alive by copying human art.

Instead, she succeeded at it.

No wonder Shades are so attracted to her.

Because her very existence is a lie. Art. A replica of life.

She blows out a sigh, shoulders slumping as if her very soul has deflated. Her lower lip wobbles and she drags it between her teeth. "Okay," she whispers, her voice cracking. Lowering her arms to her sides, she gives me a sad smile. "Do it. I want it to be you."

My heart shatters like it's been severed in two. Three. A thousand tiny fragments.

Everything in my rent-open chest screams *No,* while my mind says, *Yes, this is what you must do. You cannot let an Incarnate live, no matter how human it seems. Kill this thing and be done with it. King Kaelum's vial of blood is no more and one of his Shades has become Incarnate. This monster has ruined decades of planning. Decades of work by the rebellion.*

There was always a chance that some of the king's Shades had already become Incarnate and been killed. But I was determined to try anyway. And I got close. So fucking close. I only had two Shades left to find.

Inana was one of them all along.

She's the reason the rebellion will fail. The reason the king will never be made mortal again.

She gives me a knowing nod, tears streaming down her cheeks, carving rivulets in the blood that paints her face, then slowly turns around. "Please, Dominic," she says, pulling her hair over her shoulder to bare her nape, as if to aid me in beheading her. "Let it be you."

I hate the sound of the word *please* on her lips, so sorrowful, when last time it was uttered in pleasure. My feet move before my mind knows what I'm doing, squelching in the gore on the road. Then I'm behind her, the scent of blood and flesh and something intoxicatingly *her* filling my lungs. I wrap my arms around her, pinning hers to her sides, and crush her back against my chest in a fierce embrace.

"Don't be gentle," she says, relaxing in my grip. "I'm ready to go. I don't deserve to live. I remember what I did now. I remember it all."

Sloth curves around her legs while Lust and Pride encircle her too, caressing her bloodstained cheeks, her hair. Her own shadows rise from her, mingling with mine. I don't understand how she's come to *have* shadows. Incarnates are merely a single Shade that copied a human and consumed their flesh. They can wield their own shadowed substance, but these are clearly separate, the same way my three Shades act separately from me. How is it possible? How is *she* possible?

My vision clouds over as if in answer to my growing desperation. I find myself in the same dream I already witnessed, the one that showed me what happened between Inana and Henry. I thought my perspective had been that of a helpless bystander, but that wasn't it at all. It was how *she*—the Shade—saw this event. But, no, this isn't a dream this time; these must be Inana's current thoughts, the memories tormenting her. I'm experiencing them now the same way proximity allowed me to experience her dreams.

I watch everything happen all over again, but this time, when the Shade's fingertips reach for Henry's back, I don't launch out of the vision. I experience the satisfying crack of bone, the warmth of his sinew and blood, the gurgle of his final breaths. Then I experience the Shade grieving for Inana, trying to help her. It's been watching her for so long. It remembers more about her than about the life it lived five centuries ago, when it once shared a soul with a king. Now the woman it admired, the woman who used to tell it the most enchanting stories when no one was looking, is dying. It burns with rage for her. Rage Inana feels too.

Next I witness Inana's final, fury-laced breath as she surrenders to the Shade. With a battle cry, the Shade consumes her body. Not in the way I always assumed a Shade would eat a human to become Incarnate. Instead, it assimilates her, wrapping its arms around Inana's body and drawing her into its shadowed form, not with a smothering violence but a sorrowful, parting hug. Color spills over the creature, like an inkblot spreading over paper, the more and more they merge.

Until there's only one of them.

I watch through Inana's newly Incarnate eyes as she stares down at her hands, her body, the bloodstained floor. She rushes to her feet and stumbles out of the cell, legs wobbly. The guards outside the jailhouse stand at attention, hands flying to the hilts of their swords, but Incarnate-Inana flicks her wrists, sending tendrils of shadow from her fingertips to sever their heads from their necks.

"Revenge," Inana mutters, remembering her body's last request. Then she runs across the field outside the village, into the woods. There she collapses at the base of a tree, mind racing with confusion, with tangled memories she doesn't understand. Rage bubbles up inside her, and shadows leap from her fingertips, whipping through the undergrowth and cleaving branches in her fury. She doesn't know how to stop it. Her mind is fraying at the seams.

Seams.

Sewing.

Calm.

A memory rises to the surface, of a needle gliding in and out of flesh. No, it was fabric.

Inana takes a needle from her cuff and begins to sew with threads of shadow until her pulse evens out, until her breaths come easier. She sews and sews and sews, a tapestry of shadow.

Night falls, and Shades inspect her work. One is so fascinated that it presses itself close beside her, its arms brushing hers, its head resting on her shoulder. It watches and watches, lulled by the beauty of her art, until it sinks more firmly against her. Then melts into her body.

Inana gasps, feeling something other than rage now. She feels pride.

King Kaelum's Wrath.

A new Shade's Pride.

Her mind clears little by little.

The memories continue in a similar fashion, and soon Inana begins telling stories while she sews, the story of the woman who lost her heart. After she assimilates a third Shade, Lust, then a fourth, Gluttony, she leaves the forest, hungry for human contact. For food. For shelter.

She finds work at a textile mill, where she upgrades her art to real silk and thread. Her stories grow longer and more complex, though she knows better than to engage in art before an audience. It's her secret. Meanwhile, her fellow workers keep their distance. "She's been through something," they whisper when they look at her with sad eyes, throwing around words like *trauma* and *amnesia.* They understand, for she isn't the only one there with a dark past. They leave her be.

Once she assimilates Greed, she finds it harder and harder to relinquish her stolen moments sewing daisies. Art makes her feel alive, so why should she stop? Why should she ever stop?

Just before she's caught by the proprietress, she assimilates Envy. Her mind is clearer than ever, though most of her memories of escaping the duke remain locked away. By the time Rockefeller takes her from the textile mill's stockade, she's a dazzling array of emotions and human yearnings. Among his performers, she's just like everyone else. A little broken.

She no longer remembers the Shades that merged into her body. They're part of her soul now, and everything she experienced before she lived in Nalheim is a blur, a fever dream.

Her seventh Shade, Sloth, is a squirrel. She doesn't notice when it burrows into her palm the night she touches the dragon Shade, when she encourages it to change forms. Or when it leaps from her hand when she's reaching for the cork she lost. She doesn't realize it emerges from her skin in a burst of frustration when she stands outside the cave, angry she can't take a walk in the snow. She doesn't know it's a piece of her until it slaughters the priests in the cell.

The visions melt away, returning me to the present. Inana remains limp in my arms, her body heaving with sobs.

"I remember it all now," she says. "I'm not a woman with a patchwork heart. I'm a monster with a patchwork soul."

I hug her tighter, her sorrow burrowing deeper into my heart, darkening the too-bright places where my own darkness was once cut away. Maybe that's why she makes me feel a full range of emotion. Maybe that's why I can enter her dreams, her thoughts. Because she's nothing but darkness and half my soul has too much light. She fills it. Shadows it. Makes me whole.

"Do it!" she shouts. "Do it before I hurt you. Just get it over with."

"I'm not going to kill you, Inana," I say, my voice cracking.

"I'm not Inana."

"I'm not going to kill you, love."

"Why not?" Her voice is so sad. So hopeless.

"I can't," I say, and my next words come out stronger. Fiercer. "I won't."

"I'm a monster, Dominic."

"Then be a monster," I say, my lips against her temple. "Be *my* monster. Be a monster to the ones who created you."

She stiffens in my arms, then angles her head, her eyes locked on mine—those beautiful gray irises that she stole from a dying woman. That beautiful flesh stained with the blood she spilled in her reckless fury.

"Stay," I say through my teeth, speaking straight to her original Shade. Her Wrath. It rises to meet mine, mirroring it, dancing with it. "Burn it down with me."

Her rage is my rage. My rage is hers. She may have once been King Kaelum's Wrath, but she's mine now. My lips spread wider, and her wrath, greed, lust, pride, envy, sloth, gluttony, every sin her dark and beautiful soul comprises, hums back, resonating with me, until her lips curl too.

"Let's burn it all down," I say. "Let's make them fucking pay. Together."

ACKNOWLEDGMENTS

This book began as a 1,300-word short story I wrote for myself in 2016 as an exercise to process heartbreak. That story was similar to what is now the first two chapters of *The Lies that Summon the Night,* in which an outlaw known as The Seamstress performed for an audience, weaving a tale of her own heartbreak. She disguised it as a fantasy/horror story about a girl who had her heart torn apart by a monster and had to learn to stitch it back together herself.

The Seamstress has stuck with me ever since, my companion in healing. I've always wanted to give her a story of her own, to take her on a journey beyond that tavern (there was no Wretched Lair back then) and through something epic, dark, and beautiful. Now her story has come to fruition and I couldn't be more thrilled that you hold it in your hands. I have so many people to thank for making this possible.

Thank you to my agent, Kimberly Whalen, for championing this book and giving me the courage to step out of my indie-author bubble and into the world of traditional publishing. This is such a dream come true and it wouldn't be happening without you. I'm so grateful to you and to your co-agents for bringing this book to countries and languages across the world.

To Alicia Clancy and the entire team at Delacorte Press, thank you for believing in this book (and validating that Sloth is indeed a very good boy). It's such an honor to work with you and I am so grateful for your bringing my book to life. In the UK, thank you to Kelly Smith and the team at Zaffre. Your enthusiasm for this book was infectious from the start and I am so thankful for you bringing this book to the UK.

Thank you to my beta readers/critique partners Alisha Klapheke and Hanna Sandvig. I'm grateful you were open to my bait and switch, giving you a dark and bloody fantasy after all the fun and fluffy, cozy fae rom-coms I gave you before. Your feedback and encouragement are so appreciated.

Thank you to Sarah Horgan and Micaela Alcaino for the most gorgeous US cover I could have ever wished for. Micaela, your covers are iconic and it's a dream come true seeing your art on this book. Thank you to Charlie Arpie for the most stunning and beautifully creepy map of all time! And to all the other artists I worked with while drafting this book: Alexandra Curte, Vii Morte, Amira Naval, and K.D. Thank you for providing the visual motivation I needed with your gorgeous illustrations!

Thank you to all my author friends who supported me along the way, everyone who has ever said a word of encouragement or even just a friendly hello in person or on social media. And to all my readers, both new and old, thank you so much for being with me on this journey. It means the world to me when you give my books a chance. Every share, review, and word-of-mouth recommendation fills me with such joy. Thank you for reading.

Last but not least, thank you to my family. To my husband and daughter, you are the lights of my life and I'm so glad you love and accept my weird self. To my pets, as always you continue to be my emotional support squishmallows and I am so grateful you let me shove my face into your fur. And that I'm not allergic. To all the squirrels and birds in my yard, thanks for hanging out and being a great break-time distraction when writing gets hard. I'll pay you back with peanuts.

ABOUT THE AUTHOR

Tessonja Odette is a Seattle-based author of fantasy romance, epic romantasy, and fairy-tale retellings. Her different series range from cozy fae rom-coms to dark and twisty fantasy. In her books you'll find witty banter, sizzling romance, and breathtaking magic. When she isn't writing, she's watching anime, squeezing her pets, or dancing to the music only she can hear.

tessonjaodette.com
Facebook.com/tessonjaodette
Instagram: @tessonja
TikTok: @tessonja

ABOUT THE TYPE

This book was set in Caslon, a typeface first designed in 1722 by William Caslon (1692–1766). Its widespread use by most English printers in the early eighteenth century soon supplanted the Dutch typefaces that had formerly prevailed. The roman is considered a "work-horse" typeface due to its pleasant, open appearance, while the italic is exceedingly decorative.

ELDEEN
DUNWAY
CASSIA
MOUNTAINS
EASTERN
PASS
THORNFAL
SOUTHERN
PASS
NALHEIM
TARUN